Also by Paullina Simons

TULLY

A WYATT
BOOK for

ST.
MARTIN'S
PRESS

RED LEAVES

Paullina Simons

*A Wyatt Book
for St. Martin's Press
New York*

Design by Pei Koay

"We Just Disagree." Words and music by Jim
Krueger. © 1976, 1977 EMI Blackwood Music Inc.
and Bruiser Music.
All rights controlled and administered by EMI Black-
wood Music Inc.
All rights reserved. International copyright secured.
Used by permission.

Library of Congress Cataloging-in-Publication Data

Simons, Paullina.
     Red leaves /   by Paullina Simons.
         p.   cm.
     "A Wyatt book for St. Martin's Press."
     ISBN 0-312-14715-5
     I. Title.
PS3569.I48763R43   1996
813'.54—dc20   96-21592
                                                      CIP

First Edition: September 1996

10   9   8   7   6   5   4   3   2   1

For my Kevin,

and for Bob Tavetian,
you're in our hearts

CONTENTS

RED
LEAVES

PROLOGUE

At Greenwich Point Park, where the saltwater air from Long Island Sound fused with the earthy smell of fallen leaves, two children climbed stairs leading to what once was a castle. They were alone.

Earlier they had walked past the parking attendant, who seemed to know them well and waved them on with a smile. The park was large and it was a long walk to where they wanted to be, but the sun shone and it was still warm. The girl carried a white-and-red paper bag, while the boy carried his baseball cap and a kite. They walked around the western end of the bay and found a picnic table near the beach. The girl immediately wanted to take off her shoes and feel the smooth stones under her feet, but the boy said no. He wanted to eat first. She sighed and sat down. They ate. The girl didn't sulk for long; she was happy to be here.

Afterward, she kicked off her white canvas shoes, stood, and happily headed for the water. Many of the stones were covered with slimy moss, but she didn't mind. She picked up some of the scattered mussels around the beach and inspected them. She threw down the open ones, remembering what her father had told her: "If they are open, it means they are dead and no good." She put the closed black shells in her bag. The boy brought over some crabs, and she put them in her bag also.

For fifteen minutes, they tried to figure out if the moving ripples in the bay about fifty yards away were waves or otters. The girl said they were otters, but the boy laughed. Waves, he told her, just waves. She wasn't convinced. From a distance, they looked like they had black backs and were diving in and out of the water. They dove in place, so maybe he was right, though she didn't want him to be right. He thought he was always right. Besides, it would be fun to think they saw otters in their park.

The girl headed back up to the path. He ran past her, pulling her hair along the way. She moved her head away from him but hastened her step, trying to skip on the stones.

She was a pretty girl. Her short hair clung neatly to her head. Her impeccably tailored white blouse was starched, and her jeans were ironed and creased. Her white jacket didn't have any grime on the sleeves as is common for children her age. Her canvas shoes were bleached white and the laces looked new. Taking off her shoes and walking on the slimy moss was the only sloppy childlike luxury the girl would allow herself.

The girl liked the picnic part and the kite-flying part on the other side of the sprawling park. It was the in-between part that made her slightly weepy. She wished they could be at the green field already, unwinding the kite string. When the kite was high in the air, the girl would let go the string and run after the boy, yelling, "Higher, higher, higher . . ."

Fall was her favorite time of year, especially here, where the fierce salt wind blew over the red leaves of the white oaks.

"You wanna head right on to the field?" she called breathlessly to the boy, her voice catching. She stopped to put on her shoes, and he stopped, too, turned around, and walked back to her.

"We are. Instead of what?"

"Instead of going up to the castle," she said.

He stared at her.

"Okay," he said, shrugging. "I thought you liked the castle."

She didn't answer him at first and then said apologetically, "I do like it. I'm just tired, that's all."

He motioned her to come. "Come on, don't be such a baby."

She tried not to be.

They walked on the path between the tall, straight oaks, around to the little boathouse, to the wall.

The boy hopped up onto it. The wall was only three feet off the ground on one side, but it separated the walkway from the water on the other. Every time the girl climbed onto the wall, she feared that she would fall into the water. And if she did, who would save her? Not he, certainly. He couldn't swim. Holding hands was impossible. The wall was only twenty inches wide. No, she *had* to get up on that wall to show him she wasn't afraid.

But she was afraid, and she was exhilarated. She already felt moist under her arms. "I don't want to do this," she whispered, but he didn't hear, for he was already far ahead of her on his way to the castle. She told herself to stop trembling *this* minute, and, sighing, got up on the wall after him.

Little more than the high-hilled view of Long Island Sound remained of the ruined castle grounds; the view and the tangled walls of forsythia spoke softly of the castle's once glorious splendor.

A castle with knights, princesses, armor. A castle with servants and white linen. A castle with secret rooms and secret passages and secret lives. I have secrets, too, the girl thought, taking tentative steps on the wall. The princess in her white dress and shiny shoes has secrets.

"Wait for me!" the girl yelled, and bolted forward. "Wait for me!"

I

THE GIRL
IN THE
BLACK BOOTS

To our strongest drive,

the tyrant in us, not only

our reason bows

but also our conscience.

—FRIEDRICH NIETZSCHE

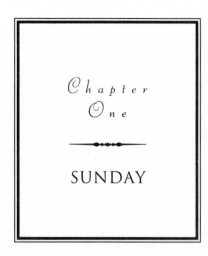

The four friends had been playing two-on-two basketball for only a few minutes, but Kristina Kim was already sweating. She called time out and grabbed a towel. Frankie Absalom, the referee, and Aristotle, her Labrador retriever, both looked at her quizzically. She scrunched up her face and stared back.

"I'm hot, okay?"

Frankie, bundled up in a coat, ski cap, and blanket, smirked. "What's the matter?" he teased. "Out of shape?" Aristotle panted, blowing his dog breath out into the cold air. He was not allowed to move during the Sunday-afternoon games, and he didn't, though in a canine form of rebellion, his tail wagged.

Jim Shaw, Conni Tobias, and Albert Maplethorpe came over. Kristina took a bottle of Poland Spring out of her Jansport backpack, opened it, poured water on her face, and then wiped her face again. It was a chilly day in late November, but she was burning up.

Jim squeezed Kristina's neck. "What's the matter, Krissy, you okay?"

"Come on! Come on!" said Albert. "What are you doing? Stalling for time?"

Kristina wanted time to move quicker, to fly till one o'clock when she was to meet Howard Kim at Peter Christian's Tavern. She wanted to get the lunch over and done with, and she was so anxious about it she couldn't think of anything else.

"I'm out of shape," Kristina admitted to Frankie, ignoring Albert's remark. She let Jim rub her neck. "The season's starting next Saturday, and I'm terrible."

"No," Conni said. "You're fine. Yesterday you were fine."

Kristina waved carelessly, hoping no one would notice her flushed face. "Oh, that was just an exhibition game."

"Krissy, you scored forty-seven points!"

"Yeah, yeah, I know. But Cornell wasn't playing all out."

"I didn't know they knew how," said Jim, now massaging her shoulder.

"What time is it, Frankie?" Kristina asked.

"Twelve-oh-seven."

"Come on, you guys, let's play," said Kristina. "The teams?"

The first game was couples against couples. Albert and Conni against Kristina and Jim.

"You okay, dear?" Jim asked, touching her back.

She thoughtfully looked at him and stroked his cold cheek. "Nothing. Hot as hell."

Conni shivered. "Yeah, I'm sweatin' myself." Squinting at Conni, Kristina smiled, thinking, she's teasing me. Conni did not smile back. Biting her lip, Kristina said to Albert and Conni, "You guys want a handicap?"

They half-mockingly sneered. "Get the hell out of here with your handicap. Put your hair in your face. That'll be our handicap. Besides, we're going to win," said Albert. Conni didn't say anything.

They lost 20–16.

Kristina was a tall, long-legged girl with a mass of jet-black hair falling into her face and halfway down her back. She didn't like to tie her hair back. Her raven mane was a distraction to the other team, and during the Ivy League play-offs she had been ordered to tie it up. She did, but by the end of the game the hair was all over her face anyway.

Here on the driveway of Frankie's fraternity, Phi Beta Epsilon—one of the least notable frat houses on Webster Avenue or Frat Row, as the Dartmouth students called it—Kristina never tied her hair. They played at an old regulation post with a rusted, netless hoop. Kristina didn't care. Two-on-two was great practice for her. It made her quicker.

Today, however, her hands were slippery; they kept dropping the ball, which even the five-foot Conni intercepted from her. Kristina tried to pass the ball from one hand to the other behind her back but she failed completely, and Conni and Albert got the ball and the shot. They all laughed at her, but Kristina's mind was on Howard; she didn't laugh back. Usually she could spin in the air as she jumped up to sink the shot. Not today, though she was clearly the best player out of the four.

At the end of each successful shot, Kristina high-fived Jim and held on to his fingers the way she always did. He let her, but the moment she let go, he let go also.

Kristina chewed gum as she played. Once when she came down hard on her feet, she bit her tongue. She spit out the gum and some blood with it.

Frankie kept penalties, shouted fouls, and kept score on a Post-it note. Chewing gum, he sat on a folded blanket, legs drawn to his chest. His ski cap was pulled over his ears.

When they came back to him, Kristina asked the time.

"Fifteen minutes after the last time you asked me," Frankie said. "See, each game is fifteen minutes. That's how I know. In a hurry?"

"No, no," Kristina said hastily, pouring water all over her face. "Come on, let's play."

"Give us a break!" exclaimed Conni. "Five minutes."

"No, I'm pumped," Kristina said. "The teams?"

Conni looked at Kristina levelly. "Gee, Krissy, I don't know. What do we usually do after Albert and I lose to you?"

"We play the boys?"

"Now that's an idea."

Kristina wasn't going to let Conni's peeved sarcasm get her down. "Great. You boys need a handicap?" Conni was her handicap, but Kristina would never say that out loud.

Jim pushed Kristina against the basketball pole with his shoulder. "I have a good feeling about this game," he said, kissing her lightly on the cheek. She turned his face toward his and tried to kiss him on the lips, but he moved away from her. There was coolness in his eyes.

He's upset about last night, Kristina thought. Later. Later.

Kristina and Conni beat Albert and Jim 18–16. "Wow, you boys came very close," Kristina said when the game was over. Jim's game was off. He ran a little slower, threw the ball a little lower, and didn't intercept the ball from Kristina or block her. She could almost swear Jim was gritting his teeth as she played, but then she wrote it off as her guilty imagination. Then what is that crunch underneath his jaw with every dribble of the ball? Kristina thought.

"Don't you patronize us, Miss All-Ivy," said Jim. "After we're done here, let's run a mile and see who's gonna come close to who."

Kristina thought she could run a mile in four flat right about now. What's the time? What's the time?

"What's the time, Frankie?"

From his sitting position, he glanced up and handed her the watch. Twelve forty-three. Kristina was wet from sweat. Seventeen more minutes.

In fifteen minutes, Kristina and Albert beat Conni and Jim 40–8. Kristina ran after every ball, marking and blocking even Conni, whom Kristina usually left alone. As if running faster would make the time go faster.

"Good game," Kristina said afterward, breathing hard.

Conni said, "I really prefer basketball as a spectator sport. Like when I go to see Krissy kick Crimson's butt."

"Yes, but you're a good sport, and that's the only thing that matters," said Kristina.

"Is it? The only thing that matters?" Conni asked pointedly, looking at Kristina. "Me being a good sport?"

"Sure," said Kristina noncommittally.

Albert stepped in. "No," he said, putting his arm around Conni and smiling suggestively. "There are plenty of other things that matter." That made Conni smile and allowed Kristina to grab her backpack off the brown grass.

"I'll catch you guys later."

"Wait!" Conni called after her.

Coming up to Kristina and lowering her voice, Conni said, "I thought you were going to help me, you know—with the—uh—you know—the . . ." glancing meaningfully in Albert's direction.

"Oh, yeah, cake," Kristina whispered.

"Shhh . . . !"

"Shhh . . . sorry." Kristina was quieter, but inside her engine was revving so high she could barely hear herself speak. "I gotta go now." Now, now, now, her inner voice was shouting. "I'll come by later, okay?"

"Kristina! The nuts, the hazelnuts, they all gotta be chopped, finely. It'll take me forever. And then the icing—come on."

Leaning down to Conni's ear, Kristina said, "I have to tell you something about that. . . ."

Just then Jim and Albert walked over to them, and Kristina didn't get a chance to tell Conni that Albert hated nuts, especially hazelnuts.

"What are you guys cooking up here?"

"Nothing, nothing," said Kristina quickly.

Conni threw her hands up. Jim laughed, and Kristina tried to move away. "I'll see you later," she called out to them, catching Albert's eye. He was staring at her. She looked away and wiped her wet forehead.

"Wait up!" Jim caught up to Kristina. "Hey." They walked in silence down Webster Avenue, to North Main Street, amid the bare trees. Some students on the front lawn of Alpha Beta Gamma House were setting up a huge turkey piñata.

Kristina was hoping Jim wouldn't notice how fast she was walking and wouldn't ask her about last night. He didn't, but what he did ask was worse. "Wanna have lunch?" Jim said.

"Lunch?" Kristina was flummoxed. She hadn't really expected to disappear after their weekly basketball session without Jim's noticing, but in the almost three years they'd been going out, Kristina had never told Jim about Howard, and she wasn't going to start now when a new period in her life was about to begin. They turned right at the corner of North Main Street.

"Jim, I've just got to write that death-penalty piece for the *Review*. I'm late with it as it is."

He squeezed her neck as they were walking. "You got a little time."

"Yeah? That's not what you said yesterday."

"Yesterday?" He took his hand away. "I didn't see you yesterday, Kristina," Jim said pointedly, and Kristina flushed.

"Yes, you did. Yesterday morning."

Jim shook his head. "No. Not in the morning. Not last night."

Kristina tried to suppress a sigh, but it escaped anyway between her dry and tense lips. "Oh, yeah, last night. I went to Red Leaves House last night."

"Red Leaves, huh?" said Jim. "How often do they make you work Saturday nights?"

Red Leaves was a home for pregnant teenagers where Kristina had done work-study since her freshman year.

"They usually don't. But Evelyn—you know—"

"Yeah, I know of Evelyn. What about her?"

"She's real pregnant—"

"Oh?" said Jim. "That's not unusual for Red Leaves House, is it?"

"And depressed," continued Kristina nearly without stopping. "She needed me, so I—I stayed over."

"Stayed overnight?"

"Sure. I've stayed overnight there before."

"Yeah, yeah, yeah."

His tone was still skeptical, but relief showed on his face. Kristina laughed and said, "God, you look like I just told you you won the lottery." She ruffled his hair without breaking her stride.

"No," he said, his face becoming impassive. "This is much better."

Kristina was almost shaking with anxiety. Thank God they were walking and Jim couldn't see her legs trembling. She took his hand. They were just past Baker Library and near Tuck Mall, down which they all lived. She wanted Jim to leave her there and not follow her to Main Street.

"You're cold," Jim said.

"No, why do you say that?" Kristina said, taking her hand away and wiping sweat off her face again. "I'm like hot lava."

"Your legs, they're twitching."

Kristina was wearing black spandex shorts and a Dartmouth-green T-shirt. "You're right, I'm freezing," she said.

Eyeing her carefully, Jim said, "Hey. What's going on with you?"

"Nothing," she said quickly, smiling as widely as possible. "Nothing at all."

She saw that he didn't believe her, his suspicious expression deepening. "Come on, have lunch with me," Jim said.

"Can't, Jimbo, sorry. Gotta do the work before Thanksgiving. Have way too much stuff to do."

Sighing, he said, "Oh, well, I'll come with you to the office then. I've got some work to do there myself." Jim was the editor of the *Dartmouth Review*.

"Oh, God!" Kristina exclaimed. She was at the end of her rope. "Jim, please! I just need a couple of hours. I just need to think and sit, and just be alone to put together my thoughts. Okay?"

He stopped walking, and she stopped with him but continued to walk in place.

"Will I see you later?" he said.

"Jimbo," Kristina said, mustering a tone of tenderness. Mixed with her frustration and anxiety, his nickname came out quick and husky, caressed and spit out at the same time. She cleared her throat. "Jim, of course you will. We're studying at four, remember? I've got basketball practice at two. I'll see you, okay?"

"Why don't you just move in to Leede Arena?" Jim said grumpily. "You're always there."

"Jimmy, I have to go to practice. You know that. I didn't become All-Ivy on talent alone." She grinned.

"Is your work suffering?" His tone was still sour.

"Well, I'm not making Dean's List this semester, if that's what you're asking."

He nodded, and then almost as an afterthought said, "You know, I looked everywhere for you last night. Everywhere."

She didn't say anything, and he continued, "Even in the library stacks."

Reaching out, Kristina touched his face. "I'm sorry. I should've told you I was at Red Leaves."

"I wish you would've. I couldn't fall asleep till, like, one. Kept calling your room."

"One, huh?" Kristina managed a smile. "That's about two hours past your bedtime, isn't it?"

"Ha-ha," said Jim.

"Gotta go, Jim," Kristina breathed out. "I'll see you later."

He leaned over and kissed her, and she kissed him back and walked away, stepping up her pace until she was running. The laces on her torn Adidas were loose, and Kristina stopped for a second to tie them, dropping the backpack she was carrying. She ran from McNutt Hall to Collis Café before she noticed. She ran back, picked it up, and sprinted under the Dartmouth-green awnings of Main Street straight toward Peter Christian's, the basement joint.

Oh dear, here we go, Kristina thought, as she took three deep breaths and stepped inside the darkened restaurant.

"Sorry I'm late," Kristina said, plopping herself down across from Howard, who smiled politely.

"This is not too bad," he said, speaking precisely and slowly, looking at his watch. "It is only fifteen minutes." He put two sugars into her coffee and added some milk. As always Kristina thought it was strange and incongruous to hear him speak such perfect English. She leaned over to kiss him.

"Why are you so wet?" he asked, wiping his cheek.

"We were playing basketball. I get all sweaty." She smiled, taking a napkin and running it over her face. Howard just looked at her.

Kristina took a sip of coffee and grimaced. "The coffee is cold," she said, putting her cup down. She didn't want Howard to see her fingers trembling.

"You sound like *you* have a cold," he said.

"Howard." Kristina was amused. "Are you making a play on words?"

"Why are you surprised by that? I do have a sense of humor," he said seriously.

"I know you do, Howard," said Kristina, gently patting his arm from across the wooden table. "I know you do."

"You do have a cold, don't you?"

"Yes, yes I do." She didn't really, but she knew it was important to Howard to show concern.

"Where is your coat? You are wearing shorts?"

"Forgot my coat." She shrugged as if it didn't matter.

"You still do it."

"Do what?"

"Refuse to dress properly for wintertime."

"I find it invigorating."

"Viruses, they can be very invigorating. Strep throat. Pneumonia."

"Never had any of those things," Kristina said. He was nagging at her, playing mother, but it was all right. "Always been healthy as an ox."

They waited to talk properly until after they ordered. Kristina wanted to

13

order a salad with the delicious spicy mustard dressing, but it was her first meal of the day—the saltine crackers notwithstanding—and she didn't want to be having mustard and vinegar for breakfast. She ordered carrot cake instead.

She tried to will herself to be less nervous. But she was wired. Last night she hadn't had much sleep. And this beautiful morning, she had been up at seven. The bare-treed Vermont hills had sparkled in the sunlight, but now there was only anxiety as she thought about an upset Jim and the patient Howard—solid and polite, looking out at her from his black-rimmed glasses, with his gentle, unsmiling eyes.

"How've you been?" she asked, trying to calm down.

"Good, Kristina, things are quite good. Busy."

"Well, busy is good," she said. He didn't reply. "Isn't it? Busy, it's very good. You must be so . . . pleased . . . that you're, you know, busy." She knew she was rambling. God! "Many interesting cases?"

He considered her for a moment. "How interesting can corporate law be? So let's see these papers, Kristina."

Kristina nervously took the manila envelope out of her backpack. Passing it to him, she said, "Everything looks okay."

Howard paused before opening it. "Is everything okay? I am not so sure."

Kristina chose to misunderstand him. "No, really. Everything is letter-perfect."

With a glance through the documents, Howard laid them aside. "We never got a chance to speak about this. Has something happened?"

Something *had* happened. Kristina's grandmother had died. But Howard didn't know that. Nor would he.

"I just think it's for the best, that's all," Kristina said, playing with her fork. She tasted the cream cheese icing of the carrot cake. It was good, but she just wasn't hungry anymore.

"Is it really for the best?"

"Sure. Of course."

"Why? Why all of a sudden did you want a divorce?"

He was wearing a suit, and he looked so nice and familiar a pang of sadness hit her. She thought, does this mean I'm not going to see him again? I'm so used to knowing he's there.

Shrugging, Kristina put down her fork. The coffee was cold, the cake was cheesy, and her stomach was empty. "It wasn't all of a sudden. I thought it was time."

"Why?"

"Howard, because I'm turning twenty-one, because I want to get on with my life. I mean, what if I want to marry someone?" She paused. "What if *you* want to marry someone?"

"Is there someone you want to marry, Kristina?"

"Not yet. But who knows?" She smiled. "Mr. Right might be just around the corner."

"Hmm. I thought Jim was your Mr. Right."

Kristina coughed. "That's what I meant. Jim." She was glad they were talking. Her hands calmed down. She wasn't as hot anymore.

Howard leaned forward and, lowering his voice, which was already calm and low, asked, "Was this *your* idea?"

Kristina sat back from the table. They were sitting in the corner behind the stairs; the cellar was dimly lit and gloomy.

"Howard, I don't know what you're talking about."

"I asked if it was your idea."

"I know what you asked. I just don't know what you mean."

"Kristina, it is a yes-or-no question."

"You think everything is a yes-or-no question," she said, on edge.

"Pretty much everything is," he said easily. "Let us try it again. Kristina, was this your idea?"

She felt impelled to answer him. "Mine, like how?"

"Yours, like did you think of this all by yourself, or did someone else suggest we go ahead and get divorced?"

Incapable of answering him, Kristina said, "Who else could possibly—" and then stopped. Howard was looking at her squarely in the face, and since she knew *exactly* what he meant, she thought it pointless to pretend any further. So she lied. "Yes, Howard. It was my idea."

Howard stared at her impassively, but there was something heartfelt behind the serious brown eyes.

"Eat your cake," Howard finally said in a gentle voice.

"Who cares about the cake?" she said sourly.

"I care about the divorce."

Kristina sighed deeply. "Howard," she said, "I know. But believe me. Everything's gonna be okay."

"Kristina, I find that impossible to believe."

"Why?"

"Kristina, your father asked me to take care of you."

"He didn't ask you, Howard, he told you."

"Wrong. We made a deal."

"Yes, and I think you've kept your end of the bargain. But one, I'm turning twenty-one tomorrow. And two, Father is dead now. It's time, Howard."

"A deal is a deal. We didn't stipulate age or his death in our agreement."

"Oh, Howard." Kristina sighed and then said quietly, "Give up."

"I cannot," he said.

"Please don't worry about me. Things are going to be just great, I promise." Kristina wanted to believe that.

He looked away from her and, nodding, said, "All of a sudden."

"Not all of a sudden! Five years. Come on. It's better this way. I was nothing but a means to an end to you."

Kristina saw hurt on his face. Her words must have made him feel terrible. "I'm sorry," she said quickly. "You know what I mean. You're a good person, you deserve better." She hoped she was saying the right things, but she was restless. She fidgeted with her napkin, then drummed her dirty fork against the wooden table. "Come on, you've gone above and beyond your deal to take care of me. And if you had these doubts, why didn't you say something in September when I first told you I was filing?"

Now it was Howard's turn to sigh. "You came to me and asked for an extra thousand dollars. I felt I had a right to know why you needed it. If you had had the money yourself, would you have even told me, or would I just have been contacted by your attorney?"

"Howard. I don't have an *attorney*. I hired some shyster for a thousand noncontested bucks. He didn't even know how much the court fees were. First he said a hundred, then three hundred. I mean, the whole thing—that's why I wanted you to look everything over."

"Nothing I can do about it now," said Howard, pushing the manila envelope aside. He cleared his throat. "It is very important to me that you are all right. That you are safe," he said.

"Howard, I'm all right, I'm safe." Smiling, Kristina added, "The only time I'm not safe is when the other team tries to foul me on the court."

"How often does that happen?"

"All the time."

"Still love playing?"

"Kidding me? It's what keeps me going. I scored record points in our exhibition game against Cornell last week." She grinned proudly.

"I still do not know how this happened—you playing basketball."

Shrugging, Kristina said, "How does anything happen? Divine providence. That school you sent me to. It was the only decent sports team they had."

"Oh, no," Howard said, rubbing his head. "Not philosophy again."

Kristina, her mouth full of carrot cake, told him what the British philosopher Bertrand Russell said once of his lifetime pursuit. "As I grew up, I became increasingly interested in philosophy, of which my family profoundly disapproved. Every time the subject came up, they repeated with unfailing regularity, 'What is mind? No matter. What is matter? Never mind.' After some fifty or sixty repetitions the remark ceased to amuse me."

Steadying his gaze, almost smiling, Howard said, "Have I ceased to amuse you?"

"Not yet, Howard," she said, smiling.

They both fell quiet.

"Have time for your major?"

"Two majors. Yeah, I got nothing but time," Kristina said. Unlike Jim, who was double-majoring because he was on track for a career and a life, Kristina was double-majoring because she was bored stiff, because she wanted to fill her wandering mind with other people's meaningful thoughts, so that her own little by little would leave her, would fly and be gone, so that there was not one minute of the day when she had an idle mind or idle hands to do the devil's handiwork.

"How is Jim?"

"Good. He's the editor of the *Dartmouth Review* this year."

"Ahhh." Howard smiled lightly. "Does he give you good marks?"

"No," she said, mock-petulantly. "He's tougher on me than on anyone. He says the *Review* is too much hard work. He's looking forward to graduating."

"What does he want to do after he graduates?"

"Go to law school." She tried to keep the proud edge out of her voice, but failed. "He wants to be a Supreme Court Justice."

Howard seemed utterly unimpressed. "That's nice. What about you?"

"Me? Grad school." That's all Kristina had been thinking about lately. "What else is there to do?"

Howard smiled. "I do not know. Get a job?"

"Howard, please. This is a liberal arts college. What do you think we're qualified to do? All we are is good readers. We're not bad on the Mac either, but that's it."

"Eventually, you will have to get a job."

She snorted. "Please. What for? And in what? With my majors, what am I good for?"

"I do not know," Howard said slowly. "What do other philosophy and religion majors do?"

"They teach, of course," Kristina responded happily. "They teach philosophy and religion."

Howard smiled. Kristina smiled back. She was going to miss him.

Kristina sensed that Howard wanted to ask her something. His lips pursed and he took on the concentrated look he got whenever he was faced with difficult questions. There were so many difficult questions. Howard usually avoided them, but today he wrestled with himself. In the end, tact won. In the end tact always won. Kristina wanted to surprise Howard just once and answer his unspoken questions, but today there was no point. Grandmother was dead. Howard and she were now officially divorced. And tomorrow was her twenty-first birthday.

"How is, what is his name . . . Albert?"

"He's fine," Kristina said quickly. "They're all fine."

"What does he want to do when he graduates?"

"I'm not sure." She shrugged, feigning indifference. "Says he wants to be a sportswriter."

"A sportswriter?"

"Yeah, too bad he can't write."

"I see."

"Or a fisherman." Kristina shook her head.

Howard asked slowly, "Can he fish?"

"I think so," said Kristina, trying to sound jovial.

"He went to an Ivy League school to be a fisherman?"

"A very good fisherman," Kristina said, wanting to change the subject.

Howard was quiet. "Are you going to marry Jim?"

She smiled ruefully. "I don't know if he wants to marry *me*."

"Of course he does."

Kristina shook her head. "No. I don't think so."

Howard was watching her carefully.

"You worry too much," said Kristina.

"I worry about you," he answered.

"Look at me," she said brightly. "I'm fine."

"Yes," he said, sounding unconvinced. He stood up. "Let's go."

"I can't spend the day with you, Howard," Kristina said apologetically.

"I know," he said. "I am flying out tonight. I have not even booked my room at the Inn. There is a blizzard warning for tomorrow."

"What else is new?" said Kristina.

Putting on his coat, he asked her, "Have you got any plans?"

"For the blizzard? None."

"I meant for the holiday."

"I know what you meant," Kristina said. She smiled. "I think I might go down to Delaware with Jim." That wasn't exactly true, but she hadn't told Jim yet. She needed to stay in Hanover—the Big Green was playing UPenn at home on Saturday—but who the heck wanted to stay at Dartmouth for Thanksgiving? She just didn't want Howard thinking she had no plans.

"I thought you did not like going with Jim anymore."

God, what a good memory he has! Kristina thought.

"Well . . ." she drew out. "I just don't think his family likes me, that's all."

"No?"

"No."

"Why?"

"I don't think they like my hair," she said. The last time I was there, they were . . . they couldn't stop thinking, I could tell, they all wanted to ask me, they were just dying to ask me, just why oh why was a nice girl like me not spending Thanksgiving with her own family?

Kristina had asked Jim to prime them ahead of time on the status of her illustrious fallen-apart family. She knew that well-mannered Mrs. Shaw was still dying to ask, dying to say something. Her unspoken questions lingered in the air until they got stale and rotten, and Kristina never went back with Jim after the sophomore year.

"You should go with Jim. I am sure he would like you to."

"I'm sure he would," she said, wanting to explain how hard it was for her to spend Thanksgiving with Jim and his well-traveled, well-spoken parents enveloping her with a suffocating blanket of concern and affection.

Kristina contemplated going down to Cold Spring Harbor with Conni and Albert. But since the beginning of the year, Kristina and Conni had not been getting along. Tension between them was thick, and it hung in the air in the same unpleasant way Jim's parents' questions hung in the air.

When they became roommates in their freshman year, in Mass Row, sharing a two-room double with a bathroom and a sitting room, every night was poker or blackjack night, every night was a sleepless night, because they couldn't stop talking. Kristina and Conni took some of the same prerequisite courses together, they ate at Thayer and Collis Café together, and went to the Hop to watch movies together. They studied together in the library, and her first Christmas at Dartmouth Kristina went with Conni to Cold Spring Harbor, where for three weeks she almost had a good time. Constance Sarah Tobias had a fine family. Conni's older brother, Douglas, was a hoot, and her parents were distant enough not to bother Kristina.

Being together became a little tougher after the problem between Jim and Albert. Soon, though, things went back to normal. Or so Kristina thought. Normal was relentless studying and term papers, lectures and study halls, Sanborn and Baker and Feldberg libraries. Normal was baked ziti at Thayer and club sandwiches at Collis, and Hopkins Center movies and frat parties on Saturday night and Sunday-morning hangovers and two-on-twos. Kristina thought they were all getting along fine, but she hadn't read Constance right.

Kristina tried hard to forget the incident last winter on the bridge, and she forgave Conni her momentary lapse of reason.

Kristina suspected it was when she and Albert went to Edinburgh, Scotland, on an exchange program in the sophomore spring semester that things changed permanently among the four inseparable friends. But what do you do about old friendships? What do you do about your college friends? Even after Edinburgh they all had continued to study together and eat together and go to parties together. We're like family, Kristina thought, feeling suddenly very cold. No matter how tough things get, we can't break it off with one another.

Howard paid the check and they got outside. Instead of putting his gray wool coat on himself, he put it on Kristina. She squeezed it around herself, wishing she wouldn't have to give it back. It was warm, and it smelled like Howard, some serious cologne he always wore. Yves Saint Laurent?

"Kristina, I want to tell you something."

"Yes?"

They stood at the head of the stairs to Peter Christian's for a few moments; Kristina's mind was reeling.

"There is no more money, Kristina."

She relaxed. "I know."

"You know? What do you plan to do?"

Kristina had lots of plans. As of tomorrow. Today she was dead broke. She was thinking of borrowing a few dollars from Howard to buy Albert a birthday present, but her conscience didn't let her.

"I'll get by. Don't worry."

"Listen," Howard said, struggling with himself. "If you need a little, I've—"

"Howard!" Kristina squeezed his forearm. "Please. I don't need anything. Really."

"You're still working at Red Leaves?"

"Yes. There's enough money."

They walked a few feet to the Co-op, and Howard bought himself a sweatshirt that said, "Ten Reasons I'm Proud My Daughter Goes to Dartmouth." Reason Number Ten was "Because her SAT scores were too high to get into Harvard."

He said he liked that reason best.

"But Howard," Kristina said, "I'm not your daughter."

"That is okay. It is not meant to be accurate. It is meant to be funny. Besides, you know, sometimes I wish you were."

She looked at him, surprised. "Why?"

"So I could take care of you all the time. So that I would never have to say to you, there is no more money," he said, sounding bitter and upset.

"Howard, please," Kristina said quietly. "Please."

"Listen, do you want me to walk you back to your room?"

Smiling, Kristina said, "No, thank you."

She walked him to his car, a rented Pontiac Bonneville.

"How is your car?" Howard asked her.

"Oh, you know. Beat-up. Old. I hate that car. The antifreeze is leaking out of the heating core on the passenger side, and it smells awful. The whole car smells like antifreeze. Plus it's loud. I think the muffler may be going."

"What do you care about the passenger side? You drive."

Kristina was going to say that sometimes she sat on the passenger side, sometimes, when there were mountains and trees, and sunlight. She sat on the passenger side on the way to Fahrenbrae, to the vacation houses nestled high in the Vermont hills.

"You need money to get it fixed?"

It was amazing that with all the money he gave her, she could be so constantly broke. It was hard to imagine that a girl getting twenty thousand dollars a year from Howard could be poor—what an insult to really poor people out there!—but still, after the tuition, and the room and board, and the books, and gas for her lousy car, there was not five hundred dollars left. That's the way her father had wanted it: no money left for extras. But five hundred dollars into ten months of school didn't amount to much. About $1.66 a day. Enough for a candy bar and a newspaper. If she saved up and didn't have a candy bar, she could go to the movies once every couple of weeks. If she was really careful, she could buy a small bag of popcorn.

Kristina reached out, touching Howard's face softly. Hugging him hard and tight, she whispered, "I don't want any money from you."

He hugged her back. "Because you know, even without your father's money, I've got some of my own." He didn't look at her when he said that, and Kristina noticed, but she guilelessly said, "I'm sure, Howard. You've always taken very good care of yourself. I certainly don't have to worry about you."

He pulled away. "You need a ride back? You look cold."

She shook her head. "Thanks. I have basketball practice. Then Jim and I are studying Aristotle for a quiz on aesthetics tomorrow. And I have to write an article on the death penalty for the *Review* before Thanksgiving. You know, same old, same old."

"Death penalty, huh? Does New Hampshire even have a death penalty?"

"Sure," she replied. "You have to kidnap and kill a police officer while trying to rob a bank to get money to buy crack to sell to little kids, but there's a death penalty."

"How many people are put to death each year?"

"What, by criminals?"

Howard laughed lightly. "Funny. No, by the state."

She thought for a moment and pretended to count. "All in all, including the ones who were going to be put to death the previous year, and all the years before, let's see . . . one . . . three . . . twenty-seven—none."

He laughed. "And what position are you going to take on this today? As I remember, you used to be against."

"That was then. I wasn't allowed to have another opinion in that damn school you sent me to." Kristina smiled. "I don't know what my opinion is yet. I haven't started writing. I usually get a position somewhere in the middle of the article and then spend the last half defending my new opinion."

"You do not think killers deserve to die?"

"I don't know," she said uncertainly. "I think I'm reading too much Nietzsche. He's screwing up my common sense—"

"What common sense?" said Howard.

Kristina poked him in the ribs. "If they don't deserve to die, then what do they actually deserve? Because they do deserve something, don't you think? What do they get in Hong Kong?"

"Death."

Kristina wasn't sure about death. God was part of that somehow. There was a God out there between all her courses on eastern religion and modern religious thought, and morality and religion, between all those lofty words strung together, there was a God, and she didn't know what He was telling her. She spent most of her life dulling His presence from her existence. What did Mahatma Gandhi say was one of the seven greatest evils? "Pleasure without conscience." Dulling Gandhi's existence too, though his credo hung on the corkboard near her desk as an insolent reminder. What would have Gandhi thought about the death penalty? In general? And specifically—for the man who killed him? Gandhi would have forgiven him, Kristina was sure. Just as Pope John Paul forgave his Bulgarian would-be assassin, Gandhi would have forgiven his killer. But then it was Gandhi who wrote that the seventh greatest evil was "politics without principle." Gandhi was nothing if not principled.

"Would John Lennon forgive Mark David Chapman?" said Howard.

Kristina smiled. "Well, you're really a popular culture whiz, aren't you? I don't think John Lennon would've," she added. "He had too much to live for."

"So that is how you determine forgiveness. You think it is easier to forgive your killer when your life is empty?"

"Much," said Kristina. But the Pope's life hadn't been empty, no, not at all. Still, the Pope didn't have a five-year-old Sean Lennon.

Howard stood shifting from foot to foot. "You're cold," Kristina said, unwrapping his coat from herself. "Here."

He took his coat but did not put it on. They both stood and shivered.

"You know," Howard said uncertainly, "you're welcome to come to New York for Thanksgiving. We could go see David and Shaun Cassidy in *Blood Brothers*."

So he had asked her. Waited till the last minute, but asked her anyway. Kristina felt bad. She rubbed his suit sleeve again.

"It's all right, Howard," she said quietly. "It's only a silly holiday."

"I know," he said. "But I do not like the thought of you alone and unhappy on the silly holidays."

"I won't be alone, okay?" she said, smiling. "And I won't be unhappy. Okay?"

Kristina wanted Howard to hug her again, but he didn't. He never reached out for her first. He carried himself with such politeness, Kristina wondered if underneath his soft, mild respect there wasn't a bit of distaste. Almost as if in Howard's religion it was a sin to touch Kristina Kim.

"Am I going to see you again?" he asked.

"I hope so, Howard. I really hope so." She again felt his reserve.

"Okay, then. Happy birthday."

Kristina pumped her fist in the air. Her long fingers felt better clenched. Felt warmer. "Yeah," she said. "I'm an adult now."

"You have been an adult all the time I have known you," said Howard.

"Yes, but before you," Kristina said, "I was a child."

"Must have been a long time ago," he said sadly.

Kristina felt sad herself hearing him say that. "Not so long ago, Howard." Her nose was running, and she breathed heavily out of her mouth.

Howard was quiet for a moment and then hugged her. "Good-bye, Kristina," he said quietly.

The words stuck in her throat. "Good-bye, Howard," she said, patting his coat. She didn't want him to see tears in her eyes.

When he got into his car, Kristina turned away.

After he was gone, she stood motionless on the sidewalk, squinting into the sun. I miss him already, she thought. I must call him and wish him a merry Christmas in a few weeks.

She was pleased with how the lunch went, but mostly she was glad it was over.

Kristina looked at the Nugget Theatre behind her. *The Age of Innocence* was playing. She thought briefly of going to see it; she even checked the time, but it had already started and it was a long film. The next show wasn't until five, and by that time Jim Shaw with Aristotle's *Nicomachean Ethics* under his arm would be waiting. Afterward there was Albert's hazelnut torte. Besides, hadn't Frankie seen the film and told her it was a movie about cutlery? Hadn't he said the utensils in that film really shined in starring roles?

But she still wanted to see it. Daniel Day-Lewis reminded her of Edinburgh, where Kristina had seen *My Left Foot*.

She slowly walked to the *Dartmouth Review* office. As she went up the stairs, her gaze passed the window of the Rare Essentials boutique. She saw a pair of black boots in the window. Nice.

The death penalty could wait.

She walked inside. An attractive saleslady came up to her and asked her if she needed help.

"I'm all right," Kristina said. "I like the boots."

"Oh, they're very nice," the saleslady chimed. "They're from Canada."

Oh, from Canada, Kristina said, smiling. Then they must be nice. She examined them and then asked to see them in size nine and a half. The lady didn't have a nine and a half but she had a ten. The boots fit her loosely. Still, they were quite pretty and graceful, with leather shoelaces.

"And they're waterproof, you know," the saleslady said.

"Waterproof? And from Canada, too?" Kristina said teasingly. "What else can a girl want from a black boot? How much?"

"A hundred and eight dollars."

She didn't have a hundred and eight dollars. She had about three bucks in cash.

Kristina paid for the boots with her American Express card. That gave her six weeks to come up with a hundred and eight dollars. She could do that, she thought, smiling to herself.

"Kristina Kim," the saleslady said, ringing the card through. "That's an unusual name."

Kristina signed her name on the charge slip. "You think so?"

"It's got a nice ring to it," the saleslady said, giving the card back to her. "It sounds . . . I don't know. Asian?"

Kristina looked steadily at the saleslady. "Do I look Asian to you?"

"Of course not. It's just that—"

"Have a nice day," said Kristina, taking her bag with the black boots and leaving the store. Geez.

She liked her new boots so much she wanted to wear them right away. Had Howard said there was a snowstorm coming? She hadn't walked her stone wall this year. Maybe during this snowstorm would be her first time. First time in her new black boots.

Kristina sat down at the head of the stairs that led to the *Review* offices housed in the Chamber of Commerce building and started to unlace her Adidas.

Spencer Patrick O'Malley had just finished his usual Sunday lunch at Molly's Balloon, the same Sunday lunch he'd been having every Sunday for five years. Spencer was nothing if not a creature of habit. He laid his parka next to him on the chair, and when the waitress came over, she smiled provocatively and said, "Hiya, Tracy."

"Hi, Kelly," he said, thinking the girl would get much further with him if she would only call him Spencer.

"The usual today?"

"The usual today will be fine," he said.

The waitress brought him a margarita on the rocks with extra salt on the rim, then Molly's Skins—excellent potato skins—and a side of guacamole with chips and a beef burrito. For dessert he had Key lime pie.

On his way out, Spencer was delayed after bumping into a seven-year-old girl who suddenly started screaming. It took him a few seconds to notice two of her fingers were stuck in the crack of the door. He helped get her fingers out and brought her inside with his arm around her while the girl continued to cry. The waitress got her some ice for the bruised fingers, and then the girl's mother came upstairs from the bathroom. Everybody thanked him, and Spencer left, thinking how tough it was with kids. One minute, everything was peachy, the next—you don't know what's going on.

With his hands in his pockets, Spencer strolled down Main Street, debating whether or not to take a walk to Occom Pond a mile away. It was cold and windy, but he was dressed for it. His sheepskin parka, knit cap, and gloves kept him warm, but even with the jacket buttoned up to the last button and his hands in his pockets, and a union suit underneath his jeans and sweater, his face hurt from the cold.

Occasionally, during the bitter cold winters of New Hampshire, Spencer wished he had driven south on I-95 when he headed west from his hometown on Long Island to find work elsewhere. It hadn't mattered to him then where he was going, so why had he chosen to stop in this sleepy little town with white buildings, black shutters, and impossibly cold winters?

Wondering how long it would take to get frostbite on his face in this weather, Spencer stroked his chin. He was unshaven today, a luxury he allowed himself only on Sundays and only since he'd stopped going to church.

Spencer was walking up Main past the Chamber of Commerce building when he saw a girl sitting at the top of the stairs. It wasn't the girl he noticed, for it was too cold to notice anything peripherally with his big hood up. No, it wasn't the girl. What drew his attention was what the girl was doing. She was barefoot, with not even a pair of socks to keep her soles from touching the cement stairs. She was wearing shorts. Next to her stood a black leather boot; the other black boot was in her hands.

It must have been in the teens with the wind-chill factor that afternoon. Spencer felt measurably colder just looking at her. One of her feet was planted firmly on the stair while the other was crossed over her knee as she was trying to pull the black boot up. She was struggling with it, finally putting the foot down on the stair and trying to pull up the boot that way.

As if hypnotized, Spencer walked slowly toward the stairs and watched her until she got the boot on. Instead of immediately putting on the other boot, she now threaded the black laces through the holes. Her foot continued to be planted on the cement stairs. Spencer's eyes moved up from her feet to her long, bare legs, then to her dark green Dartmouth T-shirt, then to her face and windblown hair. Spencer took his hand out of his pocket and stroked his chin again.

Her skin was very pale, though her cheeks looked ruddy from the weather beating on them. She glanced away from the boots for a moment. Her eyes locked into his. She had a big, wonderful, oval face, a young face if you didn't see her eyes. The melting brown eyes had deep, solemn grooves around them, making her look older. Yet the eyes themselves were black-lashed, sweet and vulnerable. The combination of the innocence of the eyes and the lines around them made for an unsettling picture.

Clearing his throat, Spencer said, "You know, our bodies lose one degree of heat per minute."

"Ahh," she said, the corners of her lips pulling up into a smile. "Thank you."

"Yes. And I've been watching you for about five minutes. Maybe six."

She flung her hair back, her hands not letting go of the laces. "How do I look?"

He saw her eyes and her chapped lips smiling at him. He maintained a serious expression—it wasn't difficult, for Spencer tried to be a serious man. "Cold," he replied.

"Actually, according to your calculations, I should be dead by now. A degree a minute, huh?"

"Not dead yet," he said, nearly smiling. "But severely numb. Frostbitten. Lost all feeling in your limbs."

She touched her foot. "You know, maybe you're right. I don't even feel cold anymore."

"See?"

He saw her lips stretch into a mischievous smile. "Well, then maybe you should stop distracting me, so I could put on the other boot and have at least a chance at survival."

Spencer stopped talking, watching her until she'd laced up the other boot. "Where are your socks?" he asked.

"In the wash," she said, standing up. "And who are you?"

She was looking straight at him, and she was beautiful. Objectively, undeniably beautiful. Tall, thin, model-like beautiful, even with that unruly hair. The eyes were bottomless, Spencer thought, in their inexpressible emotion. Spencer felt a familiar pull in his stomach. He was still young enough to remember his high school days when he felt the pull every time he walked down the hall, looking at the girls in their white sweaters clutching books to their teenage breasts.

Walking up the stairs, he took off his glove and extended his hand. "Spencer Patrick O'Malley," he said.

She took his hand and shook it gently. Her hand was warm, and that amazed him. A warm hand on a barefooted girl in November in New Hampshire.

She asked, "Spencer, like Spencer Tracy?"

Spencer took a deep breath. "Yes. No relation."

"You look nothing like him. Kristina Kim."

"Nice to meet you, Kristina. Can I give you a ride somewhere so you can get warm?"

"No, thank you. I'm going up to this building here."

"The Chamber of Commerce?"

"No, the *Review*," she said.

"Ahh," he said. "Aren't they a bit extreme?"

"No." She laughed. "But the reaction to them is." She was still holding on to his hand; then she slowly took it away. "If you have a Kleenex, I'd appreciate it," she said, sniffling.

"I don't, I'm sorry." He looked into her animated face. Her lips were smiling, too. "You must be from up North," he said. "Cold-blooded."

"I'm not from up North," she said. "But I am cold-blooded." She paused. "When I was a young girl and used to go and visit my grandmother near Lake Winnipesaukee in the winters, I would break the ice in the lake and put my feet in the water to see how long I could stand it."

Spencer absorbed that for a few moments. "How long," he asked slowly, "could you stand it?"

She smiled proudly. "My record was forty-one seconds."

He whistled. "Forty-one, huh? How does frostbite figure into that?"

"Prominently," Kristina said. "It was still a record."

"Bet it was," said Spencer. "Was it a competition?"

"Sure," she said. "You don't do something like that just for the heck of it."

"No, of course." He raised his eyebrows at her. "Something like that you'd need to do for a really good reason."

Kristina smiled mischievously at him. "That's right."

Spencer was curious. "Who were you competing against?"

"Oh, you know." She waved her hand vaguely to punctuate her vague answer. "Friends."

This was curiouser and curiouser. "Hmm," he said. "Some friends. A little girl in the woods—"

"On the lake," she corrected him.

"On the lake," he continued. "Sitting there, breaking ice, looking for a hole in the ice to put her bare feet in. That just sounds so . . ." He couldn't find the right words. He remembered his own childhood and going out on the ice on the lake near his house. Even when the lake was frozen solid for weeks, he was nervous about stepping onto the ice, because ice was water to him, and he had heard of only one man who could walk on water, and Spencer was sure as hell it wasn't himself. "So . . . intense," he finished. "Who was watching you?"

"Grown-ups can't watch over you every minute, you know," said Kristina, looking at her boots, and Spencer, thinking back to his own childhood, knew she was right. Grown-ups had rarely watched over him.

"Why would you do that?" he asked her slowly. "Why would you put your feet into freezing water?"

Shrugging, she said, "Because I was afraid."

"Afraid of what?"

"Afraid of doing it."

28

"With good reason."

"I did it," she said, "to show that I wasn't afraid."

"Show who?"

"Me," she replied, a little too quickly. "Me . . . and my friends."

He saw that she was shivering. He wanted to give her his own warm parka, but he didn't think she'd take it. She didn't seem the type.

"Hey," he said on an impulse. "You want to go grab a cup of coffee?"

She shook her head, walking past him down the steps. He followed her. "Come on. A cup of coffee. It'll make you warm."

"Warm?" she said. "It's twenty degrees outside. I'll get back outside and just be cold again. I'd love to, really, but I've got a million things to do today."

"What've you *got* to do today, Kristina? It's Sunday. Even God rested on Sunday."

"Yeah, well, did God have basketball practice? Did God have a quiz on Aristotelian aesthetics tomorrow? Thanks. Maybe another day." She looked up at him. There was something in her black eyes, something impenetrable and yet broken. He really wanted to take her for coffee.

"Come on," he said. Spencer O'Malley was determined. It had been a while since he'd asked anybody for coffee. "It'll be quick, I promise."

Kristina sighed and smiled.

"Come on," he repeated.

She tilted her head to the side. "Are you buying or crying?"

"Both," he said quickly, not wanting to show her how pleased he was.

"Well, then, let's go to EBA. They have Portuguese muffins that are to die for," she said.

"I know," said Spencer. "I buy them by the dozen."

They made a left on Allen Street and strolled to Everything but Anchovies, where they sat in the back next to the upright Coca-Cola refrigerators.

Spencer took off his mittens, coat, hat. He saw her watching him.

"What's with the hair?" Kristina said.

Spencer ran his hand through it. He had just had it shorn to his scalp. "Oh, you know."

"I don't. Are you in the army?"

Spencer rather liked his new buzz cut. The lack of hair made his deep-set blue eyes appear more prominent. He liked that.

"It's just something we did." He didn't want to tell her that one of the women at work had been diagnosed with cancer and when she began her chemotherapy, he and his colleagues, not wanting her to feel awkward, had shaved their heads. Ironically, she had come to work in a wig. However, it was the men's unbidden act of solidarity that counted. And Spencer, the mildest-looking of men with his subdued Irish features, aside from his exaggerated Cupid mouth, actually looked tough with his cropped hair.

Touching his chin, Spencer wished he'd shaved. But Kristina didn't seem to mind.

Kristina ordered a muffin and a hot chocolate. Spencer hated hot chocolate but ordered the same.

"Spencer Patrick O'Malley," Kristina said. "You go to Dartmouth? Like, who doesn't in this town?"

"I don't," said Spencer. "I work for the police department."

"The Hanover Police Department?"

"Sure."

"Really?" She livened up. "Wow." She seemed impressed. She leaned into the table. "What do you do for them?"

"I'm a detective," he said. "A detective-sergeant." He'd been promoted from plain detective only a few weeks ago, but he wasn't about to tell this girl that.

"A detective? Wow," she said. "Do you do a lot of . . . detecting?"

I detected you, didn't I, out of the corner of my eye, he wanted to say to her. "Plenty," he said. "I detect cars that are parked in the wrong place, I detect meters that are out of time, I detect drunk drivers on a Saturday night."

She looked at him uncertainly, with interest and curiosity, with warm, soft brown eyes.

"So you play basketball?" he asked her.

"Yeah."

"I sometimes watch men's basketball."

"A mistake," said Kristina. "We're much better. We won the title last year."

He looked at her hands, which were long and slender, capped with beautifully manicured red nails. He preferred the short, clean unpolished look on girls, but long nails were somehow right on her.

Pointing to the nails, Spencer said, "Hard to dribble with those?"

She studied her nails lovingly, smiling. "I've adjusted. Listen, the other team, they need all the handicaps they can get."

"Hmmm," said Spencer thoughtfully. "Quite rare for a university girl to have those long nails. Especially a basketball player."

Kristina shrugged. "I like them."

"Are you good?"

"Very good," she said, smiling wryly. "First-team All-Ivy three years in a row."

"Ahh," he said, impressed, but not letting on. "What is All-Ivy exactly?"

"You don't know what All-Ivy is? Some detective!" She sat there in a mock snit for a few seconds. Spencer almost laughed aloud.

"For your information, All-Ivy players are voted on by the league coaches, out of the nine Ivy League schools. For each position, there's an All-Ivy player. The league votes on five players for the first team, five for the second team, and then five for honorable mention. I'm the senior center. I'm the only first-team All-Ivy player in Big Green basketball right now—" She stopped suddenly, blushing.

Spencer, smiling, leaned over his hot chocolate and said, "Kristina, are you trying to impress me?"

Looking flustered and red, she said, "No, of course not."

"Because I'm impressed," he told her, and she outwardly relaxed and smiled.

"Are you a good detective?"

Spencer was going to rattle off a list of his credentials and successful cases as a joke, but he didn't. Nodding, he said, "They say some detectives have skill as interrogators, and some as crime scene investigators. To be a good detective you should be good at both."

"What are you good at, Detective O'Malley?"

The question sounded suggestive to him. He raised his eyebrows.

"You must have a categorical imperative," she said.

He looked at her blankly. "A categorical what?"

"You know." Kristina shrugged, taking a big bite of the muffin, chewing it thoroughly, and swallowing before continuing. "A categorical imperative, one that represents an action as objectively necessary in itself, without reference to any other purpose."

Spencer's eyes widened at her. "Oh, yes, of course. I got a number of those."

Kristina took another bite. "No, just one," she said. "You only have one. Kant. *Metaphysics of Morals.* It means—"

"I kind of figured out what it means, and yes, I suppose I wouldn't be an officer of the law if I weren't driven—without reference to any other purpose—" he mimicked her—"to do my job."

"Do it well."

"Do it the best I can."

"So what are you good at?"

He decided to take her at face value. "I'm like a hound. I like to think that I have a good sense of intuition." Spencer paused. "But my partner, Will, would disagree with you. He says I'm a dog whose nose has been ruined by too much pepperoni."

"You must be thinking about my dog," said Kristina. "You seem like a good listener."

"I am a good listener," he admitted. "I'm also a good observer. I watch people and I usually find out more about them by how they sit and look at me than by what they say."

She smiled. "What do you find out by looking at me?"

Spencer smiled back. "That you are not afraid of me. You stare me right in the eyes."

"Are you saying I'm in your face, detective?"

"Yes, that's what I'm saying." He was trying to be serious. "You're looking right at me, and you are not afraid."

"Got nothing to be afraid of," Kristina said, looking away, and Spencer noticed that.

Leaning closer and speaking softer, Spencer said, "What are you afraid of, Kristina?"

"What, like in general? Or most?"

He thought about it. "Most," he replied.

"Death. No, not death. Dying," said Kristina. Spencer nodded.

"How about you? What does a cop fear most?"

"I don't know about a cop, but me, I'm most scared about having to live with my conscience. I like to sleep at night."

"Has your conscience been bothering you?" She smiled.

"Not so far."

She nodded, sipping her drink. "In your line of work, you can't afford to make mistakes, I guess. To be wrong about people."

"You're right." Spencer took a sip of his drink. Where was she heading with this? "I'm not often wrong about people."

She smiled coyly. "Think you're wrong about me?"

He willingly smiled back. "I'm right on about you. You are brave and smart." He wanted to add that she was also very beautiful, but of course one did not say those things to a Dartmouth girl over coffee. Besides, she didn't need to be told that.

"Are you flexible, detective?"

"I'm as stiff as a board," he said. "One of my many failings."

"You don't seem like you have many of those," said Kristina.

"You're trying to be gracious. I'm full of bad habits."

"Yeah? Like what? And who isn't?"

"You, for one."

"Me?" She laughed. "I have more bad habits than you've had dinners."

"Name one."

She thought for a moment. "I'm compulsively neat," she said.

"Really? I'm compulsively sloppy."

"I really like to win at basketball," she said.

"I really like to close my cases."

"I never wear enough clothing outside and always catch colds." As if to prove that, she sneezed.

"Oh, yeah? I always bundle up too much and sweat profusely."

"I constantly do things to make my life really complicated."

"I constantly do things to make my life as simple as possible."

She paused. "Sometimes I drink."

He paused too. "Huh! Would that I only drank *sometimes*."

And then they smiled at each other.

"Are you twenty-one, Kristina?"

"Tomorrow," she said, inexplicably excited. "Finally."

"I see. You didn't tell me you drink, okay?"

"Drink? I meant drink coffee."

"Good. We won't mention it again." He paused. "So you're happy to be turning twenty-one? For all the usual reasons?"

She nodded. "And *then* some," she said, raising her eyebrows. But she didn't offer to explain and he didn't pursue it.

They drank their hot chocolates and nibbled on the Portuguese muffins— a sort of English muffin but bigger, thicker, and sweeter.

"So Detective O'Malley, have you had any interesting cases? I have to write this article on the death penalty for the *Review.* I'm thinking of writing something about the criminal."

"Well, that would be pretty revolutionary of you," Spencer said. "In today's day and age." He was getting a good feeling about her.

"Can you tell me anything about the criminal?"

"Like what?"

"Like why do people kill other people?"

Spencer thought about it. She was confusing him. She was too pretty. "Power," he said at last. "Power and intimidation. That's all it's about."

"Power and intimidation, huh? Serial killers, abusive husbands, rapists, all of them?"

"Yes. All of them."

Kristina smiled. "That's really good. I like that."

"Enough about the death penalty. Tell me something about yourself."

"Like what?"

"Like anything. What year are you in?"

"I'm a senior."

"What's your major?"

"Philosophy and religion."

"That's interesting. So what can philosophy tell us about why men kill other men?"

"How do I know? I don't study anything as concrete as that. Nietzsche tells us we shouldn't be upset at evil, and we shouldn't punish the deviant."

"Why is that?"

"He says because the criminal is only exercising his free will, which society gave him, and for which it now wants to punish him, punish for the very thing it told him made him a human being and not an animal."

"This Nietzsche, he's obviously never lived in New York," said Spencer. Kristina laughed.

"You know, I don't know if I agree with that," said Spencer. "Society didn't give man free will. God did. Society just reins in the excesses of free will in those who can't rein it in themselves."

"You may be right," said Kristina. "But Nietzsche doesn't believe in God."

"Well, I," said Spencer quietly, "don't believe in Nietzsche."

Kristina was looking at him with an expression of great amusement.

"What?" he asked her.

"Nothing, nothing," she said quickly. "Where are you from, Spencer?"

"Born and bred on Long Island," Spencer said.

"Oh, yeah? My best friend is from Cold Spring Harbor."

"Cold Spring Harbor? I've read about that place in books. I don't think mere mortals like me are allowed there."

"Don't be silly. Where are you from?"

"Farmingville."

"Never heard of it."

"No one has. Anyway, I'm from there."

"So what brings you here, Spencer?"

"I don't know. Got tired of chasing after speeders on the Long Island Expressway. So I got into my car and drove north."

"And stopped in Hanover?"

"And stopped in Hanover. I liked Dartmouth Hall. I spent my first night here in the completely unaffordable Hanover Inn, and heard the clock tower out of my window playing songs. My first day they played a slow version of 'Seasons in the Sun.' "

Kristina laughed. "You stayed in Hanover because the Baker tower played 'Seasons in the Sun'?"

"I stayed in Hanover so I could give all you posh Dartmouth girls and boys parking tickets." Spencer said it seriously, but he was kidding, and Kristina laughed again. Spencer liked that Kristina could tell when he was kidding.

"Now I live in Hanover so that I can feel like I'm going to Dartmouth without actually spending twenty-five thousand a year on my education."

"Without actually getting an education either."

"Touché," he said, shaking his head. "Good. You think I don't get an education watching all you people?"

"Really?"

"Really."

"You like your job then?"

Spencer nodded. "Very much."

"What *don't* you like about it?"

"The worst part is every time there's a big case, they bring on the gang from Concord—" He saw her quizzical expression and explained. "The assistant district attorneys, their own investigators, and sometimes even the state police guys from Haverhill. It really pisses me off. Like I can't do my job or something. I tell them, I can issue parking tickets with the best of them, give me a chance."

Kristina laughed. "What was your biggest case?"

"That Ethiopian premed student hacking his girlfriend and her roommate with an ax."

Kristina widened her eyes. "Oh, that was horrible."

"Yes, it was. I was the first officer on the scene."

Kristina made a disgusted face. "You found the bodies?"

"Yes."

"Yuck. Was it awful?"

"As awful as you can imagine."

"I can't even imagine." She lowered her voice. "I've never even seen a dead body."

"Really? Never?" Spencer found that hard to believe. He'd been going to funerals of his parents' relatives since he was two.

"Never." She cleared her throat. "My grandmother—she died just a few months ago, but I didn't go to the funeral."

"Why not?"

Shrugging, Kristina said, "I wasn't invited."

"You weren't invited to your grandmother's funeral?" It was Spencer's turn to widen his eyes. "What kind of family do you have?"

"Not a very close one," she admitted, changing the subject. "The Ethiopian, do you think that was power and intimidation?"

"That's all it was," said Spencer. "The girl didn't want to marry him, and he wanted to let her know how he felt about it."

"I see. What's happened to the guy now?"

"He's behind bars for life."

"Ahh. Just punishment."

"Just? I don't know. He killed two people in cold blood. Maybe he should have died himself."

"Do you think he should have, Spencer?"

"For premeditated murder? Yes."

They were done drinking their hot cocoa and eating, but Spencer definitely did not want to get up and go.

Kristina asked him if he was the boss at work.

"I wish. No, there's the chief above me. Ken Gallagher."

"Irish, like you."

He nodded.

She seemed thoughtful. "I didn't know policemen made enough money to live in Hanover."

"I know—you kids drove the price of this town way up. Three-bedroom houses start at two hundred and sixty thousand. Two-bedroom apartments rent for nine hundred."

"You must be making good money."

"Nah—I gave up smoking."

"What, so you could afford a place in Hanover?"

"That's right."

Smiling, Kristina said, "Didn't give up taking girls out for coffee, though."

"Did." He paused. "But I just fell off the wagon."

"I see."

"What kind of a name is Kim?" Spencer asked her.

"An unusual one?" she offered. She didn't seem to want to talk about it, so he left it.

"Go back much to visit your family?"

"Not much," said Spencer. "You?"

"Not much," said Kristina.

"Your folks, they must be pretty proud of you, going to Dartmouth and all. Me, I just went to a state university for a year and then joined the force."

"Do you miss home at all?"

Spencer nodded. "I miss my brothers and sisters."

"Oh yeah?" She smiled. "How many have you got?"

"More than you've had dinners," replied Spencer, repeating Kristina's own expression. "Eight. Five brothers, three sisters."

"My God, I've never in my life met anyone with that many siblings. I barely *read* about that many siblings."

"Yeah, we had a big family."

"Are you guys Catholic or something?"

"No, no, Protestant," said Spencer. "Of course we're Catholic. With a last name like O'Malley?"

Kristina sat back. "Gosh, how did your mother do it?"

"I don't know. I think she was done by her fifth kid. I was pretty much looked after by my sisters."

"Still, though—nine kids."

"Eleven," Spencer corrected her. "Twin boys died of pneumonia when they were babies."

"Oh, no."

"Yeah."

They were silent for a while.

"Eleven names your mom had to think of," Kristina said thoughtfully. "I had difficulty thinking of one."

Spencer studied her face before he asked, "Did you have . . . reason to think of one?"

"No, no," she said quickly. "But you know, people—boyfriends, girlfriends talk. I thought of Orlando. Or Oscar."

"These are not budgies, Kristina, these are babies. Oscar? Orlando?"

"See what I mean?"

"Don't feel bad," Spencer said. "When I was born, my mother forgot she'd already named one of her sons Patrick O'Malley, so she named me Patrick O'Malley."

Kristina laughed.

"I didn't think it was so funny. Finally one of the kids told her. Not my brother Patrick, mind you. So she renamed me Spencer. Spencer Patrick O'Malley."

"After the actor?"

"Yeah, Mom really loved Spencer Tracy." He paused. "I would've preferred Patrick."

Kristina, licking the tips of her fingers, stared at Spencer. "I like Spencer."

Tilting his head, Spencer said softly, "Well, thank you."

"What's your mom doing now?"

"Being a grandma. Eight of the nine children are married."

"They have lots of kids?"

"You could say that. Twenty-one already. You know, be fruitful and multiply."

"God almighty. You really took to heart the multiply part. Are you . . ." She paused. ". . . one of the married ones?"

Why had Spencer steered the conversation this way? But once steered, he wasn't going to be rude to this beautiful, curious, fresh-faced girl with black pools for eyes.

"I *was* one of the married ones," he said slowly and quietly.

"Ahhh," she said with an understanding look. "Didn't work out, huh?"

"You could say that. She died in a car accident."

Kristina put her hand to her mouth. "Oh, I'm sorry."

He waved her off. "It's okay. It was tough at first. I'm learning to live with it now, you know. It's been a few years."

"How many?"

"Five."

"Is that why you left Long Island?"

"Kind of," he replied.

They sat. The waitress had brought the check, but they still sat there. Kristina made no move to go.

"So what was her name, your wife's?" asked Kristina.

"Andrea. Andie."

"That's a nice name. Was she pretty?"

Pausing for a few moments, Spencer reached into the back of his jeans and pulled out his wallet.

"Aren't you guys required to carry a weapon?" Kristina asked, trying to look behind him.

"Not off duty," Spencer said, showing her a picture of his Andie. "Here."

Kristina stared at the picture. "She looks so young," she said. "She looks kind of like . . . me."

"Really?" said Spencer. "I hadn't noticed." Was that just a coincidence that his Andie looked a little like this girl? Yes. Yes it was.

While Spencer was paying, Samantha, the owner of EBA, came over to Kristina, patted her on the head, and said, "Great game last week, Krissyface. How many points?"

"Forty-seven," said Kristina. "Fifteen rebounds."

"It's almost not fair, is it? Those poor girls at Cornell, they just never win."

Smiling and getting up, Kristina said, "They'll never win. As long as there is breath in my body."

"Atta girl!" exclaimed Samantha.

On the way out, Spencer whispered to Kristina, "I gotta come and see you play."

"Please do. We're playing—" She stopped. "A week after Thanksgiving. Friday and Saturday. Come then."

Sticking out her hand, Kristina said, "It was real nice to meet you, Spencer. Thanks for the muffin."

Spencer shook her hand gently. "Anytime, Kristina."

She looked at the clock outside Stinson's. It read 3:45. Shaking her head, Kristina said, "Want you to know, I blew off basketball practice for you."

"Hmmm," Spencer said. "Was I worth it?"

She smiled, waving to him as she hurried away.

After she turned the corner, Spencer stayed put for a minute, and then walked and turned the corner himself, wanting to catch another glimpse of her.

Kristina's heart was beating so fast she wanted to skip to its pounding along Main Street. Blew off basketball practice looking into the blue-eyed, full-lipped face of a man with no hair who looked at her in a way she hadn't been looked at for a long time. Spencer Patrick O'Malley. "Spencer Patrick O'Malley," Kristina whispered his name to herself, and began running to Tuck Mall, her backpack in her hands.

When Kristina got back to Hinman Hall, where she lived, her room was unlocked and empty. Aristotle wasn't there, nor was Jim. She dropped the backpack on the floor and picked up a hairbrush. But her hands were numb from the cold; they wouldn't obey her. Kristina felt bad she had been such a mess for Spencer. Some first impression. Spencer himself hadn't shaved, true, but he was just so cute it didn't matter.

Sitting down on the bed, Kristina waited for a few minutes. Her hands were tingling, and she put them between her knees to keep them warm. She knew she wouldn't wait long.

There was a knock on the door. Albert peeked in.

"There you are," he said, opening the door further and letting in the dog. Aristotle bounded in, jumped on the bed, and then on Kristina. She petted him without taking her eyes off Albert.

"I walked him."

"Thanks. Where's Conni?"

"She is incommunicado this afternoon. Don't tell me she's baking me a cake?"

"I won't tell you," Kristina said absently. She was still thinking of Spencer.

Albert continued to stand in the doorway. She wanted to ask him to come in and close the door, but Jim was going to be coming by any minute.

"Going with Conni to Long Island for the holiday?" Kristina asked Albert.

"Yup. Same as last year. Want to come with us? Or are you going with Jim?"

"Oh, yeah, sure. . . ." Kristina trailed off.

He took a step toward her. "So come with us," he said.

Sitting on the bed, Kristina shook her head, never taking her eyes off him. Albert had wanted to be a gymnast when he was younger but had grown too fast, gotten at once too broad and too angular. Now he wanted to be a Zen Buddhist. His long, dark hair was slicked back in a ponytail. He had a small gold loop ring in the left ear.

"Listen," Kristina said. "I gotta tell you some—"

"How did it go?" Albert interrupted her.

For a moment, Kristina didn't know what he was referring to.

"Howard," he said impatiently. "How did it go with Howard?"

"Good." Kristina paused. "Everything's done."

"And?"

"And nothing," she said, rubbing her hands together to warm them up.

Albert came closer to her. "Was he okay with it?"

"Yeah, he was okay with it," Kristina replied. "He did ask me if the divorce was my idea."

Albert laughed loudly. Kristina for once thought his laugh sounded gaudy. "Did you tell him the truth?" he asked.

"The truth?" said Kristina. "Exactly what is that?"

"A conformity to fact or actuality," replied Albert.

"Ahh, of course," said Kristina. "Well, I told him it was my idea. Is that a conformity to fact?"

"It's good enough, Rocky," Albert said, smiling and coming closer to the bed. "It's good enough."

Kristina loved it when he called her by the old familiar nickname, but she put out her arms to stop him from coming too close. She didn't want to stop him, but it was broad daylight.

"Listen," he said. "I have an idea for Thanksgiving. What would you think of—"

He stopped abruptly. Jim Shaw was standing in the doorway.

"Jimbo," Kristina exclaimed weakly. "Hey. Ready?"

Albert nodded to Jim, who curtly nodded back.

"I'm ready," said Jim, and then stood motionless and silent at the door.

Tense, Kristina petted Aristotle and then broke the awkward silence, "How's your birthday been so far, Albert?"

"Good," he replied. "It'll get immediately worse once I taste Conni's cooking."

"You call it cooking?" asked Kristina, trying hard to lighten the mood.

"At least she's making you something," Jim said in a voice tinged with hostility, and then the three of them just stood there again.

"Well, I'm sure it'll be very nice," said Albert with an edge to his voice. Kristina was surprised to hear it. Albert never had an edge to his voice.

"Krissy, let's go," said Jim.

"Yeah, Krissy," Albert said mockingly. "Run along now."

Flustered, Kristina got up off the bed, picked up her books off the floor, and walked toward the two guys.

"Don't forget your coat," said Albert. "It's freezing out."

"Where's your coat?" Jim asked, standing with his backpack swinging in his hands.

Kristina looked around her messy room. Though outwardly Kristina maintained that a clean room was a symptom of a diseased mind (for how could she, while studying the world's greatest thinkers, be bothered with such mundane earthly issues as cleaning?), inwardly she hated untidiness and made a point of spending as little time in the room as possible. Once upon a time she had been the neatest girl in the world, but it had become clear to her even before Dartmouth that an untidy room made it easier to hide stuff from Howard. When everything was in its place, Howard found it.

Every once in a while, though, Kristina compulsively cleaned everything up before throwing it all around again.

She wished today had been a clean day, because today she couldn't find her coat.

"Wonder where my coat is."

"Sometimes it helps to put coats in the closet when you want to find them again."

"Thanks, Jim. Where's my coat?"

"You weren't wearing it this afternoon," Jim said. Albert was quiet.

"I usually don't wear my winter coat when I play basketball," Kristina said. She didn't mean to snap, but she had just remembered where her coat was.

It wasn't at Red Leaves House, because Kristina hadn't spent last night there. She had left her coat up at Fahrenbrae Hilltop Retreat.

It was her only coat. Her mother had bought it for her fifteenth birthday, and six years later, the red cashmere was faded and there were some permanent stains on it. It remained one of her favorite things. Next to whiskers on kittens and hot apple strudel.

She didn't look at Albert as she walked past him and said to Jim, "Come on, let's go."

"Kristina, put something—"

"Come on, Jim," she said, raising her voice.

She saw Jim widen his eyes at Albert, who shrugged his shoulders and smiled, folding his hands together in a prayerful Zen salute.

Jim followed her.

"You should try locking your door once in a while," he said. "It's the house rule, you know."

"Yeah, and what happens to the dog?" she asked.

They walked down three flights of stairs and went out the side door closest to the woods and the steep hill. Nearby there was a long path with shallow wood steps that wound down to Tuck Drive far below and then to the Connecticut River. Between the wood steps and Feldberg Library was a fifty-foot-long concrete bridge that led to Feldberg's service entrance. Three-foot-high walls made of crystalline stone flanked the bridge, which was suspended over a steep wooded gradient and a concrete driveway seventy-five feet below.

"Hey," Jim said, pointing to the bridge. "You haven't walked that thing yet."

Kristina glanced at it and then at him. They continued to walk away from the bridge. "Haven't been drunk enough," she said. "Hasn't been cold enough."

"Oh yeah, I forgot. You don't do it unless it's subfreezing. Otherwise it's not a challenge, right?"

"Right," she replied, thinking, he is trying to bait me. Why?

"They're expecting a snowstorm tomorrow, you know," Jim said.

"Well, maybe I'll walk it tomorrow then," Kristina said mildly.

Jim didn't reply, and they hurried on to Baker Library.

They studied in the Class of 1902 room. Kristina's mind was far away from Aristotle, as she recalled earlier Thanksgivings. Soon it would be Wednesday and her friends would be gone. Were the mess halls even open during the holidays? She couldn't recall her first year. She remembered eating a lot of soup at Lou's Diner and Portuguese muffins at EBA. And oranges in her room.

Jim kept reading and occasionally asking Kristina a question or two about the material, but she had just had enough. Let's go, she wanted to say. Let's go, let's get out of here, let's go back and eat Conni's creation and sing happy birthday to Albert.

Kristina stroked Jim's hand. There was a time you used to like me so much, she thought, or was that just my imagination? You're very smart, you've been all over the world, and you have a bright life ahead of you. But what's happened to us? We're getting so bad at this.

She stood up.

"Jim, let's go back."

"Krissy, I'm not done."

"I know," she said. "But Conni's baked a cake. And I gotta walk my dog."

"Albert will walk him," said Jim.

She closed her books and picked them up off the dark cherry table. "I'm going to go. Please come."

He looked back into Aristotle. "No," he said. "I'm going to stay here and finish my work."

Aristotle wrote that piety required us to honor truth above our friends. Kristina shook her head. *Nicomachean Ethics* was always hardest on Kristina. And Kant's *Metaphysics of Morals.* Kristina had fought most of her life against her own categorical imperative. People who didn't always impressed her. Spencer impressed her.

Men are good in one way but bad in many, wrote Aristotle. Kristina wondered about that. To her badness had always meant lack or suppression of conscience.

Gently touching Jim on the neck, Kristina kissed the top of his head. "Jimbo, I'm sorry." And she *was* sorry for innumerable things. "I just don't feel like studying right now. Come back soon, okay? We're going to have cake."

"Yeah," he muttered without looking up.

They were gathered around the complex torte Conni had made for Albert. The cake had uneven puffs of mocha icing, ground nuts sprinkled over the top, some chocolate chips, and twenty-two candles.

Conni, though dressed up for the occasion, did not seem to want to celebrate. Underneath the perky pink lipstick, her lips were tense, and the blue eye shadow couldn't hide the hardness around her eyes.

The five of them were looking at the cake as if it were a slaughtered lamb. Aristotle, however, gazed at the cake as if it were the last piece of food on earth.

Frankie Absalom arrived. Usually it was hard to get Frankie out of Epsilon House, but there was little that Frankie wouldn't do for Albert, his old roommate.

Albert had moved out of the room he'd shared with Jim and in with Frankie during the last semester of the freshman year when Jim and Albert decided it would be best if they didn't room together anymore. Now Albert had a single a couple of doors down from Kristina, and Frankie was an Epsilon brother.

Kristina glanced at Conni, who forced a happy smile and started to sing "Happy Birthday." Everyone sang, including Albert, who sang loudest of all.

"Albert!" exclaimed Conni. "Make a wish, and blow out the candles. But make a really good wish," she said suggestively, standing close to him with her hand in his back pocket. Kristina thought Conni was trying too hard to act normal. What was bugging her, anyway?

Albert glanced at Conni to his left, and Kristina to his right, and Jim across the table from him, and said, "A really good wish, huh? Well, all right." He closed his eyes and blew out the candles, every one of them. Conni and Kristina clapped, Frankie hollered and began singing "For He's a Jolly Good Fellow," while Jim just stood and halfheartedly said, "Yeah." Aristotle barked twice.

Kristina stood stiffly as Conni fussed over the cake and plates and plastic forks. She did not want to be here. The high of this afternoon, first with Howard and then with Spencer, was replaced by depressing thoughts. Conni had told her a few days ago that Albert and she were thinking of getting engaged. Oh, that's nice, said Kristina. How nice. Are you going to have a party? Engaged to be married? Gee, that's swell.

And then Jim had been acting awful today. Never a particularly affectionate guy, Jim had been acting stranger and stranger. Tonight, he doesn't even want to stand next to me, Kristina thought sadly. Some couple. Maybe *we* can become engaged to be married.

Frankie was talking heated nonsense to Jim, but then Frankie always talked in a heated nonsensical manner that reflected his eccentric attire—plaid shirts and striped pants, hot neon track suits, and jeans so big they had to be held up by rainbow-colored suspenders. Conni handed a piece of cake to Kristina, who ate it, nodded, and said, mmm, it's good. The cake was dry and terrible. She watched Albert's face when he put the cake in his mouth and chewed slowly. Oh, he said, this is not bad at all, not bad at all. And Conni stood beside him and beamed, her hand never detaching itself from his shirt. She laughed in delight.

Conni's high-pitched, squeaky voice grated on Kristina, but her laugh was infectious, and Kristina liked that. Conni also made it a point to dress sexy. She wore black bras and black underwear, bustiers and too tight jeans, and occasionally stockings and garters under her skirts. Kristina felt that sometimes Conni dressed to upstage her, because Kristina never dressed up. She was a jock and dressing up was uncool. Track suits and spandex shorts, and leggings, and Dartmouth sweatshirts, were cool. Jeans were cool. Basketball players did not wear bustiers.

She and Conni had been best friends until Kristina started playing basketball. That's what Kristina said when asked what had happened to their friendship. But it was a lie. It wasn't basketball that had happened to their friendship.

Why is she laughing so loudly? thought Kristina as she sat there trancelike, not laughing at all. Jim, too, was stone-faced. Albert bantered with Frankie, flirted with Conni, and when he hoped Conni wasn't looking, pushed his cake toward Kristina, who immediately pushed the plate back to him. Kristina lifted up her eyes and saw Conni watching Albert push his cake plate toward her. The laughter faded in Conni's blue eyes. Kristina ignored the plate, didn't even glance at it.

They had all chipped in and bought Albert a Pierre Cardin watch, because he was never on time, anywhere. Rather, Conni and Jim—the only ones with money—chipped in.

Kristina wished Jim would stop looking at her with that unhappy expression. What right does he have to be unhappy? she thought. He studies as much as I practice, he works at the *Review* as much as I work at Red Leaves. He is the one who never wants to sleep over because he has to be in bed by eleven.

Trying not to look at Jim, Kristina sat across from him at the table, an old university-issue Formica table with steel reinforced legs. She felt bad for him without even knowing why. Kristina fed Aristotle the rest of her cake, and the rest of Albert's cake, too. They got up; other people were waiting to use the kitchen facilities. The party was over.

The Hinman lounge was a semicircular TV room and kitchenette, attached like a peninsula to the front of Hinman Hall. The kitchenette, or the ironically named Hinman Café, didn't even have a refrigerator. It had an ice maker, where the students stored their drinks, an electric stove, a microwave, and dirty dishes in the sink. The chairs in the TV lounge were so old they must have come with John Holmes Hinman, Class of 1908.

Kristina and Jim sat in the low maroon chairs, while Conni and Albert sat together on the torn brown sofa, and watched the 32-inch Mitsubishi. Other residence halls had rear-projection screens. Not Hinman. Kristina remembered Mass Row fondly, where in their freshman year they had study lounges, separate kitchens, and a TV lounge with a 50-inch Sony in it.

Conni held Albert's hand. She was always holding some part of Albert,

Kristina thought uncharitably, and then caught herself and felt ashamed. She *is* his girlfriend. That's what she's supposed to do.

Frankie had gone back to Epsilon House. Aristotle lay on the floor. The four friends watched TV and didn't talk, though Kristina could recall a time when they gabbed so much that other students often asked them to leave. They usually left, and went up to one of their rooms and played cards on the floor and argued politics and philosophy and God and death. Or they argued about movies that no one ever got to see, but argued about in principle anyway. Most of the arguments were in principle.

Only the history major Jim wanted facts in his arguments. Albert would try to explain that philosophy and religion majors were not that interested in facts, but Jim didn't understand. Conni was a sociology major, and Kristina wasn't convinced Conni knew the difference between fact and theory. When they first became roommates, Conni had once looked up innocently at Kristina and said, "Krissy, what's socialism?"

A year earlier the four of them discussed the party conventions, then the presidential debates, and then the lurid revelations in *Penthouse* about a would-be president.

After the elections, the junior year was spent talking about health care and gays in the military. None of the issues really affected them: Conni and Jim were on their parents' insurance, Kristina and Albert never went to the doctor. And as far as Kristina knew, no one was planning to join the military, not even Frankie, who had plenty of opinions on gays in the military, on any men in the military for that matter.

They were university students. Everything was fodder for a good fight, including harvesting practices in Iowa, where none of them had ever been. But nothing *meant* anything. Jim was passionately opinionated. Albert was the devil's advocate. Kristina was moderate. And Conni had few opinions.

Once, Conni had *meant* something to Jim. When Jim found out that Conni wanted his roommate, Albert Maplethorpe, that had *meant* something, too. Jim had somehow worked it out. He seemed to have forgiven Albert, and he and Kristina had started going out. The four of them became very close. So close that in their freshman year, very late at night, having downed many beers, they played truth or dare. They didn't do anything outrageous, but the conversation took a definite X-rated turn.

That was as far as it went, because Kristina wanted to keep them all friends, and they all managed to remain good friends. It would have been a shame to ruin their intimate, eager college friendship over the Albert and Conni thing, which was supposed to mean nothing.

46

Except Kristina knew that Constance Tobias didn't think so. Albert meant *everything* to Conni. Earlier this year, a classmate had asked Conni, "Albert still your boyfriend?" and Conni had replied, "Now and *ever*."

After watching the news at eleven, they all got up. Kristina stretched. Conni lifted up her face to Albert, who obliged and kissed her. Kristina lowered her eyes.

"Well," Conni said, grabbing Albert's hand and thrusting her chest at him, "good night now. I have a seven-forty-five tomorrow."

"Kristina, will you walk the dog?" Albert asked, looking straight at her.

She had been lost in thought and it took her a while to answer. "Yeah, sure, course I will." She tried to smile.

"You don't want me to walk him?" Albert said patiently. "I don't mind. I know you're afraid to go out at night."

Jim moved forward. "She'll be fine, thanks."

Kristina gave Jim a quizzical look. "I'll be fine, thanks," she said.

"They'll be fine, Albert," said Conni, pulling on his arm. "Let's go."

After Albert and Conni left, Jim said gruffly, "Want me to walk him? I'll have to get my coat."

Shaking her head, she said, "It's okay, Jimbo. I'll walk him."

"You don't have your coat either. Where did you leave your coat, anyway?"

"Don't know," Kristina said quickly, wondering when she could drive up to Fahrenbrae and get it. Tomorrow she had classes, basketball, and then Red Leaves at two. Well, I'll have a long weekend to go get my coat. I'll have plenty of time.

She should have let Albert or Jim walk the dog; she really didn't want to walk him. It was late and she was tired. Aristotle was a fiend for the dark spooky woods behind Hinman and Feldberg. Kristina wasn't.

"So, you want me to walk the dog or not?" Jim asked.

"No, that's okay. I'll do it." She paused. She was so tired. "You want to stay over?"

"Stay over?" Jim repeated.

"Yes," she said, trying to smile.

"Krissy, I have a seven-forty-five tomorrow."

"I know. I do too."

"I'm really beat," he said. "Maybe tomorrow night?"

She looked at him, resigned. "Yeah, sure, Jimbo. Maybe tomorrow."

47

He must have caught something sad in her tone, because he said, "Tomorrow is your birthday? Yes, yes, definitely tomorrow."

She managed a smile. "Good." She kissed him. "You're not mad at me anymore, are you, Jimbo?"

His mouth was tense when he said, "No, why? Should I be?"

"No, you shouldn't be," Kristina said without looking at him. "Well, good night."

Kristina walked Aristotle quickly in the cold night. He was pulling the leash to the wooden steps in the woods. "No, Aristotle," Kristina said firmly, pulling him to the lighted common area in front of Hinman. "I'm not taking you there, you dog. You should know that by now." Aristotle obeyed reluctantly. After he sniffed around the ground for a bit, Kristina walked him to her bridge. It was poorly lit, but she walked the length of it and let Aristotle pull her a few feet into the darkness of the woods to do his business. Her heart already thumping, she waited for Aristotle to finish while she listened to the woodland's muffled noises. When Kristina heard something crack nearby, she yanked on the dog's leash. "Come on, Aristotle, let's go!" she breathed, and ran back.

After Kristina got back to her room she turned off the overhead light and looked out the window onto the courtyard and Feldberg Library.

It was nearly midnight.

She took off her brand-new black boots and remembered Spencer O'Malley.

A handsome young detective looking at me like I was the best cup of hot chocolate he'd ever had. A nice man with cold hands whose pupils dilated at the sight of me. But what can I do with dilated pupils now? I thought my mission was to *right my life*. What year was that my New Year's resolution? Like, every year. I've been trying to do that since I was eleven. Every year that was the first of ten items stuck to my bulletin board with a blue tack. Ah well. That's my mission again for 1994, but this time I really mean it.

Kristina took off her jeans and put on clean black underwear. She took off her sweatshirt and bra and put on the pink tank top she slept in. When she was younger, she had been proud of her sleek toned lines, of her fair color. She looked like her mother. As a teenager, her hair had always been short, and her mother hadn't allowed her to go to school in anything but dresses. She had once been a proper young lady, but at Dartmouth she played basketball, where speed and stamina counted most. At Dartmouth she didn't own a single dress.

Kristina went out in the hall to the bathroom to brush her teeth and wash her face.

When she returned, Albert was sitting on her bed in the dark. Locking the door behind her, Kristina came to sit next to him on the bed, relieved to see him. He wiped her still wet cheek with his fingers. In return, Kristina brushed the hair away from his face. His ponytail was unbound, and his hair hung loose past his shoulders.

"I can't stay long," he said. "I could barely get out as it was. Told her I had to get my condoms. She said she had some. I said I wanted the colored ones. Red, white, and blue. With the rocket's red glare . . ."

"You're so patriotic." She smiled, moving closer to him. He wiped her other cheek and forehead. She stared him straight in the face, her eyes inches away from his eyes, gently running her fingers through his hair. "I understand," she said softly. Their arms were touching.

"I wanted to talk to you about something," he said.

"Anything," Kristina said tenderly. "What is it?" She was so happy he had come. Earlier she had thought it had to stop. She *knew* it had to stop. But when she was with him, alone, she didn't want to stop anything.

"Let's go somewhere," he said.

"When?"

"Now. For Thanksgiving."

She sat quietly by his side in the dark; silently she sat and looked out the window.

"Go where?" Kristina finally said.

"To Canada!" he breathed out. "We'll rent a car and cross the river, to the other side, make a right, and just keep on driving. We'll find some nice little cottage, somewhere nice. In Quebec. On the way back, we can stop in Montreal. What do you say?"

Albert looked back at her stare. "What? We got no money again?" he said with a peculiar lilt to his voice.

"No, we—" She stopped. "We got a little. Howard gave me some for my birthday."

"How much is a little?"

She thought very quickly. "Ten thousand dollars."

Albert watched her intently. She tried to keep her face impassive. "That's enough to get to Canada," he finally said. "Or is that money all for you?"

Rubbing his arm, Kristina said, "Don't be like that. It's for us."

49

"It's not for us," he said. "It's for you."

"For us," she insisted.

"For you," he repeated, with the same peculiar lilt to his voice. Then with his right hand he cupped the side of her face. "Rocky," he said gently. "Want to?"

"Please," she whispered. "We can't. I'm playing on Saturday."

Albert sneered. "UPenn. I can beat them myself with my eyes closed and shooting into their net. Your third team can beat their first, with or without you."

"Albert, I can't skip the game!"

Shrugging, he said, "Not like you haven't done it before. It's no big deal. The coach yells at you for two minutes and then you dazzle her at practice for a week and everything's okay."

"Yeah, well, she told me last time I missed a game that she'd make me sit out, like, a month, if I did it again."

"Kristina," said Albert, smiling. "The coach knows she'd be cutting off her nose to spite her face. The only thing she'd do without you is lose, and lose big." Albert drew Kristina closer to him, squeezing her. "You're too good."

She squeezed him back.

Albert prodded on. "Come on, Rock. What do you say?"

She put her arm tighter around him and shook her head. "What, disappear for a few days? And then? We got to come back, you know. We have to come back and live here. There's no escape."

"Who wants to escape? I just want us to go—"

She interrupted, "If we could drive to Alaska, you'd say go there. If we had more money, you'd say, let's never come back to this place, let's travel the world, and be free of this life, of Dartmouth, of Howard—"

"We *are* free of Howard," Albert said sharply.

She continued, "—of Connecticut, of Luke and Laura, of Jim and Conni. You'd even forsake Aristotle, if it would mean . . ."

"Mean what?"

"Mean no one would know us. You'd forsake everything. Wouldn't you?"

Albert placed his hand on her chest to feel her heart. "Wouldn't *you*?"

Kristina tried to pull away from him. "Not everything. Not everything." She choked up. "Though God knows, I want to—"

"Do you?" he asked intensely. "Do you want to?"

"To be free? More than anything," she said, equally intensely. Her brown eyes flashed at Albert. But he misunderstood her meaning.

"Then let's go!" he whispered. "Edinburgh, Kristina! Remember Edinburgh?"

50

Remembering Edinburgh made her hands weak. Her fingers tensed and relaxed, and her heart squeezed tight with memories of Edinburgh. "Sure, I remember. But what then? I'd still have to come back and face Jim. And what about Conni? Remember how it was when we came back? It would be just like that, only worse."

"I'll make something up." He smiled tenderly. "I'm good at that."

"No," she said. They were speaking in hushed tones, and her *no* was an octave higher.

Albert said, "It's no big deal. I'll do anything to get away for a few days."

"What's the big hurry? We've just been to Fahrenbrae."

He waved at her impatiently. "Fahrenbrae is too close to here. We can go far into Canada for a few long days. We'll go sledding. Remember how much you like sledding?"

"Sure, I remember," Kristina said, getting weaker, the fight sinking out of her. "God, we just can't."

"Rock, stop," he said kindly, keeping his arm around her. Keeping her to him. "Stop fighting me."

"It's just a holiday," she said.

He was not easily dissuaded, but he took his arm away.

"This is no good," Kristina said with a miserable, hollow laugh.

"I agree," he said. "What do you think we should do? Stop?"

"Yes," she said immediately and laughed mirthlessly.

"Oh, Kristina. *Oh, Kristina!* How many times a year do you think we can continue having this conversation?"

"Until we stop."

"Well, gee," he said. "I don't exactly remember you saying that this morning at Fahrenbrae."

"The hills were too beautiful," she replied quietly, with emotion in her voice. "You were too beautiful."

He leaned into her face. "I'm not beautiful now?" he asked softly.

She averted her eyes. "Too beautiful."

They were silent. She imagined going to Canada with him.

"Albert, I know you agree with me. We have to stop. We have to get sane. You go with Conni. I go with Jim—" Kristina stopped. "Or not. But whatever. Go our separate ways."

"We've done this before. It didn't work. I don't know how to get sane." He paused. "Do you? I didn't think so. We're just crazed all the time."

Her mouth was dry when she whispered, "Yeah, crazed."

"Crazed!" he exclaimed. Grabbing her, he pulled her close to him on the bed. "Rocky, why are you doing this to me? Why do you do this to me all the time?" he said hotly, feverishly kissing her open lips, his hands gripping her wrists so tight it hurt.

She shut her eyes and pulled his head into her face, closer, if that were possible, into her, his lips overwhelming hers, pushing them apart with their intensity, their violence.

She groaned, moaned under his arms. He pushed her down on the bed. "Kristina," he whispered. "What are we going to do?"

Her only response was a stifled, raspy moan. Albert pulled her up to lift her pink tank top and expose her breasts, and then pushed her back down on the bed again. She whispered, "We're going to go a little crazy. And then we're going to escape forever."

"Escape?" he whispered into her mouth, grinding against her with the hardness in his jeans, hurting her, making her ache and moan with pain and desire. He was grinding as if he were trying to push himself whole inside her. "Escape? What are you talking about? There is no escape."

"Sweet hell," she whispered. "Almost like heaven." His big hand covered her mouth roughly. "I don't want to be damned," she said through his closed fingers. She wanted to cry.

He bent down to her breast, putting her nipple between his teeth. She stroked his arms, his head, his hair, his face. "Kristina, Kristina," he whispered back. "We're not damned. We're in love."

"No," she moaned as his hands moved down to her thighs. "We're damned."

She arched her back to help him take off her panties.

He pulled himself back up to her face and kissed her lips. "Rocky, darling," he said. "Rocky, Kristina, Rocky . . ."

"Oh, Albert," Kristina whispered. "Please . . . please . . . let's stop."

He pulled back for a moment, to look at her, his hands near her face and neck. "How can I stop?" he whispered fiercely. "How can I when you make me so fucking weak, I can't see straight . . ."

When he pulled off his jeans and she reached down to feel him, he was ready for her. She moaned softly into his neck, and he breathed hard, clutching her with his hands, propping himself up, one hand underneath her back, thrusting into her.

———•◦•◦•———

A knock on the door stopped them.

"Kristina?"

It was Conni.

52

Kristina instantly fell silent and put her hand over Albert's mouth, whose heavy belabored breath continued to be the only sound in the room.

The knock came again. "Kristina, I'm looking for Albert. You know where he is?"

Kristina held her breath, held Albert with her arms, and then let out, "Conni? No, I don't see him. Listen, it's real late."

The doorknob turned.

"Could you open the door, please?" Conni said impatiently.

"Conn, I'm so tired, I can't see straight," said Kristina, as she stifled Albert's moan. "I'm half asleep," Kristina finished, finding his mouth with her hand. "I'll talk to you in the morning, okay?"

"Could you just open the door for a second? I need to talk to you."

"Conni, tomorrow, okay?"

Conni banged loudly on the door. "No, it's not okay, Kristina. No it's not okay. Open the door."

"Conni, leave me alone, will you? I had a long day. I'll talk to you tomorrow."

Conni continued to bang on the door and carry on, but Albert and Kristina stopped listening. Albert turned Kristina over. Kristina put her face in the pillow to muffle her sounds. She felt Albert's hand in the back of her head, pushing her face into the pillow, his body hard behind her.

But Conni's banging and yelling did not subside.

Finally, Kristina heard someone out in the hall telling Conni to shut the hell up or they would call security. Conni wouldn't stop. A few minutes later somebody came to the door and asked Conni to come away. She refused. The security man knocked on the door and asked Kristina to open it. By this time Albert and Kristina were spent. Albert's hands were stroking her, caressing her. He blew on her perspired face to cool her.

Kristina told the security man she was trying to sleep, wasn't well, and wasn't dressed. Eventually he led Conni away.

Later when they were lying next to each other in the little bed, Kristina said quietly, "God, Albert, we can't live like this."

"You're right. Let's go to Canada."

"What, forever?"

"Yes," he said. "Let's go to Canada forever."

She pushed him lightly. "Boy, you'll say anything right now, won't you?"

He smiled. "Anything." He was lying sideways, propping himself up on his elbow. He blew on her face again and then kissed it.

Kristina wondered about Conni. What *was* Albert going to tell her?

"Canada, huh? Albert," Kristina said, "why Canada? Seems far away."

"The farther the better," he said. "Tell me you don't want to go."

"I didn't say that," she said cautiously, thinking.

"Let's go," he beseeched her. "We've got the money—you said so your-self. There's nothing stopping us."

She wanted to ask Albert about his imminent engagement to Conni. How are you going to take me to Canada and get engaged to her at the same time? she wanted to ask.

Albert poked her gently. "Well?"

"And when this money is gone, then what?"

"Then nothing. Then we'll get more money," he said.

"From where?"

Albert pulled away from her and stared at the ceiling.

"Howard and I are now officially divorced," Kristina said. "Grandma is dead."

"There must be some money tucked away somewhere," said Albert.

"What are you talking about?" Kristina said, a little shrilly. "There's no money, I'm telling you."

"So? We'll get jobs. We'll have money."

Smirking, Kristina said, "You're gonna get a job, Albert?"

"Sure, why not?" He put his hands behind his head. "I'll try anything once."

Now Kristina lay on her side, propped up by her elbow, and stared into his face. She wanted to tell him about the money, but she was just waiting for the right time. When he was married to Conni, maybe. She smiled at her own little joke.

"What's so funny?" he asked.

"Nothing, nothing," she quickly said. This was not a good time.

"Rocky? If I break up with Conni, will you break up with Jim?"

Oh, not this again. She wanted to say, break up with Conni? Is that before or after you get engaged? But she didn't.

"Albert, please," she said. "Please."

He gritted his teeth. "I just don't know about that Jim of yours."

Getting defensive, Kristina said, "Why, because he's a nice guy? Because he treats me well?"

"Because having sex with you is against his religion." Albert said meanly. "Some relationship."

"Well, I didn't know he didn't like to have sex when I started going out with him, did I?"

Staring passionately at her, Albert said, "No, Rocky, not just not like to have sex. Not like to have sex with *you*."

"But it's easier for you this way, isn't it?"

"Yes," Albert said instantly. "At first I couldn't stand the thought of him touching you." He paused. "Of anybody touching you."

"Well, how do you think I feel about you and Conni?" Kristina said. They fell silent. Kristina was thinking about Thanksgiving. To be with him. Not to be alone. Not to be with Jim or with Conni or with Howard, or alone, but with him, far away—in Canada.

"We don't have to go anywhere," Albert said. "The ten grand, the ten thousand goddamn dollars we have. We could save it."

"We could," she said tentatively.

"Yeah. We never have any money." He pulled away farther. "*I* never have any money."

"What do you need money for?" Kristina asked. "Conni always pays for everything."

"Not just Conni, dear Rocky," said Albert, staring at her in the night light. "Not just her."

And then they slept together in her room, naked on her narrow bed.

Chapter
Two

MONDAY

K ristina rushed to get ready for her seven-forty-five Modern Christian Thought class. To save time, she put on the same clothes she'd
worn on Sunday.

Albert was sitting on the bed, next to Aristotle spread out on his back.

"Get him off," Kristina said. "His hair gets on everything."

Albert didn't touch the dog. "His hair is already on everything."

"Albert!" she said, raising her voice. "Aristotle! Down!"

The dog got down sheepishly. He knew he wasn't supposed to be on the
bed.

Sitting next to Albert, Kristina rubbed his leg. "What are you going to tell
Conni?"

He looked sullen. His black eyes were sunken in his face, as they always
were after a night of little sleep. His pale face with huge black eyes made him
look slightly cadaverous.

"Don't worry," he said. "I'll think of something."

Kristina, unsmiling inside or out, said, "I'm sure you will. Tell her you fell
asleep in your room."

"Rocky, you'll never make a convincing liar. What, and didn't hear her
make a public nuisance of herself? Yeah, good."

Kristina looked outside into the blue post-dawn darkness. It looked very
cold. She felt bad for Conni, standing outside their door, banging, fearing the
worst, being lied to.

Albert said, "I'm going to tell her you hadn't walked Aristotle and I went to walk him. I'll tell her I went through the woods to Frankie's and was so tired I fell asleep there."

"What if she called Frankie?"

"Frankie doesn't pick up his phone after midnight."

"What if she went to see Frankie?"

"She didn't. She wouldn't."

"Well, aren't you going to have to inform Frankie of your little plan?"

"Yeah, it's not a problem."

"Oh, I see. Frankie is a stooge for you, isn't he?"

"Not a stooge, just my friend," Albert said, getting up off the bed and eyeing her grimly. "What's gotten into you?"

Kristina shook her head, feeling worse and worse. "Nothing, I just . . ." What had happened to starting over? Starting a new life? Hadn't she been beginning to do that yesterday? Wasn't that what she had told herself?

"Conni will believe it, you'll see." Albert took Aristotle's leash and fitted it over the dog's head. "Remember, she wants to believe it. Why would she want to hear the truth? What's she going to do with the truth? That's the most important thing to remember. All I have to do is let her believe what she wants to believe in the first place. It's that simple."

Getting off the bed, Kristina said bleakly, "Is it that simple? It's really the dumbest excuse."

He shrugged. "So think of a better one."

Picking up her books off the table, Kristina said, "We can't do this, Albert. I can't do this."

He came to her. "You say that now . . ." he drawled suggestively, running his free hand over her back.

"I mean it." She pushed him off her. "I just—I can't do this anymore. I'm starting to hate myself, and—" She broke off.

"And what?"

"Nothing."

"And? You're starting to hate me?"

"I didn't say that."

"You didn't have to." His black eyes blazed. She backed off, not used to seeing his rare temper.

"I gotta go," Kristina said.

He shrugged. "Where's your coat?"

"Fahrenbrae."

"Ahhh," said Albert. "So take my jacket."

"What about you?"

"I've got two." He unlocked her door and peeked outside. "All clear," he

58

whispered and walked quickly down the hall to his room. She followed him.

"I can't take your jacket," Kristina said. "Jim or Conni is going to see me wearing it, and what am I supposed to say then?"

"Make up something clever."

"Yeah? Oh, I left my coat up at this place Albert and I shack up at, and then he let me borrow his."

"No, something cleverer than that."

She sighed deeply. "I'll see you, Albert."

He studied her for a moment. "I'll see you tonight," he said, handing her his brown leather jacket. She shook her head and backed away toward the glass doors that led to the side stairs.

"Rock," Albert called after her, almost as an afterthought. "Happy birthday."

She nodded, unsmiling.

"Will you at least think about Canada?" he asked her.

Shaking her head in disbelief, Kristina smiled ruefully at him.

The glass door slammed shut behind her.

After her last class, Kristina had basketball practice, then showered and went to her car. Her long hair was still wet when she got in and started up the car. The Mustang coughed and spluttered for a few moments.

Nice car, she thought, trying to goad it on. Come on, come on, nice, dear, sweet car. I'm gonna take care of you when you get sick. You're my friend. You're nice, come on. And then the engine finally began to run smoothly. Kristina closed her eyes. Thank God. You piece-of-shit car.

Someone knocked loudly on her window. Kristina opened her eyes. Conni stepped back, her arms folded.

Oh, no, Kristina thought, rolling the window partway down.

"Hi, Conn, what's up?" she said. "I'm late."

"You're always late," said Conni.

"Doesn't make me any less late," said Kristina pleasantly. Inside she felt terrible.

"What's up?" said Conni, furiously curling a strand of hair around her index finger. "How come you didn't open the door last night?"

"I told you I was real tired. I was asleep when you knocked."

Conni stared steely-eyed at Kristina. "Sleeping, huh? You could've opened the door."

"Could've, yes," Kristina said. "But didn't want to. I was naked and tired. And it sounded like you had company in the hall."

Conni narrowed her eyes to slits. "Did you have company in the room?"

Kristina got scared. Was this where it was going to happen? Right here, in the parking lot? "Constance," she said slowly. "What are you accusing me of?"

"Nothing," Conni said quickly. "Nothing. I was just mad you wouldn't open the door. Usually you never even lock it." She paused. "And I know you weren't with Jim."

"How do you know that?"

"Because I was looking for Albert."

"In Jim's room?"

"Anywhere."

Kristina sighed. "Conn, how often have you found Albert in Jim's room? Albert never goes to Jim's room. Never."

"How do you know that?"

"Because that's what Jim tells me." Actually it was what Albert told her. Albert didn't feel comfortable with Jim anymore.

Relaxing a little, Kristina said, "I'm sorry you were upset. Next time I'll open the door, okay?" She rolled down her window.

"You know," Conni said, "I was just . . . I just didn't know where Albert was. He said he was going up to his room for a minute."

"Ahh," said Kristina and didn't know what else to say. "I hope he showed up eventually."

"No," Conni said tearfully. "That's the whole thing."

There was a pause, while Kristina looked away from Conni, who seemed to be collecting her thoughts as she stepped from foot to foot in the cold. Kristina turned to face the front windshield and the parking lot and Hinman Hall ahead. She could see her own windows up there on the third floor. How nice it would be to be alone up in the room right now. She looked over to the right and stared at her bridge vacantly. Kristina's Bridge. Maybe if it snowed soon . . . Kristina could have a few drinks, and walk her bridge, and not be scared anymore.

She turned back to Conni, who obviously was trying hard to come to grips with something.

Clearing her throat, Conni said, "Krissy, umm, listen. Was the dog with you?"

"With me when?" Kristina asked, wanting to roll the window back up.

"Last night."

Kristina's heart was pounding. She is trying to trap me. But what can I say? I don't even know if she spoke to Albert today. She is definitely trying to corner me into something, but what?

"I don't know," Kristina replied vaguely. "Listen, I really gotta—"

"Albert said he walked Aristotle for you last night."

Kristina kept her face passive, but inside she was relieved.

"Yes. He came by, and took the dog," she told Conni.

"He did?" she exclaimed. "So you saw him?"

"Briefly," Kristina replied.

"And then?"

"And then what? Then I locked the door."

"Why did you do that?"

"Because I wanted to go to sleep, and he was gone a long time."

"How long?"

"I don't know, Conni. He never came up to bring the dog back." She didn't know what else to say, and Conni still seemed dissatisfied. So Kristina said, "Maybe he'd gone to Frankie's?"

"That's what he said he did. But he said he came back and knocked, you just didn't answer."

"What time was this? I didn't hear him," said Kristina without missing a beat, but thinking, God, Albert, I wish you had talked to me about this.

"How long was he gone before I came up?"

"I don't know. Maybe a half hour."

This wasn't the first time Kristina had been interrogated by Conni. She wished it could be the last time, though. Since Edinburgh, Conni had been increasingly suspicious about Kristina and Albert. When Conni and Kristina roomed together in their freshman and part of their sophomore years, Kristina had never fallen under suspicion, but Conni had been sure Albert was seeing someone else.

Kristina lifted her black eyes to Conni, who was staring at her with the expression of someone who had just swallowed an unbelievable excuse, had bought it, and was now hating herself for it. Feeling very bad, Kristina said, "Conn, I thought he was with you. I thought he just took Aristotle down to your room and stayed there."

"Well, he didn't," Conni said, struggling to keep her voice even.

Reaching out, Kristina took Conni's arm. "I'm sorry you're feeling down. It'll be okay. You know Albert loves you."

"Do I? Do I know that?"

"Sure you do," Kristina said comfortingly. "It's obvious. Every time he looks at you, it's obvious."

Conni stared at her. "You're kidding, right?"

"No, of course I'm not." What was she getting at?

"The way he looks at *me*?" Conni laughed aloud. "You are kidding me. Kristina, have you ever seen the way Albert looks at *you*?"

Kristina had. She knew how Albert looked at her. Turning up a blank expression, she said, "Conn, I don't know what you're—"

"Kristina!" Conni became agitated. "He looks at you, and you at him, like—I don't know, like you've been—I don't know—friends for life. Like he is about to go the front and die and he's looking at you for the last time. God, it makes me crazy. Don't tell me you don't see it!"

"Conni, I'm sorry, I really don't."

"Yeah, Albert says the same thing. 'Conn, you're crazy,' he says. 'Conn, it's probably just hunger.' 'Conn, I look at Frankie the same way,' or 'Conn, you silly. What about the way I look at you?' "

Kristina was beginning to feel sick to her stomach. "What do you want me to say, Conni?" she said weakly.

Conni continued as if not hearing Kristina. "I said to him, it's not that he touches you, because he doesn't, and it's not that he says things to you, because he doesn't, it's just the way he looks at you. I asked him not to look at you anymore." Conni took a deep breath and swiped the hair off her face in a manic gesture. "God, this is just so ludicrous."

"I agree," said Kristina quietly. Glancing at the dashboard clock, Kristina got out of the car and went to put her arms around Conni, who didn't protest but didn't hug back either.

"Conn, I'm sorry you're so upset. Come on, girl." Kristina's arm remained around her shoulders.

"Am I crazy, Krissy? Am I just plain nuts?"

"Yes," Kristina said, still feeling queasy. "Bonkers."

"Krissy," Conni said, "once I saw you guys."

Kristina missed a beat, maybe two, imagining the worst, before she said, "Saw us where?"

"In Baker Library, sitting in the reserve corridor, looking into the same book."

"When?"

"I don't know. A few weeks ago."

"We were studying. Nietzsche, I think."

"Not one part of your bodies was touching, yet I just felt so bad when I saw the two of you."

"Conni," Kristina said softly, soothingly. "We were just studying."

"Yeah, I know," said Conni in a depressed voice. "That's what Albert told me. I mean, look, I know he loves me, I know that, okay? I just can't help feeling these things sometimes. I'm sorry."

Kristina hugged Conni tighter, incredulous. How did I get *her* to apologize to *me*?

Conni's face brightened slightly, and Kristina felt even worse. I'm not going to lie anymore. That's my new motto, too. I'm going to right my life and I'm not going to lie anymore.

Getting back into the car, Kristina shifted into reverse and said, "I gotta go."

"Go, go," said Conni, stepping away from the car. "Thanks for talking."

"Sure," said Kristina, hating herself as she drove to Red Leaves House.

At Red Leaves, Betty, her friend and boss, had bought Kristina an ice cream cake. It was the thought that counted, because Kristina'd hated ice cream cakes since childhood.

Betty's assistants and some of the resident girls at Red Leaves had pitched in to buy her a black leather handbag.

Kristina thankfully made a hazy wordless wish that had to do with the smell of pines and the mountains and cold and hope, and blew out the candles. Then she cut the cake and Betty served it, while Kristina went to sit in her favorite chair in the living room.

Despite hating ice cream cakes, Kristina ate every bite and asked for seconds. Afterward, she took her wallet and assorted letters and papers and magazines out of her backpack and stuffed them all into the new handbag. Seeing the pleased, affectionate faces around her made Kristina feel better about her life.

Betty was a woman of about thirty, a graceful, slightly severe-looking woman with pale skin and a sharp nose. Red Leaves House was hers. It had originally belonged to her parents, John and Olivia Barrett, local philanthropists who wanted to do something for their community. They had already contributed plenty to libraries, charities, homeless shelters, and soup kitchens. Red Leaves House was their primary charitable cause. Because it was the first of its kind in the area, it had gained immediate notoriety.

In her freshman year, Kristina had picked up a brochure about Red Leaves House at the Dartmouth-Hitchcock Medical Center and agreed to work there as part of her work/study program. She had been coming every Monday and Thursday afternoon for the last three years. Kristina wished it paid more, especially during the lean months. More important, it got her away from Dartmouth College for two days a week, and getting away from Dartmouth College was essential for Kristina from time to time. Also, all the pregnant girls adored her.

The drawback was being around babies. Kristina got reluctantly but intensely attached to these infants. When the babies left Red Leaves House, with either their mothers or their adoptive families, Kristina felt as if her own were being taken away from her.

Quitting wasn't an option. Quit and do what? She was loved by the girls and liked by the other counselors, and Kristina was the only one from Dartmouth. It felt like being on another basketball team—Kristina was the All-Ivy center of Red Leaves.

Before Kristina went upstairs, she and Betty chatted.

"How are your friends?" asked Betty. "Still see them much? You sound like you're always so busy."

"Yeah, I'm busy, but I see them all the time. I'm writing a piece on the death penalty for Jim, and Conni and I went to the movies last Friday night. Saw—"

"And Albert?" said Betty. "See much of him?"

Suppressing a smile, Kristina eyed Betty. "Yeah, I see him once in a while. He's doing well."

"Oh, good, good. You know you're welcome to invite them over here one Sunday if you're not busy. You guys were a big hit with all the girls when you came a few months ago and played basketball in our driveway. Maybe you can do that again sometime." She spoke shifting her gaze from left to right and not looking straight at Kristina.

Kristina smiled and touched Betty's arm. "Thanks. Yeah, sure. Sure. Maybe I can round them up the Sunday after Thanksgiving. How would that be?"

"That would be good," said Betty, controlling her voice.

"Where's Evelyn?" Kristina asked.

Betty told Kristina, "Go upstairs. She's not feeling well. She's been asking for you."

Kristina started upstairs. Betty called after her, "She can't spend a day here without asking when you're working next. What do you do for that girl?"

"Oh, you know," demurred Kristina. "I stick pins in a doll named Evelyn and kill chickens on Fridays."

"Nice."

Fifteen-year-old Evelyn Moss, pregnant with twins, had come to Red Leaves House last summer when she was barely out of her first trimester. A tall, pretty strawberry blonde, Evelyn, racked with morning sickness, was very depressed. Kristina spent her summer term at Dartmouth working at Red Leaves and talking to Evelyn, who slowly turned into a thickset shadow of her former slender self. During the summer all Evelyn wanted was not to be pregnant anymore. She trailed after Kristina, ate nonstop, and gained too much weight. Her blood pressure was out of control.

Evelyn ate through her second trimester and cried through her third. The feeling of not wanting to be pregnant anymore gave way to not wanting to give up her babies. Kristina told Evelyn that that too was normal, but Evelyn would not listen.

Kristina tried convincing Evelyn with statistics. "They're all against you, kid." Kristina told her about the number of teenage mothers who are high school dropouts, the number on welfare, the number below the poverty line, and the children's psychological problems. Nothing Kristina said would bring relief to Evelyn, who now wanted only one thing and would not listen to reason. Evelyn's parents had told her she had to give the children up for adoption, and Evelyn was still at an age when she listened to her parents.

Kristina could hear Evelyn crying in her room as she opened the door and entered.

"Hi, Evie. It's me," she said brightly. Evelyn cried harder.

"Nice welcome," Kristina said, sitting on the bed next to the girl and patting her belly. "How are you holding up?"

Evelyn couldn't talk.

"Come on, honey, come on, girl. Hang in there. Only a few more weeks to go."

"No more weeks to go," Evelyn sobbed. "My show fell out."

"Oh wow," Kristina said excitedly. "Oh wow."

Evelyn grabbed Kristina's hands. "Krissy, please talk to my mom, please! I don't want to give up my babies!"

Evelyn had told Kristina about her parents, who had lived in Lyme their whole lives. They had simple dignity and pride, and they could not allow their only daughter to have a child out of wedlock at fifteen. That would be a first in seven Moss generations. For Donald and Patricia Moss it meant having to send their daughter to Red Leaves and telling all the neighbors she had gone to visit a sick aunt in Minnesota. Evelyn couldn't very well return from Minnesota with two babies who did not know their father. Evelyn had confessed to Kristina during one of their many weepy talks that Evelyn herself was not *precisely* sure who the father was, though she had a couple of strong hunches. When both boys were individually confronted by Evelyn's parents, they denied any impropriety, admitting, however, that if there was any impropriety, it was all Evelyn's. The two boys were scared and didn't want to get married at fifteen. They wanted to finish high school.

Kristina knew it wouldn't help to talk to Evelyn's parents. "Evie," she said gently, "I'll try to talk to your mom next time she comes, okay? I'll talk to her." She paused. "But Evelyn, even if they are adopted, it'll be okay. I promise. They'll be so loved."

"Oh, please!" Evelyn snapped. "Don't you understand anything? I don't want to give them up!"

Kristina patted the girl's belly. "I do, Evelyn, I understand everything," she said quietly.

Evelyn tried to move away from her. "How could you possibly?"

What could Kristina tell this grieving, crying girl? "Evelyn, they'll be loved," she repeated. "And you'll have a life. They'll have wonderful parents. They'll have two grown-up, wonderful parents—"

"I don't want them to have parents!" Evie cried. "I want them to have me!" Evelyn was sitting on the bed in front of her, looking flushed, uncomfortable, and heavy. She was breathing hard.

"Evie, don't get yourself all excited," said Kristina, trying to calm the girl down. She smiled and tried to make a joke. "I don't know how to deliver babies."

"Betty does," Evelyn replied seriously. "She delivered a baby once when her car broke down and they couldn't get to the hospital in time."

Kristina knew about that. But they hadn't broken down, they had been in an accident. The baby had not been saved. And Betty had suffered a spinal injury that had left her with a permanently bad back.

"Can we have some sanity here? Nobody but the doctor is going to be delivering your babies."

"That's right. My babies."

"Evelyn, please."

Evelyn fell back on the bed. Her large belly remained up, nearly perpendicular to the rest of her body.

"I want them to stay inside me forever," she whispered.

Kristina took off Evelyn's socks and started rubbing her feet. "When I was a young girl," she said quietly, "I thought that was possible. I thought babies just stayed inside you until you wanted them to come out."

Evelyn went on plaintively, "Just stay inside me forever, never leave me, never leave their mommy . . ." She started to cry again. Her belly heaved. It was the only thing moving in the small bedroom.

"You know," Evelyn said, sniffling, "I've even been thinking of names for them. "Joshua and Samuel. Josh and Sam. Do you like that?"

Kristina wanted to tell Evelyn what Betty had trained her to say when counseling pregnant teenagers about giving their babies up for adoption: that one was never supposed to give the baby a name or think of it in personal terms. One was never supposed to buy the baby anything, or knit anything, or think of spending the first few days with the baby. Josh and Samuel. Well, wasn't that just cozy? Josh and Sam were the two boys who had dallied with Evelyn Moss and then refused to own up. Kristina thought Evelyn was insane for even thinking about them.

"Did your parents come yesterday?" asked Kristina.

Evelyn nodded. "Mom said it will all be over soon, and then we can go back to being a family again." She wiped her face.

Kristina wanted to say having babies changed everything forever, but she just rubbed Evelyn's belly, feeling little legs and feet push against the skin.

Then it was five o'clock and time to go.

Downstairs she thanked everybody again for her cake and purse and left.

About to get into her car, Kristina heard a tapping from one of the second-floor windows. She looked up. It was Evelyn, who opened the window and shouted out, "Krissy, are you going to come to the hospital when I have my babies?"

"Sure I will, Evie," said Kristina. "Sure I will."

"Good," Evelyn yelled out of the window. "You're not going away for Thanksgiving, are you? I'm going to go into labor any minute!"

Going away for Thanksgiving. Well, today was already Monday. Tomorrow was the last full day of classes. The chances of going away anywhere for Thanksgiving were looking slimmer and slimmer. The odds against it were lengthening like the pre-dusk shadows. Kristina knew Evelyn could use her support.

"No," she said. "I'm going to stay put. Have Betty call me as soon as you go into labor. I'll come to the hospital."

"And hold my hand?"

Kristina nodded. "And hold your hand," she said softly.

Evelyn blew her a kiss and disappeared from the window.

———

Usually, Kristina drove home down Route 120 and made a left onto East Wheelock and a right onto College Street to get to Tuck Mall, but today she went a little farther west in Lebanon and made a right onto Route 10. It was a nicer road during the day, and in the summers she regularly took Route 10. She liked the view from the road. Tonight it was dark, though, and she didn't know what had made her drive down to Route 10, except maybe she was thinking about Evelyn and adopted babies, and her mind, distracted from being in ten different places at once, hadn't thought quick enough to make a right onto Route 120. Kristina made her way on Route 10 at thirty miles an hour down the winding two-lane road as she thought of Joshua and Samuel. And subsequently Albert and Canada. Albert was right. Canada would be wonderful. Like Edinburgh.

The three months they had spent at Edinburgh in the spring of 1991 had been the happiest months of her life.

They had no money, the dorms were old and cold, and they got no studying done. Kristina lost fifteen pounds in Scotland, eating soup mostly and spaghetti. They saved their pennies to go out to the pubs on Friday nights. Kristina remembered the cobblestone streets, the Tudor houses, the churches, the first she'd been to on a regular basis, and the Mull of Kintyre. They went there for New Year's Eve, staying in a tiny bed-and-breakfast, got drunk on bitter and ale with the locals, and then spent New Year's Day by the stark Irish Sea. She remembered the mountains, she remembered the lakes, the dandelions and daffodils coming to bloom. She remembered herself and him at Edinburgh. She remembered most of all how she had felt then—no hopelessness, no despair, no shame. Just the two of them, freed by their anonymity.

Until one day, as a lark, they stopped by a street fortune-teller and gave her two quid to read Kristina's palm. Kristina went behind the dirty paisley curtain, and the hunched woman grabbed her hands and turned them over. Kristina tried to pull her hands away, but it was no use. The hag was strong. The old woman's heavy Gaelic brogue Kristina barely understood, but the contorted expression of horror on her face was etched into Kristina's mind. The expression of horror she understood well. She'd seen that expression before. The old witch wouldn't let go of Kristina's hands; she kept mumbling, then yelling; she became frenzied. Finally Albert stepped inside and pried their hands apart. As they hurried away down the street, Kristina could still hear the old woman holler shrilly after them. The fortune-teller was the only thing that had marred their one-hundred-and-thirty-day idyll.

The wind was howling outside, and it was very cold. Route 10 had no streetlights, only oaks and maples and plenty of American mountain ash, whose leaves were so delicate and pretty and yellow in autumn. Now, three nights before Thanksgiving, the trees were mere silhouettes on the side of the road.

Kristina drove with her mind in Edinburgh. In the moments before the curve near the reservoir, she was thinking about going to Scotland to live. Deeper in her subconscious, she was thinking of Thayer dining hall and whether they would have macaroni and cheese tonight as they always did on Mondays or whether they would go on some unspecified and certainly unjustified holiday schedule when they only served hamburgers and heroes.

The radio's country station was playing "We Just Disagree."

> *And do you think*
> *That we've grown up differently?*
> *Haven't been the same*
> *Since you lost your feel for me . . .*

68

As she went around the bend in the road, she saw an oncoming car, and because it was dark, and she judged the narrowness of road conservatively, Kristina instinctively turned the wheel to the right. But the lights were rushing headlong toward her. The other car still seemed perilously close. She turned the wheel a little more and heard the noise of her right tires hitting gravel. The Mustang bobbled, and the wheel became unsteady in her hands. To compensate, Kristina quickly turned the wheel to the left.

She overcompensated.

The car jerked, and she panicked and slammed on the brakes. The Mustang swerved, the brakes locked, and the car reeled sideways on the narrow road—directly into the headlights of the oncoming car.

Kristina heard the insistent and unremitting noise of the horn and the screeching of the other car's brakes. The instant the Mustang was bathed with light, there was a loud crash and Kristina was thrown against the driver's side window. She heard glass breaking.

The Mustang swirled around twice and flew backward down the embankment. Kristina's life came to a standstill. She had just enough time to think, ohno, ohno, ohno, I'm going to die, I don't want to die, I don't want to die! and then the car turned over once in midair, and came down with a thump to stand on its tires, a few feet from the water.

—•••—

Kristina opened her eyes and closed them again, opened them and closed them. She could see nothing at first, it was so dark. She thought, am I dead? Open-eyed, yet unable to see, just dead. No feeling anywhere. Nothing moved. Dead. But something gave away life. Something. She couldn't figure it out at first, something real-life, familiar, unotherworldly.

She heard the radio.

> *So let's leave it alone,*
> *Cause we can't see eye to eye*
> *There's no good guy*
> *There's no bad guy*
> *There's only you and me*
> *And we just disagree . . .*

She reached over to turn the damn radio off and thought, I don't think they play easy-listening music in the afterlife.

She felt no pain. On the other hand, that was good. Who wanted to feel pain? On the other hand, dead people felt no pain.

There was a rustling of leaves, branches, the sound of feet shuffling down the slope, hurrying. Somebody at her driver's side window. A man, with terror in his eyes and a bloody nose, mouthing, are you all right? Are you all right?

Kristina tried to roll down the broken window, but it was jammed. Actually, she couldn't get a grip on the handle. Her hand was not obeying her. The fingers were not closing.

She tried to nod, but that didn't work either. I'm all right, she tried to reply, but couldn't hear herself. She just wanted to get out of the car. Wait here, she heard the man say. Wait here, I'm going to go and get help. Just you wait, he said.

She leaned back in her seat. Well, I'm not going anywhere, she thought. Where would I go? And then she thought: home. I wouldn't mind going home.

But where was home?

My room. My messy room with my little bed and my desk and my dog lying on the bed smelling up all the blankets with his dog smell and dog hair. It's the only home I have, and I want to be back there right now.

She reached down and tried to pry the seat belt off herself. Was the car still running? She couldn't hear very well. The seat belt had locked, and was digging into Kristina's rib cage and right hip. What possessed me to put one on tonight? she thought. Well, doesn't God protect the wicked and the damned?

She clicked open the seat belt and moved her right hand across her body to the door, which would not open. And the window would not roll down. The headlights of the Mustang weren't on, though she was sure they had been on. What had happened?

And then she felt cold. She wondered if it was because she was dead, and getting colder by the second. But no, her right hand was moving, and her legs were moving sluggishly. The passenger window was broken.

She slowly moved over to the passenger seat and tried to open that door. It was jammed. So she got up with her knees on the seat and tried to climb out through the broken window. Climbing out was not easy. She couldn't lift her left arm to prop herself up. Finally she nearly fell out with a thump down to the ground. She fell on her good arm, but not her good side. She was still feeling no pain.

Shit, Kristina thought. Hope I'll be okay for Saturday's game. Hate to sit out the first league game of the season.

It was very dark. She tried to orient herself. Where's the lake? Okay, it's in front of me, because behind me is the hill, so if the lake is in front of me, that means it's on the left side of the road, which would be west, and that means Hanover is just a few miles north as the crow flies.

First she had to get up the brutal hill. She couldn't see. She groped around, lost her footing, and fell—on her left side. A sharp rocket of fire exploded in her arm, and she fainted.

She came to some time later. It was still dark, still no sign of police or an ambulance, still eerily quiet.

All she wanted to do was get back up on the highway and start walking home. Maybe someone would pick her up. She didn't want the man to come back with help. Help invariably meant an ambulance, which—from everything Kristina knew about ambulances—would probably take her to the hospital.

Kristina hated hospitals. She had been in one only twice in her entire life, and once was when she had been born.

She certainly didn't plan to be taken to a hospital tonight by a well-meaning stranger just because of a locked seat belt and sore ribs.

So she got up off the ground and tried again, groping at something to hold on to while with one good hand she dragged her body up the hill.

Two cars went by. She heard them slow down—probably to see the car that had hit hers—and then speed on ahead. But the few seconds gave her enough light to see that the highway was only another ten feet up, and there were some shrubs she could hold on to.

Hurry up, hurry up, she kept telling herself. Hurry up, Krissy, hurry up, Rocky, pull yourself up. She slipped on the hard ground every couple of seconds. Like a football team after a penalty, moving ten yards back after winning the territory, she kept slipping.

She felt a rock with her knee. Oh, that hurt. I felt pain! That's so great. She grabbed on, pulled herself up, felt in front of her for something else to hold on to; there were a few pebbles, but little else. Where are those damn shrubs? As she struggled up the hill, she whispered haltingly, *Hear not my steps, which way they walk, for fear the very stones prate of my whereabout.* . . . *Hear not my steps, which way they walk, for fear the very stones prate of my whereabout.* . . . *Hear not my steps* . . .

Kristina heard other cars coming, thank God, and here was some more light. Not far to go at all, we're almost there. But there was nothing to clutch now, and in desperation, she started to claw at the ground with her hand. Her left arm was immobile. She felt her nails bending back and breaking, but she didn't care. What was important was getting back up. With her new black boots she kicked into the ground like a rock climber.

Finally, Kristina climbed up onto the two-foot-wide shoulder, and rested for a moment to catch her breath. She felt fluid dripping from her head. Kristina told herself it was sweat.

The man had said he was going to get help, but how he would do this was a mystery to Kristina, since his car was smashed and off the road. She didn't give it any more thought than that. She was glad he hadn't come back. In a childish gesture, she wiped the dirt off her knees.

Then she began to walk to Hanover. Slowly at first, but then faster and faster, she eventually broke into a slow jog on the shoulder of Route 10, just to get farther away from the Mustang, the reservoir, her new purse, and the man who had gone to get help.

When she got up to Hinman, she realized she had left her keys in the ignition and had to shiver near the doorway until someone came out and let her in.

Aristotle wasn't in her room. The bed had not been made from this morning. The desk had all kinds of stuff on it, and the computer was covered with dirty glasses, Post-it notes, and scattered papers. Her clothes were all over the floor.

She was home.

Locking the door, Kristina sat down on the bed and slowly examined her hands. They were dirty and bloody from clawing at the ground. Most of the nails were broken. The nail polish was chipped. She stared at them and then tried to get the dirt off the index fingernail, until she asked herself what she was doing and stopped.

She had left all of her identification in the car. Great, just great, she thought. The police were sure to have a bunch of questions for her. Miss, could we give you back the stuff that belongs to you, please? You forgot it all in your inexplicable hurry to get away from the scene of the accident. Why were you in such a hurry? Is there something you should be telling us? Were you drinking?

And then Kristina remembered Spencer O'Malley and wondered if maybe he would come to investigate her. She smiled lightly to herself. That wouldn't be half bad.

Drinking. Now that wasn't a terrible idea. Her mouth felt wet already at the thought of the old Southern Comfort. Reaching over to her night table, Kristina opened the top drawer and took out a nearly empty bottle. There wasn't enough to comfort her. She got up, went to her closet, and reached up to get an unopened bottle from the top shelf. Then she sat back down on the bed, opened the cap with one hand, opened her mouth, tilted the bottle, and poured forth enough liquor to comfort herself and forget about her car and about her three friends who at this time were certainly waiting for her to come and celebrate her twenty-first birthday with them.

The pint bottle was a third empty when she was done. She hated seeing the bottle emptying, but when she was finished she felt immeasurably better. The shock of the accident was wearing off, and she was beginning to throb and ache.

Slowly and uncertainly, she sat on the bed, bent over, and started to un-lace her boots. The arduous procedure would have taken her five or six min-utes under the best of circumstances. Tonight, under the haze of alcohol and the distant blur of pain, it took her three times as long. She thought she might even have nodded off in that position, hunched over her boots, as if she were about to throw up.

It was difficult undressing. She pulled off her sweatshirt with one arm over her head. Her pink tank top came off the same way. The five-button-fly jeans were as hard to remove as the boots. She had to wriggle out of them in the end. The left arm just wasn't pulling down those jeans. Then the socks. Then the underwear. And when she was naked, Kristina walked unsteadily to her closet and stared at herself in the full-length mirror on the back of the door.

Her face was covered with blood that had streamed down her right tem-ple and cheek and neck, clotting and drying below her collarbone. So it wasn't sweat she had felt dripping off her, she thought. Her black eyes shone blacker than ever, glistening with the warm wet dilation of Southern Comfort. Her knees were skinned, and her left arm hung limply at her side. Kristina looked closer. Her left shoulder was a swollen, maroon-colored mess. God.

Shit.

Shit, shit, shit. During her first year, in a rough-and-tumble practice, six weeks before league play began, two girls had knocked into each other, one suffering a dislocated shoulder. The poor kid had to sit out eight weeks, and soon quit basketball altogether. Kristina had been glad not to have been on the receiving end of that one.

She became so frightened, she actually thought of going to the hospital. Anything, dear God, anything. I have to play basketball again.

However, the idea of getting the shoulder looked at terrified her. What if it was bad? She couldn't deal with thinking about it. She pretended it wasn't even that painful and tried to be brave. She gritted her teeth and moved her left arm. It's okay, it's okay. It won't be so bad.

Her right rib had the beginning of a large ragged black-and-blue mark that looked like a Rorschach blot.

Kristina moved closer to the mirror; her face was almost touching the cool smooth surface. There was something stuck near her right temple, above the eye. Kristina lifted her hand to touch it. It was a piece of safety glass. It was not a big piece, Kristina thought, trying to comfort herself as she pried the glass from her skin. The empty bloody gash the glass left behind was scarier than having the glass in her head.

Kristina went to have a shower after taking another sip of Southern Comfort. Her hand holding the bottle was steady.

The hot water felt wonderful on her aching body but miserable on her shoulder, so she turned it off. Washing under cold water felt only marginally better. Every once in a while she would try to move her left arm and wince from the pain. But she didn't feel like screaming, Kristina told herself. It wasn't that bad.

When she was trying to dry herself, another student, Jill, entered the shower rooms. They nodded to each other, and Kristina continued to pat her body. Jill looked over at Kristina and stared.

"Hey, what happened to you?" she said.

"Nothing, why?" Kristina said quickly. Rather, she tried to say it quickly, but the words came out dead slow, methodical and precise. It was more like *Nooo-thinnnn-ggg. Whyyyyyy?* Alcohol always made Kristina walk and talk slow but think she was walking and talking fast.

"I don't know," Jill said. "You look . . . terrible. You need help or something?"

"Thanks, but you know, I just gotta get to my room, and I'll be all right. Really," she said, staring into Jill's disbelieving eyes. "Honestly."

"What happened to you?" Jill repeated. "Did you get hurt at a game or something?"

"Yeah, that's it," said Kristina. "That Cornell, they'll do anything to win."

Jill smiled thinly, helped Kristina dry her back, and then went and got her a bucket of ice and carried it to Kristina's door.

When Kristina opened the door to her room, Aristotle greeted her. Albert was sitting on her bed, looking at her accusingly. Is that really accusingly? she thought, trying to get a better look at his expression. What did I do now?

"God, what the hell happened to you?" he said, getting up and walking over to her.

Kristina pondered his question as she put down the ice bucket and threw the towel off her body. Albert was in a bad mood. His tone was inflammatory, not distressed.

74

She didn't reply. *He's mad at me. He doesn't realize I almost died.* Kristina decided to tell him.

Albert's tone softened. "What happened, Rock?" he said, standing up and coming close to her. His fierce-tender way of looking at her usually made her crazy. This time it nearly made her cry.

"What are you upset about, Albert?" Kristina asked quietly, putting three ice cubes on her shoulder.

"Everybody's been waiting for you for two hours. You said you were coming back at six."

"I don't know if you noticed," she said slowly, rubbing the ice over her arm, "but I've been hurt. My car was totaled."

"I didn't know your car was totaled."

"No, how could you?" said Kristina tearfully.

Kristina sat nude in front of him. He looked at her breasts and then at the big black bruise on her side. The expression in his eyes made her feel better.

"Look at you," he said in a throaty voice, coming closer to her. "You look so—what is that?"

She rubbed her side with the ice. *That's nothing,* she thought, and said so.

"God, what happened to your face? And your shoulder? It's bleeding."

She shook her head. "It's nothing. It's not bleeding," she said, not even wanting to look at it. "It's just . . . discolored." Then, "It could be worse, you know."

"I don't see how. How?"

"I could be dead." *Should be dead,* she thought, and stood up.

"You've been drinking."

"Not then." Kristina thought he meant she was drinking and driving, but then he didn't even know what had happened to her.

"Not then, when?"

"Just now. I drank a little now. To take the edge off."

"The edge off what?"

"The edge off the pain."

"What happened to you?"

"My car turned over."

"God, how?"

"An oncoming car hit me."

"Hit you? Where?"

"On the side of the Mustang."

Albert stared at her perplexed. "No. I mean, *where?*"

"Route Ten."

"It swerved into your lane?"

75

She vaguely remembered the other car's headlights, being caught in them, trying to avoid them.

"No," she said. "I swerved into his."

"Why?"

"Why? I don't know," Kristina said slowly. "It seemed like a good idea?"

"Kristina!"

"He seemed really close."

"I see. So you drove into his lane to get farther away from him?"

She wanted to answer him, but turning her head away from him, she caught their reflection in her full-length mirror. She was standing naked in front of him. He was dressed in black jeans and a black sweater, black-headed, pony-tailed, black-eyed. They stood a foot apart, arguing about semantics. Is this what my life has become? Kristina thought. A bad Marx Brothers movie. Grotesque, ridiculous. Aristotelian theater where the absurd is the norm and the norm does not exist.

Kristina shook her head and moved toward the closet. "I gotta get dressed," she muttered.

"You have to get that shoulder checked out. Can't you move your arm?"

"I can move it okay," she said. "I just choose not to."

He stood solicitously next to her. "Maybe it's fractured."

She shook her head again. "The sockets would be popping out of the skin. It's swollen. I think it's just a sprain." She was trying her best to minimize it.

"You don't know anything. You should get it looked at. Go to the infirmary."

"No!" she said. "No doctors. You know how I hate them." Kristina didn't want to tell him how scared she was. Basketball meant nothing to him, but to her it was her whole life. That, and Red Leaves. And him.

Kristina walked over to the bookshelf and sifted through the pile of books until she found a soiled paperback copy of the *Family Medical Encyclopedia.*

She handed the book to Albert and said, "Look up 'shoulder.'"

He scanned a page. "Doesn't say anything useful."

"Now look up 'joints.'"

After reading for a few moments, Albert said, " 'Sprain . . . painfully twisted or wrenched joint . . . following some kind of violence . . .' "

"Perfect," said Kristina.

Albert continued, " 'Violence may dislocate or fracture the ends of the bones that make up a joint.' " He looked up at her. "What did I tell you?"

"Thank you, Dr. Maplethorpe," she said. "Read on."

" 'X-ray pictures from several angles should be taken to make sure the bones have not been fractured or dislocated.' " He stopped reading. "See?"

"Go on, go on," she said impatiently.

" 'Blood may seep out and discolor the skin,' " he read aloud. " '. . . The synovial membranes are inflamed and reacting by pouring out fluid.' "

"Gee, that all sounds so nice," said Kristina, bending down to take more ice. She groaned. Bending down hurt her ribs.

Glancing at her, Albert went on, " 'The immediate treatment for a sprain is application of cold wet bandages or ice bags to keep down the swelling. . . .' " And louder, he finished, " 'Medical attention and x-rays should be obtained to make sure a sprain is just a sprain.' "

"Well, I'm not going," Kristina said stubbornly. "It's fine. It'll be much better tomorrow. Tomorrow, we'll go and get some kind of infrared massager for heat treatment."

"Tomorrow you've got to go to the police."

"I'm not going to the police," Kristina said. "If the police want me, they'll come to me."

"When they come to you," Albert pointed out, "they'll bring handcuffs. Why are you being so stubborn about this?"

"Who's being stubborn? I don't remember you going to the doctor when you broke your toe."

He stared at her, perplexed. "When?"

"Two years ago."

A look of recognition passed over his face. "There is nothing they can do for toes. Besides, I had no money."

"So? I had money."

"I didn't want your money!" Albert yelled. "Do you understand?"

"Perfectly!" said Kristina. "Better than you think."

"Look, I don't care what you do."

"I'm sure of that, Albert," Kristina retorted.

He ignored her comment. "Don't go to the doctor. Don't go to the police. See if I care."

"I see already."

Falling silent, Albert sat down in the lounge chair. Aristotle sidled up to him, dragging his tongue over his hand. It was a loving gesture, and Kristina, looking at them both, thought, Aristotle loves Albert. He'd gladly spend all his days with him if I weren't around.

Bending down, Albert patted the dog on the head, and Aristotle, encouraged, licked his other hand. Albert sat next to the window and stared at Kristina with his impenetrable eyes.

Kristina hated fighting with him. Nowadays making up was harder and harder, and nothing felt worse to her than knowing they had argued and then weren't kind to each other.

"What are you looking at?" Kristina asked him.

"You," Albert replied. "God, you're so beautiful. You're amazing. Look at you."

"Yeah, look at me," Kristina said plaintively. "I'm a mess."

"No, you're all right. You could've died." His voice was peculiar. "You're lucky you're alive, you know."

"I know," she said weakly. "I know that better than anyone."

Slowly she walked over and stood in front of him. He reached out and touched her lightly on the ribs. She flinched from his fingers. "It hurts a little," she said, trying to keep her voice even. "Albert, can you imagine it? Me, dying?"

"No," he said. "I can't. I can't imagine living without you."

Kristina wanted to tell him again that he was going to have to, but thought this wasn't a good time.

"Is the car a total wreck?"

She shrugged. "Who knows? You think I stuck around to find out how the car was?"

Quietly he said, "You should've gone to the hospital."

"What, and be even later?" she asked. "I mean, they would've probably kept me there overnight. And look at what I got just for being two hours late. Can you imagine if I was away somewhere overnight?"

"I would've thought something terrible happened to you. I would've been worried sick."

"Yeah, sure. You look really worried, sitting there."

"I'm sorry, Rock," he finally said. "I know you're upset with me. Listen, please, let's go to Canada. I'm asking you. Please."

"Albert, no. You, please. You have Conni, remember?"

"I'll work it out. Maybe I'll pick a big fight."

"I don't believe you," she said. Crouching in front of him, still naked, Kristina whispered, "Albert, please. I want to stop."

He looked her over. "You're naked."

She got up and backed away from him. "I mean it."

"Let's go to Canada and then you'll tell me if you mean it." He smiled sexily.

"No. I'm serious. I've had enough. I want us to be done. Okay?"

Kristina wasn't smiling, and Albert stopped smiling.

"You're still naked," he repeated.

"Clothes aren't the problem, Albert. I can get dressed."

"Please," he said coldly.

"The problem is us. We. We've got to stop." She looked away from him. "I want us to get over each other." She coughed, causing severe pain to her head. "I want to get over you. I want you to go with Conni to Long Island, and I don't want to think about it anymore. I don't want to lie, I don't want to sneak around, I don't want to worry about Howard. Or anybody."

When he sat there impassively, Kristina said, "We're not meant to be together."

"You're wrong." His tone was flat. He could've been saying, "You're right."

"We were never meant to be together," Kristina said firmly, knowing she didn't sound firm, knowing she couldn't shield herself from his eyes. She was stuck in front of him with nowhere to go.

"You're wrong," Albert repeated, in the same tone.

Kristina continued, undaunted, "Never. We screwed up real bad, but there's still time to have a life—good lives. Don't you want one? Conni loves you so much."

"I know. So? Jim loves you so much." He sounded bitter.

Shaking her head, Kristina said, "No, he doesn't. No, he doesn't. Not the way Conni loves you. And you know that."

Albert got up out of his chair and stood, loomed, before her. "Kristina, this is absurd. I cannot not have you in my life."

She rubbed her face with her good hand, but it was more like closing her eyes at the sight of him. "Albert—please. We can't. We can't continue."

"You're wrong."

She sighed deeply and then groaned from pain. She wasn't wrong, she was just so tired of standing, of being naked, of this conversation falling again on his deaf ears.

There was a knock on the door. Albert looked at Kristina and sat back down in the armchair. Kristina looked at Albert. Aristotle barked once and started to wag his tail.

"Hold on!" Kristina said loudly.

"Kristina?" The door opened a notch. It was Jim.

"Jim, hold on!" Kristina repeated, throwing some clothes on.

"Is everything okay?"

Jim couldn't see her, for she was behind the door and out of his line of vision, but she knew he could see Albert sitting in her chair. Thank God he wasn't sitting on her unmade bed. Aristotle ran to the door, and his behind started to move from side to side just like his tail.

"I'm fine," Kristina said. "Come in."

Jim came in, looking at them suspiciously. But Kristina knew Jim wouldn't act on an emotional impulse; he didn't trust emotional impulses. Jim glanced at Albert, then at Kristina again. She was wearing her pink tank top and a pair of pull-on Dartmouth green shorts. At first his gaze was hard, but then he saw her face. Kristina knew she was a sight. There was a bloody gash where the glass had been, and her eyes had a glazed look that she knew was from alcohol. Jim could easily have mistaken the look for signs of concussion. Her tank-top collar was dark with dried blood.

"God, what happened to you?" Jim said, giving Albert a stare that made Kristina suspect Jim thought Albert had beaten her.

"Nothing," she answered, touching her face. "I was in an accident. My car crashed. Everything's okay. I'm fine."

"You look terrible."

She felt terrible. The alcohol was wearing off.

"I feel pretty good," she said, trying to smile.

"Did you go to the hospital?"

Kristina remembered clambering up the hard ground, just to avoid going to the hospital. "No, I felt okay, so I came home."

Jim became agitated. "You felt okay so you came home?"

Kissing Jim on the cheek, Kristina said in her nicest voice, "I'm okay, Jimbo." But her arm, swollen by her side, betrayed her. She tried to move it to show him, and failed. "Really," she said. "I'm fine."

Albert got up. "I'd better go and see how Conni's doing."

"She's okay," Jim said, not looking at Albert. "She's waiting for us. Maybe we should all go down."

Kristina managed a pasty smile. "Why don't you two go on ahead? I'll be right down."

Albert didn't say anything, nor look her way; he just walked out of the room, taking Aristotle with him. Jim looked at her accusingly for a second and said, "Yeah, fine," and then left, too.

Kristina waited a few seconds to make sure they were way down the hall and couldn't hear her before she locked the door and collapsed on the bed.

She lay there for what seemed like hours. Her eyes were opening and closing and she was looking at the lightbulb burning in the middle of her ceiling and wishing it would shut itself off, so the room could be dark, dark like it was in the car, in the middle of nowhere, when she thought she was dead. Now as she lay on her bed, she wondered why God had spared her, why he had spared her certain death in a collision of such suddenness.

It was the closest she had come to death. The Four Horsemen of the Apocalypse had come to her, looked into her face, and galloped away. It wasn't the first time she had seen them. When she was twelve, she had fallen off a wall into cold water. She was a good swimmer, but fear paralyzed her. She couldn't move her arms or legs, couldn't even scream for help. She just went down without a fight, gulping for air and feeling her lungs fill with water.

And last year she had seen them again on her bridge, when she tumbled down to what she was sure was certain death. She had survived that too, but lived her life prepared at any moment to meet God, adding up the tally of her life every time it snowed, and she, drunk beyond reason, praying under her breath, walked the ledge on the bridge, her hands outstretched.

She didn't want to die. However, most of all, she was scared that it wouldn't be God's face she would see upon meeting her master. "I have only one master on earth," she whispered, "and I'm trying to exorcise him from my life because he's no good for me, but he won't let me, he's stronger than me, and he won't let me leave him."

She opened her eyes and touched the temple that had had the piece of tempered glass wedged in it. I feel pain, she thought. Do dead people feel pain? Do they feel tenderness, anger, regret? Profound regret?

Do they feel love? A love more overwhelming than summer air?

I'm alive, Kristina thought, because I still feel pain. "I'm not ready to die," she whispered. "I'm not done living, I don't want to die. . . ."

I need a drink. I need another, and another and another. I need to pour it all over my wounds to numb them, to forget them, to not feel pain.

Leaning over she reached for Southern Comfort and then fell back on the bed. With her good hand, Kristina unscrewed the cap and lifted the bottle Comfort over her head. Closing her eyes, she poured the liquor over her face. Some of it got into her mouth, and some of it got into her nose. But some of it got on her cut, too. It stung then numbed her bruise, and that's what she wanted. She poured the rest on her shoulder.

Kristina dragged her aching body from the bed and put on a track suit. The track suit's biggest advantage was that it wasn't the same jeans and sweatshirt in which she had faced the darkest unknown. Kristina had always believed one should be well rested and nude—as newborns—to face one's darkest unknown, and she had been neither.

<hr/>

Her friends were waiting for her downstairs in the Hinman lounge. Albert was reading a textbook and taking notes. Jim was writing. Conni was biting her nails.

"Hey," Kristina said weakly.

They looked up at her.

"Krissy, what happened to you?" Conni got up immediately and went to Kristina, peering up into her face. "Jim told me you were in an accident. I was so worried." But those were only words. Conni didn't look worried. She looked bitter. She looked as if she was trying to contain anger with a fixed smile.

"I'm all right," Kristina said. "Really. I'm fine now."

"Accident?"

"Yeah," Kristina said. "I crashed the car." Kristina figured if she said that often enough, she soon wouldn't want to cry.

She tried not to show she was unsteady on her feet. She felt herself moving with deliberate slowness toward the cake, as if in a fast-forward search on a cheap VCR, with all the horizontal lines on the screen. And soon maybe someone would say, "Geez, this is awful; I want a four-head model." And turn her in.

They all stood up, Aristotle barked, somebody lit the candles. Kristina didn't count them, but it looked like a lot of candles. About twenty-two, she guessed. She noted that no one had baked her a cake. This cake had been bought at the Grand Union on Main Street. Pepperidge Farm German Chocolate Cake. So what if it was her favorite and everyone knew it. Nobody had baked her a cake.

Last September when it was Jim's birthday, Kristina had knocked herself out to make his favorite lemon meringue pie. The egg whites took an hour and three attempts because she wanted to show Jim she cared.

Kristina stood in front of the lit candles, in front of the kind of cake she bought often for herself, and dimly heard someone say, "Make a wish, Kristina."

She thought of her Mustang, and of Albert pressuring her to go to Canada and about to be three hundred miles away from her for Thanksgiving—about to be three hundred miles from her forever, really—and of Jim, wanting her all to himself and not wanting her at all, and of Howard in New York, and of her mother, lost, a million miles away, and of her dead father, and of herself nearly dead too, without a decent coat.

She thought of the pipe music from Edinburgh, and she closed her eyes, bent over the cake, and blew, thinking, I hope Donald and Patricia Moss let Evelyn keep her babies. . . .

Then she sat down.

Aristotle nudged her in the calf. Kristina sluggishly cut the cake. She gave the first piece to Jim with a labor-camp forced smile. She gave the second piece

to Conni without a smile. The third piece she gave to Albert without even looking at him.

Aristotle nudged her in the calf again. She smiled down at him under the
table, cleaned the knife off with her thumb and index finger, and put the fingers under Aristotle's nose to lick.

"Krissy, aren't you having any cake?" Conni asked her.

The alcohol's magic was wearing off. She wished she had some with her.
Pursing her dry lips, she sat silently staring at the cake, feeling Aristotle's
tongue licking her fingers. After he was finished, she gave him some more. The
dog liked store-bought German chocolate cake as much as the next Labrador.
And Aristotle never got offended that someone hadn't baked him a cake for
his birthday or that he wasn't going to Canada. Aristotle's life was very simple. Three walks a day and a comfy bed to shed all over.

Kristina saw a card on the table but didn't move toward it. Conni pushed
the card across the table to Kristina.

"This is from all of us," Conni said, smiling open-mouthed and happy. "Go
ahead, go ahead, open it." Reaching under the table, she pulled out a bottle
of Southern Comfort with a red bow taped to the side of it. "This is a little
something from all of us, too," Conni said. "We thought you might like it."

"Conni's idea," said Albert.

"Not!" said Conni in a high-pitched voice, laughing. "Yours!"

"Not!" said Albert, smiling.

"Totally yours," said Conni again.

Why are they squabbling over whose idea it was? thought Kristina as she
stared at the bottle. "You guys got me a bottle of liquor?" she said incredulously.

Albert said, "We thought you might like it."

Shrugging, Kristina opened the card, wishing she hadn't shrugged. Her left
shoulder burned with pain.

"Wow," Kristina said without enthusiasm. Yesterday she would have been
grateful for a fifteen-dollar bottle of Southern Comfort that would keep her
going through Thanksgiving. If it hadn't been for Kristina's turning twenty-
one, if it hadn't been for the fact that she and Albert couldn't go to Canada,
and if it weren't for the fact that she had almost died, Kristina Kim would have
been delighted to get Southern Comfort from her closest friends.

"No, guys, really," she said, staring into three drawn, disappointed faces.
"Wow. I'm sorry. It's a great present. I'm just hurting, my body hurts, you
know. I had a little to drink a while ago to dull the pain, and it's made me seem
ungrateful, but it's fantastic, really."

She leaned over to one side and kissed Conni on the cheek. Then she leaned over to the other side and kissed Jim on the mouth. Albert was sitting across from her at the table, and she wasn't about to get up, and he did not move either, so she just said, "Thanks, Albert," and he said, "Don't mention it. It's our pleasure."

Conni asked, "Krissy, how are you going to play basketball? Look at your arm. What are you going to do? I'd go to the hospital or the infirmary if I were you, really, something, you know? 'Cause you don't want to just collapse or something, I mean, I'm just trying to be helpful."

Kristina waved dismissively with her good arm. "This is my dribbling arm. I don't need the other arm."

"You need it to shoot the ball," said Albert.

"I'll shoot it with one hand," said Kristina. "UPenn needs a handicap."

"You're not that good," said Jim. He had said little.

"Oh, yes, I am," said Kristina, managing a small, genuine smile. She didn't want to tell them how badly frightened she was about her injuries, about what they might mean for basketball.

Livening up a little, Kristina talked about the Christmas tree going up in the middle of the Dartmouth Green, though Jim was Jewish and didn't care much about the tree, so they talked about *Schindler's List* instead, and how they couldn't wait to see it. They talked about Lorena Bobbitt's unmanning her sleeping husband, and about the Menendez brothers levying their unique brand of justice on their parents in a home-style execution, "chunky-style," as Albert pointed out.

"Well, you know," Conni said, "there's speculation that one of the brothers was—is—gay, and he didn't want the other brother to find out, and the father apparently was threatening to out him, so—"

"Yeah, but even if it's true, why did the other ungay brother need to participate?" asked Albert. "It's bullshit, if you ask me. Frankie is not going around killing one or both of his parents."

"Bad example," said Kristina. "Frankie is an only child."

"He's just too busy at DAGLO to kill his parents," said Conni, referring to Dartmouth Affiliated Gay and Lesbian Organization.

They all smiled.

"Don't be so sure," said Jim. "Who knows what kind of secrets the family may have had? Nobody knows what's inside a family."

"That's true," agreed Kristina quietly. She hurt all over.

"That's bullshit," said Albert. "It's one thing if you're burying the corpse of your sainted twin brother in the backyard, but you don't just summarily execute two people in cold blood unless you're after something."

84

"Unless you're really sick, you mean?" said Conni.

"No, not sick," said Albert. "Just . . . detached. From themselves, from their parents. You have to forget a part of yourself to do murder."

"A part of yourself most people don't forget," said Kristina.

"I don't know. Maybe," Albert allowed, staring at Kristina. "But who are we to judge other people, though? Are we so perfect?"

"Yes," said Conni, smiling.

Kristina couldn't smile at all. "We know what is right and what is wrong. Shooting your parents is wrong."

"Oh, come on," said Albert, waving his hand dismissively. "Nietzsche says if there is one absolute truth it's that there are no moral facts."

"Bullshit," said Kristina quietly. "I don't buy it. There are. Moral truth is not an illusion, no matter what Nietzsche says. There are things that are categorically wrong. Killing your parents has to be one of them."

Albert said, "The brothers maintain the parents abused them." When Kristina didn't answer, he said, "See, there's always another side."

Mock-shivering, Conni said, "Brrrr, great conversation, guys. Myself, I love my parents. I couldn't even *imagine* conspiring with Douglas to shoot them. Though I'm not so sure about Douglas."

They all laughed. Conni glanced at Albert, rubbing his arm lovingly. "Must be hard for you, Albert," she said. "No parents."

Albert said, "And no religion, too." They were all quiet. He shrugged. "It's been too long. College has a way of making you forget the outside world. Life is just this and nothing else."

Conni touched Albert's upper arm and said affectionately, "Your tattoo, though. You'll never forget your mom with that thing on you forever."

Albert raised his eyebrows. "I thought you liked my tattoo, Conn," he said. "Isn't it roguish and devilish?"

"Oh, yes, oh, yes." She giggled and blushed and widened her blue eyes at him.

Jim went to get more beers, and Kristina fed Aristotle some more cake. Conni said, not looking at anyone in particular, "I guess that's why you guys seem so close," and, without missing a beat, without pausing, without inflection, "Both of you not having moms and all."

"I have a mother," said Kristina. "She's just very sick." She saw them glance awkwardly away from her. Jim returned with beer.

"Krissy, come with us, me and Albert," Conni offered, trying to sound chipper. "My parents will be so happy to see you again. Come on. It'll be fun. If there's snow, we'll go sledding down to the Sound. We'll build ice statues."

"Oh, no!" exclaimed Albert. "No ice statues! Remember she built an ice penis?"

Conni laughed hysterically. "Yeah, wasn't that great?"

"Oh, yeah, your parents really thought so."

"Oh, never mind them, they love Kristina. Come, Krissy."

Kristina shook her head. "I think I'm going to stay put."

"Stay put?" said Jim.

Kristina explained about Evelyn Moss's babies. "Plus I got a game on Saturday."

"With that arm?" Jim scoffed. "Yeah, in your dreams."

"Just you watch," Kristina said defiantly.

"Well, when were you going to tell me, Kristina?" said Jim, tapping loudly on the table. "It's Monday night already. I thought you were coming with me."

"I can't Jimbo," said Kristina, her shoulder burning. "Evelyn is having her babies any minute. I promised her I'd be there."

"As you wish," Jim said irritably.

"Go with Jim, Kristina," said Albert. "Evelyn's got parents and siblings. She doesn't need you."

"Yes, she does," Kristina answered, offended. And I need her.

Jim said without turning to look at Kristina, "Do you want me to take you to the infirmary? Maybe you've suffered brain damage."

"How could you tell?" said Conni and laughed at her own joke. "But seriously, Kristina, you should go."

Albert stayed quiet.

"Says who?" Kristina asked.

"If I were you, I'd go," Conni said, opening another can of Bud for herself. "What if something horrible happened?"

"Something horrible did happen," said Kristina. "An oncoming car hit me. My Mustang went off the embankment, turned over once, I think it was once, and landed. I'm still not sure if I'm alive or dead."

Jim reached out and caressed her neck. "Go to the infirmary," he suggested. "They'll tell you."

"They won't tell me, they'll arrest me for drunk driving."

"Were you?" asked Conni, cautiously. "Were you . . . drinking?"

"Of course not! But they're not going to know that."

"So go tomorrow."

"Tomorrow I'll be all better."

Leaning over the table with her elbows, Conni said, "Seriously, Krissy, weren't you scared? Sounds like a nasty accident."

"Scared? Yes, I was scared. And it was nasty. I mean, think about it." Kristina could barely get the words out. "Somebody could be coming right now to tell you I was dead. The police. Dead. I mean, what would you do?"

"Finish the cake?" offered Jim. Nobody laughed.

"Jim!" said Conni. "Krissy, it would be awful, just awful. But don't think like that. Think positive. You're okay, you're not dead."

"But I could've been dead. Easily."

"It wasn't your time to die," said Jim, tapping on his bottle of Miller.

"Why not?" she asked. "I mean, I didn't just avoid an accident. I was *in* an accident. Remember the driver's ed course? Head-on collisions result in the most fatalities of any type of car accident. Why aren't I dead?"

"Jim's right," said Conni. "It wasn't time yet."

"How do you know? Maybe I was meant to die."

"No." Jim tapped on his beer. "If it was time you'd die."

Slowly, Kristina said, "How do you know—when . . . when it's time?"

"You don't. You just die."

Kristina shuddered. "See, that's just awful. That's the most awful thing. Never knowing. At any moment, you could die, and you just don't know. And why? Why would you die? I mean, I know why old people die, but why would I die?"

"You didn't," said Jim, getting up and throwing his Miller away. "You didn't because you're too young to die, and it wasn't time. You'll now live till ninety telling all your great-grandkids about the time you almost bought the farm on your twenty-first birthday."

"Yeah, great, maybe a bedtime story," said Kristina.

The conversation wound down. They talked about the promised snowstorm—twenty to twenty-eight inches starting tomorrow afternoon and snowing well into the night and the following morning. Many people had already left to beat the snow. Others were leaving a day later to wait it out. Kristina asked Conni when they were leaving. Wednesday morning, Conni replied.

Kristina could barely get up, and when she did, she noticed Albert's fists were clenched. Unclench your stupid fists, she wanted to tell him. Who is he so angry at? Jim? Conni, for believing everything, for buying *everything*? At her? For not going to Canada with him, as if going meant solving everything, instead of solving nothing?

They all cleaned up, except for Kristina, whose arm was starting to hurt with an intensity alien to her.

When they all got up to leave, Kristina bravely said, "I'll walk the dog."

"I'll walk him," Jim said quickly. Kristina had been hoping Albert would offer, but she guessed that was impossible after last night. Besides, she and Jim could use the time to make up or to fight; both were equally likely. Kristina wished that tonight she could be left alone to lick her wounds.

"G'night, Kristina," said Albert. "Happy birthday."

"Happy birthday," Kristina repeated. Inside her was a welt of pain, a knot that tied her up and broke her and spilled what was left all over the floor.

She stumbled out of the kitchen with Jim close behind her.

She wished she could tell Jim what she was feeling. The confusion, the fear, the aching, and the sense of a short-lived life. Kristina didn't want to be alone.

She wanted Albert.

She wanted to feel as she had always felt with him, that she wasn't alone in the world, that there was someone who was with her, and that someone was the person she loved most. And that person was Albert.

Kristina wanted Albert. But Albert was with Conni.

"Jim? Would you please walk Aristotle tonight?" she asked. She looked down at her ragged old sneakers. "Please."

Jim walked Aristotle, and Kristina didn't come with him. She said she wasn't feeling well, and that was true, but it was also true that she didn't want to be out there in the dark. While he was gone, Kristina slowly took off her clothes and haphazardly changed the sheets.

When Jim returned he had to put on a clean pillowcase because Kristina couldn't do it. He didn't undress and they didn't talk. He just sat on the bed and looked at Aristotle, while Kristina walked around the room. It was better to move around—she didn't feel as stiff as when she was sitting. After ten minutes of circling around, she sat gingerly in the lounge chair. It still smelled like Albert.

Kristina sat mutely in her chair. Maybe I should go to the infirmary, she thought. My body, my body. It's aching, it's hurting bad.

Finally Jim looked at Kristina, coldly. "You've been drinking, Krissy."

"So have you." she replied, rubbing her rib, her leg, her head. "Three Millers." Even when he was upset with her he couldn't stop calling her Krissy, not Kristina, not Kris, not honey, not pumpkin, but *Krissy.*

Shaking his head, Jim said, unsmiling, "Miller Lites, and only two. No, I mean you've been drinking a lot."

"It's not so bad," Kristina said slowly.

"Yes, it is," he said, matter-of-factly. "I watched you go up the stairs. You were like on a high wire with a pole in your hand. Immobile. Too bad it's not snowing. Otherwise you'd be out there on that bridge, wouldn't you?"

She smiled. "Want me to go on that bridge, Jimbo?"

Shrugging, he said, "It doesn't matter."

Kristina thought that once it had mattered. "I used to scare you so much when I used to do that," she said ruefully.

"Yeah, well . . ." He trailed off. "Besides, you don't want to go up there. You need two arms for balance."

"I'll show you," she said. "I'll be the one-armed circus artist, balancing myself on the wire—"

"Yeah, and I'll be the one picking up what's left of your body off Tuck Drive below."

Will you be that man? Kristina wondered to herself. Will *you* really be the man who will pick up my broken body off the concrete?

"I've never fallen yet," Kristina said. That time last February didn't count.

"Krissy, statistically, the odds are against you," said Jim, slowly, quietly. He doesn't want to be in this conversation at all, thought Kristina.

"Jimbo, it's not statistics. It's guts. No guts, no glory."

"I see. What about the bullfighters? They have plenty of guts. And the bulls every once in a while show us plenty of their guts."

Kristina smirked.

"I mean, aren't you scared to do it?"

"I've told you, of course I am."

"Oh yeah. That's the point, isn't it? To be scared shitless."

"No, the point is to be scared shitless and still do it."

He paused. "Yeah, but naked? Why do you have to do it naked?"

Smiling, she said, "It's the exhibitionist streak in me. In my freshman year, I saw a couple of guys at Epsilon House after one party take off their clothes and run screaming down Tuck Drive to the river and jump in. I just thought it was the funniest thing."

"Krissy," said Jim, "somehow I don't think those guys should be your role models."

Tilting her head to one side and biting her lip to keep her aching body in check, Kristina said quietly, "Jimbo, why are you asking me about this now? I didn't think it bothered you."

He shook his head. "Who said it bothered me? I don't care. I was just curious."

"I'm not gonna go," she told him. "I have to be really drunk. Otherwise I'm not steady enough. And it has to be snowing."

"Why?"

"Seems safer somehow," she replied. "If I fall and there is snow underneath."

Jim snorted. She hated when he did that. It was so derisive. "Krissy, all it takes is the wind, and down you'll go to the concrete, snow or no snow."

Nodding, she said, "That's why I only do that when there's snow on the ground. There's no concrete then. Just soft downy snow of angels. Clouds of snow. I imagine," she said, fighting for her words, "falling into that snow below and bouncing up, bouncing on a trampoline of cloud snow. I imagine being . . . really happy."

—·—·—

"You're not happy, Kristina?"

She stared at the ceiling. "Not really," she admitted.

He was quiet. "Not happy in general, or . . . not happy with us?"

Not answering his question, she said, "Are you happy with us?"

"No," he said immediately. "Not at all."

Kristina nodded, then said carefully, "Want to talk about it?"

Breathing heavily, Jim said, "No. I'm tired. Look," he said, getting up. "I think maybe I won't stay after all. We'll talk another time."

"You don't want to stay over?" she said. "But it's my birthday—"

"Yeah, well." He looked at her accusingly. "I wanted to stay over Saturday night."

"I told you I was at Red Leaves."

"Yes, you told me, you told me." He took his coat and petted Aristotle. "Bye." Kristina was unsure if he was talking to her or the dog.

"We'll, uhhh . . ." said Kristina, maneuvering herself out of the chair. "We'll talk another time. Sure thing, Jimbo."

"What's that supposed to mean?"

She sighed. "Jim, you never want to talk about us."

"Nothing to talk about, Krissy."

"Oh, no?"

She thought back to a few hours ago, to turning over in her car and landing on the hard ground that had no snow. Where was that soft snow to cushion her, to envelop her, to protect her from her fate?

"Jim, do you love me?" asked Kristina, coming closer to him.

Hesitating, he said, "Of course. Do *you* love *me*?"

Not answering him, Kristina lightly touched the side of his face and said, "I don't think you're being honest with me, Jimbo. I don't think you love me."

He hesitated again, sneering at her, blowing out heartily. "Come on. You mean anymore?"

"I mean ever."

"Don't be ridiculous."

"Am I? Am I being ridiculous, Jim?"

"Yes."

But she noticed he conspicuously didn't comfort her, didn't hug her, didn't make any attempt to show her she was wrong.

"Let me ask you something, Jim. Do you love Conni?"

He laughed uncomfortably. "What kind of question is that? I did once."

"Still."

"Once," he said firmly.

"She was the love of your life, wasn't she?"

Jim paused. "I was very smitten once, yes."

" 'Very smitten once,' " she repeated.

"At that time, yes," he said.

"Ahh, give me a break." She lifted up her arm in supplication. "Be honest with me, Jim. Just once."

"Is that what you want?" he said harshly, his straight face contorting for a moment. "You want honesty? Is that *mutual* honesty, Krissy?"

Taken aback, she composed herself long enough to reply, "Yes. Mutual honesty. What do you want to know?"

He stared at her for an awkward moment, and then disdainfully said, "Give me a break. Just forget it. I'm gonna go."

She raised her voice. "What do you want to know, Jimbo?"

"Nothing."

"That's what I thought," she said mildly. Her mouth was beginning to lose all feeling.

He left.

Kristina collapsed on her bed and tried to lift her arms, only half succeeding. As always they had left their argument unfinished. He usually left in the middle. She didn't pursue him, he went back to his room, or she to hers, and the next day they got together and talked about political science or the next article for the *Review* or what to have for breakfast, or Conni and Albert, and went on as if he hadn't left in the middle of telling her he'd never loved her. And she let him leave in the middle.

Lying on her back, Kristina had the sensation that she was flying. Flying through the dark New Hampshire skies, flying toward the hills of Vermont. Flying toward Fahrenbrae, over Fahrenbrae, over *them,* running after Aristotle. She closed her eyes. She didn't want to be flying over them anymore. She just wanted to feel her Albert close by. Wanted to see his lovely face, touch his ponytail, press her lips against his dear homemade tattoos.

There were bad dreams and there was pain. When she awoke she was sweating, and the fingers on her left hand felt numb. That did not worry her. What worried her was the tears streaming down her face, running from her eyes to her ears into her matted hair. Tears! That's what woke her. She felt herself crying, and when she opened her eyes, she couldn't stop. She hurt all over.

Slowly getting out of bed, Kristina went to sit in Albert's lounge chair. The streetlights shined their cold yellow light on the dirty white curtains. She wiped her face. What's wrong with me? she thought. It's just another stupid Thanksgiving weekend.

When she was a little girl, Kristina never cried. There was never any reason to. She hadn't cried, but she had many fears: A dark and quiet house without her mother; her aunt's car accident; hurricanes; dying.

In her teenage years, Kristina learned to control the fear with some success.

She wiped her face. She thought about coming so close to dying. She was flashing through the accident, through the car and the reservoir, through clawing her way up, away from death. Touching her broken fingernails, Kristina shuddered. Is this what woke me up? Was I flashing through dying?

Had she died, what would have happened to her money now that she and Howard were divorced? She would have died without so much as a scribble. Who would take the dog? Who'd get the contents of her dorm room and safety-deposit box at the bank? And everything else?

She rubbed her eyes till they hurt. In the dark it struck her—there was unfinished business in the room, in Hinman Hall, in Dartmouth.

She had come to Dartmouth to right her life. It was ironic that three years later nothing had changed. Where had she gone wrong?

Dartmouth was such a beautiful college. A picturesque, serious, tiny place, in the middle of the mountains on the banks of the Connecticut River, the natural border between New Hampshire and Vermont.

The idea of Dartmouth had appealed to Kristina when she was a high school senior and trying to find a way out of an impossible life. She would go to Dartmouth, study hard, get a good job, find a nice man, get married, have children.

Kristina had thought that by acting normal, doing normal things, having a normal boyfriend, her life would take a different course. A *normal* course.

So she came to Dartmouth, she studied hard, she helped out at Red Leaves, she had played basketball, she met a nice man.

Jim and Kristina had really tried. Even after Scotland, even after the three months she spent barely thinking of Jim, they had tried to get back on track. She had thought she wanted a life with him. He wasn't a bum, a brash, pony-tailed, tattooed performance clown with no future.

Kristina had chosen James Allbright Shaw. He was her guy.

But Jim didn't love her. She hadn't anticipated that.

College. You'd think it would be easy to fake love with so many things in common, with courses and studying and partying and sitting around Thayer three times a day. College was the great suppressor, the warm blanket that covered them all and made them safe. How could you not fall in love in college? Most of the girls and guys she had known in the last three years had fallen in love. Most of them more than once. She knew a girl who had gone through seven boyfriends her freshman fall semester, and was now back with boyfriend number one.

Anybody could fall in love in a tiny cold town in the middle of the hills. Four thousand students, two dozen parties a weekend, study halls full of Ivy Leaguers, football on Saturdays, winter carnival; everyone read the *Dartmouth,* everyone protested something, everyone shopped at the Co-op and ate at EBA. The differences between guys were muted. Everybody was a liberal arts major. Everybody came from a nurturing family, everybody placed a value on education and hard work and the future. There were no differences other than the ones between the sexes. And the college handbook tried to suppress even those.

Today it was Jim, yesterday it could've been Barry, who had asked her to go to Cape Cod two years ago, tomorrow it could be that nice-looking young detective who had watched her strap up her boots and bought her coffee. Spencer Patrick O'Malley.

Yet Kristina sat here in the virtual dark, with a swelling in her head and Southern Comfort in her blood, wearing only her bra and panties, and tears ran down her cheeks into her mouth.

Jim didn't love her. Even Dartmouth College couldn't hide it.

It was all wrong between them. He stroked her neck and gave her great back rubs. But Jim never looked at her the way Spencer O'Malley looked at her. He never looked at her the way Kristina had once seen him looking at Conni. Kristina was not arrogant about her beauty—it sometimes left her cold, and she would understand if it left a guy cold too. But it shouldn't be leaving her boyfriend cold. Albert was never left cold by Kristina, but she tried to tell herself this wasn't about Albert. Kristina didn't want to reproduce the feeling she had with Albert—she wanted to be rid of the destructive, obsessive, fierce longing forever—it wasn't love, it was insanity. She wanted sane love.

Outside it got lighter.

Getting up from the chair, Kristina went to her nightstand. The Southern Comfort bottle was bone-dry. She wondered where her gift bottle was. She had forgotten to bring it up.

She walked circles around her room and then sat down on the bed. Right your life, rang in her head. Right your life.

That's what I'm terrified of, Kristina thought, wiping her wet face. Not just death, no. I'm terrified of the future.

Kristina remembered last winter carnival when she and Jim built that huge snowman in the middle of the common. It took them two hours, and Jim was well frozen by the end of the day, but wouldn't leave until they found the hat and coals; he even ran to Collis and got half a carrot. Kristina had been surprised Collis had anything as fresh as a carrot. Jim had loved her a little then, despite Edinburgh.

Kristina would've liked to hear Jim say he didn't love her. I don't love you, Kristina. I could've saved you with my love. Lifted you out of the dark morass you're in and made you happy—and free. I could have freed you with my love—could've taken you and made you forget the mad man, the dark man. But I don't love you, so you're not saved, not at all. Play basketball, hide behind the game. Write *Review* articles. Take care of Evelyn. But you're not saved.

Kristina threw on some clothes, slipped out of her room, and made her way downstairs to Jim's room.

"Jimmy, wake up," she said softly, sitting down on the bed and prodding him with her right hand. "I want to talk to you."

He groaned, turning his back to her. She shook him again. "Please. Wake up, Jim."

He was groggy. "What time is it?"

"It's early. What time is dawn?"

"Ohhhh," he moaned. "I have class tomorrow. Please."

"No, *please*," Kristina said.

Then Jim sat with his back against the wall. "What?"

Wiping her face, Kristina said, "Jimbo, I don't know. I think it's over between us."

"Think?" he sneered.

"I'm really sorry, Jim," she said, unable to look at him. She stared at her knees instead. "I can't make you happy."

"Yes, because you really tried."

"I have tried."

"You haven't tried. You're too busy trying for basketball and Red Leaves House and even the *Review*—"

"I'm only on the *Review* because of you."

"Don't do me any favors," he snapped.

"Listen, you haven't exactly made me happy either."

"Krissy, you're impossible to make happy."

"How would you know?" she said loudly, standing up and beginning to limp in agitated lines from corner to corner. "What have you ever done to try?"

"I went out with you, didn't I?"

You pig, thought Kristina. "Don't do me any favors."

"Tell you what," he said. "It's a really good idea we don't see each other anymore. I haven't been happy in a long time."

"Never."

"Oh, yes," he said. "Before I met you."

Kristina's heart sank, but she managed to say, "Somehow I find that hard to believe." Her lips were quivering. She was about to cry. He was about to make her cry, but she wouldn't let him. She knew he had difficulty talking about personal things. That was his way. So be it.

Jim laughed an awkward laugh. "I can't believe we stuck it out this long."

"Jim, don't say that. Things weren't always like this."

"Oh no?"

"No. Only since I realized how you feel about me. Or more precisely, how you don't feel about me."

Staring at her coldly, still not moving from his place on the bed, he said, "What are you talking about?"

Kristina was still pacing, still aching, her bad arm hanging limply down her side. She became choked up and couldn't tell him what was on her mind.

"Forget it, Jimbo. I came here hoping maybe we could talk."

"No, you didn't," Jim retorted contemptuously. "You woke me up hoping I'd make you feel better about yourself, just like you always want me to do. Well, I wasn't about to ignore my work to make you feel better about yourself. I'm not a psych major."

"That much is clear," Kristina mumbled. "God!" she exclaimed. "I don't want you to make me feel better about myself. You've got it all so wrong."

She wasn't going to cry in front of him. Not now. She wasn't. She tried to make her voice as calm as possible when she said, "I'm going now."

"Bye, Krissy," he said, his voice breaking.

When he didn't make any move to stop her, she left.

Kristina sat down dejected on her bed. Instead of feeling better, she felt much worse. God, she thought. I woke up and was feeling so bad, I couldn't see in front of me. But now look at the way I feel.

Everything was quiet and blue in the dawn winter light. Aristotle whimpered.

"Aristotle, I know how you feel, dog," Kristina said. "I know exactly how you feel," she said sadly, lying down on the thin carpet next to him. She kissed the top of his head, and fell asleep after an instant of aching.

Kristina slept through her two morning classes and basketball practice. She hurt too much for basketball. When she woke up on the floor, Aristotle wasn't there. Someone had taken him out and, as a careless afterthought, thrown a blanket on her. Careless or not, she wanted to know who it was. Albert? Jim? Conni?

She woke up with an awful feeling of heaviness and depression that she couldn't shake. She couldn't believe she had been left alone for so long. Usually somebody came into her room and woke her up.

She realized as she struggled up that it wasn't depression. Her body was throbbing.

How long would they have just left me on the floor? she wondered, running the brush through her knotted hair. How long would I have lain here? Would they all have gone off? Wilmington, Cold Spring Harbor, and left me here without Aristotle. She looked at the clock. It was already afternoon.

Getting dressed was agony. The shoulder was worse today, but Kristina was able to lift the aching arm about waist high. She held it there for a few excruciating seconds before gently lowering it.

Suddenly there was a knock on the door. She didn't recognize the knock, but when she heard it, her heart sank.

"Who is it?"

"Police. Open up."

Kristina raised her eyebrows and heaved a depressed sigh. Not this, too. On top of everything else.

"Wait a minute, please," she said. "I'm getting dressed."

The knock came again. "Open the door, please. Now."

"Goddammit," Kristina muttered under her breath and went to the door in just her track-suit top and underwear.

Opening the door, she faced a young, short, heavyset police officer, sticking his police ID into her face, and Spencer O'Malley.

Spencer, standing two feet back, suppressed a smile. The patrolman became extremely flustered.

"Officers, how do you do?" Kristina said in her most formal voice. "If you could give me a few minutes, I'd appreciate it."

Spencer said nothing but smiled at her, while the other officer, red-faced and awkward, said, touching his police badge with his hand and trying hard not to look at her, "Take your time."

Kristina thanked them and closed the door, reappearing a moment later with her track-suit pants on. "Now," she said smiling. "What can I do for you?" She didn't acknowledge Spencer O'Malley, but she did notice that he was holding her new purse in his hands.

The heavyset officer introduced himself as Patrolman Ray Fell and did most of the talking. "Miss Kim?" He wore thick, black-rimmed glasses and had a mass of unruly, curly black hair. He looked more like a computer nerd than a cop.

"Yes, that's right," she said.

"Do you drive a brown 1981 Ford Mustang?" And he read off the license plate number.

"Well," she said evasively, "the answer to that has to be no."

"No?"

"No, I no longer drive a Ford Mustang."

Spencer O'Malley smiled again. Sergeant Fell furrowed his brows and his voice became firmer.

"You are listed as the driver of said vehicle."

"I no longer drive it as of yesterday," she said.

"Has it been in an accident?"

"Yes," she said. "Definitely."

"Miss Kim, did you leave your car after the accident?"

"Well, yes," she said, looking at Spencer O'Malley. Unlike Raymond Fell, he was dressed in street clothes.

"Do you know that it's a crime to leave the scene of an accident?" said Ray Fell. "It's called conduct after an accident, and it's a class-A misdemeanor. The driver of the vehicle is not allowed to leave the scene of an accident if there's been any body or property damage."

"I'm sorry," she said. "I didn't know that."

"You didn't know to wait till the police came?"

"No," she said. "It was very dark, and I just wanted to get out of there." She paused. "I was going to have a tow truck get the car today and take it to a junkyard."

"Miss Kim, you have to file an accident report, don't you know that? Did you notify your insurance company?"

"No," Kristina replied. "I was going to do that all today."

The officer nodded. "Could you come with us to the police station to have a little chat, please?"

"Officers," she said, "I want to do everything I can to cooperate. But I have a calculus test that I absolutely can't miss."

"Miss Kim," said Fell, raising his voice, "obstructing the police department in their investigation of the accident is a class-B misdemeanor, punishable either by a fine or a jail term. Now, would you like to come with us?"

"My intention is not to obstruct," Kristina said seriously. "I would very much like to come with you. What about later this afternoon? Maybe at four or so?" She had a few errands to run first.

"No, Miss Kim. Come with us now."

Detective O'Malley stepped forward and put his arm on the young cop's shoulder.

"Miss Kim," said Spencer, "have you been to the hospital?"

Kristina shook her head.

"Perhaps we could take you to Dartmouth-Hitchcock. Your face looks pretty banged up." He looked at her bad arm. "Someone should take a look at you."

Kristina thought that someone had.

"Sergeant," Fell said quietly, turning to Spencer, "I thought she was supposed to come with us now."

Spencer nodded. "I know, I know," he said. "Don't worry, she's not going anywhere." Turning back to Kristina, Spencer said, "But a doctor should take a look at you, Miss Kim." He enunciated "Miss Kim" slowly, almost tenderly.

Kristina stared up into Spencer's light blue eyes. "I really feel all right," she said. "I can always go to the Dartmouth infirmary, thanks. But would this afternoon be okay?"

"Not possible. You're already facing probable grounds for arrest," said Fell. "It's police procedure to fill out the accident report immediately. You left the scene. It's a misdemeanor. You have to come with us."

Coughing, Spencer O'Malley again placed his hand on Fell's shoulder. "Raymond," he said. "Could you wait for me downstairs, please?"

Ray Fell was reluctant to leave, but as little as Kristina understood police hierarchy, she knew Ray Fell had been given an order he had to obey.

After Fell left, Spencer turned to Kristina and smiled, handing her her purse. "I didn't think we'd meet again so soon."

Taking her bag from him and dropping it near the door, Kristina replied, "Well, don't you know? I staged the whole accident just so we could meet."

Without missing a beat, Spencer said, "You didn't have to go to all that trouble."

"No trouble."

"You're in a lot of trouble, you know. You made the patrolman quite upset."

"Thanks for helping me out." Kristina wanted to ask Spencer to come inside, but her room was such a mess, and she was embarrassed by it. She didn't want Spencer O'Malley to think she was a slob. She made a mental promise to clean it as soon as she could. Thank God she brushed her hair.

"You did commit a crime, you know."

"I didn't know it was a crime, did I?"

"Why didn't you just wait for help?"

Kristina felt impelled to tell Spencer the truth. "I don't like hospitals much. Plus yesterday was my birthday. We were having a party."

"Ah, happy birthday. Was it a nice party?"

"Very nice," said Kristina.

"Twenty-one feel old?"

"Yes, how'd you know?"

"Because I recently turned thirty. And it felt *really* old."

She was thinking how young Spencer actually looked, even with his stubbly hairdo. He looked like a lanky kid just out of the army.

"Do you really have a calculus test?" he asked her gently.

"Well . . . if I took calculus, then yes." Kristina watched his expression and then said, "I don't really have one. But I kind of have to get to the bank before three."

"What, rearranging your finances at twenty-one?" Spencer was joking.

Kristina said, "Something like that," and looked away.

Standing in front of Kristina with his arms crossed, Spencer said, "Tell you what. Do you want me to hold your accident report on my desk until after the holiday?"

"You can do that?" she said eagerly.

He shrugged. "Sure. I'm in charge, I can do anything. Just don't let my boss find out. He'll cream me."

"Okay," she readily agreed. "But what's the catch?"

"No catch," said Spencer. "But . . ." He became flustered and trailed off. Kristina watched him turn red. Inquisitively she peered into his face. He became redder and stammered for words. "What I was trying to say, was—I was wondering if you—you and I maybe could—you know—grab some dinner or something."

Kristina smiled. "Dinner, huh?"

"Yeah, if you wanted to." He lowered his eyes.

"Dinner where?"

"At Jesse's. They have the best steak there. You like steak, don't you?"

"I love steak," Kristina said. "I don't get to eat it too often."

"Is that a yes?"

"It's an I don't know," she replied, her heart beating a little faster. She almost wanted to touch his shorn hair. "I'm so busy around here . . ."

"It's an evening. What's an evening?"

She bowed her head. "When were you thinking?"

"Friday?"

"What, this Friday?"

He scratched his head. "Yeah, why not? Oh, wait, it's Thanksgiving weekend."

"Yeah," she said. She really wanted to go out with him this Friday, but she didn't want him to think she had no life.

Then he made it easy for her. "How about the following Friday?" he said.

"Okay," Kristina said, grinning. "Okay, Spencer O'Malley. You can take me out to dinner in exchange for not putting me in the slammer."

"Don't be silly. No one was going to put you in the slammer. It's procedure. We live and die by procedure at Hanover. Will you be able to come next Monday? Or do you want me to swing by and pick you up?"

"No, no, don't worry. I'll get there myself."

Spencer smiled. Kristina noticed he had a beautiful smile. Perfect teeth. "You're not going to come, are you?" he said, obviously trying to hide the pleasure at her saying yes.

"No, I will, I will." She was thinking it would give her another chance to see him but saw that he remained unconvinced. "Uhh . . . about next Friday—what time?"

"Any time that's good for you. I get off at five."

"Well, we're playing Crimson—the game should be over at ten. Is that too late? We can go at, like, ten-fifteen."

"You're going to the game?"

"What do you mean, going?" said Kristina. "I'm playing."

Spencer shook his head. "Not with that shoulder you're not."

Kristina felt a stab of fear. "What do you mean?"

"I mean—you're not going to be able to play with that arm."

She didn't want to talk about it. Not even with him. "It'll be all right," she said dismissively.

He was looking at her with an amused expression. "Should I pick you up here?"

"Depends. Are you going to come in a police vehicle or an unmarked car?"

"Whichever you prefer, Kristina."

She smiled, unable to hide her pleasure. "Come in a police vehicle then. With sirens. Okay?"

"Okay," he said. "I'll bring an extra siren, just for you."

"And I'll get dressed up," she said. "Just for you." I'll have to buy a dress, she thought.

"Deal," he replied, and then impulsively reached out and touched Kristina's face. Before he went, he said, "It looked like a terrible accident. Your car was in bad shape." He looked her over. "Worse than you. You're lucky to be alive, you know."

"Aren't we all?" she said, but inside Kristina knew he was right.

"Listen," Spencer said. "Promise me something. If your arm doesn't get better by tomorrow, you'll go and have it checked out."

Kristina said sheepishly, "Does it look that bad?"

Nodding, Spencer said, "It looks bad. Looks sprained. You can't move it, can you? You never know. Sometimes it's something more serious. Promise me."

"Okay, Detective O'Malley," said Kristina, trying to move her arm. "I promise."

She extended her right hand, and he held it briefly. His hand was warm and strong. As he backed away toward the fire doors, Spencer said, jokingly, uncertainly, "And no standing me up. Or I'll have to arrest you for lying to a police officer."

"Oh, is that a misdemeanor, too?"

"Capital crime."

Laughing, Kristina said, "Don't worry. I'll be here with bells on."

"See you later."

"See you, Spencer."

She watched him go through the doors and then turn around and sneak a look at her. Kristina's body stopped throbbing for a moment after seeing that. The heat of pleasure soothed her aching skin.

She closed the door behind her, then went back and locked it. She sat in front of her Macintosh and opened a new document. She quickly typed in the date—*November 23, 1993*—and the time—*2:29 P.M.*—and then, *To Whom It May Concern.* Deleting that, she typed, *Dear Sir or Madam.* Yes, that was better. She wrote a short note, printed it, and closed out of Word. When the computer prompted her to save the file, she clicked *NO.*

It was snowing when Kristina went outside. Steady flutters were building momentum. Kristina wondered if Albert and Conni and Jim had left for the weekend. No, they couldn't have, she reasoned. Aristotle's not in my room. They wouldn't just take Aristotle without letting me know first.

Cold in her faded blue track pants, Kristina hobbled to the bank. She could have put on a second sweatshirt, but what Kristina wanted was her mother's coat back. Maybe she could call Spencer O'Malley and ask him to drive her up to Fahrenbrae. No. Too many questions. Fahrenbrae wasn't real to anyone but her and Albert, and she wanted to keep it that way.

The bank was closing at three. She had to hurry.

But hurrying was difficult; in the accident she had banged her knee on the underside of the front panel and now it hurt like hell. At East Wheelock, across from the Hanover Inn, she slowed down to a limp and waited for the cars to pass. Why am I in such a hurry? she thought. So I don't make it. There is always tomorrow. The banks are open tomorrow, aren't they? And there is going to be hardly anybody around. I can go then. It really doesn't matter. But she wanted to have her note notarized immediately.

"Sorry, closed," said a guard holding the keys in the door.

"Listen, I just want to put something in my safety deposit box and check my balance, that's it. Please," she panted.

He called over an accounts representative, who reluctantly let her in.

"Please be quick," she told Kristina.

I'll be nimble, I'll jump over a candlestick, Kristina thought. "I'll be just a sec. Thanks."

She waited to be let into the back vault room.

"Hi, Mr. Carmichael. Would you be able to notarize something for me?"

Mr. Carmichael, a thin, gray-bearded man of fifty-five, rolled his eyes, then smiled at Kristina with kindly expression.

"Closed, Kristina," he said patiently. "Do you understand closed?"

"I do. Mr. Carmichael, you can do it, can't you?"

He sighed. "What do you need?"

"Just notarize my signature here." She took out her paper, but folded it so that he couldn't see the contents of the letter.

"I have to see the whole document, Kristina," he said. "You know the rules. I've notarized stuff for you before."

Kristina had no choice but to show him the contents of the letter.

After reading it, Mr. Carmichael glanced at Kristina, who hoped her face was blank.

Mr. Carmichael said, "Okay, sign right here." She did, and he got his notary stamp and notarized her signature, and then they used their keys to open her safety deposit box and Mr. Carmichael left her alone.

She put the notarized letter carefully into the manila envelope containing the divorce papers and then quickly rummaged through the contents of the box. She thought a moment, then took out a pencil and scribbled on the back of an old letter. She buried it in the box and left.

"Have a nice Thanksgiving!" Kristina called out to Mr. Carmichael. "And thank you!"

He waved. "Anytime, Kristina. Have a nice holiday."

Yes, it's going to be just peachy, she thought, wishing she had her coat, wishing she had a drink, wishing her head would stop throbbing. She was glad she had made it to the bank. Tomorrow she intended to sleep till the sun went down.

It was now snowing hard. The snow was no longer coming down in little flakes, but in thick clumps that looked like snowballs. They fell out of the sky and onto Kristina's hair and face and the ground. The cars on Main Street moved slowly, quietly burrowing their wheels in the snow. The sidewalks had white fur on them, the Dartmouth-green awnings were white, and the trees stood still and black and bare.

Kristina crossed Main Street and debated going to Peter Christian's to buy some carrot cake to take home—there had been a time last summer when she subsisted on carrot cake—but decided it might be better tomorrow when everyone had gone and she could go in and have a nice quiet lunch and read the paper.

Kristina hadn't eaten since last night's cake. In the last twenty-four hours she had had the Red Leaves ice cream cake, the German chocolate cake, and Southern Comfort. Some diet. Still, she wasn't hungry. Her head hurt.

Remembering yesterday made her cold again. *Was it only yesterday when I almost died? Why does it feel like such a long time ago?* She reached up and touched the swelling on the side of her head. *Not that long ago,* she thought. *No, here it is, right here.*

What if something is wrong? What if I have a concussion? Kristina thought, walking slowly back to campus. *What if I have a concussion or a hematoma, and I'm going to bleed to death from the inside out? Blood will drip out of the veins in my brain and run down my body until it all collects in my swollen feet and legs, sloshing about in the big slop pot that is me, and then one morning I'm just not going to wake up.*

Kristina felt very cold. She went to the Dartmouth chapel and sat in the warmth for a few minutes, thinking of Evelyn, and of babies, and of Albert. She wanted to put a candle up for the little ones, but there was no place to do that. She left.

Kristina spotted Albert near Kiewit. Her mood darkened. He stood in the snow talking to a friend. Kristina sped up reluctantly. Her legs sped up, but her mind was slowing down. Albert began to walk northward to Frat Row. Kristina sped up some more, slightly dragging her right leg behind her.

"Albert!" she finally yelled, out of breath in the falling snow. "Wait up!"

He turned around and came toward her. Kristina was panting when she caught up to him and found herself with nothing to say. They stared silently at each other.

"Jim stay the night last night?" Albert finally asked, and Kristina felt his palpable question reverberate through her cold bones. She hated it when Albert was this way.

"No, he didn't," she told him, rubbing her hands together. "We broke up."

He was quiet. "You did? Why? It wasn't working out?"

"Yeah, well, we weren't working out like you and Conni."

"Who said anything about me and Conni working out?" He fell quiet. "I'm just glad about you and Jim, that's all."

"I bet you are."

"I am. So what now? Should I break up with Conni?"

"Break up with her?" Kristina was aghast. "What for?"

"So that we could go to Canada. And other things."

"Look, stop pushing this Canada thing on me. I told you, I can't go. Why are you so persistent?"

"I'm not persistent. So what are you going to do, then?"

"About what?" Kristina said sullenly.

"About you and Jim."

"Nothing. Maybe start seeing someone else." She saw a look of pain fly through his eyes. Barely audible, Kristina said, "Albert, please." The heaviness inside her chest wouldn't lift; her heart squeezed and shut and hurt. She breathed out heavily and asked, "Did you take Aristotle out this morning?"

"Yes," Albert said. "He loved the new snow."

"Bet he did." She realized Albert was the one who had covered her on the floor.

Leaning closer to Kristina, Albert said, "Remember last year? When we took Aristotle to Fahrenbrae and got snowed in for three days? How much we ran around then. How much we loved the snow. I drank and you made me coffee, and late at night, we would take off our clothes and run naked down the Vermont hills, screaming all the way. You always won—I always got cold first. And back at the cabin, you'd blow on my frozen feet and wrap blankets around them. Remember that, Rock?"

"Sure, I remember, Albert," Kristina replied, beaten, exhausted. "I haven't denied my feelings. They never change." Shivering, she rubbed her throbbing arm. The cold was making it feel better. "Let's go back. I'm cold."

Leaning closer to her and lowering his voice, Albert said, "I'll win now, being out in the cold with you. I'll win for once."

She didn't back away but didn't respond in kind either. "Come on," she repeated. "I'm freezing."

He said, "I was going to go and see Frankie."

"Oh," Kristina said. "Want me to come?"

"No," Albert said quickly. "I won't be long. I think he wants to talk to me alone. Man to man."

"Oh, yeah?" Kristina said. "Well, you better run along then, if Frankie wants a man."

Albert eyed Kristina. "What's that supposed to mean?" he asked, reaching out to brush the snow off her hair.

"Nothing, Albert," Kristina said. "Nothing."

"Go back," he said gently. "You're freezing." She saw his black eyes filling up with her. "Poor you," he added tenderly. "We gotta go and get you your coat."

"Don't poor me. I'm fine."

"Fine," he said, a little cooler. "I'll see you later then?"

"No! I mean—I guess. I mean—I want it to be over between us, Albert," Kristina blurted out.

"I got it, I got it," he said coldly. "Who are you trying to convince?"

"Me," she said without hesitation. "But this time I mean it. I want you to go your own way and me mine."

"That's the way we planned it, Rocky," Albert said, his eyes blazing at her. His skin became flushed; he actually looked warm.

"Don't Rocky me," Kristina snapped. "I want to have a life, don't you understand?"

"With who? You and Jim are over, you say me and you are over. With who, Kristina?"

She didn't rise to the bait. "A life away from you. Is that even possible?"

"No," he said, bluntly, resigned. "It's not. I realized it long ago. Why won't you realize it?"

"Because it's not true," she said desperately.

Stepping closer to her until he was just inches away from her face, Albert said quietly, "Look at your beautiful lips. God, I want to kiss you. Right now."

"Stop it," she said weakly. "Enough, Albert."

"Okay, listen, if you don't want to come to Canada, come with us to Long Island, Rock. I don't want you to spend Thanksgiving here by yourself. Come on. It'll be fun."

"You don't mean it. Fun for who? For Conni, who knocks frantically on my door? For me? For you, who'll sit there for four days watching me? Thanks, but no thanks. I had a home once. I don't want other people now wishing pity on me, wishing turkey on me. Mr. and Mrs. Tobias, or Mr. and Mrs. Shaw and all their children, sitting and asking me questions and passing me the turkey, the pumpkin pie, the apple pie. Well, I don't want their charity. And I don't want yours."

As if not hearing her, Albert said huskily, "I wish for you, Kristina. There is nothing else I wish for on this earth."

"That's what we are," Kristina said. "Impossible wishes."

"I wish we could live in Edinburgh. Never leave the bed-and-breakfast, never leave our bed."

Unable to help himself, Albert reached out and intensely stroked Kristina's cold cheek. "God, Kristina, God," he said. "Come with us. It's better than being here."

"See, that's where you're wrong," she said, not moving away from his hand. She never did move away. He knew that, and she knew it.

"Please. Come."

"No."

"Please." He was still stroking her.

Finally, Kristina moved. Now was as good a time as any. "Tell me, is it true?—Conni told me last week that you guys were thinking of getting engaged this Thanksgiving?"

"No, it's not true," Albert said instantly and then, "Conni was thinking of getting engaged this Thanksgiving."

She looked incredulously at him.

"That's the truth," he said. "We talked about it, but she was the one to bring it up."

Laughing, Kristina said, "God, Albert, you just never stop, do you? Never. Lying. Not even to me."

"I don't know what you're talking about," he said gravely.

"I see." Her breath left her body in a puff of vapor. "It was my under-standing," she said, "that engagement implied a degree of mutual attach-ment."

Albert just stared at Kristina bleakly, blankly, darkly. He was stepping from one foot to the other to keep warm.

She, however, stood immobile. "How were you going to do that, Albert? Take me to Canada and get engaged to Conni all during the same holiday?"

"I wouldn't have gotten engaged to Conni."

"You would've postponed it a week or so? Or is her whole family plan-ning a special Thanksgiving engagement turkey feast?"

"I don't know what they're planning."

"Yeah, okay." She stepped away from him. He didn't follow.

"Poker night tonight, Rock," he said to her. It was almost a plea. "Us four and Frankie. Penny ante."

Kristina didn't answer, and he called out, "Please come. We need you."

Saying nothing, Kristina turned her back to him and started walking toward Tuck Mall.

"We'll have to get you your coat back," Albert yelled after her.

Kristina waved at him without turning around.

Aristotle wasn't in Kristina's room. It was snowing hard, and she hoped he wasn't outside. She just wanted to get her dog and bring him upstairs and lie down with him for a few minutes.

She went down to the second floor to Conni's room. The door was open. Kristina glanced in. The room was clean as usual. The alarm clock's digital blue display read 3:10.

Kristina eventually found Conni studying near the glass windows of the Hinman lounge. What surprised Kristina was seeing Frankie Absalom, studying next to her. They were completely absorbed. Neither looked up.

Kristina stood and stared in confusion. Hadn't Albert said Frankie was waiting for him at Epsilon House? And if not Frankie, then who? Kristina emitted a low laugh. Was Albert running around on Conni?

Maybe Frankie had forgotten he had invited Albert to come over. Kristina pulled back her hair and walked up to them.

"Hey, guys," she said. They looked up and nodded unenthusiastically.

"How are you feeling today, Krissy?" Conni asked.

"Fine, thanks," lied Kristina. "Have you seen Aristotle?"

"I think I saw Jim with him on Main Street about an hour ago. Near the *Review* office. Where've you been all day?"

"Oh, here and there," Kristina said vaguely. "Sleeping mostly. Frankie, aren't you supposed to be with Albert?"

Frankie looked puzzled. "Huh?"

"Frankie, don't be so eloquent. Aren't you supposed to be meeting Albert in your room right about now?"

"Huh?" Frankie repeated.

"Frankie!"

"Kristina, I have no idea what you're talking about. I haven't spoken to Albert since his birthday."

"I see," said Kristina.

Frankie went back to the books. Conni stared uncomfortably at Kristina, who managed a friendly smile, waved with her good arm, and left.

Kristina went back to her room, lay down on top of her bed, and then pulled up the blanket over herself. She tried to nap, but the heaviness inside her wouldn't let her. She got up and tidied up a little, played a computer game, called Jim's room, stared out the window, lay down again. Nothing. Her heart was a hard ball. She buried her head in the pillow and cried.

She couldn't sleep. She wasn't tired, she just wanted to feel better, and she thought sleep would bring her relief. But there was no sleep. Every time she closed her eyes, an image of her car crashing into the oncoming vehicle flew up in her eyes, crashing, turning over, thud. Crashing, turning over, thud. Crashing, turning—

She got up and called Spencer O'Malley at the Hanover police station. He'd already left for the day. She got his home number from information and called him there. He wasn't in. She didn't know what she would've said to him if he had been in; she just wanted to hear his kind voice.

Jim finally brought Aristotle back, but didn't stay long. Kristina didn't have the energy to make him stay. The dog would have to do for now. She let Aristotle jump on the bed and then curled up next to him.

She thought of walking the bridge later, but she had no Southern Comfort. She then spent part of the next hour rummaging through her closet, trying to find something to soothe her throat, to calm her shaking hand, to ease the throbbing in her shoulder and her ribs. To ease the aching in her heart. There was nothing.

Kristina remembered the Southern Comfort she'd gotten for her birthday. Where was that bottle now?

It was time for her to go downstairs for poker, but she didn't care. Unlocking the door and letting it shut behind her, she made her way quickly down the stairs, and then just as quickly went back to get Aristotle, who was less than enthusiastic at the prospect of going out. But he went anyway, as if he understood that his mistress needed the company. She made her way down Tuck Mall in the white dark and then to Main Street. She headed to Murphy's Tavern. There was no liquor store in Hanover. Stinson's grocery store sold champagne and beer, as did the Grand Union, but who the hell wanted champagne and beer? One of the bartenders at Murphy's, a real nice guy, would sometimes let her buy a bottle of Southern Comfort, if there were no cops around and she asked nicely.

Murphy's was closed. Closed because of the snow. She looked down the street as if hoping an hombre with tequila in his belt would sidle up and offer her a shot.

She remembered Spencer lived on Allen Street, close to EBA, so she walked there, and stood in front of the two-story building, looking up at two lighted windows. She didn't know if they were his windows, but they were the only lighted windows on the short block. His name was on the doorbell. She thought of buzzing *S. P. O'Malley,* but didn't.

"Aristotle," she called to the dog, who was sniffing the clean snow in hope of something delicious. "Aren't we something, out in this weather, cold and miserable. Well, you're cold. I'm miserable. Are you miserable, too, Aristotle?"

The dog wagged his tail happily.

"I thought so. You look miserable." She patted his back. "Come. Let's go back."

They walked slowly, snow kicking up at their feet. Kristina looked down at Aristotle's bare paws. She looked at her own feet. She had unlaced sneakers on. "Now, that hardly seems fair," she said. The dog stopped walking at the sound of his name. Stopping too, Kristina kicked off her sneakers. She wasn't wearing any socks. Bending down, she picked the shoes up and kissed Aristotle on the top of his wide blond head.

The bell tower clock at Baker struck once. Kristina didn't look up.

The Hinman lounge was empty when Kristina got there. She looked up at the digital clock that had been broken for months. It read 2:10. Is that 2:10 P.M. or A.M.? she thought. She helped herself to a beer, sat down, and waited.

In a little while they'd all arrived but Frankie.

"It's a mirage. Krissy's early," said Conni.

"I'm not early. You're all late."

"We're not late," said Jim. "Look at the clock."

"Yeah," Kristina said. "Two-ten. Where were you guys?"

"Conni's room," Jim replied.

Conni said, "We were figuring out a strategy to beat Frankie."

Then Frankie walked in, took off his coat, and bellowed, "Where have you guys been? Conspiring against me?"

"Ahh, he's finally arrived," Conni drawled. "Could you have taken a little more time?"

They sat down at one of the round tables. Kristina sat across from Albert, who narrowed his eyes at her, and she pretended to ignore him.

"Aristotle's paws are wet and freezing," Albert said. "Where did you take him?"

"For a walk in the snow. You know he loves the snow, don't you, Albert?" Kristina said, staring straight at him. "He just loves that snow."

"Let's play!" said Frankie. "Anything to drink?"

"Nothing good, that's for sure," replied Kristina, getting up. "Plenty of Miller Lite, though."

"Perfect. Hand me a beer, woman, and let's get to it," Frankie said, stretching out his hand. Slapping it, Kristina handed him a beer.

Albert put a jar of nickels, pennies, and dimes on the table. They each took their five bucks' worth and anted up two pennies. Albert dealt. He played straight poker with nothing wild. Frankie won that hand with three of a kind. Conni dealt next. Five-card stud and jacks were wild. Frankie won that one also, with a straight. Everybody liked Frankie but nobody liked to play cards with him because he always won. And he was so jovial about it, too, as if he couldn't understand why their weekly games were such a big deal that they had to take his winning and laughing about it so seriously. He called them poor sports and sore losers, and they couldn't even call him a bad winner. He always put his winnings back. But it was the principle of the thing.

When they played, they were never jovial, and they never put their winnings back. Albert needed the money. Constance was raised to keep her winnings. Jim kept his because it was inconceivable that he should put back what was rightfully his. Kristina knew Jim loved to win. He was ruthless at Monopoly. And Kristina rarely won. Maybe twice in three years. To put the money back would have turned her victory into a defeat. Among the five of them, Kristina was well known for losing most often.

Unlucky in cards, Frankie would tell her, lucky in love. Jim would smile, back in the days when he did smile, and Kristina would think of Albert and want to say aloud, "Fucking lucky." But she smiled gracefully too, because to lose gracefully was an art. And she had mastered that art out of necessity. She was lucky in love and a gracious loser, and what else was there on snowy winter nights at Hinman Hall in the River Cluster at Dartmouth College?

The only one who seemed to be having a good time was Frankie. Loudmouthed, gum-popping, laughing, winning Frankie. His cheeriness was not contagious to Kristina, who felt her oppressive malaise invading her fingers.

The rest of them sat holding their cards like armor. Usually the game was livelier. Kristina didn't know what was bothering the other three, but she knew what was bothering her.

"So, Albert," Kristina said, after ten hands were played. "How was your chat with Frankie this afternoon?"

Everyone looked up. It was surprising and strange to hear Kristina address Albert. It rarely happened. And now this odd question with unknown implications.

Frankie was looking into his cards, a big gum bubble bursting out of his mouth. "Two cards for me," he said, and took two cards from Albert. Frankie turned to glance at Albert's impassive face. But Conni's face wasn't. And Jim was just pretending to be impassive.

"What time is it?" Jim asked.

Frankie looked at his watch. "Ten to eleven."

"Ah," Jim said, looking over his cards. "Make this my last hand."

"What's the matter? A little past your bedtime?" Frankie teased.

Jim didn't reply.

Kristina persisted. "Frankie, how was your chat with Albert this afternoon?"

"Albert?" said Frankie, smiling his genial smile. "What the hell is she talking about?"

"Yes, what *are* you talking about?" said Conni.

Looking at Albert with raised eyebrows, Kristina said, "Albert?"

He stared into his cards. "What, Kristina?" he said wearily.

"How was your chat?"

"We didn't have one. Frankie wasn't there."

Kristina nodded, looking at her hand—a queen of diamonds, three aces, and a queen of spades. "No cards, thank you," she said, pushing her remaining money into the center. "I raise you that." She pointed to the pile. Conni and Jim folded. Albert saw her, Frankie saw her and raised her three pennies. She had to borrow three pennies from Conni to see him.

He had four kings.

She threw her cards down. "It's so peculiar," Kristina said. "I could've sworn you said Frankie needed to talk to you. Man to man, remember?"

Albert stared across the table at her. Frankie scratched his head and asked, "Albert, what is she talking about?"

"Yeah, Kristina," said Conni. "What are you talking about?"

Jim remained quiet. So did Kristina. "Nothing, I guess," she said, staring pointedly at Albert. "Nothing, right?"

"Yes," he said. "Nothing."

Frankie blew a big bubble while shuffling the cards. "Well, gee, Krissy, as you know, I always love to see Albert."

"But not this afternoon, right, Frankie?" Kristina said. "This afternoon you were studying with Conni."

Conni laid her cards aside. "What I want to know, Kristina," she said, "is what do you care?"

"Good question," Jim muttered next to Kristina.

"Fine, let's drop it," said Kristina.

"No, let's not drop it," said Conni. "Now I'm curious."

"Are you?" Kristina asked. "Are you curious?" Taking the card deck from Frankie's hands, she passed it to Conni. "You deal."

Conni shoved the cards aside. Jim and Albert laid their hands on the table. Frankie looked at everybody with a befuddled expression.

Albert leaned over to Conni and said quietly, "Conni, you deal."

Conni didn't pick up the cards. "I don't think I want to play anymore," she said.

"Constance, come on," said Albert. Whenever Albert called her Constance, Kristina knew he was getting angry.

"Come on, nothing!" Conni exclaimed. "What's going on, Albert? I want to know what's going on here!"

In a strained voice, Kristina said, "Yeah, Albert. Why don't you tell her?"

He flashed his black eyes at her. "There's nothing to tell."

Frankie got up, still smiling. "You know what? It really seems like time I be going. This is very good time that I be quickly and without dawdling going."

Albert got up, too. "Don't leave, man. This is stupid."

Frankie smiled, turning to the rest of the table. He tipped his proverbial hat as he said, "Good evening, ladies and gentlemen. If this is all over my uncommon stroke of good fortune, you may keep my winnings for luck."

"No, thanks," mumbled Kristina.

Frankie lightly tugged on Kristina's hair. "And you, miss, I came here tonight, first because it's poker night and second because it's snowing, and isn't there a tradition around here when it's snowing?" He extended his hands as if balancing on a high beam, closed his eyes, and tiptoed carefully on an imaginary straight line on the dirty wooden floor. "Come on. All the guys in my house get drunk and watch you. They wait all year for it. I think half of them are already collected at the windows of Feldberg, waiting for you."

"Are they drunk?"

"Since September," replied Frankie, making Kristina smile.

"They'll have to wait a long time," said Kristina. "*I'm* not drunk."

Conni snorted. Albert sat back down next to Conni, leaned over, and said very quietly to her, "Cut it out."

"No, I will not cut it out," Conni said loudly, challenging him.

"Cut it out," Albert repeated, slower, quieter.

"No," she said sourly. "Not until you tell me what's going on."

"This is my cue!" said Frankie cheerfully. "I'm gone! Krissy, this is a very nice snowstorm. Please oblige, will you, by getting drunk pronto. Here, here's the rest of my Miller. I'll be up at the library waiting for you. I even brought my binoculars." Reaching into his coat pocket, Frankie pulled out a pair of small, ladylike gold-plated binoculars. "I got them from my dear sainted mother. She asked why I wanted them, and I told her that nothing ever happens at the opera that's half as exciting as what happens at Dartmouth, and she said well at least you're getting an education, dear. Oh yes, I said, a fine, fine education." And he flipped the binoculars to his face. "Will I see you later?"

Kristina couldn't help smiling. She even took a swig of the beer. "Frankie, will you ever give up? What do you care about me on that bridge?"

"Are you kiddin'? I become the hero of Frat Row. I get to cut classes for a week and copy everybody's notes. Everybody loves a hero!"

Patting him on the arm, Kristina said, "Yes, they do, Franklin. Yes, they do. You'll watch out for me on the bridge, won't you? Make sure I don't fall?" Kristina glanced at Conni, who flushed and looked away.

Frankie just stood there, stumped, and then scratched his head. "I'm not getting in the middle of this, no sirree Bob, not me, I'm staying far away from this one, thank you very much. Good-bye!"

"Get the hell out of here, Absalom," said Albert.

"See, all I want," said Frankie, "is to"—he saw Albert's face—"get the hell out of here. That's the only thing I want. The only thing I ever wanted. And that's the truth. Bye!"

Before he left he winked at Kristina and held up the binoculars to his face. "We made a deal," he whispered to her. "Drink up."

"Yeah, yeah, yeah." And she laughed.

After Frankie left the room, the four of them sat silently staring at the cards on the table. Kristina broke the silence by saying, "Want to play some more?" But that didn't break the tension.

Conni snapped, "You have to go, don't you? You have an appointment on the bridge you gotta keep, don't you?"

"Oh, lighten up, Conn," said Kristina. "You're taking all this much too seriously."

"No, I don't think so," Conni said. "I think I'm not taking this seriously enough. And Jim is not either."

Kristina glanced at Jim. "I think Jim is taking this just fine. Right, Jimbo?"

"Leave me out of it, will you?" Jim said impatiently. He stood up suddenly, not looking at anybody. "Ahh, just forget it. Forget the whole thing." They looked up at him with their peeved, surprised faces.

Conni stood up and then sat back down with a humph. Her fingers were nervously, angrily thumbing the cards. "Jim, what's going on?"

"Nothing," said Kristina.

"Let's drop it," said Albert.

"I don't want to drop it!" Conni nearly yelled, shooting up out of her seat. The cards spilled to the floor. "See, I think there is something going on here, something really sick, under my very nose, and I swear to God, if you don't tell me what's going on right now, I—I—I—" she stammered.

Conni isn't very good at making useless threats, Kristina thought.

"Right now," Conni repeated. "I'm tired of these games."

Wide-eyed, Kristina stared in mock surprise at Conni until Conni saw Albert mouth *stop it* to Kristina, who ignored him.

"Why—are—you—" Conni could barely get the words out. "—you mouthing anything to her?" she nearly shrieked. Though the question was directed at Albert, Conni was looking straight at Kristina. Conni's hands were shaking.

She was the only one standing. Nobody answered her. Nobody even looked at her.

"Right now, right here," Conni went on, plaintive and panting. "I want to know what's going on, and I'm not leaving till you tell me." Her frame heaved.

"Look," said Kristina, standing up too. "This is no place for this conversation."

"No!" exclaimed Conni. "This is a great place for this conversation. Kristina, I want you to tell me the truth."

Kristina laid her arm on Jim's shoulder, who threw it off, standing up also. He was agitated, and his green eyes were perplexed and angry. "This is a conversation? The truth about what, Constance?"

"The truth about Kristina and Albert," said Conni.

Jim stood mutely next to Kristina, as if he were pricking up his ears to hear her response.

Kristina said nothing for half a minute, but when she finally spoke, she said, "Tell you what, I want to hear the truth about you and Jim."

"Me and Jim?" Conni was more irritated than flustered by the question. "What the hell are you talking about?"

"Ahh, forget it," Kristina said, waving her good arm and mimicking Jim. "Forget the whole thing." She turned to go, and then stopped. "By the way, Conni—Albert, he's standing right there. Why don't you ask him?"

"Because I'm asking you," Conni said, without even glancing Albert's way.

Jim had moved away from Kristina. "Conni, don't be such an idiot," he said rudely. "Isn't it obvious? She just told you."

"I didn't hear it," said Conni.

"She just told you!" screamed Jim, turning to Kristina. "Didn't you? Listen, I don't want you to ever tell me anything again!" His face was red and contorted by anger. "Never," he nearly hissed. "I don't want you to tell me anything, ever again, do you understand? I don't want you to come near me, I don't want you to ask me to walk your dog, I don't want you to ask me to help you study. I don't want you to talk to me again, understand?"

Conni wasn't the only one who stared at Jim open-mouthed. So Jim *was* able to get angry at something other than criticism of the *Dartmouth Review,* or the president, or crime. But he really knew how to pick his battle sites. Several students had come in to watch television and had obviously heard the whole outburst. They now stood uncomfortably at the door.

"Jim, man, come on—" Albert started to say before Jim cut him off.

"Screw you," Jim said, pointing at Albert. "I don't know what kind of sick game you're playing, but I don't want any part of it. Any part of it at all."

Albert faced down Jim, who finally whirled around and left the room, pushing his way past three students who couldn't get out of his way fast enough. On the way out, Kristina saw Jim turn back to look at her with not just anger, but hate.

Turning to Conni, Kristina said, "See what you've done?"

"Me?" But Conni said it less angrily, as if Jim's calling her an idiot and his subsequent outburst had calmed her instead of incensed her.

"So Jim thinks you're running around on him," Conni said, in an offhand, casual voice that belied the gravity of her words. Conni was obviously hard at work trying to forget just *who* Kristina had been accused of running around on Jim with.

"I'm done with both of you," said Albert. "I'm going to my room."

"Albert, wait," said Conni, while Kristina said nothing.

"No, stop. I'm tired of this, and I'm tired period. I'm tired of you people accusing me of crazy things," he said, despite the fact that no one had accused *him* of anything. "I'm tired of you pointing fingers, and of you not taking my no for an answer," he added. "If you feel that strongly about it, Conni, then just break up with me. Better yet, break up with me and go back out with Jim. I hear he's available. You don't trust me, and I can't stand it. I don't want to have a relationship where I'm not trusted. Trust me, or leave me, that's your choice. I'm tired of these games."

"I don't want to leave you," Conni said quietly. "I just want you to tell me the truth, and I'll never ask you or doubt you again."

Kristina waited. She waited without curiosity or anticipation. She knew Albert, and she knew telling the truth was not Albert Maplethorpe's forte. She knew he would never tell the truth. She suspected that Conni knew that too, but chose to overlook it, and that was *her* categorical imperative—denial. Albert's was eternal equivocation. His word, which had no collateral, no support, no weight, and no history, would be good enough for Conni. Kristina waited for Albert to face down Constance Tobias and assert his imperative.

Albert Maplethorpe did not disappoint her.

The showdown was a letdown. The only thing that happened was that now no one was talking to anyone else. They had never before let anything like that happen.

Kristina went upstairs. It was eleven fifteen when she got to her room.

The snow was still falling heavily. Kristina desperately wished she were drunk tonight so she could walk her wall. Frankie Absalom was waiting. With a big sigh, she sat down at her computer, thinking about starting the *Review* death-penalty story, but wanting to go to bed instead and wishing for her heart to stop squeezing and hurting her.

At eleven forty-five she went to walk Aristotle, coming back a few minutes before midnight.

A knock on the door startled her and made her heart start pounding. What's going on with me? she thought nervously.

The knock was light, not angry; it could only be one of three people, and Kristina hardly wanted to talk to any of them. Kristina didn't go to the door right away. She was waiting to recognize the knock.

The knock came again.

Finally, she opened the door. "Look, Jim—" she began.

It was Conni. She looked disheveled, and her hair was messy. Her blue eyes were trying to smile, but Kristina could see Conni was battling with herself.

Kristina opened the door wider. "Come in."

Conni shook her head. "No, I gotta get back. Albert's waiting for me. And I need to pack too. We just wanted to bring you this." Pulling her arm from behind her, she gave Kristina the birthday bottle of Southern Comfort. "We thought you might want to have it while we're gone. I said I'd bring it to you. I wanted to talk to you, anyway."

Kristina felt warm relief flowing through her veins. She gladly took the bottle and threw it on the bed. "I like it very much. Thanks."

"Listen, I'm sorry about before," Conni said, not looking at Kristina.

"Come in," Kristina repeated. Aristotle wagged his tail. Conni didn't move. "You've got nothing to be sorry for," said Kristina.

"Well, Albert says I do, and I think he's right."

"You've got nothing to apologize for," said Kristina firmly.

"No, I do. I do. I was out of line down there. Nothing was wrong, I don't know what I got so bothered over."

"Yes, you do," said Kristina. "You know why you got bothered. Why are you always pretending that nothing is wrong?"

Kristina saw fear in Conni's eyes, as if this was not the conversation Conni wanted to have the day before she got engaged at Thanksgiving. "I'm not pretending, okay?"

"Yes, you are," Kristina said. "Why?"

"I'm not!" exclaimed Conni, and then, quieter, "So what do you think I'm pretending about?"

Her body throbbing, Kristina leaned down to Conni and whispered, "Pretending what's true isn't true, Conni."

Kristina might as well have slapped Conni, who recoiled and staggered back a foot from the door. She took a few seconds to regain her composure. "You're lying. I know you are. I don't suspect anything, for one. They're just the normal doubts everyone in a relationship has. I trust him, I have to. Otherwise, how can I stay in a relationship with him? If I don't trust him and still stay with him, then I have no self-esteem and no self-respect. So I have to trust him, do you see?"

Kristina shaking her head, said, "Yes. I see."

All of a sudden, Conni slapped Kristina across the face, leaving a bright red mark, and then, before Kristina had a chance to move, slapped her again across the other cheek.

Now it was Kristina's turn to stagger back. "What are you doing?" she said. "What do you think you're doing?"

"You deserve worse," Conni said. "For trying to break us up. I thought you were my friend."

"I am your friend," said Kristina, rubbing her cheek.

"You're not my friend," Conni went on. "Otherwise you'd know how much I love Albert."

"I know how much you love Albert," Kristina said. "I also know all the other things you don't know."

"You don't know anything. Nothing. You're just cruel. You have everything. All I want is Albert. Can't you see he's weak?"

Kristina laughed. "Weak? Albert? Conni, he's the strongest person you'll ever know."

"He is weak. He doesn't know his own heart."

"Better than anybody. Better than you, better than me. Albert is true only to himself. You'll see that."

Conni lashed out, grabbing Kristina's hair, yanking it hard. But this time Kristina was ready. She had to bring her right arm across her body, and tilt her head, but she grabbed Conni's hair very hard, and pulled. "Listen, you," Kristina panted. "Listen, stop behaving this way, stop it, you're nuts!" But Conni wouldn't let go. Trying to stop Conni, Kristina dug the tips of her nails into the skin under Conni's eye, piercing the cheek and making Conni yelp.

Conni let go. Kristina didn't.

"Listen, I'm going to tell you something," Kristina said, standing very close, looking down at Conni. "I know you always manage to get mad at just me, but I'm telling you, *I'm* not the one you should be mad at."

"Oh! Let go of me," Conni whispered vehemently. "Let go!"

Kristina let go. Bloody scratches marked Conni's left cheek.

Conni touched her wounded face. Kristina receded into her room.

Panting, trying to get her breath back, Conni said, quietly, malevolently,

"Now I'm going to tell you something. I asked Albert about you and him, and you know what he said?"

"Of course I do," said Kristina.

"He denied everything."

"Of course he did."

"Well, now I have a choice—either I believe my boyfriend, who I love and who I'm going to marry, or you, just a friend. And I have decided for better or worse to believe Albert, because it's what I can live with, okay? And I never want to talk about it again."

"Okay," said Kristina. Inside, she was sick. Sick for Conni, sick for herself, and furious at Albert.

Still holding her cheek, Conni backed away, and then turned around and ran down the hall and through the fire doors.

Kristina wanted to say to Conni, okay, so you think you figured him out. You alternate between going off the deep end and swimming in denial. And when you snap, you never snap at him, only at me.

Kristina sat on her bed and thought about Conni.

Then she looked at the clock.

Twelve thirty.

Kristina slowly took her clothes off. The feeling in her chest was so strong and so despondent that she slumped onto the bed. She grabbed Conni's bottle, held it between her bare legs, and unscrewed the cap. She was going to take a slug, but the open bottle disgusted her. Opening her legs slightly, she let the bottle fall to the floor. She didn't want that foul drink, not even for a walk on the bridge, not even to ease her heart.

Kristina turned off the lights and went to the window. The soft, untouched snow was beautiful. The first snow of the year. Ordinarily, many students would be out, but tonight they had all gone home or were asleep. The Feldberg Library across from Hinman was still lighted. Kristina wondered if Frankie was really waiting for her to walk the wall.

She was going to do it. There was something about walking that wall in the snow while drunk that rid her of all the bad inside her. She felt like a flightless bird, ready for takeoff, one with nature, her footsteps softened by the snow. The alcohol in her blood steadied her step so that if at any moment she was to meet her maker, she'd be ready.

After yesterday, Kristina had realized she wasn't ready at all.

And today she was scared. "Forgive me," she whispered. "Forgive me for living, for not wanting to see You yet, for wanting to live. Dear God. I want to live well. I just don't know how." She bowed her head. "Please show me how."

Yesterday she had been given another chance at life, and she was going to take it. She had been given a chance to do right, to live right. But how?

Give up Albert, she thought. Give him up. Let Conni have him, let her have him and get on with your life. Without him.

The yellow streetlights cast a lonely hue on the blue-white snow.

Usually, she walked the bridge without shoes, but that was before she had the black boots. She finally had something decent to wear. Her ribs and shoulder hurt and the boots were a bitch to put on with only one arm working, but she slowly managed.

She had laced one boot when there was a knock on the door.

Her heart started racing. She was panting even before the second knock.

Kristina didn't want to open the door. But Aristotle's tail wagged as it wagged for only one person, and Kristina wanted to say have a happy holiday to him. Have a great wonderful holiday at Cold Spring Harbor.

Outside her door stood Albert.

"Come in," she said to him, moving her naked, one-booted body to face him, desperately wanting to touch him.

"Came to see how you're doing."

"I'm doing great," she said, moving back inside the room and sitting down on the bed near her other boot.

"I thought you'd be walking your wall," he said. "You never could resist a dare." He carelessly plopped himself down in the lounge chair and looked around the room. His eyes stopped at the bottle of Southern Comfort, which had leaked into the carpet.

Kristina said quietly, "Where are we going, Albert?"

"Going nowhere, Rocky. You know that." He looked out the window, then reached over and closed it. "It's cold," he said.

"Leave it open," Kristina told him. "I get so hot at night."

He got up. "Listen, if I don't see you tomorrow, have a great Thanksgiving."

"Yeah," answered Kristina, looking away from him, ready to cry. "Thanks. You, too. You have a good one."

"You sure you don't want to come with us?"

Now she looked up. "Yeah, I'm sure, Albert. Sure."

He came over to her, but Kristina backed away from his hand. She looked up at him with a mixture of anger, regret, and love, all doing battle on the frontline of her soul.

Albert reached out to touch her, but she backed away farther and he stopped. "Let me help you with your boot," he said gently.

Kristina let him. He knelt down in front of her, and she gave him her foot.

She was naked and she saw him looking at her with longing, his lips slightly parted.

"Do you want me to lace it up?"

"Yeah, sure," she said, and Albert did, kneeling in front of her for a few extra moments. His hand reached out to caress her thighs, but she closed her legs and tried to move away. He lifted his hand and touched her face.

"What happened to your cheeks? They're all red."

"You, Albert. You happened to my cheeks," said Kristina.

He didn't ask, and she didn't offer. Getting up off the floor, he moved to go. "I'll see you, Rocky."

"Yeah, sure," Kristina said, turning her face away from him. "See you."

She felt him watching her for a couple of seconds and then he left.

With her boots on, she fell back on the bed as the ceiling swam in front of her eyes. Please don't cry, she said to herself. Stop feeling this way. Cheer up, you're going out in subfreezing temperatures. If that doesn't brighten your spirits, nothing will.

In a few minutes Kristina got up, prodding Aristotle with her foot on the way out, and headed down the stairs.

She walked out the side entrance. The cold and blowing snow hit her. She hastily wrapped one arm around her breasts. I'd better do this quickly, she thought. But she knew she couldn't do it quickly. She must watch every move and walk as if she were in slow motion. She had spent the day delirious with pain, rambling and tossing with bad feelings. She wanted the cold to numb her, to make her feel better.

Kristina looked up at Feldberg Library, trying to see Frankie by one of the windows. He was her nightwatchman, but Frankie hadn't said he'd be waiting for her all night. Kristina smiled to ward off the spirits and crossed herself as she came to stand by the head of the bridge.

Up you go, Kristina, up you go. The stone ledge was three feet high and nearly two feet wide. She slowly climbed on top of it, favoring her right knee, and stood up. She tried to extend both her arms at her sides before she took a step. Only the right arm obeyed her.

With the left arm at her side, Kristina extended her right arm, and, trembling, took two, then three, then four tentative steps, whispering, *Hear not my steps, which way they walk, for fear the very stones prate of my whereabout.* At this end, if she fell, it wouldn't be bad. It was only three feet down to the bridge on the right of her and about the same down to the snow-covered ground on the left of her. Then the embankment on the left got much steeper, eventually

122

stopping at the utility driveway. Kristina moved along the ledge, suspended seventy-five feet in the air. She was a naked bird with her one wing out-stretched, her long legs stepping carefully, her black boots making slow and deliberate marks on the snow-covered wall, her black eyes fixed ahead, whispering haltingly, *And take the present horror from the time, which now suits with it.*

The black boots were helping her gain traction, but fear raged in her heart. *Whiles I threat, he lives. Words to the heat of deeds too cold breath gives.* She shivered and shifted to one side, her right arm insufficient to keep her balance. Against all reason, she tried to lift her left arm, and the sudden and sharp pain made her jerk involuntarily, and when she jerked she slipped on the snow and fell.

She slipped sideways and backward, hitting her right leg on the sharp side of the stone. She thought her heart would explode. For a moment she just sat on the ledge in an awkward position, too terrified to move, and then she inched her way down onto the bridge.

Oh, God, oh God, oh, God, she kept stuttering. Her heart would not calm down. God, that was close; God, that was close.

Kristina had never been this scared, not even during the crash.

Well, this is no fun, she thought. Losing to Frankie in poker is more fun. Thank God I'm all right. Amid the superficial relief, black fear beat her from the inside out.

She walked unsteadily to the end of the bridge, whispering inaudibly, *"I go, and it is done: the bell invites me. Hear it not, Kristina; for it is a knell that summons thee to heaven or to hell."*

A little path wound behind Feldberg Library at the edge of the pine woods. One yellow bulb lighted a service door to the building.

I'm crazy, Kristina thought. Crazy. Never again. Never, ever again. Spencer Patrick O'Malley, I promise, I will live long enough to have dinner with you.

Brushing the snow off her chest, Kristina Kim crossed herself and thanked God. As she began to walk back to Hinman, she thought she heard a voice calling her. *"Kristina . . . Kristina . . ."* She looked around but couldn't see from where the voice was coming. I must be imagining things, Kristina thought, peering into the darkness, her heart slipping into the abyss.

II

SPENCER
PATRICK
O'MALLEY

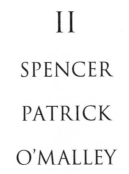

"Vox Clamantis in Deserto"

(A VOICE CRYING IN
THE WILDERNESS)

*Rage, rage against the
dying of the light.*

—DYLAN THOMAS

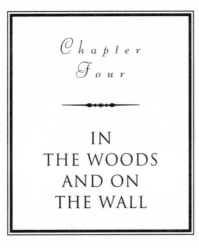

Chapter Four

IN
THE WOODS
AND ON
THE WALL

S pencer was looking into Kristina Kim's empty auto accident file, drinking his seventh cup of coffee, when the dispatcher buzzed him on the intercom. He had been thinking about Kristina all week, hoping she wasn't going to stand him up tomorrow night. He hadn't heard from her and it was now Thursday, a week after Thanksgiving.

After he heard from the other driver's insurance company last Tuesday, he called Kristina's room. When no one answered, he assumed she was in class. When he called from home Tuesday evening and again there was no answer, he assumed she hadn't returned from her Thanksgiving break.

But what if she had returned and was just blowing him off? The unsettled feeling didn't tie in with what he had been thinking when he had last seen her— that Kristina seemed as pleased to say yes as Spencer was to hear it. Had he been wrong? He didn't think so.

"Trace, we just got a call about something at the college."

"Something?" said Spencer absentmindedly. Then he became alert, then irritated. " 'Something' is very vague, Kyle. What the heck does that mean?"

"Sorry, I don't have more information," Kyle said. "A student called up, real nervous, saying he thinks he may have found something that may belong to a person. Something like that."

Spencer rolled his eyes. "Like what?"

Kyle was quiet. "Look, it's probably nothing, but go check it out."

"Did you get a name?"

"Yeah. Milton Johnson's the kid that called."

Spencer closed Kristina's accident file and stuffed it into his drawer. Then he got up. "Kyle, who'd you send already?"

"Fell was in the area. I sent him."

"Great," Spencer muttered. Then, louder, "Why don't you radio him and tell him I'm coming right over." And then, quieter, while putting on his parka, "Maybe, possibly, they think . . ."

On the way out, Spencer knocked on the chief's door. The door was slightly ajar, but Spencer had been trained never to presume, never even to nudge the door.

"Chief?"

A grunt from inside the office. That was a good sign. Spencer came in. "Chief, I'm going to run down to the college. Some kid called about finding something weird."

"Weird?" Chief Ken Gallagher said gruffly. Graying and overweight, he was sitting behind a shiny metal desk, and Spencer couldn't tell what looked more out of place, the desk or the chief. Spencer and Gallagher were both Irish, and in the spirit of Irish camaraderie, they occasionally had a drink of whiskey together. Spencer became certain the chief had a soft spot for him when Spencer was promoted to detective-sergeant, over others like his partner, Will Baker, who had seniority. But the chief was as brusque with him as with everyone else in the department.

"So what are you waiting for? The boys from Concord?"

"Certainly not, sir," Spencer quickly responded.

"Good. Go check it out. Ask Will for help."

Spencer didn't think he'd need his partner's help to examine a lost-and-found item. "Yes, sir."

Spencer was nearly through the glass exit doors when he turned around and called out to Kyle, behind the bulletproof glass of his dispatcher's office, "Where?"

"What?" said Kyle.

"Where am I going?" Spencer shouted, walking back a few steps.

The dispatcher checked his log. "In the woods, behind Feldberg Library. Between Tuck Drive and Feldberg."

Spencer left. He didn't know where Feldberg Library was, but he knew Tuck Drive, leading down to the river, was a dark, winding road, nestled between hundred-foot-tall pines. He would drive there and hope to spot Fell's police vehicle—a white Crown Victoria with cornflower-blue stripes.

As Spencer walked to his car, something began to gnaw at him. Feldberg Library. Hinman was close to the river, it was one of the half-dozen or so dorms in what was called the River Cluster. The woods near Hinman dropped down onto Tuck Drive below.

Hinman. Spencer walked faster.

His light blue Chevy Impala, rusty and beat-up, was parked on the side of the building next to the Hanover Country Club and golf course. For the last several years, the police and fire departments had shared offices in the modern building. Spencer had liked it better when police had their own space. In the old building the desks and the chairs were old, the floorboards were old, the window frames needed paint, the heavy wooden doors creaked, and the toilets had the high-up tanks and the nineteenth-century pull chains. It wasn't sterile and it wasn't clean, but Spencer considered it fitting for working and living in a small old town.

Backing out of his space, he made a right on Route 10 and drove carefully to the college. The roads, even covered with salt, were slippery. He made a right at College Street, getting momentarily stuck behind a double-parked driver waiting for a space. Spencer beeped the horn; the guy didn't move. One reeling, high-pitched noise from Spencer's red siren, however, and the other driver decided parking could wait.

The small Christmas trees that lined the common square in front of Baker Library looked festive with snow on them. At night the trees sparkled, with Christmas lights reflected in the snow on their branches. Spencer had sometimes seen the trees glittering on December evenings.

Tuck Drive was empty. He drove toward the boathouse on the Connecticut River but saw nothing. Not even Fell's police car.

The road, the trees, the boathouse were covered with snow. The town had had a week of freezing weather after the blizzard before Thanksgiving that had covered Hanover with twenty-six inches of winter. Last night, everyone had been expecting more snow, but only one or two inches had fallen.

Turning his car around, Spencer drove back up Tuck Drive. Through the trees up on a hill past the turning with the bridge hanging over the service drive, he saw a small crowd of people. He recognized Fell's hat and the black shirt of his uniform. Spencer parked his car on Tuck Drive, left the police lights flashing, and started up the hill.

"Wait, wait!" Fell yelled, when he saw Spencer. "Careful."

Fell was telling him to be careful. It was almost humorous, except that Ray Fell was very serious. As if Spencer didn't know how to be careful. Circumventing the cluster of people by about thirty feet, Spencer made his way up the hill.

Snow seeped into Spencer's boots, melting into his socks and making his feet first cold, then wet. Damn boots. Not worth the cow they were cut from.

"What's up?" Spencer said, coming up fast to Fell.

"I don't know yet," replied Fell. "I'm keeping the people at bay."

Spencer looked at the handful of students gathered around, not moving anywhere except from foot to foot. They didn't look as though they needed to be kept at bay. One of the boys stood a little apart from the rest, looking forlorn. Spencer made a mental note. That was probably Milton.

"What's going on?" said Spencer.

"Don't know yet. I was waiting for one of you guys to arrive."

"Where's your partner?"

"Out sick."

"Where's Milton?"

"Who?"

"The student who called," Spencer said patiently. "Milton Johnson."

Fell pointed to the forlorn-looking boy. Spencer nodded. "Have you talked to him?"

"Yeah. He pointed me to over there." Fell waved down the hill. "I don't know, Sergeant Tracy. I think he's just imagining things. I didn't see anything."

Feeling less patient, Spencer said, "That's fine, Ray. I'll go check it out. Why don't you go to the car and get us police tape and some sheets, just in case, all right?"

"Sheets?"

"Yes, Ray, so we don't walk all over the evidence."

Spencer watched him lumber off around Feldberg, then turned to the woods. The birches and the oaks were gray. The conifers were heavy with snow. Spencer saw old tracks on the ground, under an inch of yesterday's new snow, leading down off the path. He walked between two young Norwegian pines and stopped. His eyes followed the footprints, five, ten, fifteen feet down the hill to a cluster of conifers. There was something there. Squinting to see better, he reached into his pockets to get his notepad and pen. His hands were cold, and he kept fumbling while looking downhill. What is that? he thought, his heart beginning to thunder in his chest. *What is that?*

And then his hands fell to his sides. The pencil and the notepad fell from his hands.

Next to the evergreens at the end of a snow-covered mound, Spencer O'Malley saw two black boots poking up out of the snow.

No, he thought. No. He staggered on the path. No, they weren't boots. He was too far away. They were just black rocks, or hats, or bags, or junk left on the side of the road. He slowly made his way down the hill.

They're just black stumps. My imagination. It's working overtime. It's been a long day and I need a drink. He stood ten feet away from the mound and stared at the boots. Oh, God. Oh, shit. No.

Spencer liked the way Dartmouth Hall looked in wet weather, its sterling whitewashed walls highlighted by the wide ebony shutters, the building peeking through the soggy green trees like snow in spring. It was Dartmouth Hall that had gotten his attention when he first laid eyes on Hanover.

But in the wintertime, all Spencer saw was the black shutters peeking out of the snow, much like the black boots before him.

The shutters, however, didn't startle him, didn't frighten him, didn't reduce him to a derivative of a detective, of a human being, of a man. When he saw those boots, Spencer realized in an instant of self-loathing and fear that he wasn't a man, he was just a boy playing detective and hoping no one would catch him.

Spencer crossed himself and silently said two Hail Marys.

Fell was calling down to Spencer from the path. Spencer motioned him to come. They stood side by side. "Did you bring the sheets?" Spencer said hoarsely and then cleared his throat.

"Yes." He handed one sheet to Spencer. "Do we need it?" He looked impassively at the mound.

Spencer laid the sheet out in front of the mound and then searched in his pockets for the notebook, and for a tissue. "I think we may have found a body, Fell," he said.

Fell looked closer. "We did?" he said with surprise. "Where?"

Spencer didn't find a tissue. His notebook was still on the ground up the hill. "Ray," he said. "Do you see a pair of boots in front of you?"

"Boots?" He looked again. "Is that what they are?"

"Well," said Spencer slowly, "what do they look like to you?"

"I don't know," Fell replied. "Is that what Milton was pointing to? I kind of looked where he pointed but didn't see anything."

"No, I guess you didn't," said Spencer. "Look, make sure no one comes down here and go up and wait for me."

"What are you going to do?"

"Just wait for me up there, Ray."

⁂

Spencer stood motionless for a few moments and then slowly walked on top of the sheet to the mound. Up close, the boots were strikingly black against the white snow.

Everything else, however, looked to be in its natural place, and the mound looked like a snowdrift. Spencer instantly became convinced it was a snowdrift. He then recalled someone on Main Street wearing similar black boots a few days ago, and he squatted down to the mound, breathlessly relieved. *It's not her, it's not her.*

Spencer put on his leather gloves and started to scrape away at the snow. First slowly, then faster and faster, he frantically dug through the mound. He couldn't feel anything except hard old snow, and he was thinking, it's nothing, it's just boots, somebody played a bad joke, and then he felt something that wasn't snow.

Shutting his eyes, he brushed the snow away and felt a human hand through his gloves. His heart sank and he opened his eyes, emitting a low groan of pain.

It was Kristina's hand. Long fingers, stiff and unyielding, no jewelry. The beautiful nails were broken, the red nail polish chipped. The hand was neither clenched nor relaxed, just stiff in the deep freeze, like ice, or like meat. Spencer's head made a shuddering, jerky motion. He was unable to control it and was vaguely embarrassed by it, as he was by all things uncontrollable. He knew his head made that motion only under extreme duress. He knew now was *the* time to have his wits about him. Except for the jerking of the head, Spencer was outwardly composed.

He slowly took off his gloves, lifted her icy arm, took her hand into both of his, and held it.

Another anguished moan escaped his dry throat.

He gently laid her hand down and stood up. His head shuddered again.

Spencer stood in the woods with his arms at his sides and tried not to blink. He wished the crowd would move away. And Fell would leave too. Spencer wanted a little privacy with her. Before the examiner and the coroner and the undertaker saw her, before Concord and the major crimes unit at Haverhill saw her. Before the ground would see her, or the oven. His knees were shaking. *Please, dear God,* he whispered. *Please let me take this like a man, let me do my job like a man. I know I can do this,* he said. *I know I can, and I will.*

He willed himself to steady, and then listened to the woods. What had happened?

Not a branch out of place. Not an evergreen leaf, not a bush, and the snow covers everything. I mean, what did she do? Come here to die? Did she just walk over, lie down in the snow, and die? Did she stumble, did she hurt her head and lose consciousness, and then freeze to death? The mound is perfect and symmetrical. Only nature in blizzards blows mounds like this and then leaves them serene for the sun.

But the footsteps barely covered by snow showed that someone had been near her as recently as yesterday afternoon. Spencer squinted into the snow, trying to see better. To the right side of the shoe prints were other tracks. These were small, round, four-toed, and shoeless.

Spencer breathed deeply, nodded to himself, and went back up the hill to Ray Fell.

"What's going on there?" Ray was antsy.

"There's a—" Spencer paused to get his voice on even keel before he continued. "—a *body* down there, Ray. Please go and immediately call Will, the hospital, and the funeral home. Oh, and bring me back a camera and several more sheets."

Having recognized Kristina's hand, he realized there was no hope anymore, and he wanted her out of the snow as quickly as possible.

"A body?" Ray gasped, and immoderate excitement shone in his eyes. "My God! Wow."

Spencer gritted his teeth. "A body, Ray," he said loudly. "Do you understand what that means? It means someone has died. Wonder if you'll say wow when you have to call her parents and tell them their little girl is dead."

Embarrassed and red, Ray said, "I'm sor—"

"Please go to the car, call Will and everyone else, and bring me the camera."

Ray looked befuddled.

"Raymond, the camera?" Spencer asked.

Fell was not in possession of the camera he was supposed to carry with him in the patrol car at all times. Something about the cold and not wanting to leave it out in this kind of weather and something about an aunt wanting to see the camera used during crime investigations.

Spencer waved at Fell impatiently and said, "Go to the car and get me more sheets. You have those, right? Your aunt didn't want to see those too, did she?"

"No, sir," said Ray Fell. "Do you want me to call Will right away or bring you the sheets right away?"

"Both, Ray, both," said Spencer, turning away from him and going to pick up his notebook and pen from the ground nearby. Damn Ray.

He jotted down the time of his own arrival, what he'd seen, what the mound looked like, the black boots, the footprints, the paw prints, the hand. And then went to talk to the students.

"Which one of you is Milton Johnson?"

The small, thin guy in the back raised his hand as if he were in class.

Spencer sighed, motioning him to come closer. "You don't have to raise your hand," he said. "Just speak up. You are . . ."

"Milton Johnson," the boy said, timidly looking away from Spencer.

"Milton, do me a favor, and please look at me when you talk to me. All right? We have a body here, and when you don't look at me, I can't help it, I think you have something to hide. Okay?"

The obviously frightened Milton blinked rapidly, unable to stop his teeth from chattering, but managed to look up at Spencer.

"Now, Milton, when did you notice something?"

"Just a f-f-few hours ago," stammered Milton.

"What did you notice?"

Milton pointed up to the second-floor windows of Feldberg. "I was just sitting on the sill on the second-floor stairwell, taking a break from studying. Looking out the window. Not studying. Avoiding studying, avoiding it, you know."

"I know," said Spencer helpfully.

"Anyway, anyway . . ." continued Milton, his body now a mass of tics and fidgets.

"Are you an engineering major, Milton?"

"Engineering, yes," Milton quickly replied. "That's why I was at Feldberg, the engineering library. Plenty of room. Quiet."

"Go on, Milton," said Spencer.

"Oh. Yeah. Okay, okay." Milton scratched the side of his face and then his hair under his coat hood.

Spencer was glad his own only physical nervous habit was an involuntary shuddering of the head. Maybe engineers could get away with being a mass of nerves. He couldn't imagine a cop having those physical tics.

"So anyway, there I was, sitting, and out the window, you know, it's kind of nice out, sunny, and I'm looking down and at the trees, kind of absent-mindedly, you know?"

"I know," said Spencer. "Go on."

"And I noticed something, I don't know. From the second-floor windows it was hard to tell what it was, but I kept looking and looking, and for some reason, I just became a little, I don't know, obsessed with figuring out what it was, you know?"

"Go on. What did you think it was?"

"That's the whole thing. I couldn't tell. I mean, strangely, it looked like . . . well, it really did look like tips of boots. Even from up there." Milton pointed.

"So you went downstairs."

"Yes."

"And?"

"I walked around back, carefully, and then came to about here"—Milton pointed a few feet away from where they were standing—"and I looked down, and it kind of still looked like boots to me. Plus now, on this angle, I noticed there was a mound. Like maybe there was someone under there. So I called the police. I said I didn't know what it was."

"Yes, you did, Milton, and we appreciate your call. How close did you say you came to the mound?"

"Just down to here." He pointed to about four feet away, still on the beaten path.

"Okay. You'll have to come down to the police station to make a statement. Okay?"

Milton became a nervous tic again. "Yeah, yeah, sure."

"Milton, one last question," said Spencer, jotting the last of the conversation down on the notepad. His hands were cold and moving slowly. "Do you have a dog?"

The other students chuckled. Milton scratched his neck, then his hand, then his other hand. He looked small and sickly.

"No, sir, I don't have a dog."

"Milton is allergic to dogs," said the girl in the black wool coat.

"Milton is allergic to everything," someone else chimed in, and Milton, as if to prove just that, broke into a scratching frenzy.

"I see," said Spencer, smiling lightly. "Milton, do you come into contact with a lot of dogs?"

"No, sir. Well, you know Hanover, sir. They're everywhere, the damn things. I try to stay away from them as much as possible."

"Smart move, Milton," agreed Spencer, checking his notepad. "You live in Mass Row, see a lot of dogs there?"

"No, sir. We're not allowed to have dogs on campus."

"Ahh," said Spencer alertly. "Any students disobey the rules?"

"Plenty," said the girl in the black wool coat. "It's one of those rules hard to enforce. Too many people break it."

"One more question, Milton," said Spencer. "Did you come down here yesterday, by any chance?"

"Yesterday? No, uh-uh." Milton shook his head, and then couldn't stop shaking it. "I didn't come to Feldberg yesterday," he said, his head still shaking. "Too many classes. Studied in my room. Why? You think I was here?"

"Unless you were here, Milton, no, I don't think so. Relax. You can go back home if you want to. Someone will call you later today, all right?"

"Yeah, sure, no problem," Milton said, trying to sound brave, but his hands twitched.

Spencer waited impatiently for Ray.

After Ray returned with the sheets, he and Spencer took the police tape and spent several minutes taping around a twenty-by-twenty-yard area surrounding the mound. Spencer tried to concentrate on the sticky tape and not think of anything else. POLICE LINE—DO NOT CROSS read the black letters on the tape, which, except for the letters, looked much like the yellow sticky fly traps that hung from the ceiling of Spencer's mother's kitchen.

As they were rolling the yellow tape around the makeshift posts they cobbled together with twigs, Spencer felt his feet break through a crust of ice and sink deep into the snow, up to his knees. For a brief, unreal moment, Spencer wondered if the black boots kept Kristina's feet from being wet and cold.

Spencer looked at their tape work. To get the tape around the trees, they had to break some of the branches, which were now lying on the ground, marring the impeccable white blanket that covered the earth. With their police tape they created more disarray than death had made.

After they were done, they went under the yellow tape into the crime scene and spread two more sheets down on the ground to protect the evidence.

"Careful," Spencer told Fell in an irritated voice when he saw him step on the snow. "See the tracks?"

Fell stepped back on the sheet and squatted. They were about five feet away from the mound.

"Kind of," he said slowly. "But they look old."

Spencer, also on his haunches, turned to him. "Fell, that's a good thing. We want them to be really old."

"Old?"

"Very old. She—" He stopped. "The body," he corrected himself, "has not been here since just this morning. It's covered by snow. You remember the last heavy snow?"

"Well," said Fell uncertainly, "it snowed last night."

"Yes, it did. Did it snow enough to cover a person?"

"I don't know," Fell replied coolly. "I wasn't out last night."

Straightening up, Spencer said just as coolly, "Ray, you were on the four-to-midnight shift. What do you mean, you weren't out last night?"

Fell became flustered. "Yes. I meant out walking."

"You didn't see the snow from inside your car?"

"Yes. I saw. It snowed."

"Yes. Not much, though," Spencer said, backing away. "This morning on the radio, they reported an inch and a half. Do you think an inch and a half is enough to cover a person?"

Averting his gaze, Fell said archly, "No, sir."

Spencer nodded. "Good. Neither do I. So what was I saying? Be careful of the tracks."

The snowstorm before Thanksgiving was enough to cover her, he thought, looking at the mound. The snowdrifts alone reached six feet in places around town. A chill passed through him. Has she been here since before Thanksgiving? He surreptitiously crossed himself, his head jerking. It just can't be.

Spencer's thoughts were interrupted by the arrival of his partner, Will Baker, the Dartmouth-Hitchcock medical examiner, and two ambulances.

"Did we need *two* ambulances?" said Spencer to Will, a balding, paunchy man with a goatee, who came under the tape and stood next to Spencer.

"Ray wasn't specific on the phone. He didn't know how many bodies you'd found."

Spencer shook his head. "There's only one body," Spencer said testily. "She doesn't need the entire hospital."

Will studied Spencer. "What's the matter with you? And how do you know it's a she?"

"Well, unless the man once had fine, long, well-polished nails, it's a she," said Spencer.

"You touched the body?" Ray Fell said, sounding slightly repulsed.

Spencer considered him briefly before ignoring him. "Can you go and question the other students, Ray? Get their phone numbers."

Stretching his hand out to Will, Spencer said, "Where's the camera?" Will handed him a Nikon 28-85. The two men hunched down in front of the mound. "So what do we have here?" Will asked quietly.

"A dead girl," replied Spencer.

"I see." Will fell silent. "Trace, who dug her hand out of the snow?"

Spencer thought before answering. "I did."

"Why?"

"I didn't know it was a body until I saw the hand."

Will looked sideways at Spencer. "The boots didn't give you an idea?"

"No," said Spencer, not elaborating further. "Look," he said to Will, pointing at the prints next to the mound.

Will looked carefully. "What do you think of these?" he asked.

Spencer replied, "Someone was walking a dog and stumbled onto the body."

"You think it was a dog?"

"As opposed to what? A wolf? A cougar? A fox? How often are they walked around here? The paw prints are right next to the boot prints."

"Boot prints?"

"Good winter shoe. Very fashionable. Deep grooves, thick lug sole with the trademark single lug in the heel. Doc Martens. About size ten. A little big for a girl. Probably a guy, five ten or so. Medium-pressure impression. He's not too heavy, maybe one-sixty."

As Spencer was talking, he noticed something else. At the side of the right boot, he saw a small hole, maybe three inches deep, clawed out with some urgency, as if the animal was desperately trying to get to whoever was underneath the mound. Spencer almost heard the whine of the animal. Brushing the snow back from the hole, Spencer noticed skid marks on the icy crust where the reluctant animal had been pulled away.

He stood, trying to control his head, to no avail. "Not just a dog," said Spencer. "But *her* dog."

After taking pictures of the surroundings, of the mound from all sides, of the footprints, the paw prints, the skid marks, the dug-out hole, Spencer shivered as he watched the paramedics dressed in white begin to dig out the body with gloved hands, careful not to throw the snow over the footprints.

First they exposed her boots, which were laced onto bare ankles, and then her bare calves, and her knees. Spencer began praying for some clothing on her, but when they got to her naked thighs, he began to suspect the worst.

Helplessly, he yanked up the sheet from under his feet, ready to cover her. God, she was naked, all this time in the snow *and* naked. His eyes burned.

The paramedics delicately stopped and turned to Spencer, who stared at them dumbly with the sheet in his hands. Will patted Spencer's back. "It's all right, man," he said. "You go right ahead," he told the paramedics.

Spencer didn't want to see them scrape snow off her genitals. He turned away. Then, dropping the sheet, he grabbed the camera from Will. He desperately wished he were sitting after hours on a high stool in a dimly lit bar, holding a glass in his hand. He shuddered.

"Careful," he said under his breath. "Please. Be careful."

The paramedics uncovered her bare stomach and hands and arms and chest, gingerly brushing the snow off her frozen white breasts. Spencer lifted the camera, which shook in his hands.

The men began to expose shoulders and her neck—

"Careful!" screamed Spencer. "I asked you to be careful, goddammit!"

They turned to stare at him. Will, his head bent, placed his hand on Spencer's back.

"Do *you* want to do this?" asked one of the men.

In other circumstances, Spencer would have. But in other circumstances, it wouldn't have mattered to him if the men were careful with a corpse. He shook his head. "Just be careful is all I'm saying," he said, much quieter.

He could only bear to look at her body in quick glances. There were marks on it: cuts on her knees and calves, dark blue bruises on her ribs. They could have been from the car accident. On the other hand, a maniac could have mauled her. How else could you explain her being nude in the middle of the woods?

Her left arm even in death looked unnatural lying at her side, as if someone had put the cover on a jar improperly with the grooves out of alignment.

"Careful," he kept muttering under his breath. He lifted the camera and shot another roll of film, walking around her, coming close to her, not letting himself see her through anything but the lens of the Nikon.

Will came up behind him. "Spence, can you do this?"

"Yes, of course," replied Spencer. "Everything is okay."

"Then I want you to look at something." Spencer and Will knelt down near the body as if to pray for the dead or to examine evidence.

Spencer was praying. Quickly, mutely, he mouthed a Hail Mary before he answered Will with a statement of his own. "Her eyes are closed."

"Right," Will said. "Unusual, wouldn't you say?"

"Impossible, I'd say."

"Could she have gone to sleep and died in her sleep?"

"Nobody goes to sleep in this weather," Spencer replied.

"Nobody goes outside naked in this weather either," Will said. "Yet, there she is, with nothing on except her boots, and with her eyes closed."

Spencer got up and turned to face Will. "I think she was killed. And whoever killed her closed her eyes."

"How likely is that?" Will said skeptically. "Does a rapist close his victim's eyes? And where are her clothes?"

Spencer, exasperated, wanted to retort and snap at Will, but he was too cold and too upset. It wasn't worth it. It wasn't Will's fault Kristina was dead.

The paramedics were ordered to go back up the hill and wait until the police and the doctor had examined her. The medical examiner pronounced Kristina Kim dead at three forty-five in the afternoon on Thursday, the second of December, nineteen hundred and ninety-three.

The paramedics were impatiently calling down to the detectives. They wanted to leave, to get out of the cold. Fed up, Spencer finally yelled back, "Wait, please! We'll be done in a while. Then you can take her."

"How is she?" one of the students yelled down.

"She is down for the count," Spencer heard somebody shout back, and tried to no avail to shake off the words when he realized it was he himself who had yelled that. What could be worse than the memory of his own flippant voice wrecking the center inside his conscience? *Down for the count.* Had he seen so much death that it had made him immune to pain, even his own? Even to the pain of her dog—he was sure it had been hers—that had sat at the snow mound and dug with his paws and whined and cried and hadn't moved, needing to be pulled away from his frozen mistress.

Spencer heard the question again, "How is she?" and realized the student was yelling, "Who is she?" and Spencer had misheard. His eyes welled up. This time he didn't answer.

They had about an hour of light left, and here in the trees, hidden behind the north side of a building, it was darker

Spencer and Will looked through the trees, and the snow, looked at the soles of Kristina's boots, looked at her hands and nails, looked at her eyes and through her hair. They shot five rolls of film. Three-quarters of an hour went by in utter silence.

In the growing darkness, Will finally said to Spencer, "So what do you think, Trace?"

Spencer concentrated on maintaining his voice as he answered. "It's odd, isn't it? There's nothing here."

"No, nothing. Except the marks on her body."

"Yeah." He wanted to tell Will they were old, but he didn't want to have to explain how he knew that. "But her legs—" He paused, having difficulty continuing. "Her legs are closed. She was left in pristine condition. There are no gunshot or knife wounds, no marks around her neck."

"Maybe she was poisoned," suggested Will.

"What is this, ancient Greece?" said Spencer. "What else?"

"She got drunk, fell down, and died?"

"On her back? And naked? What else?"

They stood near the body. Spencer didn't look at it.

Will quietly said, "She knew her attacker."

After a silence Spencer asked, "Where are her tracks?"

Will shrugged. "Under the snow?"

"Yes. She was lying under that snow as if she flew here, not walked here, not stumbled here. If she was killed, where are her attacker's tracks?"

"Under the snow," repeated Will.

"Yes. Her attacker knew what he was doing. He was careful. He left no trace of himself."

Will motioned to the paramedics and then said to Spencer, "We'll find him, Trace. Murder is hard."

"It's easy, Will." Spencer pointed to Kristina's body. "Look how easy."

"No, I mean, it's easy to trip over all the details. Planning means lying, and lying means remembering. You'll see. We'll find him."

Turning away and looking at the woods, Spencer nodded.

The paramedics brought down a stretcher. Spencer helped them lift Kristina's corpse onto the gray canvas. He took a white sheet from the ground, brushed snow off it, and covered the body. Will went up to help Ray question the students. Spencer was interested in Kristina's dog. Who walked her dog? Spencer asked Will Baker to find out. He reminded Will that her death was a suspicious homicide, however, and it was good to ask all kinds of questions. The less time people had to make something up, the better.

The paramedics carried Kristina's covered body up the hill, past the curious students, past the police officers, to the ambulance with the flashing lights at the end of the stone bridge. The attendants turned on the siren and sped away to Dartmouth-Hitchcock. A big crowd had gathered nearby to see what was happening.

Spencer stood apart from everyone, with his hands in his pockets. He took out his leather gloves and put them on. While Spencer watched the ambulance go, he noticed a petite girl slip by quietly into Hinman's side door. There was nothing at all remarkable about the girl—she was small and it was dark. What *was* remarkable was that she walked past the crowd, past the ambulance, and didn't stop. In fact, she seemed to drop her gaze and quicken her step. Rubbernecking was a profound human instinct, much like blinking. Spencer didn't know how she could stop herself; it flew in the face of his experience as a detective-sergeant and as a human being.

There was no one behind Feldberg. It was too dark. Baker and Fell were finished. Spencer warned the students at the bridge that the area within the tape was a police-protected area and anyone found inside it would be arrested and charged with disturbing felony evidence, a class-B misdemeanor, punishable by several months in prison. That seemed to impress the group.

"Who was it?" someone asked.

"A girl named Kristina Kim. Do any of you know her, or of her?"

In the back a girl started to cry. Shining a flashlight in the crying girl's direction, Spencer broke through the crowd and came near her.

"Does this mean yes?" he asked gently. "You do know her?"

The girl wiped her face. Spencer waited. He was cold. He'd been outside too long; even his parka was not helping him. It was fifteen degrees Fahrenheit out on a dark December night.

"I know of her," said the girl finally. "God, she was the best basketball player Dartmouth ever had. She was just the best. Last year she set a Dartmouth record with seventy-four blocks. She'd regularly score twenty to thirty points in a game. I think last year she scored twenty-seven points when the Big Green won the Ivy title."

The girl needed a moment to calm down. "You think someone might've killed her? Like maybe somebody from another college?" she asked.

"What? Because they wanted her out of league play or something?" Spencer asked, not wanting to smile.

"Yes, oh, you have no idea how serious the Ivy League takes its sports."

"No, I guess I don't," said Spencer, patting her shoulder. "Please calm down. Do you know who she hung out with? She had mentioned something—" Here Spencer stopped. What was he saying? Kristina had mentioned something about a former roommate to him at EBA, but what was he telling this girl? He glanced at Will Baker, who stared at Spencer inquisitively.

Spencer shrugged and shook his head.

The girl stopped crying.

"Nothing, never mind. Know anybody she was friendly with?"

"Let me think." She scrunched up her forehead in an attempt to remember. "I don't know. I think she went out with the editor of the *Dartmouth Review.*"

Spencer felt a pang in his heart. So she went out with somebody. How silly of him to have thought she was unattached.

"Know his name?"

"Jim. Jim something. Shore, I think. Maybe Shaw."

Spencer said in a loud voice, "Anyone here from Hinman?"

One person raised his hand.

"Well, isn't this interesting?" said Spencer to Will. It was loud enough for all to hear. "Hinman is the closest dorm to here, in fact, there are no other dorms, only the library, which, by admission of the students, no one uses. Yet we have twenty people collected in the middle of a crime scene, all from somewhere else. I find this all very interesting, Will, wouldn't you agree?"

Will agreed.

Six more people raised their hands.

Shaking his head, Spencer took down their names and phone numbers. What did they hope to accomplish by keeping quiet? He figured they must be budding lawyers. Wouldn't utter a word without legal advice.

Spencer thanked the girl for cooperating, asked again the perfunctory questions about when was the last time anyone saw Kristina Kim alive, and got no satisfactory answer, which was as he expected.

Afterward, he stood quietly for a few minutes with Will.

"Wow," said Will. He was a good, easygoing cop, never raised his voice. He was a perfect complement to Spencer. He kept Spencer in check.

"Wow what?" asked Spencer.

"Wow nothing. Just wow." Will scrunched up his face. "Tracy, how the hell did you know who that girl was? How did you know her name was Kristina Kim?"

Spencer looked over at Fell, standing a few feet away, shifting from leg to leg in the cold, obviously wanting to be part of the conversation. Calling Fell over, Spencer said, "Ray and I came to see her last week about a car accident, didn't we, Ray?"

"Who?"

"The girl. The dead girl. Kristina Kim."

"Oh? I didn't recognize her, Sergeant Tracy."

"No, of course not." Spencer observed Ray for a few seconds.

Squaring his shoulders, Ray said loudly, "Waiting for further instructions, sir."

Spencer said, "Go on back to the station, Ray. We'll join you there."

Will said softly, "He's not a bad cop, Spence. He's steady."

"Yeah, steady rotten."

"No, no. Just . . . inexperienced."

"Will, he forgets everything! Everything. He'd forget to go to his own funeral."

Will smiled, and said wow again.

Leaning even closer to Baker, Spencer said, "Wow what?"

"Really, nothing. I was just thinking that Kristina—that could be my kid someday."

"You've got two boys."

"You know what I mean," Will said. "She'd been dead a while, the girl. How long you think?"

"When did enough snow fall to bury her?"

Will was silent. "I think the blizzard Tuesday before Thanksgiving."

Spencer nodded mutely. He couldn't bear to think of her in the snow for *nine* days. When he had left her last Tuesday in the afternoon, it had just started to snow. She'd been alive then. So sometime between 1:00 P.M. Tuesday and Wednesday morning when it stopped snowing, Kristina had died.

"Yeah. I think that's a pretty good bet," he said at last. "Before Thanksgiving."

"It was so cold that night," said Will. "She must have frozen immediately. Did you see? No decay, no lividity."

"Hey," said Spencer weakly, in an attempt at humor. "Maybe if we thaw her, she'll still be alive?"

Will shook his head. Spencer asked him to go notify the dean of students that there had been a death at the college and to interview anyone else who might have seen her in the last week or so. Then he remembered basketball. "Will, do me a favor, too, and talk to the women's basketball coach. See if Kristina played in last Saturday's game." He was just sending Will away; Spencer knew she couldn't have played. He had seen her shoulder.

Will was wrong about the lividity too. Spencer caught a glimpse of her back and legs as he helped lift her onto the stretcher. They were a mass of black bruises and marks, pools where the blood had settled after it stopped circulating. There was no decay because there was no rigor, and there was no rigor because she had frozen before rigor had had a chance to set in. In the hospital she would thaw and decompose at the same time.

Spencer felt very cold.

He waited to be let in at Hinman Hall's side door, and went upstairs. At the third floor, he stopped by Kristina's door and knocked. The door was not locked, but Spencer knew he had no right to enter without a search warrant.

Opening the door slowly, Spencer peeked into her room. The light was on. The computer was playing a screen-saver of some kind. The bed was not made. Books and clothes were scattered over the room. The clothes on the bed could very well have been the clothes she took off the night she died. A bottle of Southern Comfort lay on the floor near the bed.

Spencer badly wanted to enter the room and damn the protocol, but he knew better. What was the point of finding anything if he wouldn't be allowed to use it? The court would first throw the evidence out, and then the chief, egged on by the Concord prosecutorial zealots and sticklers for detail, would throw Spencer out. He'd be out on his ass, out of a job, and without a suspect.

Reluctantly Spencer let the door close.

And then he looked up and down the hall and knocked at the door directly across from Kristina's. A fastidious-looking Asian student opened the door. Spencer began to tell him who he was and what had happened, but the student calmly cut him off.

"Wait, wait, wait," he said. "You want to speak to him." He pointed down the hall. "Three-nineteen."

"Why three-nineteen?"

"They were friends," said the student and made a move to shut his door. Spencer put a foot out to stop the door and took out his badge.

"I don't like your attitude," he said firmly. "What's the name in three-nineteen?"

The student, looking at Spencer's foot inside his door and then at Spencer's badge, said, "Maplethorpe. Albert. May I?"

Spencer took his foot away, and the door closed.

Spencer slowly walked over to 319. On the mauve door, next to the magnetic note board, there was an art representation of Anubis, the god of death, jackal-headed and frightening, and a Bulgarian proverb that said, *If you wish to drown, don't torture yourself with shallow water.*

Is there anything more I need to know about *Maplethorpe, Albert*? Spencer wondered, knocking on the door until it opened and a handsome, long-haired young man stood in front of him. He wore only black shorts.

Spencer showed his police badge. "Are you Albert Maplethorpe?"

"I am, yes," Albert said, pulling his hair back and tying it up in a ponytail.

"Were you friendly with a girl down the hall, Kristina Kim?"

The young man's black eyes flashed something at Spencer. What was that? "Friendly, yes."

"She was found dead today."

Even in the dim light of the hallway, the young man looked as if he'd been hit, and hard. All the blood drained away from his face.

Without turning around, Albert said, "Conni, come here. It's about Kristina."

The girl came to the door. She, too, was barely dressed, even though it was winter. "What's the matter? What's happened?"

"This is Detective . . ."

"Excuse me," Spencer said to the girl. "Could I get your name, please?"

"Conni. Constance Tobias," the girl stammered. She was visibly nervous. In a way, she reminded Spencer of twitchy Milton.

"What's happened?" Conni said in a small voice.

Turning to her, Albert said, quietly, "They found Kristina dead today."

Conni broke down. She cried so immediately, so furiously, and so hard that Spencer was taken aback. Albert's arm went around her shoulder. "It's all right," he whispered. "It's all right." Conni cried harder.

Spencer watched her very carefully. In a matter of seconds, Conni went from apparently normal to hysterical.

Clearing his throat, Spencer said, never taking his eyes off her, "I'm terribly sorry. You knew her."

"Knew her?" sobbed Conni. "She was our best friend."

Our, echoed Spencer to himself. Well, this is interesting.

"I'm sorry again. I'll try to be brief."

Conni could not stop crying. She was shaking, and her nose was running. Albert's comforting hand on her shoulder did nothing to stifle her sobs. In fact, she sobbed harder.

Spencer watched them carefully. Conni Tobias was a small, pretty girl, pretty, that is, theoretically. It was hard to tell at this moment whether she was pretty or not. Her face was wet and red.

She was wearing a tank top and short shorts. She was thin and big-breasted. Spencer looked down at her bare feet, and then into the room behind her. He was trying to see some shoes.

His gaze reverted to Albert, who was muscular without being brawny, and good-looking without being perfect. Spencer noticed a small gold hoop in Albert's left ear and an elaborate tattoo on his left arm. That was interesting. Tattoos were rare on Dartmouth College students; Spencer stared at it. It was the picture of Anubis, this time with wings, and underneath him the initials KM.

"Nice tattoo," said Spencer. "Who's KM?"

"My mother," said Albert. "Kay Maplethorpe."

"I see," said Spencer, suspicious. "Couldn't just write 'Mom,' huh?"

Albert flashed his teeth at Spencer. "Pathetic for a guy to write 'Mom' on his arm."

"Disagree," said Spencer. "Love for your mother is a commendable thing. The sort of thing that will get you elected to public office."

"Thank God, I will never run for public office," said Albert.

Conni was still crying. Spencer was wary of people who reacted too swiftly to devastating news. Paling was good and nonreactions were good. From mothers and fathers he expected hysteria. From friends he expected less, yet this girl was giving him more and more and more.

Also, nobody had asked what had happened to Kristina.

"Are you sure?" said Conni. "Are you absolutely positive about her?"

"Miss Tobias," Spencer said evenly, "it is my job to tell the difference between people who are dead and people who are alive. Your friend was found frozen in the snow, where she had obviously been a number of days. We don't yet know how she died, but we are sure that she is, unfortunately"—he swallowed; the word stuck in his dry throat—"dead."

"Would you like to come in?" asked Albert.

Spencer leveled his gaze at Albert. He could've meant come in so that the students curiously poking their heads out of their rooms won't be privy to our informal talk, or he could've meant come in because you look like you need to sit down.

"No, thank you," said Spencer. "I was wondering if Kristina had a dog."

"Dog?" said Conni, sniffling. "Yes. Dog. She's got a dog. Where's Aristotle, Albert?"

They both looked back at the room and then at each other.

Spencer waited. "Is Aristotle the dog?"

They nodded.

"Funny name for a dog. Did you misplace Aristotle?"

"Why do you ask if she had a dog?" asked Conni, wiping her face.

Spencer made it his policy never to answer questions from people who had no business asking them. He didn't answer this one.

"Do you know where the dog is?"

"It's not here," said Albert.

"That much is obvious. It's a big dog. Maybe a Labrador, isn't it?"

"Yes, how did you know?"

Again he did not answer.

When Spencer was young he had had a golden retriever, old and half-blind. The dog had died in the wintertime. Its slow-moving paws on the snow in their backyard were etched into Spencer's childhood memories.

"Albert, Conni," Spencer said firmly. "All I want to know is whether you've seen the dog and where the dog might be."

"Maybe Jim's got her," said Conni uncertainly.

"Jim Shore?"

"Jim Shaw. He's her boyfriend," Conni said mournfully. "Did she fall?"

"Fall?" Spencer was instantly alert. "What do you mean?"

"Nothing, nothing," Conni said quickly. "Just thought maybe that's how she died."

"Where would she fall from?" Spencer never put his notepad down.

"The bridge," said Conni. "That awful bridge she walks on."

"The bridge at the side of Feldberg Library?" He remembered driving under the bridge; he also remembered walking across the bridge in a procession after the paramedics who were carrying Kristina. "Why would she fall off the bridge?"

Albert shook his head. "She walks the ledge. There and back."

"Why would she do that?"

Shrugging, Albert said, "For fun. She'd have something to drink and then walk that stupid thing." Albert shook his head violently. "We just thought she might've fallen off this time."

"How often did she do that?"

Albert and Conni both shrugged. "Once in a while."

"While drunk?"

"Yeah, the drink steadied her," said Conni.

"Steadied her?" Spencer wrote it down on his pad. He breathed in heavily before asking the next question. "She was—naked—when we found her." *When I found her.* "You know why she might be naked?"

Albert said simply, "She walked the ledge naked." He paused. "Did she fall?"

Spencer answered this time. "No, she did not fall. Why would she walk naked in the freezing cold?"

"We don't know," said Conni, sniffling. "We've been asking her that for three years."

"I see. Where does Jim Shaw live?"

On the first floor, Conni told him. Spencer informed them that they had to dress at once and come to the police station to answer a few more questions. He then turned to go.

"Oh, one more thing," he said. "Do you know where her parents live? I need to call them." When they didn't answer, Spencer said, "We need someone to come identify the body."

Conni started to cry again. Albert looked terrible. "Her father is dead. We don't know where her mother is," he said.

"I see," said Spencer. "Do you know where her home is?"

Albert turned away from Spencer and toward Conni. "Conn, do you know? Where Kristina's from?"

"I think New York. She graduated from some prep school in Brooklyn Heights. I'm not sure, though," she said, her voice trembling.

"Yes. That must be it." Albert turned back to Spencer. His gaze was impenetrable. "Brooklyn Heights."

Spencer felt uneasy as he left.

He waited for five minutes after knocking on Jim Shaw's door. No one answered. There were no sounds coming from the room. Spencer thought Jim might be out walking the dog, and so he leaned against the door and waited. Another student walked down the hall and said, "Can I help you?"

"No, thank you," said Spencer pleasantly.

"If you're waiting for Jim, I saw him out earlier. Can I give him a message?" The student seemed curious.

"No, thanks," repeated Spencer.

"I don't know how long he'll be," said the student. "Sometimes he's gone quite a while. Sure you don't want to leave a message or come back?"

"Positive," Spencer said. He had a feeling Jim wouldn't be too long.

And he was right.

About fifteen minutes later, around six o'clock, the yellow Lab came barreling down the hall.

The dog ran up to Spencer, who bent over and lavishly petted him. Spencer had always loved dogs and wished he were allowed to have one like his childhood pet in the little apartment. He also got a good look at the shoes of the dog's present owner.

"Good dog, good dog, Aristotle," Spencer said, straightening up and facing a bundled young man wearing a ski cap and scarf. "Are you Jim Shaw?"

"I guess so," replied the young man sourly, taking off the cap and scarf. "Who are you?"

Taking out his ID and shoving it into Jim's face, Spencer said, "From now on, let's get it straight. I am the only one allowed to ask questions, okay? I need you to come with me."

"What for? I haven't done anything," said Jim loudly.

"See, that's my trouble with you, Jim. I think you either did plenty or not enough. In either case, I'd like you to accompany me to the police station so I can ask you a few questions."

"I don't know what you're talking about," said Jim, but Spencer, looking into Jim's flushed face, into his racing eyes, thought Jim knew precisely what he was talking about.

"Come now."

"I'm not going anywhere until you tell me what this is all about and I have my lawyer with me."

"And where is your lawyer, Jim? Do many Dartmouth students have lawyers on call? Can he get here in an hour? Because my shift was over at five, and I'm not going to wait another second. I will place you under arrest for suspicion in a capital felony and will hold you in our jail cell until I return to work tomorrow morning. Or you can come with me now, so I don't have to stand in this claustrophobic little hallway and yell at you."

Jim just stood there, dumbfounded.

"What's this all about?" he finally said, averting his eyes and staring intently at Aristotle.

"Look at me, Jim," Spencer said, wanting to put his fingers under Jim's chin and lift up his head. Jim looked up. "Your girlfriend, Kristina Kim. She's been found dead." Staring at Jim intently before speaking again, Spencer waited.

Jim blinked and blinked again. He slumped against the door, and when he lifted his hands up to his face, Spencer noticed they were shaking. "Oh no, oh no, oh no," Jim said quietly. "Oh my God, oh no." His shoulders heaved, and for a moment Spencer was afraid Jim was going to cry. Spencer wanted to stay sharp, and sympathy would destroy that.

"Keep yourself together, Jim," said Spencer, gentler. "I'm sorry to have brought you bad news."

Jim's shoulders were still heaving. He did not look at Spencer, who wished to hell he didn't have to look at Jim.

"I'm sorry, man," said Spencer with emotion. "It's awful, I know."

Jim lifted his eyes up at Spencer. In a low voice he said, blinking rapidly, "She's not my girlfriend."

Spencer shook his head. "That's good. Show grief," he said sarcastically.

"No, no," Jim said quickly. "Just wanted to clear that up in case of further confusion."

Jim stood dumbly outside his door. Aristotle paced about. Other doors opened and closed.

"I'll come with you," Jim finally said. "Let me just leave Aristotle some water."

"Actually, the dog should come with us."

"What for?"

"Jim, I see you're forgetful. The rule is, I ask the questions, you answer them. Got that? Now, the dog comes with us. Let's go upstairs."

"Upstairs where?"

"Upstairs to Kristina Kim's room." Spencer never took his eyes off Jim, who winced noticeably at the mention of Kristina's name.

"Aristotle is Kristina's dog, isn't he?"

"Yes. How did you know?"

Because I know everything, Spencer wanted to say, but it wasn't true. He hardly knew anything.

Jim said quietly, "I saw the cop cars outside. When I saw you, I thought it might be about Kristina."

Spencer tilted his head in an effort to keep it steady. "You were right. It's about Kristina."

———

When they got upstairs, Aristotle began to whine. He lay down in the hall, refusing to move or go in the room.

Jim's back was to Spencer. There was no sound coming from him. It was almost like watching someone's sorrow with the mute button on.

Jim's heaving shoulders reminded Spencer of his own deep-down boiling-over grief, and he felt bad for the boy.

Spencer pulled out of his pocket the roll of yellow fly tape, the one that said POLICE LINE—DO NOT CROSS, and stretched it over the wall, the doorknob, the door itself, and a foot or so over the other wall.

"We're done," Spencer said, ripping the tape off with his teeth. "Let's go."

They got Conni and Albert, took the dog back to Jim's room, and left for the station.

Spencer led Conni into one small room, Albert into another, told them to wait and that someone would be with them shortly.

He took Jim into a rectangular room in the back. After speaking to Will Baker about the students he had interviewed at Hinman Hall, Spencer asked Will to sit in on the questioning. They got a tape recorder and some coffee, which Jim refused.

They sat in uncomfortable plastic chairs in a room with a single light above a white round table. Will sat to Spencer's left. Under his breath, Spencer cursed the modern table that belied the gravity of any questioning he might do at it. The table looked more like a snack table at a suburban corporation's canteen.

He cleared his throat.

"Jim Shaw, this is Detective Will Baker, my partner. He's assisting me on this case."

Will nodded. Jim was motionless. Trying to inject a little humor, Spencer said, "You know your Dartmouth library? It's named after Will."

Jim raised his eyes but said nothing.

Spencer made a face at Will, and sat down. "Okay, let's get on with this. Tell us a little about yourself."

"Like what?"

"Like anything, Jim. We don't know you. Tell us anything you want us to know."

Clearing his throat and keeping both hands under the table, Jim said, "I was born in Bonn, Germany—"

"You're German?" Spencer interrupted. Will laid a gentle hand on Spencer's arm. Spencer moved away.

"To American parents. My father was a vice president in the international division of the Coca-Cola Company. We traveled a lot, and when my dad retired, we moved back to Wilmington, where the rest of my family's from."

"Any brothers or sisters?"

"A younger brother."

"Where's he now?"

"Back in Wilmington. He works for Delaware National Bank."

"I see." Spencer fell silent, sorting through his notes. Will silently rubbed his hands, and Jim looked at Spencer. Jim was a good-looking guy. He was wearing a tweed jacket over a white-collared shirt, and a royal blue wool sweater. His deep-set eyes alternately flashed intelligence and exasperation, defiance and fear. His light brown hair was parted on the side and neatly combed back. Jim looked like a good son and a good student.

"Jim, as you know, Kristina Kim is dead."

Jim remained stationary.

"Can you tell us when you saw her last? I need you to remember everything, every last detail."

Jim twitched. "It must've been last week."

"Last week when?"

"Last week before Thanksgiving."

"Okay. Before Thanksgiving. Sunday? Monday? Tuesday?"

"Guess it must've been Tuesday."

"Jim," said Spencer, "I'm not going to lead you into the right answer. I want you to tell me as much as you know. In case you don't understand how this works, I'll run it by you once. We sit here and ask you lots of questions. You answer them completely and fully, also furnishing us with details we may've forgotten to ask about. This way your conscience is clear and we in turn don't arrest you. Got it?"

"Tuesday, I told you."

"Why Tuesday?"

"Because I left for home on Wednesday, and didn't see her then."

"You sure?"

"Positive."

"When on Tuesday?"

"Late. Maybe eleven. We played cards that night."

"In the Hinman lounge?"

"Yes, how'd you know?"

"Who is we?"

"Me, Kristina, Albert, Conni, and Frank."

"Who is Frank?"

"Frankie Absalom, he's Albert's good friend. Conni was Krissy's roommate a few years back."

"I've met Conni. And Albert?"

"Albert is Conni's boyfriend."

Spencer noticed Jim winced when he said that.

"How long have they been going out?"

"A few years."

"So . . ." Spencer glanced at Will. "What's Albert's connection to Kristina?"

Jim became jittery and wouldn't answer until Spencer asked him again. "Through me, through Conni, I guess. We were good friends."

"Were?"

"Are, I mean. Are."

"You said *through* you?"

"Yes. Albert and I were roommates in our freshman year."

"So Albert and you were roommates, and Kristina and Conni were roommates."

"Yes, that's right. Can I have a glass of water? My throat is dry."

Will went to get Jim water. Jim emptied the tall glass immediately. Without being asked, Will left and brought back a pitcher. While he was gone, Spencer and Jim did not speak.

Once Will sat down, Spencer resumed. "When did you say you all met?"

"During freshman year."

"How?"

Spencer could see Jim was struggling to keep calm. This is hard for him, Spencer thought. Am I beating a confession out of him?

"I don't know how we met," Jim said at last. "It's a difficult question."

"It's a difficult question?" Spencer repeated incredulously. "Jim, let me tell you something. *That* is not a difficult question."

"Forget it, you don't understand," Jim said, shaking his head.

"Explain it to me."

"Listen, I don't know what this has to do with anything."

Spencer turned and stared at Will, who said to Jim, "You're upsetting my partner here, Jim. It's not up to you to decide what has to do with what. You're not forthcoming, and we're getting worried that perhaps you have something to hide."

"I've got nothing to hide, I just—" He broke off. "Look, I haven't been able to figure it out, okay?" he said. "I had thought that I met Conni and Kristina and introduced them to Albert . . ."

"But . . ."

"But nothing. Freshman Thanksgiving, I saw Conni and Kristina coming out of the Alumni Gym. To be perfectly honest," Jim said, clearing his throat, "I liked Conni at first. She was smaller, more, you know, inviting. Kristina— I thought she was out of my league, truthfully. She came outside in the bitter cold in biker pants and a spandex tank top."

"You thought she was out of your league because she came outside in sports gear?" said Spencer.

"No, no," Jim said quickly. "Look, I liked her and everything. We started chatting walking back to Mass Row, where we all lived. I said I had a room-mate, they giggled."

"So, Jim, you seem to have a very good idea of how you all met, wouldn't you say?"

"You don't understand," Jim said.

"Were you and Albert good friends?"

"Very good friends. We hit it off right away. We were great roommates." His face was unable to hide the tension. He was biting his lower lip. "Conni was very friendly. Kristina was funny, but not very friendly, you know?"

Spencer understood: Kristina had been too beautiful to be friendly to strangers.

Except for him. She had been friendly to Spencer. He felt himself biting his own lower lip.

Spencer knew that soon he would have to stop this line of questioning and go on to more grave matters, but for a few more minutes he wanted to imag-ine Kristina, wearing spandex shorts, giggling, *alive.*

"I was hoping to run into them again, and it wasn't long before Albert and I spotted them one morning at Thayer. They walked by with their trays. But this is the thing. Before I had a chance to wave to them, Albert did. They came over and sat at our table. Albert said, 'Kristina, Conni, this is my roommate, Jim.'"

"That was strange to you?"

"Well, he wouldn't be introducing them unless he had met them already."

"It is a small campus."

"Yes, I know. But he never told me how he'd met them. It was never very clear. Anyway. Albert and I became friendly with them, and soon—" Jim stumbled and stopped talking.

"And soon?" Spencer said.

Jim poured himself another glass of water, downing it before he contin-ued. "Conni and I kind of started going together."

"Conni and you?"

"Yes."

"And Albert and Kristina?"

"That's what *I* had thought. Wouldn't it be perfect if we could pair off like that."

"But . . ."

"But . . . Albert and Kristina didn't hit it off."

"Oh."

"Yeah. I asked Albert about it one night, and he wasn't enthusiastic. 'No chemistry' was what Albert said to me."

Spencer could see every word was a struggle for Jim. "So how did you end up with Kristina?"

"Things with Conni just weren't going as well as I thought." Jim gulped and said, "I saw that she was kind of smitten with Albert."

Spencer nodded. "I see. And he with her?"

"I didn't notice that. I saw them coming out of Baker together, going into Lou's together, talking, you know. She said they were just friends, but I could see she liked him."

Spencer shook his head in disbelief. Kristina Kim was Jim Shaw's consolation prize. It was almost laughable.

"I thought Conni wasn't Albert's type, but what did I know?" said Jim. "They've been together since then, and I think they got engaged or something during Thanksgiving. So you see, I didn't read the situation right."

"No, no," said Spencer. "What did you and Albert do?"

"Nothing for a while. Continued as we were."

"Must have been tough," said Will sympathetically.

Jim nodded. "Albert ended up moving out mid spring semester and rooming with Frankie."

"And you started going with Kristina."

"Yes," Jim said in a tired voice.

"How's your present relationship with Conni?"

"Fine. We're friends."

"What about Albert?"

"Fine, too," Jim said quickly.

"So you're friendly."

Jim paused. "*Less* friendly," he said and went no further.

"You had said Kristina wasn't your girlfriend. When did you break up?"

"Monday."

"Monday before Thanksgiving?"

"Yes."

"Monday, the day before she died?"

"It was actually Tuesday morning."

"Tuesday morning?"

"I mean, like, early in the morning on Tuesday. She came to my room at dawn or something."

Spencer relaxed slightly. He had had a brief vision of Kristina dying minutes after she had broken up with her boyfriend of three years. It did not look good for Jim.

"She break up with you?"

Jim shrugged and nodded, reaching for the glass. "Things weren't work-ing."

Spencer wondered if one of Kristina's reasons, the tiniest, could have been Spencer himself. He'd never know now.

Will nudged Spencer under the table. "May I?" he mouthed.

"Go ahead," replied Spencer.

"Jim," began Will, "I spoke to a few people in Hinman Hall to find out about Kristina's whereabouts the night we think she died—Tuesday—and a couple of people told me you guys had a big fight in the lounge that night and you stormed out."

"Oh, that!" Jim waved his hands dismissively, but Spencer noticed the hands were shaking. "Yeah, we just said a few words. It was nothing, really."

"Oh? The guy I spoke to said you were pretty mad."

"Nah, I wasn't mad." But Jim didn't offer more details. Spencer and Will exchanged glances.

"Jim," said Spencer, "maybe I haven't made myself clear earlier."

"It was nothing, I tell you," Jim exclaimed in an exasperated voice.

"Who are you trying to protect?"

"What? Nobody!"

"Are you trying to protect yourself?"

"I'm trying to protect nobody." Jim's voice was loud, and he looked hot and uncomfortable.

"Jim, did you kill Kristina Kim?"

"No!" Jim exclaimed in a high-pitched voice.

"Do you know who did?"

"No!" he exclaimed again, his face sweating.

Nodding, Spencer went on, "You said you played cards last Tuesday. When you stormed out, what time was that?"

"Probably around eleven."

Spencer looked at Jim's wrists. "Wearing a watch, Jim?"

Pulling up his sleeves, Jim showed Spencer he wasn't.

"There wasn't a clock in the Hinman lounge?"

"No, it got busted months ago. I asked Frankie for the time."

"After you left the lounge, where did you go?"

"Back to my room." Jim swallowed very hard.

"Did you pack? Did you study? Did you call Kristina on the phone?"

"No, I . . . studied a little. I was tired. I don't remember. I think I went to bed."

"And you never left your room at all for the rest of the night?"

Jim was silent for a very long time. "No," he said. "I never left my room."

Spencer stood up. "Should I read you your rights and arrest you for killing Kristina Kim?"

"No, no!" Jim exclaimed. "I didn't kill her. I'm telling you I didn't kill her."

"So why do you need a lawyer, Jim?"

Jim again was at a loss for words. Spencer's impatience and suspicion were reaching critical mass. "Jim!" Spencer exclaimed. "What do you want to do, spend two nights in jail? We can keep you here for forty-eight hours while we're investigating her death. Is that what you want? Are you going to be a lawyer? A politician? The future president? Future presidents don't go to jail, Jim!"

Spencer finally sat down. Jim was upset and couldn't continue.

"Tell us," Spencer said, with beseeching intensity. "Get yourself together. What are you afraid of if you didn't kill her? Tell us what you did that Tuesday night."

"Tuesday? God, nothing. I told you. I never left my room," Jim said quickly.

"Can you prove that?"

"What do you mean?"

"I mean, can you prove you never left your room?"

Jim said, his hands shaking, "No. I mean—how could I prove something like that? I was in my room till the next morning. No one was with me."

"Did you talk to anybody?"

"In person?"

"In person, on the phone, anything."

"No. I was awake for a while. I started to pack and then went to sleep. I didn't see or hear anything."

"See or hear anything like what?" Spencer said suspiciously.

"I don't—like anything. I don't know."

"You're saying after eleven at night when you stormed out of the lounge, no one can vouch for your whereabouts?"

"I was asleep, for God's sake! Who can possibly vouch for that except for me?"

Will said gently, "So what you're saying is you have no alibi."

Jim looked so distressed that Spencer took pity on him. "Okay, okay. What about the next morning? What did you do?"

"The next morning, the snowstorm ended, so I packed the rest of my stuff and went home."

"What time did you leave?" Spencer asked.

"I'm not sure."

"Must be hard for you to make your classes, never knowing what time it is," said Spencer.

"I have a watch, I just don't like wearing it. Don't wear any kind of jewelry," Jim added.

"Did you see Kristina Wednesday morning?" Spencer was certain Jim hadn't.

Jim shook his head.

"Did you see the dog?"

"Yes, the dog was in her room. He wasn't happy to see me. Didn't even get up from her bed."

"How did the room look?"

"You know—"

"I don't know."

"Messy."

"What did you do with the dog?"

"Nothing. I petted him and left."

"Was it unusual for Kristina not to be in her room?"

Jim shook his head. "Not unusual at all."

"Did you knock on Albert's door?"

"What for?" said Jim, a little rudely.

Spencer studied Jim levelly, with an unhurried, cold gaze. "I don't know. To say good-bye to your friend? To ask if he'd seen Kristina?"

"No, I didn't do that."

"Didn't, or wouldn't?"

There was a pause. "Didn't."

"So you left."

"That's right."

"You were gone for how long?"

"Until Sunday night."

"I trust you had a good Thanksgiving," said Spencer acidly.

"It was okay," said Jim.

"When you came back, what did you do?"

"What do you mean? Like, did I unpack?"

"Like anything. I don't care much if you unpacked. I care more if you went to see Kristina."

"I did, yes."

"And?"

"And what? She wasn't there."

"No, of course not," said Spencer. "The snow had already fallen."

Jim stared at Spencer quizzically.

Spencer wanted to reach across the table and grab Jim by the shirt collar and shake him. Thank God Will was there, because Spencer's Irish temper would have gotten the better of him. That's why he needed Will, whose steady hand on Spencer's back was like counting to ten and breathing deeply.

Getting Jim to talk was difficult, but more important, Spencer felt Jim was hiding something. There was *something* Jim Shaw was not telling Spencer, and the anger swarmed inside Spencer's chest. Spencer wanted to warn Jim that things could get real bad for the smart-aleck guy who thought he was being clever, real clever, by keeping information on a dead girl away from Spencer O'Malley.

"Jim, tell me, so you came to see her, and she wasn't in. How did the room look to you?"

"I don't remember. Probably the same as before."

"Yes, probably," said Spencer sarcastically, and Will touched him on the arm lightly—to calm him? support him? ease him? Spencer needed to be *eased*.

"Was the dog there?"

"No, the dog wasn't there."

"Okay, so the dog was there on Tuesday night, but wasn't there on Sunday. What did you make of that?"

"I thought someone might be walking him."

"Someone like . . . Kristina?"

"Maybe. More likely Albert."

"You all take turns walking the dog?"

"Yeah, something like that."

Spencer stared at Jim for the longest time. He really wished the self-righteous bastard would realize that any minute he was going to be caught. Couldn't he at the very least give Spencer some respect, considering the imminent outcome of the questioning?

Spencer was waiting for Jim to continue, but Jim had obviously answered the question and wasn't about to open his mouth until he was asked another.

"Jim, did you go see if Albert had the dog?"

"No."

"Why not?"

"Because if Albert was walking the dog, obviously he wouldn't be in his room."

"I see. So what did you do?"

"Nothing. I went downstairs to my room."

"Did you wonder who the dog had stayed with for four days?"

"Of course not. I thought he'd stayed with Kristina."

"But you just said her room looked exactly the same as when you saw it Wednesday morning."

"Look, I didn't pay careful attention. What do I know? It was messy both times. I didn't really study the room, you know."

Spencer went on, "Then what did you do?"

"Went back to my room. Called Kristina's room right before I turned the lights off."

"And?"

"And? She wasn't there."

"Okay," Spencer drew out, scratching the underside of the table with his fingers, while Will took copious notes. Spencer had stopped taking notes because he was too busy watching Jim. "That brings us to Monday."

"Monday," Jim repeated. "I don't remember Monday very well."

"Tuesday?"

"No," Jim said weakly. "Not Tuesday either."

"Wednesday. That was just yesterday. Do you remember that?"

"Not well," said Jim.

Spencer noticed that Jim would not look up from his hands, which lay flat on the table.

"Okay, let's go through this step by step. Literally. Okay?"

"Sure," said Jim.

Spencer pressed on. "Did you see Kristina on Monday?"

"No."

"Did you know Monday she was already dead?"

"No, of course not!"

"Tell me—do you know how she died?"

Jim was looking at his hands again, placed flat on the table. "No," he said. "I don't know how she died."

"You don't know how she died?"

"No, I told you."

"Yes, yes. Well, you know, something makes me curious. If you don't know how she died—you say you don't, and I have to believe you—I'm confused about something. Why don't you want to *know* how she died?"

Jim looked away from Spencer.

"Jim, I really need your attention on this one. Please look at me when I speak to you. It makes me very uncomfortable when you can't look me in the eye." It made Spencer more than uncomfortable. It made him suspicious and furious.

Jim cast another furtive glance at the detective, but was not able to meet Spencer's stare for long.

"I'm going to ask you another question. When I came to your door and informed you that your girlfriend of three years was found dead, was that the first you heard of it?"

Jim opened his mouth to speak, then closed it again. "Yes," he said after a minute. "It was the first I heard of it."

"Are you playing games with me?"

"No!"

"Why didn't you ask me how she died, then?"

"Because I thought I knew."

"Why would you think that?"

"I thought she fell off that damn bridge."

"Why would you think that?"

"Because I've been half expecting her to fall for three years."

"You have?"

"Yes."

"You mean, you thought it was only a matter of time before she died, and so you weren't that surprised?"

"Maybe," Jim said quietly.

"Do you think she was walking that bridge to die?"

"Something like that," Jim said, even quieter.

"Do you think she wanted to die?"

He shook his head violently. "Not when she wasn't drinking. Even then . . . she loved life."

"But not when she drank."

"No, not as much then."

"So if she was so full of life, why would she put her life in danger by walking a stone ledge seventy-five feet above a concrete road?"

"I don't know. She gave me some reasons. None of them made any sense."

"I'll bet they didn't," said Spencer, and felt a little better about this kid sitting in front of him. This kid that must have felt terrible things underneath that snake skin.

"Well, Jim, Kristina didn't die falling off that bridge."

Jim didn't look up from his hands, and Spencer thought, wait. He already knows that.

"Jim, a few more questions about these last three days. You told me you didn't see Kristina."

"No."

"Did you go back to her room to see if she was there?"

"Yes. She wasn't there."

"How many times did you go back?"

"Once on Monday and once on Tuesday."

"What about Wednesday? You know, yesterday?"

"I don't know," Jim said evasively. "I don't think I went there Wednesday."

"Why not?"

"I don't know. I got busy, I guess."

"Did you at any point think it was strange that Kristina was not in her room?"

"Sometimes she'd disappear. Also it was right after Thanksgiving. I thought maybe she'd gone away and wasn't back yet."

"What about the dog?"

"What about it?"

The stone wall had come down again. Jim was guarded.

"Had you seen the dog since Sunday?"

"Well, of course. I've been walking him."

"Did you walk him every day?"

"Yes."

"And where did Aristotle stay when he wasn't being walked?"

"With me."

"That wasn't strange?"

"Kristina obviously wasn't back. I took care of the dog."

"You weren't curious where Kristina was?"

"I was busy. I didn't think much about it."

"Did you see Albert and Conni after Thanksgiving?"

"Yes, once or twice."

"Did you by any chance ask them where Kristina had been?"

"No, I didn't."

"Why not?"

"I just didn't. I had a lot to do, I was preoccupied."

Spencer again felt uneasy. "Jim. Answer me. Who did the dog stay with for Thanksgiving?"

"I don't know," Jim said. "I mean it. I don't know."

"What do you mean, 'I mean it'? Do you mean you didn't mean it until now when you said 'I don't know'? Because you've said 'I don't know' a number of times. I'm wondering if you said 'I don't know' but meant something else."

"No, no," Jim said quickly. "I mean I gave it no thought before and even now I don't know. I suppose Conni and Albert took the dog with them."

"With them where?"

"To Conni's parents' house. That's where they went."

"Why would they do that?"

"I don't know," said Jim, and Spencer felt that after half an hour of interrogation, he knew even less than before. He was so perplexed that he almost forgot the most important thing. Wednesday. Wednesday before an inch of snow fell on somebody's boots, before an inch of snow fell on a dog who scraped away a hole in the ground to get to his cold mistress.

"Did you walk the dog on Monday?"

"Yes, I'm sure I did."

"Did you walk him on Tuesday?"

"Yes, I had to. He was with me."

"Did you walk him on Wednesday?"

There was the briefest pause, and then Jim said, "Yes, I suppose I did."

"You remember where you walked him?"

"All around. I really don't remember."

"Where do you usually walk him?"

"All over, I guess. We go to the river sometimes."

"How do you get there from Hinman?"

"We walk through the woods. There is a little path behind Hinman. We go down there."

"Did you go down there on Wednesday?"

"I don't know. I really don't remember."

"Really?" said Spencer. "Is that a *really* don't remember? And do you mean it this time?"

Jim looked back down at his hands, and Spencer bent down under the table for a moment and then lifted his head back up and said, "Nice shoes, Jim. What kind of shoes are they?"

Jim looked at Spencer, bewildered. "I beg your pardon?"

"The shoes, Jim. What kind of shoes are those?"

Jim briefly looked at his shoes and then quickly back at Spencer O'Malley, who now sat with his own palms pressed against the round Formica table, but that was only so he wouldn't clench them. Their gaze met, and Spencer knew that Jim understood precisely, *precisely,* what Spencer was getting at.

Heaving a big sigh, and taking his hands off the table and placing them on his lap, Jim said quietly, "Doc Martens."

*Chapter
Five*

CLOSE
FRIENDS

Spencer never took his eyes off Jim.

"What do you say, Jim?" said Spencer quietly, thinking, those hands may never do college work again. They may be folding laundry for about twenty-five to life.

"Look," Jim finally said with some difficulty. "I'll tell you what happened. But . . . I don't want you to arrest me." There was a long pause. "Please."

"I don't know," said Spencer. "Should we?"

"No, I don't think you should," said Jim instantly. "I didn't kill her."

"I'll tell you up front," said Spencer, "if you killed her, you're going to need a lawyer."

Jim hit the table. "Is that what you think?" he said fiercely. "That I killed her? Is that what you think I'm going to tell you? You are so wrong, you couldn't be more wrong."

"Spoken like a true prelaw student," said Spencer. "Jim, you must know even murderers vehemently deny their guilt. Not guilty, not guilty, not guilty, they shout, through trials and mistrials and appeals, while sitting in jail. Those words don't mean anything. What are you going to tell us?"

"Everything."

"Okay," said Spencer. "I'm just telling you, if you killed her, you're going to need a lawyer."

"I know that! Don't you think I know that? I plan to go to law school, for God's sake. Who do you think you're talking to?"

Spencer leaned toward Jim. "I'll tell you who I'm talking to," he said. "I'm talking to a kid who broke up with his girlfriend and then had a fight with her the night she died. He had a fight with her, and then he left for four days and when he came back she wasn't there. Of course she wasn't there. She was dead. The kid suspects that something is wrong, but he doesn't want to think about it. So he goes to his classes, takes her dog for walks, eats, sleeps, pretends everything is okay. Except he knows that something is seriously wrong. Because no one has seen her for days. Not he, not his friends, Conni and Albert. And then, on Wednesday, he's walking the dog in the woods, and the dog, smelling something on the ground, pulls him behind Feldberg where it stumbles upon a three-foot-high snow mound out of which stick black leather boots belonging to his mistress. The dog starts to wail and dig at the ground. The kid drags the dog away; his worst fears have proven true. Kristina is not only missing, she is dead." Spencer paused, his chest heavy. "My question to you is, why didn't you call us immediately?"

His fists clenched and his face drained of blood, Jim said, "I don't know."

Spencer laughed. Will twinged. Jim recoiled. Then Spencer turned serious. "Let's try this, Jim, shall we? For the next fifteen minutes, you don't once say 'I don't know.' Can we try that?"

Jim was silent.

"What I've just described to you, was I right?"

Jim could only nod.

"Tell me, why didn't you call us?"

Letting out a big heavy breath, Jim said, "Because I was scared shitless."

"Scared of what?"

"I don—"

"Ah-ah, Jim! No. Scared of what?"

"Scared that something was going to happen to me."

"To *you?*"

"Yes. I was afraid I was going to be blamed somehow."

"Blamed for what?"

"Blamed for her death."

"Jim, if you're innocent, why would you be blamed for anything?"

"Look what's happening! You're blaming me now. I've done nothing, I know nothing, and yet exactly what I was afraid of is happening right now."

"How do we know you've done nothing?"

"I'm telling you."

"How do we know you didn't kill her on Tuesday before Thanksgiving and venture out yesterday to find out if she was still there?"

"Why would I do that? My shoe prints are on the snow. The dog can be traced to Kristina. Why would I go back to the scene of the crime? I'd never do that."

"You're saying if you killed her, you'd never come back to the scene of the crime?"

"That's right," Jim answered carefully, thoughtfully. "I wouldn't."

Spencer whirled around to Will. "Will, are you married?"

Will slowly nodded, as if unsure where this was going.

"Will, if your wife went missing for eight days, would you be worried?"

"Frantic."

"Would you call us?"

"Immediately."

"Will, if you found your wife buried in the snow behind your house, would you let her lie there, hoping she wouldn't be found until the snow melted?"

"Never."

Spencer turned back to Jim. "See, I think Will is right on the ball. Don't you think so, Jim?"

"People react differently," Jim said. "And she was not my wife."

"Are you saying you didn't love her?"

"I'm not saying that at all. We were just not . . . that close."

Not that close, Spencer mouthed. He wanted to curse. Instead, Spencer turned his head to Will and asked, "Will, did you know Kristina Kim?"

"Not at all," answered Will, looking meaningfully at Spencer.

"If you were strolling along in the woods behind Feldberg and found her body, would you report it?"

"Immediately."

"Even if you weren't a cop?"

"Absolutely."

Spencer said coldly to Jim, "By your own admission, you came to her room every day to check if she was there. You obviously were close enough for that. You just weren't close enough to her to report her dead, is that right?"

Shaking his head, Jim said, "You just don't understand."

"You're absolutely right," snapped Spencer. "I'd like to, though. I'd like to understand what makes a twenty-one-year-old guy so afraid that he'd let his dead girlfriend lie frozen in the snow."

"I was afraid for myself," said Jim. "I know it sounds terrible—"

"It does sound terrible," said Spencer.

"I know. But that's the truth. I didn't know what to do. I panicked. I couldn't stop thinking about it. And then today when I realized how bad it would look, it was already too late to call you."

"And snow had fallen," said Spencer.

Jim flushed, as if he finally understood Spencer's meaning.

"There was snow," Jim agreed weakly.

"And what did the snow mean to you?"

"The snow meant," Jim said in a stricken voice, as quietly as he could without whispering, "that maybe my tracks were covered and her boots were covered too . . ."

"And?"

"And what?"

"And if your tracks were covered and her boots were covered, then what?"

"Then maybe it would be another while until she was found, and it wouldn't get back to me."

Spencer and Will were coolly quiet, exchanging glances. Will shook his head. Spencer shook his head and raised his eyes to the ceiling.

"Jim, I can't believe what I'm hearing. I honestly can't. It's mind-boggling," Spencer said, raising his voice, "that you, when confronted with the absolute and total death of someone you were close to for three years, would run like a coward with your tail between your legs back to your cave and hope that no one would find her."

Jim closed his eyes.

"Eventually, though," said Spencer between gritted teeth, "after a month, two months, say by February's winter carnival, would you have maybe mentioned to Conni and Albert that you hadn't seen Kristina in a while? Or do you think they wouldn't have noticed either?"

Jim rubbed his closed eyes. "Look," he said. "This has been the longest day of my life. I skipped all my classes today. I've never done that before. I was very upset."

"Could've fooled us," said Will Baker loudly. It was Spencer's turn to put his hand on Will's shoulder.

"I was hidden in the library stacks all day," Jim continued. "If it weren't for Aristotle cooped up in my room, I wouldn't have left the stacks till morning. When I came back from the walk and saw you standing by my door waiting for me, I was relieved. I would've come to you guys myself sooner or later. I couldn't live with it."

"Couldn't, huh?" said Spencer. "You're full of shit. I've been in police work for eleven years. More than a third of my life. I understand crimes of passion. I understand jealousy, I understand greed. I understand rage, and revenge, and blackmail. What I don't understand is a young man about to graduate and go to law school, a man whose entire life is going to be held up to future scrutiny, running as fast as he can the other way from his frozen naked dead girlfriend. That's incomprehensible."

Spencer turned to his partner. "Will, does it make any sense to you?"

"Not at all," answered Will.

Spencer stood up. "Jim, you're going to have to get yourself a lawyer. And a good one."

Jim nodded without looking up.

"We have no other suspects, Jim. Just you. Do you understand what I've just told you?"

Beaten, Jim remained sitting at the table, and without looking up, said, "I don't know."

"No, I don't suppose you do," said Spencer, motioning to Will to take Jim out of the room. "By the way, we need to get in touch with her family."

"Yeah," said Jim, as if in a daze, helped by Will to stand up. "She didn't talk much about her family."

"Did she go anywhere for Christmas, or Thanksgiving?"

"No," Jim said sadly. "She didn't. Sometimes she would come with me. Sometimes she just stayed at Dartmouth. Once, I think, she went with Conni and Albert to Conni's home."

"Are you saying she didn't have a mother or father?"

"I don't know. I think her father was dead. She didn't talk about her family."

"Did she have any other relatives? Brothers? Sisters? Grandparents? Aunts?"

Jim scratched his head. "I think her grandmother died over the summer."

"Died? Well, that doesn't help us any. Kristina's body needs to be identified before the medical examiner can autopsy her. We have time, of course." Spencer fell silent. "She has to thaw first."

Jim shuddered.

"Where did her grandmother live?"

"Near some lake east of here. Not too far, a big lake. Can't remember the name of it, long, funny name. Indian or something."

"Lake Winnipesaukee?" asked Will.

"Yes, that's it!" Jim exclaimed.

Spencer nodded. "Will, take some blood from Mr. Shaw, and a hair sample. And some fibers from his sweater, and an imprint from his Doc Martens shoes."

"Okay," said Will, and then leaned to Spencer, asking, "What about the other two?"

"Oh, yeah. Them." Spencer had forgotten about them.

While Will was busy with Jim, Spencer looked into Albert's room and said, "Don't worry. We haven't forgotten about you. Just a little while longer."

Albert nodded.

"Need to go to the bathroom?"

"I haven't drunk anything, so the answer is no," said Albert.

Spencer brought him some coffee, and went to tell Conni he'd be with her shortly.

Jim went with Spencer and Will as they drove in silence to Dartmouth-Hitchcock Medical Center to identify Kristina.

On the way, Jim told Spencer that there had been some weirdness on poker night he hadn't understood, about Albert's going to see Frankie and Frankie's not knowing about it; and Conni had gotten upset that Kristina would care what Albert was up to.

And no, Jim told Spencer, he didn't know why Kristina would care what Albert was up to.

It left Spencer confused.

⁕

Spencer watched Jim carefully as he walked in the cold to the hospital's modern main doors. He noted his sloping shoulders, his ashen face in the gleaming elevator taking the three of them to the subterranean bowels of Dartmouth-Hitchcock. They walked through stark-white, fluorescent-lit halls before they went through the double doors that led them to another long corridor that ended in unmarked gray doors. Will led the way, Jim followed, and Spencer closed up the rear. Spencer thought that judging by Jim's posture and stance, Jim was about to drop.

The morgue was a stark room with tall ceilings and clean tiled floors.

Sometimes the floors were less sparkling, covered with fluids from the victims that came through the morgue's doors.

Today, the floors were clean, and Spencer was grateful for that small favor.

The morgue attendant on call, a small thin gray-looking man, pulled out drawer number 515. Most of the body was covered by a sheet. The black boots were plainly visible.

Jim stood there bravely for a moment and then started to cry. Spencer, after a few seconds of staring dumbly at Will, put his hand on Jim's back and patted him brusquely. He wanted to say, "It's all right." But he couldn't trust his voice.

It was Will who, looking at Spencer, said, "It'll be all right."

"Yeah, right!" exclaimed Jim, moving away from Spencer's hand. "She is dead! It's not all right. It's terrible."

The morgue attendant stood near the covered gurney. His eyes were impassive.

"Yes," Spencer agreed quietly. "It *is* terrible. She was too young to die and

170

had too much life ahead of her," he said, welling up with emotion. He continued, "That's why we need you to help us. Help us find out what happened to her. Help us—"

"Oh, and what's that going to do? Helping you, how is that going to bring her back?"

Spencer stepped away, and his gaze became cold again. This boy was impossible. "You're absolutely right. Nothing's going to bring her back. But helping us is going to keep you out of jail. Because I'm sure Concord's DA's office will want to know why you knew she was dead yesterday and didn't report it. Why you knew she was missing for over a week, yet didn't report her missing. They'll be very curious, I can tell you that right now. They're a curious bunch."

Jim's expression went from defiant to broken. "All right," he said, pointing to the gurney. "Do I need to see any more? It's her new boots, I know them."

Yes, Spencer thought, reaching out and touching the boots with his fingers.

"Spencer!" exclaimed Will.

Spencer slowly took his hand off, not taking his eyes off the boots. "Huh," he said, squinting up at Jim. "Interesting."

Jim looked at the boots. "What?"

Stepping back, Spencer said, "Nothing, nothing."

Jim said, "Listen, it's her, all right? Do I have to see any more?"

Spencer didn't want to see her himself, and was about to say, no, no, you don't, when Will stepped in. "Yes, Jim," he said, glaring at Spencer. "I'm afraid you do."

"All right," Jim said, stiffening. "Show me, and then let's get out of here."

The little attendant lifted the blanket off the body's head. Then he removed the blanket completely. Spencer stood at the head of the gurney, looking at Kristina in front of him and at Jim to the left of him. He held his breath. He didn't want another cry of pain to escape his throat.

If ever there was a positive identification, this was it. Jim looked at her and turned away, trembling. Kristina was naked, her hands at her sides. She was still frozen, but the extremities were starting to thaw: their bluish color was different from the rest of her body, which remained white. Spencer needed to ask the question *Is it Kristina Kim?* But he couldn't speak. He motioned to Will, who said, "Jim, is it Kristina Kim?"

"Yes," Jim said brokenly without turning around. "It's her."

Though Spencer noticed—with a pang in his chest—the blueness of her skin, the whiteness of Kristina's face, he was riveted on Jim. He wanted to see what was in Jim's eyes. Tears and shaking shoulders could just as easily be remorse as grief.

Crying, Jim turned back to the body. Wiping his face in a rough gesture, he asked, "So what's going to happen to her now?"

"Nothing," said Spencer. "Nothing until she thaws. Maybe Saturday. The medical examiner in Concord has already been notified." The last sentence was more a question than a statement. Spencer looked over at Will, who shrugged.

"Fell was supposed to call the coroner."

"And the DA's office?"

Nodding, Will said, "And the DA's office."

Turning back to Jim, Spencer said, "And I'll tell you about the DA's office, Jim. They're eager. The more criminals they put away, the better their record. You dig how that works, right?"

Jim, looking as if he were barely listening, nodded.

"There's nothing they like better than a homicide. We don't get too many of them around here. I don't know what it's like around Wilmington, but in this part of the country a suspicious death is the biggest deal there is. It's front-page news, if you get my meaning."

Jim didn't move.

"If the death was an accident, fine," Spencer continued. "But if the autopsy shows it wasn't, then our little friends in Concord don't sleep or eat until they get their man. Understand?"

"What makes you so sure it was a man?" Jim asked.

"Jim, Jim. You're taking this personally. And literally. Try to relax. We don't know her death wasn't an accident."

"An accident?"

"Yeah, sure, an accident," Spencer said. "The autopsy could show she'd been drinking. She could've drunk an entire bottle of Southern Comfort, walked the wall, then taken a walk through the woods and just collapsed. Alcohol made her seem warmer; meanwhile she was colder and colder. Sat down in the snow and went to sleep. It could've happened."

"Really?" Jim said, with so much expectation, so much hope, it made Spencer almost physically sick.

"No," Spencer said sadly. "No. But never mind that, right now. You understand how important your testimony is? Taking her body temperature is useless. Worse than useless. Irrelevant. It won't tell us anything. She's been frozen solid under three feet of snow for nine days."

"But at least we know when she . . ." said Jim, trailing off as if the words were too much in Kristina's presence.

"Died?" finished Spencer, mindful of Jim's delicacies. "Do we know that? I think we don't know anything."

Moving away from the stainless-steel gurney, Jim blinked away tears. Spencer motioned to the attendant that they were done.

I hope this attendant doesn't fall asleep in public places, Spencer thought. Or someone might mistake him for a corpse, too.

The white-gray sheet was spread over her legs, then over her naked midsection, over her frozen breasts, and finally over her face and wet, black hair. Spencer lowered his head.

"Let's go," he said. "Tell you what I'll do. I'm going to send you home. I want to talk to your friends. Albert and Constance. I'll ask you to come back tomorrow. Don't go into Kristina's room. We're getting a search warrant first thing in the morning. Understand everything? Hope for your sake your story checks out. Come on, let's go."

"Why'd you do that?" Will whispered to Spencer on the way to the car. "It's against protocol. We definitely should keep him overnight."

"He's a poor scared-shitless kid," Spencer whispered back. "And I don't think he did it."

"You don't? Why?"

"Because," said Spencer. "I don't think the killer would keep coming back to Kristina's room. What would be the point?"

In the car, Spencer said, "I just want to ask you again, the dog wasn't with you for Thanksgiving?"

"No," Jim said from the backseat.

———————

After they dropped off Jim, Spencer and Will went back to the station. It was after hours, and the station was nearly empty. Albert and Conni remained separated in their rooms.

Spencer poked his head in to see Conni. "How are you doing?"

"God!" she exclaimed. "It's been so long."

"Just a few minutes longer, all right?" said Spencer. He wanted to talk to Albert first.

"That's what you said last time," she said. "Look, can I get something to eat, or—"

"No, Conni, you can't," said Spencer as he was shutting the door. "This is not a restaurant." He brought her a glass of water and some coffee, anyway.

He and Will went in to talk to Albert, who was composed. Spencer knew composure did not mean internal calm nor ignorance. All it meant was that someone could handle his or her bodily tics in front of others. It was eight o'clock. Spencer was still a long way from being done, and he was spent. He adjusted his gun holster so he could sit more comfortably, and then took it off altogether.

Albert said, "Do you need someone to identify her?"

Opening his notepad, Spencer said slowly, "Jim Shaw already identified her. What we need is someone to authorize an autopsy and to claim her body. Can you do that?"

Shaking his head, Albert said, "I thought maybe you needed someone else to look at her."

Spencer considered him for a moment. "We got a positive ID. We don't need to second it."

Shrugging, Albert turned his gaze straight ahead and shifted in his seat. Spencer watched him. There was something impressive, something no-nonsense, about his demeanor, about his unwavering gaze and his stoicism. Young people didn't regularly die in this part of the country. This was not the streets of New York. And Kristina was Albert's friend. Yet he was composed. He didn't look so beaten down as Jim, and he did not look away from Spencer's face.

Before Spencer could speak, Albert expressed remorse for what had happened and said he would do whatever he could to help.

"Well, we certainly appreciate that," said Will Baker, who took his seat next to Spencer and across from Albert.

"It was very hard for Jim Shaw," Spencer added.

"It's hard for all of us," said Albert, and somehow Spencer didn't doubt for a moment that Albert was talking about himself. Spencer turned on the tape recorder.

"Albert, before I get to Kristina, tell me a little about yourself."

"What would you like to know?"

"Where are you from?"

"Clairton, Pennsylvania."

Spencer nodded. "Never heard of it. Where are your parents?"

"I don't know. Maybe still there. We don't keep in touch."

"You don't keep in touch with your mother?"

"No."

"Why not?"

Albert shrugged. "I just don't," he said slowly.

"She was important enough to you to tattoo her name on your arm."

174

"She *was* my mother, detective."

"Any brothers or sisters?"

"No."

"Why did you choose Dartmouth?"

Albert smiled lightly. "Because my SAT scores were too high to get into Harvard."

Spencer didn't smile. "Why Dartmouth?" he repeated.

Albert stopped smiling. "I didn't choose Dartmouth. Dartmouth chose me."

Spencer studied Albert, while the tape recorder hummed. They didn't speak. Albert looked different from a few hours ago, somehow more familiar, more sympathetic. The tattoos made sense, the earring, the long hair, the impenetrable black eyes. Albert was collected and he was steadfast, but underneath, Spencer saw no fear. No fear of him, no fear of the interrogation, no fear of jail. Albert looked like a guy who had nothing to hide.

"Albert, tell me," said Spencer. "Were you good friends with Jim?"

"Yes, we were roommates in our freshman year."

"Is that how you met Kristina and Conni? Through Jim?"

"Kristina and I were in the same philosophy class together. Conni was Kristina's roommate."

Well, that explained it. Albert had met Kristina in class. He wondered why Jim didn't know that. Why had Jim been sitting there puzzling over a three-year-old memory when in two seconds and one sentence it was all clear?

Will stood up. "Can I see you for a second, Trace?" he said.

Closing the door behind him and lowering his voice in the narrow hallway, Will said, "What are you doing?"

"What?"

"What the hell are you asking him this for? I can see you're on a roll, but we already got this stuff from Jim, and it wasn't any more relevant then."

Will was shorter than Spencer, who had to bend his head to reply. "Will, I want to see if their story is the same. I want to catch one of them in a lie."

"So?" Will said wearily, rubbing his eyes. "So you catch one of them. One says one thing, one says another. You gonna go through this with Conni too, to get a third side? So what if one of them is lying? This is three-year-old shit. Who cares?"

"This is where you're wrong, Baker," said Spencer. "This is two-hour-old shit. A girl has been found dead, and her three best friends didn't report her missing for nine days."

"They were away!" Will raised his voice.

Spencer also raised his voice. "They didn't report her missing! That's all I care about, Will," Spencer said, quieter. "They didn't report her missing, and I'm going to find out why."

Will groaned.

Back at the table, Spencer continued, "Tell me something, Albert. Why didn't you go out with Kristina? Jim was seeing Conni."

Smiling bemusedly, Albert said, "Is that what he told you? Well, to be perfectly honest, I couldn't help that Conni liked me. She just didn't want to hurt Jim's feelings. And Kristina really liked Jim."

"Jim said you told him there was no chemistry between you and Kristina."

"I told him that, yes. I wanted him not to be upset about Conni and me. I also told him that Kristina really liked him."

"He didn't tell me that."

"No, he wouldn't."

Will nudged Spencer under the table.

Spencer proceeded to ask Albert the questions he had already asked Jim. When was the last day and time Albert saw Kristina? Albert said he had seen her after poker on Tuesday night after midnight, to wish her a happy Thanksgiving.

"Was Conni with you?"

"No, she wasn't."

"You're going out with Conni, right?"

"Right."

"You often visit other girls' rooms after midnight without your girlfriend?"

Albert looked at Spencer with surprise. "We're all very good friends. Besides, Kristina and I were on the same floor, and Conni was downstairs packing. It was no big deal. I went upstairs to pack my stuff anyway."

Albert said he didn't know what Kristina had planned for the holidays. Conni had invited Kristina to come with them, but Kristina had refused, something about a girl at Red Leaves House and a basketball game on Saturday.

Spencer remembered Kristina's boots. "Her boots—I noticed one of them was tied, one untied. When you went to see her, you didn't happen to lace up one of her boots, did you?"

"I don't recall," said Albert. "I might've. She'd been hurt in an accident, and her arm wasn't working well. I might have helped her with the boots."

"You mean the boot?"

"Do I?"

"Only one was tied."

Albert smiled comfortably. "Maybe one got untied."

176

Spencer studied him. "Maybe," he said.

Will said, "We'll have Ed Landers dust the boots, Tracy."

Nodding, Spencer asked, "If your fingerprints are all over the boots, would that help you remember?"

"Not really," replied Albert. "So much has happened, and it would have been such a little thing. I can't recall."

"Albert," said Spencer, "when you came to see her, was she naked? Would you recall that?"

"Sure."

"Was she?"

"I don't recall."

"I see." Spencer paused. "Because if you were kneeling in front of a naked woman, who was not your girlfriend, and lacing up her boot, you'd recall that, wouldn't you?"

"I think I would."

"Yes. I think you would, too. You wouldn't mind giving up a fingerprint sample, would you? Hair and blood?"

"No," said Albert. "Of course not."

"Did Kristina seem normal to you?"

"Yes," said Albert. "Sweet."

"Where was she headed after midnight?"

"I don't know. She didn't say."

"Did she mention wanting to walk the bridge wall?"

"I don't recall her mentioning it, no."

"You don't recall a lot of things about seeing Kristina."

"It wasn't that important." Albert smiled. "That's why I don't recall it."

"A few more questions." Spencer stared pointedly at Albert.

Politely cocking his head, Albert said, "Whatever I can do to help, I'll be glad to do."

Prodding Albert along, Spencer asked him what happened to Kristina's dog.

"We took the dog with us," Albert replied.

"Why?"

"It's not unusual. We also took him with us last year for Thanksgiving. Kristina sometimes likes a break from the mutt, and Conni's got a great back-yard for him to run around in."

"You took the dog."

"Yes."

"Well, how was Kristina supposed to know that Aristotle had gone with you?"

"I thought you said Kristina was dead?"

Spencer did not take his eyes off Albert. "I said that, yes. But you didn't know she was dead before you left for the holidays. Did you?"

"No, of course not." Albert's eyes never left Spencer's.

"And Conni? She also didn't know?"

"You'd have to ask Conni that," Albert said, smiling affably.

"Back to my question. How did you tell Kristina you were taking her dog?"

"I think Constance left her a note."

"Where?"

"I don't know. On her desk?"

"You walked into her room last Wednesday morning to take the dog and write her a note?"

"I didn't. Conni did."

"Okay." Spencer had a lot to talk to Conni about. "And then you went away for four days."

"Five, actually. We came back on Monday."

"Right. Did you return the dog to Kristina?"

"No, she wasn't around. Jim took her."

"Did you inquire where Kristina might be?"

"We didn't know she wasn't around. It was Jim who asked us if we'd seen her. And we hadn't."

"You speak for both Conni and yourself?"

"Yes, because we hadn't left each other since the previous week."

"Not even for a second?"

"No."

"That Tuesday night, you were together every minute?"

Albert became puzzled. "Which Tuesday night are you talking about now?"

"The Tuesday night Kristina died."

"Oh. That Tuesday night." He scratched his head. "I think so. I mean, not *every* second." He smiled. An open smile. "We went to the bathroom separately."

Spencer wasn't biting. "Remember what time that was?"

Albert shook his head, saying pleasantly, "I'm only joking. I mean, we weren't together every second."

"Do you remember the seconds you were not together?"

"Am I or are we both under suspicion, Detective O'Malley?" The question was asked mildly, but Albert's eyes hardened.

"Right now, even the dog is under suspicion, Albert, so the answer to your question is yes. I have a body that's been lying in the snow for a week and a half and three friends who weren't curious where Kristina was during that time. Now I'm trying to piece together what I think was the last night of her life. Didn't you worry when you hadn't seen her?"

Will interrupted Spencer. "I spoke to the women's basketball coach. She was very surprised that Kristina didn't play in the first game of the season on Saturday. Apparently, two of her teammates went to her room to see if everything was all right Saturday after the game. On Sunday, the coach herself called Kristina, to chew her out, as she put it. Kristina is their star player, and they lost to UPenn without her.

"On Monday, a couple of girls returned to the room, but they weren't that concerned, because they said Kristina had been known to miss practices and sometimes games. So Tuesday and Wednesday they just kept calling her room. They even called Red Leaves House."

Spencer nodded, scribbling in his notebook. "That's interesting, Will. Wouldn't you say, Albert? The women's basketball team is concerned enough to come to her room, to call her, to even call her place of employment. But not you guys. I'm trying to figure out why Kristina's best friends weren't concerned that she was missing for four days. Nine days actually. Why didn't anyone report her missing, at least to the undergraduate advisor, who might've notified the police?"

"That's a lot of questions," Albert said, smiling. "Which one would you like me to answer first?"

"All of them."

"Kristina leads a very busy life. She's got two majors, she writes for the *Dartmouth Review,* she works three days a week and practices basketball five and plays two games. There are often days when we don't see each other."

"Are there?" Spencer didn't believe it. "Are there many days between close friends on a small campus when you don't see each other? I went to a university with eighteen thousand students, and whether I wanted to or not, I ran into people I didn't like. As far as my friends were concerned, there was always time at night for them. There was always the phone. And somehow you just made time. Two majors or not. Red Leaves or no Red Leaves. Basketball or no. Especially when there is a dog involved. Especially when a long holiday weekend just passed."

"Look, maybe that's you," said Albert. "I'm just telling you that we all keep pretty busy."

"What about that night? Tuesday night? What happened during the poker game?"

"Not much. We played, then Frankie left, then Jim, and then Kristina went up to her room, I guess. Conn and I went to pack."

"Wait, wait," said Will. "Everything was pretty normal during the poker game?"

"During the poker game? Yeah, pretty normal."

Will and Spencer exchanged glances. "You consider," Will said, "Jim Shaw ranting and raving and then storming out pretty normal, do you?"

Albert scrunched up his face as if trying to remember and then said, "Oh, that." He emitted a short laugh. "That was nothing. He just got a little excited. It happens."

"Over what?"

"I really can't recall," said Albert. "Something silly."

"Did it have anything to do with you and Frankie?"

"Me and Frankie?" Albert was incredulous. "Nah. Nothing, I'm telling you. Everything was fine."

"I see," said Spencer. "What was the situation with you going to see Frankie and Frankie not knowing you were coming?"

For a moment Albert blanched. "Oh, that," he said slowly. "Yeah. He must have forgotten we made plans. I went to see him and he wasn't there."

"Jim said Frankie was studying with Conni, but that Kristina clearly seemed to think you should've been with Frankie."

"Yeah," said Albert. "It was all very perplexing."

"Perplexing for who?"

"For me. I had no idea what the fuss was about."

"There was a fuss?"

"No, nothing dramatic." Albert smiled. "Nothing for the papers, detective."

"I don't want it for the papers," retorted Spencer. "I want it for me."

"Of course."

"I don't get it. Why would Kristina care whether you went to see Frankie, or not see Frankie, or anything at all about your whereabouts?"

"I don't know. That's why it was just so perplexing." There was that smile again. It was beginning to annoy Spencer.

Albert said, "I had run into her on campus earlier that Tuesday and told her I was going to see Frankie. She just wanted to know what happened."

"So what was Jim so upset about?"

"He didn't seem that upset."

"No? That's not what some other people said."

"Well, he didn't seem that upset to me."

Will nudged Spencer. "Okay, fine," said Spencer. "So what did you do after Jim left?"

"We stayed a few more minutes and then Kristina left."

"And you and Conni?"

"We went to Conni's room to pack."

"But you weren't there for the rest of the night?"

"No, we were tidying up Conni's room and I realized I needed to pack myself if we had a prayer of leaving the next morning, so I told her I'd be going up to my room for a while."

"What time was that?"

"About midnight, I guess."

"And you went to your room?"

"No. I went down to the lounge for a minute. We'd forgotten our jar of change there. I picked it up and then went upstairs."

"And then?"

"I packed, listened to some music, and then went to say good-bye to Kristina."

"What time was that?"

"About twelve-thirty, twelve-forty, I guess."

"What time did you leave her room?"

"I don't know. About ten to one, maybe."

"Very late."

"Yeah, it was pretty late."

"And then?"

"Then I went downstairs to the lounge again."

"Why?"

"To get myself a beer."

"Was anyone else there?"

"Yeah, this kid Tim. He's a good guy. He was watching *Die Hard*. It had started at twelve-thirty. So I grabbed a beer and talked to him a little and watched the movie with him. Then I left to go to the bathroom and went upstairs to Conni's room," Albert paused. "The door wasn't locked, but she wasn't in her room. So I went back to the lounge. The kid had fallen asleep, but I woke him up. Told him he was missing a good movie. We sat for a while, watching. I drank my beer. Then Conni came in, looking for me."

"What time was that?"

"I don't know. Let's see, the movie was more than half over. Maybe quarter to two. Yeah, about then, because by the time we got back to Conni's room it was two A.M."

"Where did Conni say she'd been?"

"She said," Albert drew out slowly, "that she'd been looking for me. I said I'd been in the lounge. She wanted to know why I didn't come back to her room. I said I did but she wasn't in, so I had gone to watch the movie for a little while."

"How long was she out looking for you?"

"She said about half an hour."

"Half an hour?" Spencer exchanged glances with Will. "That's a long time."

"I know."

"Where did she say she was looking for you?"

"She didn't say. I didn't ask."

"So what did you do after she found you?"

"We went upstairs to her room. I stayed there. The next morning we left for Long Island."

"Did you see Kristina at any time after ten to one A.M. Wednesday?"

"No, uh-uh."

"Did you see her Wednesday morning?"

"No."

Spencer was itching to talk to Conni.

He asked Will to fingerprint Albert and take a hair and blood sample.

"I want to speak with Frankie. Where does he live?"

"One of the frat houses. Phi Beta Epsilon. At the very end of Frat Row. Past the President's House. But you won't get him—he hasn't come back yet."

Spencer perked up. "Hasn't come back yet? Why?"

"I don't know why."

"Isn't this exams time?"

"Yeah."

Thoughtfully, Spencer scratched his face. "Where's home?"

"Don't know. Boston, somewhere."

Spencer felt there was something there, he just didn't know what. Something.

"One last question, Albert. Did you kill Kristina Kim?"

"No!" said Albert immediately and emphatically. "She was my friend."

"Do you know who killed her?"

"No, certainly not."

Spencer and Will both nodded.

On the way out, Spencer said to Albert, "Two days ago we had a missing-dog report here. Some mutt went missing for a few hours and his mistress, a ninety-two-year-old widowed woman, went crazy."

"Oh, no," said Albert. "Was the dog found?"

"Yes. Dead," replied Spencer. "But isn't it a shame that Kristina didn't belong to a ninety-two-year-old lady?"

Spencer was tired, and his tone with Conni was brusque. Will was silent. After Conni told Spencer she was from Cold Spring Harbor, Long Island, he sat for a long time staring into his notebook, pretending to be reading his notes, but he was thinking about Kristina. She had told him her former roommate was from Cold Spring Harbor. Spencer remembered because he was a cop, and also because he was from Farmingville, Long Island.

A chasm the size of China separated Cold Spring Harbor from Farmingville, though the two towns were only twenty-five miles apart.

Spencer told Conni where he was from.

Farmingville, she said, her eyes pretending to be lost in thought. "I think I heard of that. Is that somewhere near Route One-ten?"

Not even close, Spencer wanted to tell her, shaking his head. *You're* near Route 110. "You're thinking of Farmingdale."

Ah, yes, she said, giggling. "Silly me."

Conni tried to engage Spencer in a conversation about Long Island: when was he back there last, did he miss it, what brought him to Hanover? But Spencer had already shut off this bubbly girl. He needed to get to the big stuff.

He let Will ask Constance how long she'd known Kristina, how was it being roommates with her, did Conni know anyone who might not like Kristina or wish her harm.

"No," Conni said, with her head bobbing, her painted eyebrows twitching, trying to smile as pleasantly as possible. "No, she was very well liked. Everybody liked her. Everybody. She was very likable, you know." Her face contorted a bit, and she added, "You couldn't help but like her. And she was beautiful, too."

His face tensing, Spencer wanted to agree that from what he knew of Kristina, she did indeed seem very likable. And very beautiful.

"I know some girls used to be jealous of her. But we all forgave her for her looks once we got to know her, she was so sweet." Conni paused. "I know some girls used to talk about her behind her back, you know, catty, like. Why doesn't she brush her hair more, or why doesn't she put a little makeup on."

"Jealous, yes, but not enough to kill her over, I would think."

Conni's eyes opened wide. "You think someone killed her? I don't believe it, I don't. Not here, not at Dartmouth. Why? I think it was an accident."

Spencer eyed her carefully. "You think so, do you? What do you know about it?"

Stammering, Conni said, "Nothing. Just what you told me."

"I told you very little."

Conni bent down to scratch her leg. She did not look at Spencer or make a comment. There is something she knows that's making her itch with worry, thought Spencer. Jim wouldn't look at me, Albert looked straight at me, and Conni is itching.

"Constance, when was the last time you saw Kristina?"

Straightening up, she looked at the ceiling as if trying to find inspiration from it. "I guess it must have been Tuesday night," she replied. "Before Thanksgiving. We were all playing cards."

"How did it go?"

"Good," Conni said, but looked away from Spencer as she said it. Only Albert had looked unflinchingly at Spencer. Only Albert had not shifted in his seat or looked at his hands. Only he seemed relaxed and concerned and only he made all the right noises. Maybe too relaxed, thought Spencer. Shit, I'm just driving myself crazy.

"Was that the last time?"

"Yes," she said, but didn't look at him, and this time Spencer demanded Conni lift her gaze.

"Yes," she repeated in a quieter voice. "That was the last time."

She's lying, thought Spencer.

"Were there any problems during the poker game?"

Conni was silent. She's weighing her options, Spencer thought. She knows I've already talked to Albert.

"Nothing serious."

"No fight?"

"No, nothing, just nerves, midterms coming up, we always lose to Frankie, you know, stupid things."

"I see. Jim didn't storm out of the lounge, furious?"

She was silent. "Nah, not furious, the game was already over."

"Did he storm out?"

"Not really."

"Do you remember over what Jim didn't really storm out?"

"No, I can't remember."

"All you guys seem to have extremely poor short-term memories," Spencer said. "Is that a problem during exams?"

Conni laughed. "Oh, you're so funny," she said. But Spencer wasn't laughing. And Conni's laugh sounded fake to him.

"What time did you come back to your room?"

"I didn't look at my clock."

"And you didn't see Kristina after that?"

"No."

"What did you do for the rest of the evening?"

"Spent it with Albert."

"In his room or yours?"

"Mine," she said, in a small voice.

"You came back from the lounge and never left each other's sight?"

"No, we did. Albert had to pack."

"Did you go with him to his room?"

"No, I stayed in mine."

"Okay, why don't you tell me everything you did until the time you went to bed."

"I really don't remember very well. It was a while ago." She seemed at a loss for words. Spencer didn't like it.

"Tell me what you remember."

"Let's see . . . Albert went to his room—"

"What time?" Spencer interrupted.

"I think right around midnight."

"Okay, and then what?"

"Then? Nothing. I packed, tidied up a bit, got my clothes ready for the trip home, went to wash."

"Okay, and then?"

"And then? Well, then, I—gee, I really don't recall. I think I called Albert's room to see when he was coming back down. His line was busy. I waited a few minutes and called again. It was busy."

"What time was that?"

"Around ten to one, maybe. I remember thinking it was pretty late for him to be on the phone."

"Yes."

Spencer waited. When Conni didn't say anything, he prompted her further.

"Then I—I waited a little longer. Then I called Frankie's line to see if Albert was talking to him."

"And?"

"He wasn't. I mean—no one picked up."

"So then what did you do?"

"I called Jim's room. No one picked up there either. I was a little surprised by that. Jim is a very early to bed type. I thought maybe Jim was with Kristina, maybe they made up."

Spencer looked at Will meaningfully. Will nodded. That Jim, Spencer thought.

"What did you do then, Constance?"

"I went upstairs to see Albert. His door was locked and everything was quiet inside. So I went back downstairs and called again, and the phone was busy. So I realized it was probably off the hook or something."

"What then?"

"I still didn't know where he was, so I went down to the lounge."

"Was he there?"

"No. Well, actually, he was, he was just in the bathroom. But I didn't stay long. I just glanced in and left."

"What did you see when you glanced in?"

"*Die Hard* on TV. One guy sitting in a chair."

"The lights were out in the lounge? Could it have been Albert?"

"No."

"How do you know Albert was in the bathroom?"

"He told me he was. He told me, he just came down for a beer and got caught up in the film."

"I see," said Spencer thinking hard. Nothing was coming to him. "What then?"

"I ran back upstairs to my room, grabbed my coat, and went outside."

"Where did you go?"

"I don't recall." Conni was looking at her hands, at the table, at Will, at her hands again. But she wasn't looking at Spencer.

"How long were you gone?"

"Maybe twenty, twenty-five minutes."

"Albert said he went up to your room around quarter past one or so and you weren't there. And that you didn't come back to the lounge till quarter to two."

Conni rubbed her face. "Yeah . . . I guess. So maybe thirty, thirty-five minutes."

"In the time you were gone, did you see Kristina?"

"No," Conni said in a high voice. "I told you, I was looking for Albert."

"What was the panic?"

"He wasn't in his room. I got worried."

"Worried about what? That he might have been kidnapped? Killed? Robbed? What?"

Jittery, uncertain, her bubbliness gone, Conni said, "I can't say."

"Try."

"I don't know. I just got worried. He said he'd be in his room, and then he wasn't."

"It sounds like you guys just missed each other. He went to say good-bye to Kristina—"

"He did?" Conni exclaimed.

Ahhh, though Spencer. I knew it.

"Yes," he said.

Conni was silent for a few moments. Her hands looked tense and white.

"It was just a misunderstanding between me and Albert," she said at last. "You know?"

"I don't know," said Spencer. "Let me ask you, where were you looking for him?"

"All over. All over campus."

"Around the back of Feldberg Library? The bridge?"

"No!" exclaimed Conni. "God, why would I look for him there?"

"Did anyone see you looking for Albert around campus at one in the morning?"

"I don't think so."

"I don't think so either. Heavy snow, freezing cold, very late. Everyone was sleeping."

Except Kristina, who was dying.

"You sure no one saw you?"

"I'm pretty sure."

"Yes. Not so good."

Silence. Then, hesitating, stuttering, she said, "That's the truth, that's what happened."

Spencer was getting a headache. This had been a long day for him. At nine o'clock in the evening, he was usually finished with work. This girl in front of him, small, perky, cute, was giving him a huge headache with her nonanswers.

Suddenly he remembered a small girl hurrying into Hinman Hall earlier. What did he remember about that girl? The size certainly matched. What else? The coat—she wore a jacket. Yes, a jacket with a white D on the back. That's it.

He asked Conni to show him her coat. It was a Dartmouth jacket. Realizing that ninety percent of the students wore Dartmouth jackets, Spencer nonetheless couldn't shake off the feeling that the girl who had hurried past a crowd and an ambulance was Conni Tobias.

"All right, back to Albert. You spent the night together?"

"Yes."

"And the following morning?"

"We got up, went to Thayer for breakfast, and then left for Long Island."

"Remember seeing Kristina Wednesday morning?"

Conni thought about it, or pretended to think about it. "No."

No, of course not, thought Spencer.

"Did you see Jim that morning?"

"No."

"Did you see Kristina's dog?"

"Oh, yes. We took him with us."

"Why?"

"I don't know. We felt bad for him."

"Why?" Spencer wasn't about to give this up.

"We thought it would be fun for him at my house." A forced smile. "We have a nice backyard."

I'm sure you do, Spencer thought. I'm sure you do, all manicured like exquisite nails. Leaves all picked up, bushes trimmed. Topiary bushes, maybe.

"Did you call your mother and ask her if it would be okay to bring a dog with you?"

Conni waved him off. "Nah, my mom doesn't mind. When Kristina came with us for Christmas two years ago, we brought Aristotle."

"Constance, you took Aristotle and didn't tell Kristina you were taking him?"

"I left her a note."

"You left her a note that you were taking *her* dog with you?"

"She knew the dog would be happy with us."

"Yes, but how could you just take the dog without telling her?"

"Well, Albert mentioned that Kristina seemed reluctant to keep the dog with her for Thanksgiving because she didn't know what she'd be doing. She's at work all the time, and at practice. In any case, we didn't think she'd mind at all. I thought she was kind of hoping someone would offer."

Spencer thought very carefully about what he'd just heard. Finally he asked, "How would Albert know Kristina was reluctant to keep Aristotle with her?"

"I'm not sure," said Conni, and her voice became uncertain.

"Do you know if she had any plans at all for Thanksgiving?"

"No, I don't. She said something about a girl she was tending to who was supposed to have twins over the holidays."

"At Red Leaves?"

Conni nodded. "How'd you know?"

Thinking that these kids badly needed a crash course in who was the interrogator and who the interrogated, Spencer said, "That doesn't sound very busy to me. Why would she be reluctant to keep her dog? She'd be staying right here." God, and I thought she'd be going home to her family, Spencer thought. As it turned out, we were both here for the holidays. Except that she was under three feet of snow.

Spencer clenched his fists and brought them under the table to lay them, still clenched, on his lap. Nothing would've changed. I was already too late.

"Kristina always felt better when we were around to pick up the slack of walking Aristotle. That's why she never locked her door, you know."

"I didn't know. She never locked her door?"

"No, never," said Conni, flushing. Spencer noticed.

"So you took her dog, left her a note, and left. When did you come back?"

"Monday afternoon. We kind of blew off our classes," Conni said sheepishly.

"Did you return the dog to Kristina?"

"Well, actually we gave him to Jim."

"Had anyone seen Kristina?"

"Not me."

"Was that unusual?"

"Not at all."

"That was Monday. Did you see her Tuesday?"

"No!"

"Did you see her Wednesday?"

"No."

"Did you see her earlier today?"

"No."

"I see. Well, having not seen her for four days, and having not seen her before Thanksgiving, did you at any moment get the least bit concerned?"

"No, not really."

"How often did you usually see her?"

"Oh, every day." There was a long pause. "We were always together. She was really like my best friend at Dartmouth." But Conni said it without effort, without conviction, and without the remorse that should've flowed like tears at the thought of having one's best friend dead. The kind of tears that had flowed earlier tonight. She dabbed at her dry eyes, hoping it would help. Conni looked at Spencer's face. It obviously hadn't.

Spencer continued, "So usually you see her every day, but now you haven't seen or heard from her in over a week, and you don't get worried?"

"No, like I said, she would sometimes disappear and no one would know where she was."

She really disappeared good and proper this time, didn't she, Conni? thought Spencer, squinting at her.

"Conni," he said, "what are you hiding?"

"Hiding?" she said, in a voice higher than her usual soprano. "Not hiding anything."

"Nothing, Conni?"

"Nothing."

"You walked past a crowd of people earlier tonight, didn't you, walked past an ambulance without even stopping?"

"What are you talking about?" she said. "What does that have to do with anything?"

"Was it you, yes or no?"

"Me?"

"Yes, you."

"Oh, me . . . no, I don't think it was me. I don't remember a crowd of people. No, not really."

"Ah. When I spoke to Albert, he told me when you had come to his room, you still had your jacket on."

Spencer almost felt bad for her.

"Oh, yes, well," she said nervously. "I remember, yes, I think I did, come—you know—I might've been too busy to—you know—stop, I meant to, it was very interesting, I was just—in a . . . you know—hurry."

The more flustered Conni became, the calmer Spencer became. He leaned back and folded his hands across his chest.

"I'm curious," he said. "How is it possible to walk past a commotion with ambulances, police cars, crowds, and not stop and ask what happened?"

Conni had no answer other than an anxious shrug of the shoulders. Spencer was getting increasingly irritated by her. Her cutesy-pie fidgets were getting on his nerves. He had nearly forgotten his annoyance with Jim, who was nothing compared with her.

Breathing in, Spencer said, "A few more things, Constance."

Spencer pretended to write in his notebook. Actually, he was making straight, short, hard marks with his felt pen.

Then he looked up at her. "That's a nasty scratch on your face."

She touched herself quickly below the eye. Spencer noticed her hands were unsteady. "Oh, this," she said. "It's nothing." Before he had a chance to ask her, Conni said, "My brother and I were playing over the weekend. I kind of got scraped up."

"I see that. Looks painful."

"Nah. It's nothing."

Spencer leaned into the table to get a closer look, and Conni moved back almost imperceptibly. That's all Spencer wanted to see, *her moving back.* He'd already taken a very good look at the scratches.

"Conni, let me ask you something. Did you kill Kristina Kim?"

She giggled and then became gravely serious. "No, of course I didn't, lieutenant."

"Detective," said Spencer.

"Detective." Conni's blue eyes smiled at Spencer.

"Okay," he said. "You won't mind giving us a fingerprint and hair and blood sample, will you?"

Becoming visibly nervous, Conni said, "Hair and blood? What for?"

"Police procedure. Just routine," Spencer assured her. "Nothing to worry about. I'm going to make Ray Fell, one of our patrolmen, give his hair and blood sample too." He was only kidding about Ray, for Will's benefit mostly, but Conni was not amused. And Will just snickered. "Don't worry, Conni," Spencer said, getting up. "Albert and Jim volunteered their prints and blood."

"They did? Jim did?"

"Sure. They want to cooperate," Will said.

"Is there some reason you'd prefer not to do it?" asked Spencer.

"Of course not, of course not," said Conni, on the way out the door.

While Will was fingerprinting Conni and taking a blood and hair sample from her as he had from Jim and Albert, Spencer went to talk to Jim.

Jim looked awful. Spencer sat down next to him.

"Just a couple more questions, Jim, and then you can go home. I talked to Conni, who told me that she called your room around one in the morning and you weren't there."

Spencer waited for a response. When there wasn't any, Spencer cleared his throat.

Jim spoke. "I was there. I just turned the phone off."

"Why would you do that?"

"Because I didn't want anybody calling me."

"Why not?"

"Because," Jim said, "I was upset, mad, whatever. I just wanted to be left alone."

"Who were you afraid might call you?"

"I don't know. Kristina. Albert. Whoever."

"Surely if they needed to talk to you they could just come to your room?"

"There was nothing I could do about that. But I could turn my phone off."

"I see," said Spencer standing up. "Is the phone turned back on?"

"Yes."

"So what you're saying is on the night of your ex-girlfriend's murder, some-body tried to reach you and couldn't."

Jim didn't say anything. Spencer left the room.

"So what do you think, detective?" said Will to Spencer when they were alone in the hallway.

"I think I'm going to go home, Will, and collapse into my chair. What do you think?"

"I think I'm going to go home and collapse into my bed," Will said.

"Drive the kids back first, will you?"

<hr />

Spencer headed home feeling the day in his bones. He thought of stop-ping for a nightcap at Murphy's Tavern. He didn't want to be drinking alone. But he didn't want to be talking to anyone either. And at Murphy's, every-body knew him. Whether he wanted to or not, he would have to do some talk-ing. Tracy this, Tracy that. Given the choice between drinking alone and talking, Spencer went home.

He thought of calling his mother. He missed her. He had missed his mother most of his life. He didn't blame her for it, he just missed her. The emptiness Kristina's death brought him made him colder, made him want to call home, hear his mother's voice, hear his father in the background, saying, "Can I? Can I? Can I talk to my son now?"

Mom, he wanted to say, *if I'm found dead, promise me you'll come and not leave me to lie on a metal gurney in a drawer.*

Spencer's throat hurt.

His tiny apartment was dark and sparsely furnished. In the bedroom, a frameless bed, a nightstand, a dresser, and in the living room, an old couch, a TV, a coffee table, and—his only housewarming purchase—a plush La-Z-Boy chair.

Plopping himself into the La-Z-Boy, Spencer reached down to the floor and lifted up a bottle of whiskey. Good old-fashioned Jack Daniel's. He was simple in his drinking taste. He was not a wine drinker, he was not really a beer drinker. He liked whiskey.

Spencer thought of drinking straight from the bottle, but two things stopped him. It did not look good for a detective-sergeant to be seen by God drinking straight from the bottle, and two, he remembered the bottle of South-ern Comfort on the floor of Kristina's room, a bottle and no glass.

So he got up and went into his so-called kitchen—really just a little enclave with a stove and fridge—and got himself a plastic glass that said, LOOK WHO'S THIRTY, from a birthday party the guys in the department had thrown him six months ago, and brought it back to the chair. Taking a swig, Spencer let his head fall back and his eyes close. Immediately the image of Kristina's black boots shot up, black against the white snow. Black and quiet, yet . . . screaming. Screaming for answers, screaming for help, screaming for life.

Except she hadn't screamed. Spencer was willing to bet a week's salary the autopsy would show there hadn't been much struggle in Kristina's last meeting with death.

Eyes still closed, Spencer took a long sip of whiskey and swilled it around his mouth. After midnight on Wednesday, November 24, Kristina Kim emptied a bottle of Southern Comfort, undressed to the bone, ruffled the hair of her dog, and in her new black leather boots walked out into the snow onto the bridge, onto the stone wall. She walked to the end of the bridge, jumped off the ledge, and then instead of going back home, walked on farther into the woods, lay down on her back into the snow, legs together, arms spread out as if learning to fly, closed her eyes, and died.

Spencer opened his eyes and looked around his dark living room for a few minutes, at the shadows on walls, at the dim light coming from Allen Street, at the square shape of the TV.

Then he got up, threw on his parka, and left the house.

He walked quickly, looking mostly at the snow on the ground and at his feet. He walked straight down past the Dartmouth Green, past Sanborn Library, and made a left onto Tuck Mall. An old Dartmouth cemetery was on the left. The streetlights near the cemetery were broken, and Tuck Mall looked ominously lit by a few yellow bulbs on the right. Tuck School of Business was right in front of him, but he needed to get behind it, so he hung a left, walked past the Feldberg parking lot, past a common field in front of Hinman and McLane halls, and saw the bridge in front of him. Exposed, bare, dark. There was a streetlight at the head of the bridge and one on the other end. The middle of the bridge wasn't well lit. Spencer looked to his right. The tall glass windows of Feldberg Library shone white light on the trees and the snow and the bridge. Spencer saw students behind those windows, peering into their books. Thoughtfully, Spencer looked at the windows and the students, and then at the bridge.

He took a few steps forward and then leaned over the ledge. It was pitch black, he couldn't see a thing, but he knew there was a steep slope running down to the concrete drive below. Spencer slowly walked across the bridge, touching the rough stone of the wall, and then slowly walked back. Checked his watch. It had taken him ninety seconds. He walked to the middle of the bridge and looked up at Feldberg. He saw the windows and the students clearly; if they pressed their faces against the glass, they could see him just as clearly.

He walked back to the far end and tried to lean over the side. He couldn't— the ledge was too high at this end. Not believing what he was about to do next, Spencer walked back to the start of the bridge, where the wall only came up to his upper thighs, and jumped up, checking his watch. Snow covered the ledge. Spencer hoped the snow wasn't slippery, nor crusted with ice. He slowly inched his way along the ledge to the darkness and conifers on the other side. His arms were out for balance, and he stepped very carefully onto the hard snow. Finally, he was there. Checking his watch again, Spencer discovered it had taken him over two minutes to walk the wall.

He jumped down, and with his racing heart went around Feldberg, into the darkness behind it. His steps were deliberate and hesitant, for he could not imagine anything being so eerily quiet, so still, so black. The trees didn't move; he just saw their outlines and shadows. There was hardly any light coming from Feldberg. The stairway lights had been turned off. Spencer couldn't see the path, couldn't see the conifers, couldn't see the police tape up ahead. Nothing. He listened to the still darkness, saw the immobile trees. They know, Spencer thought. They know what happened. Look how quiet they are; they're standing there, thinking, *We're not saying. No one's asking us. We're not talking. But we know.*

His chest was heaving. He heard noise, human noise. It was coming from two hundred feet below on Tuck Drive; Spencer knew that intellectually. Emotionally, however, the voices were in the woods, they were drawing closer, and they were coming for him. There was someone in the woods, in the tall dark trees, hiding out, waiting for him. Standing there, Spencer felt himself one step closer to death. One day, one month, one year.

He couldn't even turn around. Backing up the path as fast as he could without tripping over his feet, Spencer put his hand on his chest to steady his heart. He was panting. When he was at the bridge, he turned around and walked as fast as he could back home.

Fifteen minutes later, back in his chair, Spencer swallowed his drink in big, hungry gulps. The whiskey burned his throat.

What would possess a naked woman to step into the darkness? Wasn't she cold? Didn't she want to go back home?

Spencer willed his eyes to stay open. Had someone closed Kristina's eyes? Had someone closed her eyes to make it look like an accident? A killer wouldn't close his victim's eyes. Killers weren't usually this sensitive. But if her eyes were closed, it might look like she just fell asleep. The killer might have been someone extremely considerate, or extremely calculating.

Or both.

Another swig, and the drink was now gone. To get more would've required more effort than Spencer was prepared to make. The emptiness and the aching he was feeling inside could not be filled with whiskey. He was sure it could not be filled with Southern Comfort, not even a whole bottle of it, and he was sure Kristina's emptiness couldn't have been either.

Kristina hadn't deserved to die.

But what did Spencer know? He hardly knew her. Maybe she had deserved to die. Maybe dying had been her only redemption. But somehow he doubted it. Her dying didn't seem redemptive, it just seemed like dying.

Dying young.

Dying before one's time, dying too soon, not meant to die, why her, no, too much, too much to bear, too much to endure alone, she was in the prime of her life, she was full of life, she was so full of life, she hadn't even had any babies yet, but God knows she wanted to, God knows they were trying, Andrea, Andie. You were too young to die. I hope you remember our honeymoon, our five days in Paris, sitting in the pit of the underground because the subways were paralyzed by bomb threats, walking in the rain around Versailles, eating baked Alaska on the boat trip on the Seine, and making love on an old bed that creaked. Five days. We made plans to come back to Paris when it wasn't rainy season, maybe sometime in the spring. But spring came and you were already dead, head-on, hundred-mile-an-hour collision, when we found you, you were in the backseat of your killer's car, right through your windshield and his windshield. If he hadn't died, I would've killed him myself. You were the passenger; your girlfriend, the driver, she survived. But she was nothing to me. I didn't find her in the backseat of another car. Just you.

What killed Kristina? Andie, I kind of liked her. She reminded me a little of you. The hair, or the eyes. The sweet smile. You had a pair of black leather boots, but you weren't unceremoniously buried in the snow for nine days with nobody looking for you. When you died, we all knew. You didn't lie there for nine days without your family mourning you.

How long is Kristina going to be in the morgue, pre-autopsy, post-autopsy, before someone claims her thawed-out body, before someone steps forward and says, *It's me, she's mine, can I have her? I love her and I'm going to miss her. She is my daughter, God, my only girl! Or one of seven, she is my sister, my only sister, or my oldest.* She is my wife. She was my wife, and I loved her and I buried her and myself along with her, and for the last five years I've been trying to claw out of the grave, little by little, inch by inch. I thought I was doing pretty good, and you, Kristina, made me look forward to Friday, but now I'm looking forward to nighttime again, to the oblivion of the night, or to the high noon of the day, when the sun is too bright for me to grieve much.

Spencer fell asleep in the chair. When he awoke, just before dawn, he stumbled up and went to sink into his bed. The days of his falling asleep, clothes and all, in the chair, night in and night out, were over.

———•••••———

Spencer woke up around nine o'clock on Friday morning, about an hour late for work. He had a terrible headache. A strong cup of coffee, white and sweet, usually cured it fast. There was no coffee in the house, though. Spencer kept it that way deliberately. Got him out of the house fast. Today was no exception; there was a lot to do.

Today Spencer put on his only suit. It was similar to the one he had worn to Andie's funeral. Showered, shaved, white-shirted, and somber-tied, Spencer left his apartment, where there was no coffee and no food, and went down to the local Mobil Mart, where the smell of fresh brew almost made Mobil Mart homey.

He called in to the police station from his car radio and then drove to the Hanover city hall and courthouse, where he obtained a search warrant for Kristina's room.

While on the phone with Kyle, Spencer asked the dispatcher if Concord had been notified of the homicide. Kyle said he didn't know but he thought so. Fell was supposed to be taking care of that. Friday was Chief Gallagher's day off from the office. Friday was Gallagher's day to play golf, to drive to Haverhill forty-five miles north to the Major Crimes Unit, or sometimes to drive to Concord. Spencer asked Kyle what the chief was doing today. Kyle said he was taking his daughter to the mall to buy her a confirmation dress or something.

Just great, thought Spencer. We've got a possible murder and the entire investigation is in the hands of a thirty-year-old Irish small-town cop, Will, a former male nurse, and Raymond Fell, the guy who gives police cameras to his aunt in Cleveland. "When the Concord men come, tell them I'm at the college, and get me on my radio, okay? Where is Fell now?" Fell was in his patrol unit somewhere around Lebanon. "I hope he called Landers. I need the victim's room dusted."

"Yeah," Kyle said. "Ed called this morning. He'll be up around noon."

Spencer's first stop was the office of admissions in McNutt Hall, where he asked to see Kristina's college entrance application. He needed to find out if she had relatives. The admissions clerk was reluctant to give him the records, which apparently were confidential. Spencer had to assure the earnest girl that confidentiality was no longer an issue. What was more important was having Kristina properly buried when the time came. The clerk was suspicious and relented only after her supervisor was called. She pulled Kristina's admissions application. Spencer took it and sat down in one of the big plush couches in the comfortable and quiet room.

Last name, *Kim.* First name, *Kristina.* Any other names? *NO,* the application said. Birthdate, *November 22, 1972.* That's right, she'd just turned twenty-one, Spencer thought.

I remember when I turned twenty-one. My six brothers and my best friend Matt and I went to Port Jefferson and got tanked. There was a fight—some kid was forcibly undressed, then beaten right on Port Jeff's Main Street. Drunk as I was, I actually had to make an arrest. I had to call for help because I couldn't drive the two punks to the station myself. That was my twenty-first birthday.

Kristina's twenty-first birthday was the second-to-last day of her life.

Spencer continued reading the application. It gave some address in Brooklyn, New York. Spencer would have to check it out. He skipped down. He needed the next of kin. Ah, here it is—mother's name: *Katherine Morgan.* Address: *unknown.*

Unknown? Spencer quickly looked down for the father. *John Henry. Deceased.* Siblings: *none.*

Things were worse than Spencer had imagined. But at least there would be no parents claiming the body of their beloved daughter. God, though! Somebody had to claim her. Spencer felt it was his personal responsibility to ensure that someone came forth for Kristina.

Her application raised more questions than it answered. Katherine Morgan? John Henry what? John Henry *Kim?* What did it mean?

Other information on the application was even less helpful. Kristina had gone to a preparatory school in Brooklyn Heights. She received financial aid through grants, a small loan, college work-study—Red Leaves—and the rest of tuition, room, and board came from her maternal grandmother, *Louise Morgan.* No address for Mrs. Morgan, though. Was that the grandmother who lived on Lake Winnipesaukee?

Spencer quickly checked Kristina's high school transcripts and her SAT scores; all were very good. She wasn't just a jock.

He decided to go to the Dartmouth infirmary on North Main Street near the former Mary Hitchcock Memorial Hospital to check Kristina's emergency contact information. Louise Morgan was listed as the only emergency contact. Spencer knew there was no point in calling the number. Louise Morgan was dead.

Without leaving the infirmary, Spencer called information for Brooklyn.

"Kim," he said. First name or last? Any first names? He was going to say Kristina, but that was idiotic, so he said no.

No Kims in Brooklyn Heights, the operator told him. How about Morgan? He got three Morgans. Phone calls to each yielded him two message machines and one I don't know any Kristina, sorry. He hung up on the recordings. What was he going to do, say, I'm sorry, but this is Spencer O'Malley with the Hanover, New Hampshire, Police Department. If there is a member of your family named Kristina Kim, please call me at blah blah blah. Better yet, why didn't he just tell the truth? If there is a member of your family named Kristina Kim, she froze to death in the snow and is lying in the Hanover town morgue waiting to be claimed. *Very good, Spencer. God.* Talk about disappearing without out a trace. Maybe it really was an accident. Except for her few close friends and me, did anyone even know this girl was alive?

He decided to try something else. He called the private school she had gone to. Kristina Kim? No, sorry. Oh, when? Four years ago? Hold on? Ah, yes, Kim, Kristina. Yes, she went to our school. Home address was the one Spencer had in hand. Do you have a home phone for her? Yes, but from four years ago. Better than nothing, said Spencer. He called that number only to be told that it was disconnected and there was no new number. Another dead end.

Now was the time to use the search warrant. Her room surely would contain more information than his two hours at the college had yielded him.

But he couldn't go to the room alone. He waited for Will Baker to meet him with the fingerprint man from Concord.

Spencer did not eat as he waited impatiently for Ed Landers with his gloves and talcum powder and Will Baker with his notepad and his plastic bags. Time was ticking away. While waiting, Spencer placed a call to copy desks of the *New York Post, New York Daily News, New York Times,* and *New York Newsday* and asked them for help. A girl, listed with a residence in Brooklyn, had been found dead under suspicious circumstances and there was no family to contact. Could they maybe run something?

Then Spencer took a walk to Kristina's bridge. It was daylight and the bridge didn't look mysterious at all. He didn't get up on the wall this time, he just walked slowly across the bridge, made a right at the conifers, and strolled

scene. He proceeded to take off the yellow
more. Just the trees, and the snow and the
Kristina had been. Spencer stopped
where she had lain buried. This place
Spencer went off the path and made
g down to Tuck Drive. He looked
of two steep wooded hills. He
d the road and slowly trudged
p, low-hanging branches of trees,
nifers. The snow soaked his good-for-
ng and wet at the secluded westernmost end
rst house on his right was Phi Beta Epsilon.
ght Spencer, knocking on the door. Someone yelled for
. He went in and showed his badge to a grungy guy in over-
thes sprawled out on the couch. "Is Frankie Absalom here?" he asked.
Frankie wasn't in, Spencer was told. He'd gone home for the weekend.

"Please tell him," Spencer said, "that Detective Spencer Patrick O'Malley was looking for him and needs to talk to him about an urgent matter as soon as he returns."

The guy in the living room nodded and went back to his book, but Spencer couldn't let it go. "Listen," he said. "Sorry to disturb you, but we dug a body out of the snow yesterday, and Frankie was one of the last people to see this girl alive. I need to speak with him urgently. Can you help me?"

The grungy guy shook his head. "Can't help you, man. Don't know where he lives in Boston. Try his friend, Albert something."

"Albert Maplethorpe?"

"Yeah, him. They hang out together. Albert will know."

"I asked him. He doesn't know."

The guy shrugged; his fingers never left the pages of the book he was reading.

Spencer left Epsilon House and jogged back to McNutt, where he pulled Frankie's application and got his family's address and phone number. He called, using his calling card, from a public phone on the first floor. The building was quiet.

"Hello? This is Detective Spencer Patrick O'Malley from the Hanover Police Department. Is Franklin Absalom there, please?"

"Yes. Is everything all right?" said a concerned maternal voice.

"Everything's fine, ma'am," replied Spencer. "I just need to talk to Frankie for a couple of minutes."

"I see. Yes. Yes, of course. He's still sleeping, I t[...]
please."

Spencer heard "Franklin!" being shouted several tim[...]
voice came on another line. "Yes?"

"Frankie?"

"Yes."

"This is Detective Spencer Patrick O'Malley from the Hanove[...]
partment. Do you have a couple of minutes?"

"Yes." Frankie didn't sound groggy now.

"Could you hang up, please, ma'am?" said Spencer. "This will only [...]
couple of minutes."

The mother's nervous voice said yes, and then the other phone w[...]
hung up.

"Frankie, how long have you been down in Boston?"

"I never came back after Thanksgiving."

"Why not?"

"I just—I don't know. I needed some rest."

"I see. Well, I'm sorry to bring you bad news." Spencer paused. "Do you
know why I'm calling?"

There was no answer. Spencer waited.

"Frankie?"

"I hope—everything's all right." His voice was unsteady.

"No. Kristina Kim was found dead yesterday."

Frankie breathed in sharply, and for some minutes all Spencer heard was
erratic breathing, punctuated by dry moans.

"Frankie?"

"Y-y-yes?" His voice was broken and quiet. "God, I—"

A few more minutes passed. Spencer looked at his watch. Twelve-thirty.
Ed and Will were probably waiting for him.

"Frankie, I'm very sorry. Very sorry to bring you bad news. Just a few questions, and I'll be on my way."

"How?" Frankie interrupted. "What happened?"

Spencer didn't mind answering this time. Frankie seemed to be taking
Kristina's death to heart. Spencer felt sympathy for him.

"She was found in a three-foot-high drift of snow."

"Was she . . ." Frankie couldn't continue. After a while, he said, "Was she
hurt?"

Hurt? What a strange question.

"Like . . . how do you mean?" Spencer said slowly.

"I mean . . ." Frankie was having trouble getting his words out. "I mean, was she, you know, hurt?"

Spencer considered the question again, his eyes widening. Rummaging in his pockets, he told Frankie to hold on while he found his microcassette recorder and turned it on close to the receiver. Then he answered, "Frankie, she was found *dead* under snow. Does that fall into the category of hurt?"

When Frankie didn't answer, Spencer asked, "Or do you mean, was she raped or butchered?"

"Yes," Frankie quickly replied.

"No," Spencer answered just as quickly. "She wasn't butchered. Now, are you up to a few questions?"

"Oh sure," Frankie said. "I'm sorry. This is just . . ." He sobbed. "Awful. Just awful."

Spencer said, yes, and then asked Frankie when was the last time he remembered seeing Kristina.

"Kristina?" Frankie said, as if hearing her name for the first time. "Last time?"

"Yes." Are you buying time, Frankie? thought Spencer, wishing he could see Frankie's face.

"Well, I haven't been back this week."

"Frankie!" said Spencer firmly, beginning to lose his patience. "Please. The last time you saw her."

"Okay, let me think. . . . I guess before I left for home."

"Right. When was the last time you saw her?"

"I'm trying to remember." His voice had a different quality to it from before. "We played cards on Tuesday night."

"The last time you saw her, Frankie," repeated Spencer.

"Yeah. Tuesday, I guess."

"You guess?" Spencer said, exasperated.

"Yes, that's right."

"Frankie, listen to me very carefully now. I don't have a lot of time. A girl's been found dead. I don't want to have to come to Boston to get you, and I don't want to think you're keeping secrets. So let's have it. Last time you saw her."

Frankie breathed in and out several times before he answered. "Tuesday. Or was it Wednesday morning?" Frankie paused and then said quietly, "I saw her walking the bridge."

Yes. Still clutching the tape recorder, Spencer pressed his left hand to his heart. Yes.

"You did," Spencer finally said. "Good. What time was that?"

"Let's see." Frankie said as if he were buying time. "Let's see now. I guess it must have been around one A.M. or so. Maybe one-oh-five. Around there."

"One, one-oh-five. That's pretty precise. How'd you know?"

"I looked at my watch and thought of going back home 'cause it was so late, and then looked out the window and saw her."

"Why did you look out the window?"

"I—I was waiting for her to walk the wall."

"Were you watching her?" Spencer asked hesitantly.

"No. It's nothing like that. More, like, watching *out* for her."

"Okay, tell me what happened. Everything."

"Right. Everything. Okay."

"Frankie, are you covering up for someone?" Spencer said loudly.

"No, no one."

"Because if you are it could make you an accessory to murder."

"Of course. I know that. You don't have to tell me that. I understand. Listen—I told you everything. Last Tuesday, we finished playing cards. I won, as usual. But there was some tension in the room. We were all on edge."

"Yeah, I heard something about that." Spencer tried to hurry Frankie along. "You were supposed to meet Albert in your room."

"No I wasn't. It was a mix-up."

"He says you forgot."

"Yeah, and pigs fly out of my butt. I never forget anything. Especially," Frankie said, half-mocking-suggestively, "meeting Albert in my room."

What was that supposed to mean? Spencer wanted to meet this Frankie. "Got it," said Spencer. "Was Kristina sober?"

"Stone sober. I know that. I know that for a couple of reasons. I kissed her good-bye, I smelled her breath. She was lamenting there was nothing to drink—Murphy's was closed."

With a pain in his heart, Spencer thought, she used to go to Murphy's too?

He willed his mind back to Frankie, who said, "We offered her a beer, but she took a Coke instead. So I knew she was sober."

"There was a bottle of Southern Comfort in Kristina's room."

With a tone of distaste, Frankie said, "Yeah, she liked that stuff. We gave her a bottle for her birthday. But she never drank that bottle, never even took it with her."

"How do you know?"

"I know because Tuesday afternoon when I was in Conni's room, the bottle was on her desk. She had to move it off to make room for our books."

"How did you know it wasn't Conni's?"

"You kidding?" Frankie laughed. "Conni is strictly a beer drinker." Then he corrected himself: "Only since she's turned twenty-one, of course."

"Yeah, yeah, yeah," said Spencer. Time was ticking by. He had to go.

"Conni had been feeling bad that we had given Krissy a bottle of liquor. She said Kristina wasn't happy about it. We had talked about that for a few minutes."

"There was a spilled bottle of Southern Comfort in Kristina's room."

"There was? Huh. Well, maybe Conni brought it to Krissy after poker."

"Yeah," Spencer drew out. "Maybe. Go on."

"During poker, I was sort of needling Kristina to walk the wall. It's a really sick thing she does, but the guys at Epsilon love to see it, so I goad her on every once in a while, and sometimes she does walk it. Not often. But sometimes. She's gotta be pretty drunk, though. They collect by the window at Feldberg and watch her. It's this thing."

"Do you watch her?"

"Nah," he said casually. Too casually. "I'm usually last in line. As I said, I don't watch her so much as . . ." He stumbled on his words. ". . . watch over her," he said, haltingly. "It's really dangerous, but it's a thrill for everybody. I just kind of watch her to make sure . . . well, it doesn't matter—"

"To make sure what?"

"Nothing. To make sure she doesn't stumble. That Tuesday night, she said she might do it. So I waited."

"But she was sober."

"How long does it take to get a little tipsy?" Frankie asked. "If Conni brought her the bottle, it would've taken Kristina no time at all."

Spencer asked why Frankie had egged her on to do something so patently dangerous. If she fell, she'd be killed.

"I guess," Frankie said slowly. "You should have seen her on that thing, though, man. She glided across it and back like an angel. She had God on her side when she was there."

"I'd say the odds were against her."

"Yeah. She used to say, our whole life is against us. She crashed on Monday night in her car. She could've been dead then. I had a good feeling about her when she was walking. She was very steady. She put on a real show. And she always turned around and walked back on the ledge. But anyway, that night I wasn't sure if she was going to do it, and I wasn't going to go back to Epsilon and tell the buds unless it was a sure thing. They'd kill me."

"Sure, to come out in a blizzard," said Spencer.

"Yeah. And also I had work to do. So I went up to Feldberg. I always study up there. It's real quiet, and I like my spot. It's on the second-floor lounge, smack dab overlooking the bridge. I moved a table next to the window and a chair. I like it, it's secluded. That's where I was."

Spencer was silent. His breath was short. He knew he was hearing about the last minutes of Kristina's life, and he couldn't bring himself to question Frankie, nor hurry him along.

"By the time I saw her," Frankie said, "she was already halfway down the bridge, and very wobbly. Very. I got a bad feeling in my chest right away, watching her. I actually opened the window, but decided against yelling. I was afraid to scare her further. So I watched for a few seconds, and then she tripped. She just kind of slipped on the snow, and fell over, I nearly jumped out of my skin, I didn't have enough time to react, to do anything. She slipped, but held on to the wall and climbed back up and just lay there for a few seconds. She must've been so scared."

"She lay there naked in the snow?"

"Yes." Frankie shrugged. "I know it sounds weird. But she was a philosophy major. There are men in Tibet who pierce their bodies or eat swords or walk on hot coals and don't get hurt. She had this gift. She successfully steeled her body against the cold."

Not in the last battle of her life, thought Spencer.

"I watched her," Frankie continued, "I was still panicked. Then I saw her jump four feet down off the wall, and she never does that. She usually turns around and walks back. I understood that she must've been very scared. She was at the end of the bridge, I was real relieved. I shouted something at her. Like, hey Krissy, well done, you crazy kid. Something like that."

"Did she hear you?"

"I really thought she did. I really did. Because she stopped and looked around, kind of. She looked up and then into the woods behind Feldberg. I thought she didn't know where my voice was coming from. So I yelled at her again. She looked around her."

"And then?" Spencer was stiff, his fingers gripping the phone.

"And then she walked out of view down the path behind Feldberg."

"Into the woods?"

"I don't know. I guess. I didn't see her then."

"What did you do?"

"I thought, silly girl. I shook my head. Kind of remembered that she was scared shitless of the dark. Whenever we walked her dog behind Hinman Hall, she hung on to my sleeve and didn't let go."

Spencer was shuddering, the hand holding the tape recorder was shaking. He was remembering the black timber of the ancient Douglas firs.

Frankie continued, "I closed the window, and tried to look at my books some more. But it was late—"

"How late?"

"Plenty late. I wrapped up my books—"

"Right then and there?"

"Yes. I was tired. I closed them all up. Put them into my backpack, put on my coat, zipped in, put my gloves on, put the hood on. How long would you say that all took me?"

"Maybe five minutes?"

"Maybe. Seven, or so. Eight? No, not as much as eight. No, wait, I went to the bathroom first. Yes. So maybe fifteen minutes. Yes, that's right—"

"You were in the bathroom for ten minutes?"

"About, yes. I washed my hands, too, washed my face. Eight to ten minutes. That would make sense, because when I got back to Epsilon, it was, like, one-forty."

"About half an hour after Kristina disappeared into the woods?"

"Yes."

"And that's it."

"That's it."

"You sure?"

"Yes."

"You didn't see anybody else?"

"No."

"You didn't see her after that?"

"No."

No, of course not. That was it.

Spencer turned off the tape recorder. His head shuddered involuntarily and he dropped the receiver.

Will Baker and Ed Landers from the crime lab were waiting for him at the Feldberg parking lot.

"Where've you been?" said Will in a hushed but strident voice.

Spencer raised his eyebrows. "Looking for Kristina's killer, Will. How about you?"

Ed Landers was a tall man with gold-rimmed glasses and extremely large, protruding ears, about which Ed was painfully self-conscious. No one in the department was allowed to make jokes about them, certainly not to Ed's face. Spencer liked Ed. He was a good guy and a thorough professional, and he didn't take a lot of shit.

In Kristina's room, Spencer asked Landers to dust the Southern Comfort bottle and Baker to bag it. The bottle was half empty. Spencer found the cap nearby, and then got down on his hands and knees and smelled the floor where the liquor had spilled. The carpet smelled moldy, like a bum's clothes at Penn Station in New York. If Kristina had drunk something the night she died, this wasn't it.

Then Spencer methodically examined the room. He started with the clothes on the bed and went down on the floor on his hands and knees. What am I looking for? he thought, searching under the bed. What am I hoping to find here?

On her desk, he found Conni's note, carelessly thrown on top of a textbook. *Dear Krissy, we took Aristotle with us to Long Island. Wish you could've come, too. Have a happy Thanksgiving. Love, Conni.*

Spencer read the note several times, then gave it to Will.

The closet had some interesting periodicals in it, all bagged by Baker: *People* magazines from the seventies and early eighties, *Newsweeks* arranged as if they had been looked through recently—a November 15, 1993, issue was right next to an November 10, 1988, issue, which in turn was underneath an August 27, 1993, issue. Some recent *Life* magazines, one *Time* with the Dalai Lama on the cover. And a copy of a newspaper called *Greenwich Time* with a subscription sticker torn off. "Put that one in a separate bag, Baker," Spencer said. What would a girl from Brooklyn Heights be doing with the *Greenwich Time*?

It took Spencer three hours to sift through Kristina's papers. Landers dusted nearly everything, but Spencer didn't have much hope for fingerprints in this case unless they were right on Kristina's pale neck. He was certain fingerprinting would show that every one of her three friends and most of her basketball teammates had prints all over her desk, her chair, and maybe even her bed.

The men barely spoke as they worked. Once in a while, Spencer asked Baker to bag something, or Landers to dust a drawer or inside a closet shelf, but Landers and Baker knew their jobs very well.

The drawers in Kristina's desk and her closet contained few personal items. She had some college textbooks and term papers, but there were no journals and no diaries. Her class notebooks had no doodling on them—surprising for someone with such an untidy room. Sloppy and distracted note-taking usually went along with room contents, but not in Kristina's case. Her class notes were meticulous, written in beautiful, book-perfect penmanship. How did that mass of hair, those loose clothes, this messy room, and the spilled bottle of Southern Comfort go with such refined handwriting?

Spencer was looking for stronger, more personal clues: a photograph, a canceled check, a bank statement. Spencer O'Malley was a desperate man the day a bank statement became personal. But the clues in this room were as obscure as Kristina's admission records. This was the place she called her home, and yet it was a game of Clue with two suspects and three murder weapons missing. In fact, the room screamed to Spencer that there was something wrong.

A room kept so devoid of personal belongings was not an accident. A girl so seemingly careless would be careless with everything. Kristina was only *outwardly* careless, Spencer realized. Almost as if to make a pretense of carelessness. But why? Was it to hide the very fact that she took great pains to eliminate every single item from her room that might speak of who and what she really was?

Everything that might shed any light on her had been removed, and that shed more light on her than anything. It was like a beautifully wrapped gift that turned out to be an empty box. Kristina monthly, daily, *hourly,* emptied that box.

What came crashing into her room every hour of every day that she needed to keep it so thoroughly cleansed?

Spencer searched in vain for a photo, one single photo of anything. Or a Rubik's Cube, an Eagles cassette, a newspaper article, a picture of her mother. Anything. But what really tipped him off was the absence of canceled checks or statements or bank information of any sort. No ATM receipts. No deposit receipts. Kristina Kim had been a careful person. Spencer looked again through her purse; there was nothing in it. There was a brown leather man's wallet, very worn and old, with shredded seams and the plastic credit card dividers long gone. A cash card from New Hampshire Savings Bank told Spencer there should have been bank information. An American Express card. A Dartmouth College green debit card. Three singles. A folded, blank piece of paper. And that was it. There wasn't even a receipt for the black boots that Spencer knew Kristina had bought only two days before she died. That receipt must have been thrown out immediately, as matter of course. But why throw out a silly shoe receipt? Unless it was just a matter of habit, or unless it was in a safe place.

"Will, let me have a look at her keys again," Spencer said, and Baker dutifully took them out of the plastic bag. Ed Landers had nearly finished dusting the purse. Spencer smirked. Ironically, his fingerprints would be all over that purse. Maybe I'm a suspect, too, he thought, looking through the key set. There was nothing unusual about the key ring: big keys, car keys, and a small key that looked like a mailbox key, but he found another key, also small, but thicker, heavier, and coded. There was a number on it.

"Bingo," he said quietly. "There was a farmer had a dog, and Bingo was his name-o . . ."

"Detective O'Malley? Pardon?" It was Landers. He seemed confused. Will smiled without comment.

"It's all right. You people finish up here. I've got to get to the bank before it closes."

"It's well after three," Will pointed out.

"Yes, but the employees are there till five, proving."

Prove it all night, prove it all night, Spencer hummed as he drove back to Main and parked next to Molly's Balloon, which in turn was next to the New Hampshire Savings Bank. Spencer knocked on the bank's glass doors.

"We're closed," a grouchy-looking man mouthed to him through the glass. Spencer took out his badge and the door opened.

"Who is your manager? I need to speak with him, please."

Spencer was introduced to Mr. Carmichael.

He told Mr. Carmichael about Kristina. For the first two minutes, Spencer couldn't get much out of Mr. Carmichael, who put his head in his hands and cried. "She was a nice girl," he kept repeating. "A very nice girl."

Spencer finally said, "I'm here because I noticed a key of hers that looks like a safety deposit box key. I used to have one myself."

"Yes, she had one, if that's what you mean," Mr. Carmichael answered.

"May I see it, please?"

"Let me ask you, don't you need a search warrant to look inside it?"

He didn't need one if he didn't expect to find anything. He could just look through it and leave. But if he found something that might implicate someone and that someone would stand trial, he certainly would need one. If he didn't have one, he might as well put his own badge in Kristina's safety deposit box and go on border patrol in the north of Vermont. If they'd have him, that is. If they thought he was still fit for anything after searching through a safety deposit box without a warrant.

"I guess I do need one, yes." He glanced at his watch. Four forty-five. He had just a few minutes. "I'll be right back."

Mr. Carmichael walked him to the glass front doors. "It's incredible that she is dead, you know," he said quietly to Spencer.

"Yes, I agree."

"Do you think it was an accident?" Mr. Carmichael asked, and Spencer heard him suck in his breath as if to prepare for a response that was out of sync with a quiet small New England town on a cold December afternoon. People got five-dollar parking tickets here, and rooted for the Dartmouth Big

Green, and once a month ate Sunday brunch at the Hanover Inn whether they could afford to or not. People did not get murdered.

As he passed the curmudgeon who had not wanted to let Spencer in, Spencer leaned closer to Mr. Carmichael and answered, "No, I don't think it was an accident."

He saw Mr. Carmichael's pained expression. "What is it? What?" Spencer asked.

Mr. Carmichael avoided Spencer's gaze when he said, "Come back with the warrant, go through her things, and I'll talk to you then. Get permission to sequester the funds in her accounts."

Spencer remembered Kristina's three singles in her wallet. "She has funds in her accounts?"

Mr. Carmichael looked at Spencer meaningfully. "Come back and I'll talk to you then, Detective O'Malley."

Spencer got his search warrant in what was record time even for him—twelve minutes. Kristina's bank accounts were immediately frozen, pending disposition of her estate. Spencer rushed back to the bank, thinking, what is it that Mr. Carmichael has to tell me? What does he know?

The bank employees had gone. Mr. Carmichael let Spencer in. They walked to the back and through the vault. Mr. Carmichael found the right key on his formidable key chain, and together they opened Kristina's safety deposit box.

"I'd like to examine it in private, please," Spencer said, and knew how it sounded. It was good that he wasn't trying to suppress information. Imagine the power of the police officer who had the right to look through a dead woman's safety deposit box in private. Still . . . the trappings of the Pandora's box that Spencer held in his hands were too strong and too important to ignore.

Mr. Carmichael took him to a small empty room and closed the door.

He lifted the metal cover of the big box. His heart beat faster.

To Spencer's surprise, it was *not* filled with the stuff that Kristina cleared out of her room with the intensity and completeness of a forest fire. Spencer expected to find the receipt for the black boots stacked neatly on top of canceled checks and monthly statements. He expected to find tear-stained love letters, stacked neatly beneath the receipt for the black boots.

At first glance it was nearly disappointing. He found a photo—finally!—of a young girl, neat, short-haired, smiling, holding a kite in her hands. The picture had been taken near a body of water that looked like Long Island Sound. There was an older photo of a very beautiful young woman holding a toddler girl in her arms. Polaroid shots of teenage girls with babies. Spencer assumed they were girls from Red Leaves House. There were about a dozen photos. He would go through them again when he had time.

Now he was looking for something more specific. He found a pen from a place called Fahrenbrae Hilltop Retreat and a matchbook with the same inscription.

He'd read about Fahrenbrae in the Chamber of Commerce "Guide to Hanover" brochure. Three houses, beautifully furnished, twelve miles away from Dartmouth in the Vermont hills, renting for $125 a night. He'd remembered them because the place had intrigued him. He had wanted to drive up there one day.

Spencer found souvenirs from Scotland. Matchbooks, lighters, napkins, dirty napkins, beer-stained napkins, torn napkins with Gaelic words written all over them, words Spencer did not understand. There was a bar of soap from a bed-and-breakfast at the Mull of Kintyre. There were foil rings and red and white ribbons and nail polish with more Gaelic inscriptions on it. None of it individually meant anything. But all together, it made up a time of Kristina's life that must have meant a great deal to her.

Judging from other objects in Kristina's box, the Scottish things must have meant more to her than anything else in her life. There were no matchbooks from Brooklyn, nor torn napkins from Dartmouth College. But Scotland was in her box.

Scotland, and Fahrenbrae.

There were a dozen letters from her grandmother, dated a few years earlier, an old antique parchment stationery with Old English initials in the upper left corner: L M. Spencer read one.

Dear Krissy, my baby, I miss you honey, I wish you would come and see me more often. I know you're busy with school and work, your work is important, I know you can't come down in the summer, but I wish I could see you a little more. If ever you have more time, come see me, I'll always be glad, despite everything, and I mean that honey, I mean that from the bottom of my heart. You're still my family, and I believe with my soul it wasn't your fault. So don't be scared of me who loves you. You come and see me when you can, darling, and I'll do anything to help you.

And one other letter, on pastel pink stationery, this one with a flowery *K M S*.

Kristina,

    Why are you returning my letters? Why aren't you letting me speak with you? What have I done that you should be so angry with me? I should be angry with you, furious, yet, I've been trying, and you've been turning your back to me. Please, honey, please. Your father, he didn't mean anything by going to the lawyers, he was just mad, it'll blow over, you'll see. Forgive the letter he wrote you. I know he didn't mean the things he wrote. He misses you so much. And me too, Kristina, we both miss you.

It was signed *Mother.*

KMS? Spencer wondered. *S?*

He looked quickly for the father's letter, but he couldn't find it.

What else?

A manila envelope that contained a folded letter and a seven-page document. The letter scared him—him, a veteran of the Long Island Expressway on a Saturday night. A veteran of an ax murder. A grisly premeditated murder. A veteran of growing up in a family of eleven, veteran of six boisterous brothers.

They all found their brides, some more often than others. He found his only once, and he was a veteran of that, too. Yet, sitting here in an empty room, he was afraid to open a thrice-folded letter in that manila envelope. Spencer looked at the thick document instead.

A petition before the judge in the Borough of Brooklyn in the City of New York on this day of November 10th, 1993, being brought by a Kristina Kim of P.O. Box 2500, Hinman, Dartmouth College, Hanover, N.H., against a Howard Kim—

There it was. Howard Kim. She was married.

Married.

Married. Buried. Well, not buried yet. But Spencer should have known. Kim was not her real name. He had thought it sounded strangely . . . nonoccidental. Malaysian? Vietnamese? Korean? Something. He quickly flipped to the end of the document to see her maiden name.

Sinclair. *Kristina Sinclair.*

Katherine Morgan *Sinclair.* John Henry *Sinclair.* Now *that* made sense. Kristina Morgan Sinclair, the divorce petition said.

Howard Kim. At least now he had a name. In fact, he had more than a name, he had an address. The address was different from the one on Kristina's college application. Howard must've moved in the years since. Spencer quickly scanned through the document. Abandonment . . . three years of separation not made legal by the courts . . . there was no alimony, there were no children.

The divorce petition had been drawn in September 1993, two months before Kristina's death.

Maybe Howard Kim had killed her. Maybe he hadn't wanted to be divorced from her.

Imagine that—married. A college girl married. Spencer checked the dates. Howard and Kristina Kim had been married on the twenty-eighth day of November 1988. That would have made her sixteen years old! Still in high school. Wouldn't she have needed parental permission to be married so young? Even if she hadn't, why would a sixteen-year-old marry anyone? God, the questions. No answers, though.

Not yet, thought Spencer.

Howard was the man to talk to.

Spencer wondered if her dear friends knew she was married. He wondered if Jim Shaw, as he was making plans to make Kristina his political trophy bride, had known that his girl had already been married to someone else, and at sixteen.

Spencer got up to go, and then sat back down. There was still the matter of the letter, thrice folded.

He held it in his hands, looking at it the way he had looked at the black boots poking out of the snow. Spencer suspected that as soon as he opened the letter and read it, all pretenses that Kristina's death had just been an accident would have to stop. And despite himself, Spencer still entertained an idiotic hope that her death had been as unlucky as being hit by lightning.

He unfolded the piece of paper. He saw the date, he saw Kristina's signature, he saw the notary public stamp and the signature of Mr. Carmichael above it. He read the six lines of text over and over.

I, Kristina Morgan Kim, hereby leave the funds in my checking and savings accounts at New Hampshire Savings Bank to be divided equally among my three friends, James Allbright Shaw, Constance Tobias, and Albert Maplethorpe. Aristotle goes with Jim. Safety-deposit box contents go to Albert. My grandmother's house on Lake Winnipesaukee goes to Howard Kim.

All Spencer could think of, as he slowly put Kristina's documents back into her box, was the three singles in her wallet he had found in a crushed Mustang near the reservoir the night she almost died.

Outside Mr. Carmichael was waiting. There was only one question to ask him. They stared mutely at each other. There was nothing to say.

"How much?" asked Spencer, not wanting to know.

"Nine million three hundred and forty thousand dollars," replied Mr. Carmichael.

Spencer nodded, his mouth numbing. Nine million seven hundred and forty thousand dollars. That's a motive, or close enough for government work. But . . .

"Mr. Carmichael, you just notarized the letter for her, didn't you?"

"Yes, last Tuesday."

The day she died. The day *after* her brush with car death.

"How long has the money been in her account?"

"Since last Monday."

Spencer thought about it for two seconds. "What would've happened to her money if she had died without this letter?"

"What always happens to the money," replied Mr. Carmichael. "It would've gone to her closest living relative."

Spencer held his breath. "Like a . . ."

"Husband. Sure. Or a child. I don't know the line of succession that well."

"I think Speaker of the House is third," said Spencer.

Mr. Carmichael just stared at him.

"A husband . . . or a child," Spencer repeated. "Does ex-husband count?"

"I don't think so." Mr. Carmichael's eyebrows came together. "Isn't that all kind of moot, anyway? Now?"

"Yes, yes, I suppose it is."

But did the Speaker of the House know about the notarized letter that made it all moot? There was no husband and there was no child. *Who would have been third?*

Spencer left the bank with Kristina's belongings in a bag under his arm.

He knew what had prompted Kristina to write a brief will. It had been written on the heels of a nine-million-dollar inheritance and a near-death on Monday evening. No one but her and Mr. Carmichael knew she had written it, of that Spencer was sure. Without that will, who would have gotten *all* of Kristina Sinclair's money?

Back in his car, Spencer called in to the station. The dispatcher told him to go to Hitchcock. The medical examiner was there, waiting for permission to perform the autopsy.

"Permission from whom?" Spencer asked the medical examiner when he got to the dungeon of the hospital.

"Permission from her family," the medical examiner replied. Dr. Earl Innis was a short, balding, heavyset man perpetually out of breath.

"Her family," repeated Spencer. "I see. Well, her father is dead, her mother is God knows where, and she's got no siblings. She does have an ex-husband, though. Would you like me to contact him?"

"Yes," said Innis.

Spencer nodded. Howard Kim, I don't know how you felt about your recently exed wife, married at sixteen, dead at twenty-one, but I'll soon find out.

He called the New York operator from Dartmouth-Hitchcock and gave Howard's new address—in New York City. He got an answering machine. Spencer looked at his watch. Six-twenty. Mr. Kim should be just strolling in from work. "This is Detective O'Malley from Hanover, New Hampshire, calling for Howard Kim. It's about—"

The phone was picked up. "Yes," said a voice, in a slightly accented English.

"Mr. Kim?"

"Yes?"

"Hello, sir. It's about Kristina Kim, your ex-w—"

"Yes? Is everything all right?"

"No, sir, I'm afraid something terrible has happened," said Spencer.

The voice on the other end said, "Is she dead?"

"I'm sorry. Yes. Would it be possible for you to drive up?"

Howard Kim's voice was faint. "I'll be there at ten-thirty. I'm leaving now."

"Come to the Dartmouth-Hitchcock Medical Center. Ask the front desk to page Detective O'Malley or Dr. Innis."

Howard hung up, and eventually Spencer hung up, too.

He had four hours to kill. It had gotten dark, and that usually meant the end of the day.

The end of the day meant drink. But his day was not nearly done, so he drove to Everything but Anchovies instead, and had a bowl of chili and a turkey club. Then, because he had the time, he had meatloaf and mashed potatoes. And then two helpings of rice pudding. And then, because he had so much food in him to absorb the liquor, he went around the corner to Murphy's and had two double Southern Comforts on the rocks. It was strong stuff. How could she have drunk it?

Spencer looked at his watch. It was seven-thirty. The medical examiner from Concord was waiting to do the autopsy. Spencer was waiting for Howard. Ed Landers was back down in Concord in his lab doing his work. Will had long gone home.

Spencer walked past the little Christmas trees in the town square, and past Baker Library. He made a left onto Tuck Mall and walked to Hinman Hall in the snow. It was Friday night, *the* Friday night he had been going to take Kristina to Jesse's on their first date. Instead Spencer was waiting for permission from Kristina's ex-husband to cut her open to see if there were any clues inside her to the nine million dollars she had left her three best friends.

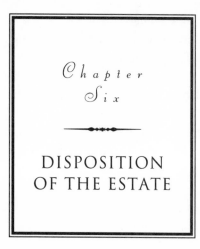

Spencer called Will Baker, asking him to come back to work. "I've brought the three kids back to the station. I want to play show and tell with Kristina's safety-deposit box contents. Come on, Will, just for an hour."

"Really for an hour, O'Malley? Tell it like it is."

"Actually for the rest of the night, Will. She is going to be autopsied tonight."

Fell had long finished his shift. It was late Friday night, and there still was no one from the Concord DA's office at Hanover. "Explain that," Spencer said to Will.

"I can't. I have no explanation."

Spencer called Fell at home. "Raymond," said Spencer calmly into the phone, "I'm looking around the headquarters, and you know what I don't see around here?"

"No, sir, what?"

"I don't see our friends from Concord, Ray. Do you know why that is?"

Silence on the other end of the phone. Spencer turned his eyes to the ceiling and cursed out loud. Will placed a helpful hand on Spencer's shoulder. "Ray?"

Silence.

"Ray!" much louder.

Will got the phone away from Spencer. After five minutes of listening and nodding, Will hung up the phone and said, "They're not here."

"No! Really? I don't believe it."

"It's true. They're not coming."

"Not coming. This is interesting. Are they deeming our matters here not important enough? Did he call them?"

Will, trying hard to cover for Ray, said, "Didn't call them, per se."

Spencer's eyes widened. "Did he *forget* to call them?"

"Didn't forget."

"Will," said Spencer, "it's been a long day, and this is not a party. I don't want to play charades. What exactly did Fell do? Per se."

"He called them, but it was after six when he did, and they had all gone home."

"What do you mean, all?"

"Don't you remember last weekend?"

"All too well."

"Everybody who worked was promised time off this weekend."

"Yeah, except me. But he didn't call them until six?"

"No, he got busy. Says he did everything else."

"What everything else?" Spencer shouted. "There was nothing else to do!"

"Tracy," said Will quietly. "What are you hyperventilating about? It's a homicide case, and it's all yours till Monday."

Spencer calmed down. That was true. That wasn't such a bad thing. "Ours, Will, ours."

"Yours, partner. I got family obligations this weekend."

Spencer thought about it. "That's too bad, Will. You should see what I found."

"In her room?"

"Oh, no. You know her room was bare." Spencer paused. "But her safety-deposit box wasn't."

Will widened his eyes. Will didn't usually get excited about evidence, but the divorce decree and the will excited him. Then the ever cautious Will said, "But the coroner hasn't determined the cause of death, has he? Conceivably, she could've lost consciousness and frozen." They were talking in hushed tones. The door to the questioning room was open and they could see Conni's and Jim's backs.

"It's possible, yes. But I'm telling you—my instincts are out on this one. She did not fall into the snow and die flat on her back with her arms out-stretched and her eyes closed by Providence."

"O'Malley, sometimes your instincts are wrong. Remember the Ham-monds?"

Spencer remembered. When they were still patrolmen, he and Will had frequently rounded up a quiet, diminutive Mr. Hammond because Mrs. Hammond called up screaming to the dispatcher. Every Saturday the wife was badly bruised, and he was too. She would scream at them to take him, to book him, to hold him in jail overnight because she was pressing charges in the morning. The husband never said a word against his wife, never offered a word of explanation for why he beat her. He rarely spoke.

One Saturday night, Spencer and Will came to the house a little before the time of her customary phone call and witnessed a crazed and obviously drunk Mrs. Hammond beating the shit out of a cowering Mr. Hammond with a one-quart aluminum pan and then beating herself in the face with the same pan before staggering to the phone. They rang the doorbell immediately. The pot was still in her hands. She was surprised they had come so quickly and couldn't understand why they had to arrest her.

Till the very last Saturday, Spencer had maintained that Mr. Hammond was the very profile of a habitual wife abuser.

"All right, all right," Spencer said tonight. "The Hammonds broke my instinct bank. But who would've known?"

"No one. All I'm saying here is keep an open mind, O'Malley. Things look one way here, but we don't know shit, and those kids out there, they're likely as not completely innocent."

"You won't say that after you see this." Spencer pointed to the manila envelope.

"Can't wait," said Will.

<hr>

The five of them sat in the questioning room. Conni sat between Albert and Jim, their chairs huddled close together, across the round table from the two detectives, in an icy stand-off. There was nothing in the bare room to look at except one another.

Spencer began. "It has come to my attention that there were a few things you guys left out yesterday when we spoke at such length. Anyone care to comment?"

But the three of them wouldn't be roped into anything. They sat there—Albert impassively, Jim sullenly, Conni watchfully—and did not say a word.

Spencer passed the divorce document to them and then Kristina's will and watched them as they read, as they shifted in their seats, or remained completely calm, or stared at him with amazement.

"Kristina was married?" gasped Conni.

"Kristina had nine million dollars?" exclaimed Albert.

"I thought Kim was a strange name for her," said Jim. "What was her real name?"

"Sinclair," said Spencer. "Kristina Morgan Sinclair."

"We roomed together for two years and she never told me she was married. Jim, did you know she was married?"

He shook his head. Albert did too.

"Nine *million* dollars," said Jim.

"Nine *million* dollars," echoed Albert.

"Where would she get that kind of money from?" asked Conni. "She was always so broke."

"She was broke," Spencer agreed. "Her grandmother left it to her. Kristina came into nine million dollars on Monday, wrote out a will on Tuesday, and died early Wednesday morning. And left all her money to you."

Conni put the letter down on the table. "This is ridiculous. I didn't know about any money."

Albert said to Spencer, "None of us did."

Jim remained quiet. "It doesn't matter. We can say what we like, right? Point is, she left us her money and then she died. Looks like she was killed." Jim suppressed a large, pained sound; it came out as a low gurgle. "But, detective, it could've been an accident. She drinks and she goes out there in the cold. She could've lost consciousness."

Nodding, Spencer said, "She could have, yes. But something tells me she didn't. Call it my gut instinct."

"You may be right," said Jim. "She was terrified of the dark."

Spencer nodded.

Will asked, "Why would Kristina not turn around and go back the way she came? That's what I want to know. What would make a frightened and cold girl continue into the woods?" Spencer nudged Will under the table and shook his head. He didn't want Will to say anything about Frankie's seeing Kristina on the bridge, not yet.

"Maybe she got scared, maybe she screamed," said Conni, giggling nervously. "*I* would've."

Will shook his head. "I don't think so. Screaming would've gone along with struggling, and there was no struggling."

"She couldn't have struggled very much even if she wanted to," said Jim, his mouth tense, his eyes glistening. "She'd been hurt badly in a car accident."

Conni said, "Maybe—" and Spencer cut her off. "Listen, it's great that you guys want to play amateur sleuths here, but can we get back to the money?"

"There's nothing to get back to," said Albert.

"Yeah," said Jim. "We didn't know about it."

"Didn't, huh?"

"She had money in the bank. So what?" said Conni, refraining from biting her lip while she spoke.

"What Detective O'Malley is trying to say," interjected Will, "is that it's worrying that the person who wills a fortune to three people just happens to die less than twelve hours later."

"Why is that so odd?" said Jim. "We didn't know about the money, so it doesn't matter."

Spencer stared at Jim, who didn't take his eyes off Spencer. He did not fidget or wince. Maybe Jim didn't know about the money, thought Spencer. But Albert gave me exactly the same look, and Conni, though nervous, doesn't seem nervous at all about the money, as if she is nervous about something completely different. Maybe none of them knew about the money. How odd. Can this kind of money have nothing to do with her death? I refuse to believe it. He peered at them more closely, hoping to unnerve them by his stare. They didn't move.

Jim said, "I mean, I know it looks bad for us and everything, but I'm telling you, her dying and the will—it's just a coincidence."

"Coincidence, huh? Let me ask you this—who would've gotten her money had she not left a will?"

Conni stared at Spencer. She seemed more relaxed than the day before, but she couldn't help fidgeting. Albert was exactly the same as the night before—composed and sensible. Jim was tense, but not nervous.

"How do we know?" Conni said. "Maybe her ex?"

Shaking his head and getting up from the table, Spencer said, "No. She divorced him, so he's not entitled to anything. Someone from her family?"

Albert, Conni, and Jim exchanged puzzled looks. "I think she told me her father was dead," Conni said tentatively.

"And she was an only child," added Jim.

"Kristina said her mother was deranged or something." Albert lowered his voice. "She told me something about her mother needing a lot of medication to stop screaming."

"She told you that?" Conni asked, turning to Albert. It was the first time she had looked at him since they sat down.

"Why was her mother screaming?" Spencer asked Albert, cutting Conni off. There was going to be no jealous bickering at his interrogation table.

"She didn't say," Albert replied.

"If there is a mother, then she would be entitled to Kristina's money," Spencer said.

Shaking his head, Albert said, "Guess so." He was pale and his dark eyes seemed darker than usual.

Their reactions unsettled Spencer's stomach. They seemed naturally surprised, then concerned and helpful. What was it about Kristina that they had failed to mention? Spencer was hard pressed to remember the confrontation with Jim. Oh yeah, Jim found her and ran away. And Conni was unaccountably missing from her room for half an hour. Albert came to Kristina's room *after midnight* to say good-bye.

"I don't understand," said Conni. "Why would Krissy leave us her money? We don't want her money. She knows that."

"Does she?" asked Spencer. "Does she know that?"

"Of course she knows that," Jim said irritably. He seemed to have gotten braver with his friends around him, though Spencer noted there was no love lost among the three of them. There was a cold, impenetrable being sitting in the spaces between them, pushing them apart with its long sharp fingers.

Spencer shrugged. "You were the closest thing she had to a family. Nine million dollars. That's a lot of money to be split three ways."

They didn't say anything. Spencer got a strange feeling while watching them. They seemed to be thinking about things other than Kristina's money. Albert was still pale, and his black eyes shone. Conni was biting her lip, while Jim looked defiantly straight at Spencer, as if to say, screw you. Hell with you. I did nothing wrong, and my life is already pretty much ruined. I don't care what you think or what you do with me. Jim didn't have to say a word, but his challenging wounded gaze screamed at Spencer across the white Formica table.

After a few minutes Albert asked, "What do you want from us, Detective O'Malley?"

"I want to know what you three were doing between twelve and two A.M. Wednesday morning, November twenty-fourth. That's it."

Conni shifted hard in her seat. Jim rolled his eyes. Albert stared straight at Spencer. "What do you want to know, detective?"

"Well, this is what I have so far—Jim says he was in his room all night, but no one had seen him after eleven, and when Conni tried to reach him at one, he didn't pick up the phone. Albert says he was watching a movie in the lounge, but when Conni went in to look for him he wasn't there. The kid Tim had been asleep for half the movie, so he isn't sure of anything. And Conni was admittedly out and about on campus looking for Albert in the snowstorm, gone from her room for forty minutes. What does this all mean—?"

Kyle stuck his head into the room. "Sorry to bother you, but the chief wants to see you pronto."

"Tell him we're in the middle of a—"

Widening his eyes, Kyle said, "Now, the chief said. Now."

Spencer shot up. "We'll be right back."

"Are we free to go?" asked Jim.

"Wait. We'll be back in a minute."

And then Spencer and Will left Albert, Conni, and Jim alone.

Kyle was waiting for them outside. "How did I do?" he asked.

"Great, Kyle," Spencer told him. Just the timing sucked.

Will went to the bathroom and to call his wife. Spencer went into a small dark room, adjoining the questioning room, turned on the monitor, sat down in a chair with his face to the two-way mirror, and listened.

At first they didn't talk much. Jim kept saying the police had no right to keep them there, and they could go anytime they pleased unless they were actually charged with something.

"Do you want to be charged with something?" asked Albert.

"What are you talking about? Of course not."

"Then shut up."

Jim gave Albert a withering look.

Conni said, "It's horrible that she left us her money. Horrible."

"Yes," Albert said. "It really is. How could she have left us her money?"

"It's horrible she's dead," said Jim. "That's the horrible part."

Yes, the other two agreed. That was horrible.

They sat for a while after that, staring at their hands.

"Well, what are we going to do now?" said Conni, looking hopefully to Albert, as if he had all the answers.

"I don't know what *you* guys are going to do, but I know what *I'm* going to do."

The mirror was across from the three of them, but Albert got up, paced absentmindedly around the room for a few seconds, and then sat down with his back to the mirror, across from Conni and Jim. Spencer couldn't see Albert's face, nor Conni's. Getting up, he moved a few feet to the left so that he could watch them at an angle.

"She is dead. I don't want her money," said Albert.

"Really?" said Conni.

"Really," Albert answered firmly. "She was my friend, and it's awful enough she is dead, without compounding her death by profiting from it," said Albert quietly, and Spencer wasn't sure if it was meant genuinely or ironically. "I don't want her money."

"You were never much for money, were you, Albert?" Conni said.

"Never. You know how I feel about it. The less I have, the better I feel. I'm sure in large doses it ruins you."

"But what are you going to do? She meant for you to have it."

"No," said Albert, and again Spencer wished to hell he could see Albert's face. "She did not mean for me to have it."

There was a pause, a silence, in the staccato conversation. Spencer watched Conni and Jim, and they watched Albert. Conni's face was tender; Jim's was cold.

Interesting, thought Spencer. There's something I haven't yet been privy to here. They've kept me out of their little secret, and by God, I'm going to find out what it is.

When the sound of Albert's words stopped lingering in the air, he spoke again. "I'm going to donate my share to Red Leaves House."

"You are?" said Conni incredulously.

"Yes. Why does that surprise you?"

"Because, Albert, you don't have any money." Conni laughed. "You've never had a penny. It's us who don't need her money, but you . . . you could actually use some."

"I don't need to *use* her money," Albert said bitterly. "I don't want her money. I won't know what to do with it, and plus, I want to earn my money honestly. I'm *going* to earn my money," he corrected himself, and ran his right hand through his black hair, adjusting his ponytail, which for some reason began to irritate Spencer.

"It was nice of her to think of us," said Conni.

When was she going to cry again? wondered Spencer. When is that giddy, emotional girl going to break down again over the death of her best friend? There was nothing on Conni's face that resembled bereavement.

"Where do you suppose she got that money from?" asked Jim.

"Yeah, and why didn't she leave any to her ex-husband?" said Conni.

"I can't believe she had a husband." Something must have just occurred to Jim, because he started up from his seat and then sat back down in a hurry, looking restlessly around the room. He seemed upset and shaken.

"What's the matter, Jimmy?" asked Conni.

"Nothing, nothing," he quickly said. "Forgot to ask the detective—something." Pause. "Forgot to ask him when she got divorced from this Howard Kim."

"Oh, Jimmy, who cares now?" said Conni. "It's all just water under the bridge. She's dead. What are you going to do, be mad at a dead person?"

"Why not?" said Albert. "You are."

Conni flushed. "I'm not mad at her, Albert. She's dead. I'm not mad at her anymore."

"No, I'll bet you're not," Albert said quietly, but Spencer heard him, and Jim heard him too, for his gaze weakened.

He looked away, saying, "Back to this money thing. You're going to give your share to Red Leaves?"

"Yes," said Albert. "They could use it. That place meant everything to her. And she meant everything to the girls she took care of. Why, they got more attached to Krissy than they did to their own babies."

"Yeah, you're right. It did mean a lot to her," said Conni. "Well, I certainly don't need her money. How would it look for a penniless orphan to give her money away but for me to keep it?"

"Like you had some sense," said Albert. "I feel wrong taking it. You should keep it."

Conni raised her voice. "I'm not going to keep her money—what are you, kidding me?"

"Think about traveling to Europe. You always wanted to do that."

"Albert, I always wanted to do that with *you*," Conni said with emotion.

"You still can, babe."

"Albert Maplethorpe, I certainly don't want to travel through Europe with you on *her* money."

"That would be ironic, indeed," said Jim. He was wearing a black sweater out of which he kept obsessively picking light dog hairs.

"It wouldn't be ironic at all," retorted Albert. "We've never been to Europe."

There was a long, pained pause. Finally, Conni said, not looking at anyone, "I think Scotland is considered Europe."

Scotland! Spencer's face was pressed to the mirror; he felt its cool, smooth surface against his skin. I get it now. God, I'm an idiot.

When he tuned back to their conversation, Albert was patting Conni's arm across the table, saying, "Let it go, babe, let it go. She is dead. Let it go."

"What, like that makes it all better?" snapped Jim.

"Not better," said Albert sadly. "Just over."

Albert then said to Conni, "We were friends, Constance, friends. Why is your imagination so out of kilter?"

Had Spencer caught Albert in an out-and-out lie? He had not seen a love letter from Albert to Kristina, nor one from her to him. Spencer had not seen the two together, or smelled his cologne on her clothes, or seen their breath intermingle in the November cold. However, he had seen something more powerful and more telling. Matchbooks and cigarette lighters and napkins from a country with impossibly green grass, a country where men wore kilts and bag-pipes played music nearly too mournful for the human ear. He had seen first-hand what Kristina Kim née Sinclair thought of Edinburgh, *Scotland,* and be-cause of that, Spencer O'Malley knew she and Albert were not just good friends.

Kristina loved Albert.

That made all the difference.

What the hell was she doing going out with Jim? Spencer pressed his palms against the mirror. If Albert and Kristina wanted to be together, and if Jim was stuck on Conni, why in hell's name did they play this stupid game of mu-sical love chairs?

Spencer's headache was getting nasty. Why, why, why? The questions of the living pressed at him. What happened to "No chemistry, man"? Or was it just a one-way street? Maybe Albert wasn't lying. Maybe they *were* just good friends.

And he was rejecting her money. She left it for him, and for her boyfriend, and for the girl who was her best friend; why would Albert not take her money? It was obvious he didn't want to. And soon, Spencer heard Jim Shaw say, "It's a good idea, Albert. This Red Leaves thing. That's a lot of money for them."

"Yes," Albert said. "Kristina mentioned they wanted to renovate. They only have a few bedrooms upstairs, and sometimes it gets so crowded the girls have to share rooms. With the money they could build an extension."

"For nine million dollars?" said Conni. "An extension and then some."

"Yes, it's a good idea," agreed Jim. "But why didn't Kristina think of it her-self?"

"She cared about us more than she cared about Red Leaves," said Conni. "But you're right. We should give the money to them. Who runs that place?"

"I don't remember," said Albert. "I'll write them a letter, and when the money becomes available send the check. They'll be very happy."

"But will you?" said Conni softly. "Will you be happy?"

Spencer did not see his face, but he saw Conni's. "Sure. She's dead. Me keeping her money isn't going to bring her back, is it?"

"Do you want to bring her back, Albert?" said Conni, and again, Spencer could not read the expression on her face. It read somewhere between intense love and intense misery.

"I'm sad she is gone," Albert said. "You should be, too."

"Don't tell her how she should feel," snapped Jim. "What do you under-stand about her feelings? Everything is black-and-white with you."

"What the hell does that mean, man?" said Albert and laughed irritably.

It was the first time Spencer had heard Albert be anything more than impassive. "First of all, nothing is black-and-white with me, and second of all, how Conni feels is none of your business, all right?"

"See, unlike you, I care about her feelings," Jim said.

Albert did not miss a beat. "Well, we certainly know how you feel about Conni, Jim. You've made it very clear. Listen, stop acting like this all the time, stop it, all right? I didn't take *your* girl away from you, and you know it."

"Yeah," Jim said, "you took both girls away from me."

"I don't know what the hell you're talking about," said Albert.

" 'No chemistry, man,' " Jim mimicked Albert. "Remember you said that to me? About why you couldn't get it on with Kristina? No chemistry, you said."

"Yeah?" Albert said rudely. "What about it?"

"It was a goddamn lie, wasn't it?"

"What are you talking about?" said Albert loudly. "Kristina is dead, we're sitting here, all under suspicion for killing her, she's left us a shitload of money, and you're going on about three-year-old crap. I mean, what's going on?"

Spencer moved away from the glass and toward the door. Any moment he was going to be needed in the small square room with the round table.

Conni spared him from intervening by intervening herself. "Guys, please," she said in a small voice, "can we just please stick to the matter at hand?" Looking at Albert across from her, she said, "I'm with you. We'll give our money to Red Leaves."

When no one said anything, Conni looked at Jim. He stared back at her, and his mouth tightened. Conni reached out and patted his arm. "Jimmy, why are you so angry? She's gone."

He moved his arm away and said harshly, "So what? Does that make it all better?"

"Yes," said Conni quietly. "Doesn't it?"

"What are you talking about, Conni?" said Jim, staring at her intently. "Don't say that, you of all people, don't say that."

Not answering, Conni stared at the table. Albert said nothing.

Spencer was amazed. Minutes passed, and the three of them began talking about other things: about the ex-husband; what would Kristina be doing married so young, and why? Why hadn't Kristina ever told Conni about Howard when they talked about everything, and then Conni looked at Albert and asked, childlike, "Everything, Albert?" and he said, "Guess so," and then they talked about Kristina's funeral, would she be buried at Pine Knoll, in which case they could come, or would she be buried in Brooklyn? In which case they couldn't take the time off from their exams. Well, Jim said, he'd take the time off, and the other two were surprised. Jim? Time off from school?

None seemed disturbed by the fact that they had vowed to give away over nine million dollars.

With a sleight of hand, Albert, Conni, and Jim gamely gave away what Spencer thought was the motive while he watched from a two-way mirror.

And the subject of Kristina's actual death was going self-consciously untouched.

Spencer suddenly thought of last week when they went for coffee—was that only last week? What had Kristina told him? She was broke. She drove an old Mustang, she bought used textbooks because she couldn't afford new ones. She had three dollars in her pocket. Had she told a single soul she was coming into nine million dollars? And if not, why not? If Spencer were coming into nine million dollars, heck, if he were coming into nine *hundred* dollars, he would tell everybody. Certainly Will. But Kristina hadn't told her three best friends. Why not?

He turned around to walk out of the room, and Will was standing at the door. "What was she afraid of, Spence?" Will said.

For a second Spencer thought Will had read his mind and was talking about Kristina. Then he realized Will was talking about Conni. "Was I talking out loud?" Spencer said.

"No, you were thinking out loud," Will said, coming closer to Spencer. "I stood behind you the whole time." Will put his hand on Spencer's shoulder. "You're taking this way too personally, O'Malley. What's gotten into you?"

Spencer ran his hand over his cropped hair. "Nothing, man."

"Relax. We'll figure it out. *You'll* figure it out. I know you will."

"Will I?"

Will nodded. "There's something else here. Something else besides the money."

"I agree."

"There's this abnormal tension among kids who are supposed to be friends."

"Yes."

Will said, "I think they really didn't know about the money. Did you see their faces? I watched them. Albert nearly fell off his chair. Conni acted like somebody hit her. Jim closed his eyes; he understood right away what it meant for them. I'm telling you it's not the money."

"I don't know, Will. It's too much money not to be the money."

"Yes, but O'Malley, Albert goes alone to Kristina's room. She is possibly

226

naked, and he is possibly tying her boots. Conni sees Albert is not in his room and goes nuts. No wonder she is obsessively looking for him all over campus at one in the morning." Will was talking quietly, but he lowered his voice another notch. "And why is Conni so uncomfortable? She keeps pulling on her eyebrows all the time."

"Yeah, I know. But Will, where was Jim?"

"Sleeping."

"Okay, if Jim was sleeping, where was Albert?"

"You're saying he could've slipped out?"

"No," said Spencer. "I'm not saying that. I'm saying, where was Conni?"

Will stopped him. "Tracy, we've been so wrapped up in looking for the motive, we haven't been looking for the killer. What if it was just some crazy lunatic? What if someone demented knew she walked the wall naked, so he waited for her, dragged her into the bushes, raped her, and then killed her because she was screaming like a banshee?"

Spencer shook his head vehemently. "Will, I know you're making this up. She was clean. And she wouldn't have gone into the woods for a psycho. Where she was found was a long way from the bridge. What did he do? Carry her tenderly in his arms? Besides, what kind of sicko would rape a woman in the snow? What did he do, bring a picnic blanket? He'd have to get down in the snow himself, and it's cold. His dick would freeze."

The two men eyed each other, and Spencer said, "Look, it's not a bad idea to say that that's who we're looking for, a crazy man. It'll give us a little more time, and might relax these kids a little."

Will nodded. "Not a bad idea. Still, though . . . I think . . ."

"Shhh," said Spencer. "Let's go."

Opening the door for Spencer, Will said, "These kids worry me. There is something weird going on."

"Yeah, but we haven't met the husband yet," said Spencer, walking out of the room. "He could be weird as hell."

Howard Kim was neat, well dressed, gravely serious, and Asian.

Spencer was not surprised. He had expected Howard to be Asian.

They shook hands. "So she is dead? I am sorry to hear that. I am sorry. How did she die?"

"She was found frozen in the snow."

Howard looked at the floor. They were standing near the front reception desk at the hospital.

"God, how horrible."

"Yes," echoed Spencer. "I'm very sorry."

"Do you need me to identify her?"

"Thanks, but she's already been ID'd. We need your permission to autopsy her."

"That will be it?"

"No." Spencer glanced at Will. "Then maybe you and my partner, Will Baker, could talk."

"Kind of like a formal talk?"

"Formal?"

"Like questioning talk?"

Spencer looked at Howard askance. "Questioning?" Spencer's voice wasn't as friendly and sympathetic anymore. "I don't know, Mr. Kim. Is there something we should question you about?"

"I am a lawyer, Detective O'Malley. I know how these things work. A young woman is dead. Everybody close to her is a suspect."

"Yes, and you, after all, *were* her husband."

Howard waved him off. "Yes," he said, "but in name only."

After that, Howard asked to look briefly at her body. They took the elevator into the dungeon. With a disbelieving, stricken look, Howard touched Kristina's corpse, now unfrozen and decomposing.

"How did this happen?" he whispered. "How?"

Spencer shook his head, trying not to look at Kristina's body. "What can I tell you? You allow us to autopsy her and we'll have more answers for you then."

Howard nodded his assent and began to cry. Spencer breathed shallowly, quickly—to keep his composure.

"I do not want to leave her here," said Howard, turned away from Spencer, from Will, and from Kristina. "Not another minute. She does not belong here. I—want to bury her. Her body needs to be at rest for her spirit to be at rest. I have to take her out of here. Please," he added.

Spencer wanted to put his hand on Howard's shoulder. "After the autopsy, the funeral home in Hanover will take her anywhere you like," he said, unable to comfort Howard. "Let's wait outside, and I'll talk to Dr. Innis."

Howard started to leave, and then took a black scarf off his neck and placed it on Kristina's body. He was sobbing. Spencer took the scarf off and handed it back to Howard. "No," he gently said. He asked Howard to wait for him in the corridor.

Dr. Innis was in the autopsy room. The three metal tables were empty. The doctor was putting on his rubber gloves. "Can we begin?"

"How long is it going to take?" asked Spencer.

Dr. Innis handed Spencer a white overcoat. "About six hours. Three for the autopsy, another three for the coroner's report. This isn't your first autopsy, is it, detective?"

Spencer's life in the last two days had been doled out in three-hour increments. It wasn't bad enough that it was ten at night. Three hours from now it was going to get worse. And Spencer was still on the job. "No, it isn't my first," he said. "Certainly not." But the lab coat in his hands made him shiver, and his head jerked.

Dr. Innis calmly looked up at Spencer. "Detective?" he said.

"Yes, yes," Spencer said hurriedly, fumbling with the white coat. "I'm fine."

"Good. Can we begin? I'll have Ralph wheel it in."

Spencer leaned against the wall for support. Had the word *it* made him feel suddenly queasy? He waited five minutes for Kristina's body to be brought over to the cold room. Glancing at him, Dr. Innis, said, "Detective O'Malley, I don't have all night. Are we ready?"

"I'm—I'm—" Spencer stammered. His back was still against the wall. "I'm sorry, doctor, if you could—excuse me for just a minute." Spencer turned and walked out of the room.

He walked down the corridor to Will and Howard. "Will, can I have a word with you?" he said. They went inside a small waiting room, and Spencer closed the door. He handed the white lab coat to Will.

"What's this?"

"Will?" Spencer said. "Feel like staying here for three hours?"

"No," was Will's quick response.

"Go on. You know once of us has to be in there."

"This is why I'm glad you're detective-sergeant and I'm just plain detective."

"As detective-sergeant then, I'm ordering you to go in there."

"No, thank you. You go. You live for that stuff."

"You're confusing me with Ray Fell."

"Yeah, well, where is he when you need him?" said Will, shaking his head. "O'Malley, it's ten at night."

"Tell me something I don't know."

They looked at each other. "Will, this is important," said Spencer.

"Yeah, yeah, yeah." Will sighed. "All right. Let me call my wife. Tell her I'm not coming home anytime soon."

It had been several years since Will stayed with Spencer all hours of the night. Spencer wished there had been more of those hours—he missed Will.

He shook Will's hand. "Will, you know I'd do it, I'd go in," Spencer said quietly. "But I just can't on this one, okay? Wish I could. I just can't."

Patting him gently, Will said without artifice, "Tracy, I don't get you at all sometimes. But you don't have to explain."

Wordlessly relieved, Spencer smiled.

"Should I wait for the death certificate if you aren't back?"

"I'll be back, don't worry." Seeing Will's slightly disappointed face, Spencer added, "We'll wait for it together, okay?" Despite the morbidity, he understood Will's anticipation. It wasn't every day they waited for a death certificate. Even rarer when they didn't know what was going to go on it.

When Spencer came out into the corridor, he said to Howard, "What do you say we go check you into a hotel, and we'll talk there?"

Howard, his bloodshot, tired brown eyes rimmed with wire glasses, nodded. "I usually stay at the Hanover Inn," he said.

"That's fine," said Spencer, thinking, *usually?*

When he and Howard were at the Hanover Inn, Howard said to Spencer, "Your partner seems like a good officer. Wish we had more like him in New York."

You once did, Spencer wanted to tell him. You once had me. But then my wife died. And who wanted me then, except a town of ten thousand people in the middle of the mountains?

Spencer wanted to help Howard with his bags, but Howard didn't have any. "I came too quick. Didn't even pack," Howard said apologetically, as if Spencer would somehow mind not being able to help him with his luggage.

"Doesn't matter. Want a cup of coffee?"

"Yes. Maybe some dinner, too. Have you eaten?"

"I have, but I'll have some coffee."

They went to the hotel's Ivy Grill. Howard ordered a shrimp cocktail and a steak. Spencer ordered a whiskey *and* a coffee and drank them alternately. One sip of whiskey, one sip of coffee.

Howard was staring at him. "Don't want to go to sleep," Spencer said as a non sequitur, by way of explaining. Explaining what?

"No explanation necessary," said Howard coolly.

Or even wanted, thought Spencer. "So Howard, tell me, how does a sixteen-year-old white girl marry an Asian lawyer from—"

"Hong Kong."

"—Hong Kong, a good ten years her senior?"

"We were in love?" Howard said as a question rather than an answer. "We could not wait to be together?"

Spencer raised his glass. "My condolences to a grieving ex-husband."

Silence.

"You said earlier you were married in name only."

Howard fumbled with his fork, which fell to the floor. He had shown little interest in eating his shrimp cocktail. The Ivy Grill was nearly empty; it was getting ready to close. "Kristina was a very nice girl," said Howard, trying to stay composed. "I tried to help her as much I could."

"I don't doubt that. When was the last time you saw her?"

"Sunday afternoon."

Spencer for an instant thought he meant this past Sunday and was filled with a kind of insane hope that maybe, just maybe, things weren't what they seemed. Maybe she had gone home, was alive for her last Thanksgiving, had some turkey, spent time with her family . . . was alive for a few more days.

"Sunday before Thanksgiving," added Howard. Spencer sank back into his upholstered chair. "She gave me the divorce papers."

Spencer didn't know what to ask next. He tried to focus himself by taking a sip—a gulp—of bourbon. "When did you see her last?"

"Like I said, Sunday before Thanksgiving."

"Yes. Yes, of course. I meant, what were your whereabouts on Tuesday night, November twenty-third?"

"Am I under suspicion, Detective O'Malley?"

"As much as anyone else is. We have to question everybody. That's our job. You said so yourself."

"Is that why you called me here? To question me?"

"Yes," said Spencer. "You were her husband until a week ago. What kind of law do you practice, Mr. Kim?"

"I practice business law in Chinatown, detective. For your information, I was in court until eight o'clock in the evening, and then I was home."

"By yourself?"

"No, wait. Last Tuesday? I went out to dinner with one of my clients."

Spencer wrote it down in his notebook. "His name?"

"*Her* name," Howard corrected. "Anna Chung."

Spencer looked up from his notebook. Howard stared back calmly. "Yes, Detective O'Malley. I have a life."

"The ink was not dry on the papers."

"I told you, we were not married in the proper sense of the word."

"How were you married then?"

Howard thought about it. "Improperly," he finally said.

The waiter took away Howard's shrimp cocktail untouched, and brought him filet mignon, medium rare, with a baked potato and garden vegetables.

"Eat, Howard," Spencer said. "I'll be brief. It's been difficult getting information from people who are supposed to be her friends and/or ex-husbands. Everyone is tight-lipped, uncooperative, or downright hostile. As if I should just mind my own business, really. As if it's none of my concern that this girl is found dead at twenty-one, dead in the snow for nine days while her friends merrily or otherwise go about their business, without bothering to check or notice or report that their friend is missing. Well, I'm going to tell you, it *is* my business. And I don't want to make an example out of you, Mr. Kim, but I've just about had enough. I've had no sleep, I'm very tired, and the girl is, after all, dead. And I will bet my mother's house that she is not accidentally dead, no matter that you and her friends would like me to think so."

"I do not want you to think anything, Detective O'Malley," Howard said coldly.

"Wait." Spencer had a sip of coffee. "So if I have to drag you to the police station and keep you there until you answer every question to my total satisfaction, I'll do just that and be happy that at least I'm keeping you up, too. Do you understand? Or would you like to call *your* lawyer?" Spencer finished.

Howard Kim slowly took a bite out of his steak, chewed it, swallowed it, wiped his mouth with a napkin, and then said, "I understand."

"Good."

"You think her death was not accidental?"

"It's a hunch I have. Call it my man's intuition. There was no reason for her to be dead. Other than she was naked in the year's worst snowstorm. You'll see—the autopsy report will bear me out. She was killed."

"Were there marks on her?"

"Not that I saw. There could've been. She might have been drinking."

"Yes."

Spencer studied Howard for a measured moment, and then said, "She liked to drink?"

Howard nodded. "She was a college student."

"Yeah, so what? I like to drink too," said Spencer. "You don't find me naked and dead."

"You weren't unlucky."

"Wrong. I wasn't killed. I'm plenty unlucky." Spencer took a quick sip from his whiskey glass.

"Detective," Howard said quietly. "I have an alibi."

"Will Anna Chung support it?"

"Yes," said Howard, even quieter.

"Okay," Spencer said. He believed him. "Still, you haven't explained."

"Yes?"

"Why would she marry you?"

"Love?"

"Not love."

"Would you believe necessity?"

Spencer thought it over. "You got her pregnant?" he asked incredulously.

"Well," said Howard, wiping his mouth and throwing the napkin into the uneaten meat, "she was certainly pregnant."

Spencer tried not to breathe so he wouldn't miss a thing. "What does that mean?"

"I mean, she was pregnant when we married."

"But not by you."

"That is right."

"God! Well, by who then?"

Howard was silent.

"And why wouldn't she marry *him* instead of you?"

"I do not know," said Howard.

"Who was it?"

"I do not know."

"You don't know? What the hell does that mean?"

Howard didn't answer.

"Where do you come in?"

"I come in on a boat. Not literally. My family, originally from Pyongyang—"

"Where?"

"North Korea," Howard said, with a slight edge to his voice, as if he were offended Spencer O'Malley didn't know where Pyongyang was. "My family immigrated to Hong Kong in search of work. I went to a British university there to become a lawyer. Kristina's father bought textiles from my father. I finished school in Hong Kong. I wanted to go to England, but England was very difficult. America was my first choice, but America was even more difficult. I am a business lawyer; I worked with my father, but I did not like it. Kristina's father could not help me for a long time. It is very hard. Everybody wants to work in America. In 1997 there will be even more people who will want to come here from Hong Kong. You know—the British must give it back to China."

China, right. "Go on."

"Then her father—"

"John Henry Sinclair?"

"Yes. Her father comes to Hong Kong about five years ago. He asks me if I still want to come live in America. He says he can work it out, if I marry his daughter. We would live in New York, where I will work and she will finish high school. At the end of five years, I can become an American citizen, and she will be twenty-one, and we can get divorced. We need to stay married that long—the immigration officials, they are very strict these days about arranged marriages—"

"Yeah, especially between a Korean man and a young American girl."

"Especially, yes. So we stay married. Kristina goes to private school in Brooklyn Heights. I go to work for a good law firm. I am still with them."

"So the divorce—you both wanted it?"

"No. She wanted it. I said okay. I applied for citizenship—there were no problems."

"If she hadn't asked you, what would've happened?"

"Nothing. I was . . ." Howard thought about it. "Indebted to her father. I would have done whatever she wanted."

How nice, Spencer thought. Everybody got what they wanted.

"Where's the baby?"

"The baby?"

"Yes, the baby."

"It was stillborn."

"Oh." Spencer fell quiet.

"I do not know the family very well. Not at all, really. Never met Kristina's mother, just talked to her on the telephone. I deal with the father. He—" Howard paused. "He was a very, very upset man. He did not talk to Kristina at all. He told me it was better his daughter married an important man, a lawyer, one of the father's colleagues, not such a disgrace."

Spencer was appalled. "You mean *that* was better than the truth?"

"I think so."

Spencer flagged the waiter for another drink, and a minute later, having forgotten what he'd ordered, flagged him down again. He finished them both and ordered another, all the while thinking, well, that explains Red Leaves House.

"Did you know she worked at a home for pregnant teenagers?" Spencer asked.

"Yes, she told me." Howard bowed his head. "Poor Kristina." He suppressed a dry sob. "Will that be all, detective? I am very tired."

"Just a few more minutes, Mr. Kim. Why did you keep in touch with her after she went to college?"

Howard coughed. "Part of the deal. Her father gave me money for her. I paid for her college education."

Spencer shook his head. "You didn't."

"Of course I did."

"Really? That's strange. I was under the impression her grandmother paid for it."

Howard blanched and moved forward in his seat, then backward, against the back of the chair, and got a nervous bend at the corner of his mouth. He tried to sound calm when he said, in a shaky voice, "That's not possible. Every year I gave her money. I know. Twenty thousand dollars a year for four years. I was very careful. She had a tendency to always spend more money than she was given. Her father warned me against giving her too much. She will use it for ill means, he said. I found out how much she needed for her tuition and room and board, subtracted her scholarship and work-study. I gave her money every year."

"That's ironic," said Spencer. "You weren't the only one very careful about giving her exactly twenty thousand dollars for four years."

"What are you talking about, detective?"

"There were letters from her grandmother in her safety-deposit box. She gave her tuition money every year, too."

Howard shook his head violently. It was a good thing he wasn't still eating, Spencer thought—the steak would've flown out of his mouth. "It cannot be," Howard said. "It just cannot be."

Shrugging, Spencer said, "Maybe she invested wisely and ended up with nine million dollars."

Howard looked at Spencer suspiciously. "What nine million are you talking about?"

"It came from her grandmother," said Spencer. The look on Howard's face—there was something awful in it, something failed and shamed and spent.

"Grandmother?" Howard came to. "Ah, yes. Maybe. How do you know?"

"It was wired to her from a bank in New Hampshire. There was a copy of Louise Morgan's will in Kristina's safety-deposit box, dated late August. The will clearly stipulated Kristina as the sole benefactor of Louise Morgan's liquid fortune. Louise Morgan's money all went into a trust for Kristina, hers when she turned twenty-one."

"Why?" said Howard. More like gasped. Opened his mouth and gasped the syllable out. *"Why?"*

"How do I know? I ask the questions. You're supposed to have the answers."

"I do not know anything. I told you, I only knew her father, and he told me nothing. He told me how to take care of Kristina. That is it. We had a deal. I took good care of her, I thought. I watched over her. I thought." Howard bowed his head. "But I did not. I did not watch over her enough."

"No," agreed Spencer, debating with himself whether or not to have another drink. "You did not."

They sat in silence while the waiters put the chairs on top of the cleaned tables and prepared to wash the floor.

Howard must have felt the need to explain, because he said, "What do I know, Detective O'Malley? I am a textile factory manager's son from Korea. I was grateful to Mr. Sinclair for the opportunity to come to America. It was my dream. I did not ask unwelcome questions. He told me this must be so and it was. I did not show my curiosity. I was right not to do so. Kristina's mother would sound very sad when she called. I felt sorry for her."

"She didn't call often?"

"No. Then she stopped calling. I think Kristina felt bad about that."

"She loved her mother?"

Howard nodded. "She loved her mother."

"What happened to John Sinclair? He is listed as deceased on Kristina's college application."

"Yes. Yes." Howard rubbed his head. "The last time Mrs. Sinclair called, she told us he had died, from heart failure. She sounded very sad."

I bet she was, thought Spencer. She lost her husband and her only daughter. "Sad" was an understatement.

"Was there a will?"

"What?"

"John Sinclair—did he leave a will?"

"Yes, of course. A man of his means does not die without a will."

Spencer waited. Howard continued. "I was sent a letter by the executor's attorneys saying that I was to receive a yearly sum of fifty thousand dollars for the next six years. That was two years ago."

"Now isn't that nice. What about Kristina? What did she receive?"

Howard looked away before he answered. "Nothing."

"Nothing?"

"Nothing."

"His only daughter, and nothing?"

Uncomfortable, edgy, Howard cleared his throat, adjusted his glasses, and said, "He had disowned her."

"He what?"

"Disowned her. He drew up a legal document, signed by himself and his wife, and disowned her."

Spencer badly wanted to wet his throat. "John Sinclair disowned his only daughter?"

"Yes."

"In legal terms, does that mean that she's not entitled to any of her parents' assets?"

"Right."

"And," Spencer slowly said, formulating his racing thoughts as he spoke, *"they're not entitled to any of hers?"*

"I do not know. I suppose so. Detective O'Malley, pardon me, but what does this all have to do with Kristina's death?"

Reluctantly deciding against another drink, Spencer said, "Maybe nothing. Maybe everything. Kristina's accounts are chock full of dollars, she divorced you—her only direct beneficiary—and her parents—"

"Parent," Howard corrected Spencer. "John Sinclair is dead."

"—parents have disowned her. This is getting crazy. And she does not die intestate, a fluke, an act of Providence. She leaves a do-it-yourself will."

"With no mention of me."

"Oh, no, she mentioned you. She left you her grandmother's house."

Howard was silent. "Who did she leave the money to?" he said stoically. Spencer could've sworn Howard was holding his breath.

"Her three friends. Who did you think she was going to leave her money to?"

He let his breath out. He seemed greatly relieved. "Nobody. I think you should talk to them."

"You can be sure I'll do that. In any case, it's all moot. They don't want to keep the money."

"Not to keep it?"

"They want to give it to Red Leaves House."

Howard fell back in his chair. "God, that is so peculiar. So strange." He took off his glasses and rubbed his eyes. "It just makes no sense."

Spencer leaned forward. "Did you want that money, Howard?"

"What can I say? I would not have minded having some of it."

Spencer did not have his man. That much was obvious. As a matter of procedure, Spencer would check out his alibi, but he had no doubt it was good.

They sat for a while longer. The floor was washed. The bill came and was paid. Their table had long been cleared. *He looks as exhausted as I feel,* thought Spencer, feeling pain behind his eyes that wanted desperately to close and wake up back on Long Island with all this behind them or in front of them. It really didn't matter, as long as it wasn't *around* them. Spencer made a mental promise to himself as soon as this was all over to go and visit his family. Maybe for Christmas.

"I think they were from Connecticut," Howard finally said.

Spencer remembered the *Greenwich Time* he had found in Kristina's closet. Getting up, he said, "Thank you for coming, Howard."

"Yes, of course. When do you think the body will be released?"

"Tomorrow. You can get her tomorrow. I'm going back to the hospital now, to talk to the coroner."

Spencer was expecting Howard to say he wanted to come, but Howard didn't. He looked spent. Spencer was also spent, but he had to go. It was worse than sitting on the Long Island Expressway looking for speeders. In those days, he had been the speeders' friend because he used to go to sleep. But now he had to keep moving in spite of how he felt.

He left Howard at the Inn and got into his car. It was well after midnight. Will was at the hospital, wanting to be home with his family. Ray was home with his family, wanting to be at the hospital. Nutty old Ray wanted to be down in the coroner's quarters looking at decomposed corpses. Would Innis even be able to tell if Kristina had first died and then frozen?

"Yes," said the doctor in answer to Spencer's question. Though the autopsy anteroom was forty-three degrees, Earl Innis was sweating profusely and frequently wiped his wet forehead with the sleeve of his white lab coat. It wasn't *totally* white, but Spencer didn't want to think about that. Will had gone home as soon as Spencer came to relieve him.

"Yes?"

"Yes," Innis said. "The answer is yes. She did not die of natural causes."

"Doctor, I would say freezing to death is not dying of natural causes."

"She did not freeze to death. She died, and then froze."

"Really?"

"Yes. Did you want a different answer?"

"No, that's exactly the answer I expected."

"Well, you were right. Congratulate your instincts."

Spencer waited. The doctor did not offer any details, standing in the anteroom to the autopsy quarters, a small hospital-white area with glass windows, glass doors, and fluorescent lights. A cold room.

Coughing, Spencer said, "Dr. Innis, umm, the cause of death?"

"Ah, yes. Would you like to see?"

Spencer shook his head violently. "No."

"Fine." The doctor began to take off his soiled gloves. Spencer was repulsed.

The doctor did not speak until the gloves were off and in the garbage container. Spencer felt better.

The doctor said, "Death by asphyxiation. She was smothered."

Spencer couldn't even say he was surprised. He had been saying those words in his head for the past twenty-four hours. The doctor's verdict was but a hollow echo of his own thoughts. Having seen nothing, having felt nothing, having not cut through any flesh or watched or smelled any part of a young woman's corpse, Spencer had thought, death by suffocation.

"I can't say I'm surprised," he said finally.

Dr. Innis raised his eyebrows. "No? Perhaps you should also be a medical examiner, Detective O'Malley. You seem too cynical to be in your line of work. A young woman dies and you immediately suspect foul play? Hope you haven't shared your thoughts with anyone. In a court of law, the defense will say I was but a pawn in your hands."

Spencer smiled wanly. "Weren't you, doctor?"

Dr. Innis didn't find that amusing. "Do you want to know what happened to her, or not?"

"Yes, yes, of course," said Spencer. "Tell me."

"The subdural matter around the brain showed signs of muscle-fiber softening, which began before she froze. If she just fell asleep in the snow, her brain would not decompose until her body temperature was too low to sustain bodily functions, so by the time she died she'd be nearly frozen anyway. No, she died, and then froze—fast but not fast enough to stop the supersensitive brain tissue from deteriorating. Normally, losing a degree and a half per hour, she'd cool to the temperature of the environment in twenty-four hours and start to lose rigor in another six or so. But it's freezing cold, the wind-chill factor must have been well below zero Fahrenheit. I remember that night. The papers said it was the coldest night in seventy years. So now she's losing more like a degree and a half *a minute*. She must have cooled to the temperature of her environment in an hour. *Voilà*—no rigor, no decomposition, and the lividity in her back is mild when you consider she'd been lying prone for nine days. Anyway, freezing slowed the more advanced dying process in the brain but didn't stop it. During the past twenty-four hours while the rest of the body thawed and decomposed, the brain was achieving . . . skeletal decomposition, so to speak."

Innis seemed satisfied he had to explain all that to Spencer, who nodded politely but hadn't heard anything he didn't already know. "I see. That makes sense. Anything else?"

"Yes. A telltale sign of suffocation."

"The eyes?" said Spencer.

"Yes, how did you know? Did you know what to look for?"

Yes, a dead naked girl with black boots and nine million dollars, and stuck in the middle of a jealous quadrangle. I'm real good at finding that. Spencer shook his head. "No, not really." He wanted not to show how upset he was.

"Yes, the eyes," said Innis. "The capillaries were broken. Broken from the pressure on the head that is caused by the severe pressure on the pulmonary artery in the neck and the absence of oxygen from the head for a time long enough to cause cessation of the functioning of the parasympathetic system and subsequent heart failure. The pressure on the eyes was so great they actually hemorrhaged up into the temporal lobes. You sure you don't want to see?"

Spencer was hurting. "Someone with great strength?" he said, his voice breaking.

"No, not at all. She was trying very hard to breathe. She fought for every last breath. The effort nearly ruptured her pulmonary artery."

"Yeah," Spencer said, struggling to speak normally. "She just couldn't fight him off."

"Do you know it's a him, detective? No, she couldn't fight. Her left shoulder was severely incapacitated."

"Yes, yes." Spencer nodded. "That was from the day before. She'd been in an accident."

"Well, that explains some of the injuries—they looked a little old. She had a broken right rib, and a cranial contusion. I'm surprised she was able to function. Did she go to the hospital?"

"No. She didn't want to."

Dr. Innis wiped his brow. "Too bad. It would've saved her life."

"How do you figure?"

"Because the hospital would've never let her out. The shoulder especially. That shoulder was an awful mess. She would've required surgery on it—she had an infected multiple fracture."

Spencer was unable to speak.

Dr. Innis looked as pleased as if he'd just found the killer, not told Spencer that Kristina was weak.

"She was in bad shape," Innis said. "Which is why anyone, including my seven-year-old granddaughter, could've overpowered her. She couldn't struggle except with her right hand."

"Do you think," Spencer asked haltingly, "that she struggled? There are no marks on her."

The doctor smiled. "That's where you're wrong, detective. You do need the state medical examiner, after all. And I thought I might be out of a job with you knowing all you know and still nodding away there. There *are* marks on her. There's a large wound at the back of her head, on the occipital lobe. Slight subdural hematoma. She probably lost consciousness."

"She was hit?" Spencer exclaimed. God, Will was right, it was a rape-murder.

"Maybe. I think she was pushed, or she fell."

"Fell?"

"Yes. She could've been backing away, tripped and fallen, hit her head on a log, a stone. It wasn't a sharp object, it didn't penetrate the skin, but there was bruising. This is just my theory, you understand. Or she was shoved. She fell, hit her head, became dazed, maybe unconscious for a few seconds. From then on it was easy. There are two symmetrical marks on the insides of her upper arms and two marks on her chest, just above the thoracic cavity. Contusions with broken blood vessels below the skin. What does that tell you, detective?"

Spencer thought about it for a moment. "Someone sat on her arms and chest. Knee marks."

"Exactly. Knee marks. Now, this girl, she was fighting for her life, trying to breathe—"

Spencer interrupted, "What was she suffocated with? A hand?"

"No, no, that would have left a nice imprint on her face. No, it was a large, absorbent object. There are no specific points of pressure from fingers on her face. Maybe a pillow? Any twelve-inch-square pillow would do."

Spencer couldn't look at the doctor.

"Detective O'Malley," Innis said, his manner becoming gentler, "I found something under her nails. Her killer might have been scratched up, gouged."

"What was under her fingernails?"

"Blood," replied the doctor. "Small hair fibers."

"Ahh. Why didn't you say so?"

"I was waiting for you to ask."

"What color hair?"

"I did not examine it that closely, detective. I have a microscope, though. Would you like to take a look yourself?"

Spencer almost said yes. But what did he know about hair samples?

"Do you have a sample for me to compare it against?" asked Innis.

Spencer almost said yes, and then stopped. They were just three stupid kids. He shook his head, and then thought of something. "Are you ruling out it was a female?"

"I never rule anything out, detective, unless I'm absolutely sure."

241

"Well, a female couldn't have raped her."

"Who said anyone raped her?"

"She wasn't raped?"

"No."

"No? You're sure? You're absolutely sure?"

"Am I sure?" Innis chuckled. "This is my job. Do I ask you if you're sure how to write a ticket, or interrogate a suspect? She wasn't sexually assaulted, there is no tearing of her vaginal walls, there's no sperm—"

"He could've used a condom," Spencer said.

"Who? The killer? What, before he raped her, he could've said, excuse me while I put this on? Very thoughtful of him. Did he ask her to hold the pillow while he was adjusting the rubber, or did he put the pillow under her bruised head for added comfort? No, detective, I already told you, whatever the motive was, sex wasn't it."

Spencer wished it had been. He couldn't believe it, but he was wishing she had been brutalized by a total stranger.

Bowing his head, Spencer said, "I'll give you something to work with as far as hair and blood samples."

"Oh, you have something? Good. I'll get it to the lab."

"Which lab do you mean, the DNA lab in Cellmark? In South Carolina? Why, that takes months!" Spencer exclaimed.

"We'll do a simpler blood and hair test in Concord."

"How long will that take?"

"You're very impatient, Detective O'Malley. A minute ago you didn't have a case."

"That's where you're wrong, doctor. I've had a case since yesterday. I just didn't have any evidence. How long?"

Dr. Innis thought about it. "A few days. Maybe a week."

"Faster than that."

"Detective, New Hampshire is a state of a million people and has only one medical examiner—me. Hanover is a town of ten thousand. You'll wait."

Spencer bit his lip but would not raise his voice at the coroner. "Was she drunk?"

"Drunk?" Dr. Howard said, panting, surprised. "Why do you say that?"

"Was she?"

"I don't think so. I mean, I won't know till the blood work comes back, but there was nothing in her stomach, completely empty."

Nodding, Spencer said, "When will you know for sure?" But he would have bet his paycheck the last time in her life Kristina Sinclair Kim walked the wall, she was sober.

"I told you, detective-sergeant," Dr. Innis panted. "A few days."

"All right. Is the death certificate ready?"

"You'll have to wait for me to fill it out. I just finished with her."

Spencer sat down in one of the chairs, muttering, "I'm doing a lot of waiting at two in the morning, aren't I?"

Dr. Innis heard him, because he turned around and said, "And I'm still working at two in the morning, detective."

"As am I, doctor," said Spencer.

"No, Detective O'Malley, now you're just waiting." And with that he left and Spencer was alone in the cold, stark room.

He was tired and his thoughts drifted, wandering to Kristina, walking backward in the snow, down the slope, why would she get off the path? And then, she's pushed, and falls, and can't breathe, she's trying to fight, but she can't breathe. Spencer's heart was aching. He tried to think of something else, of Howard Kim, of his marrying a girl he didn't know to live in America. Marrying Kristina Sinclair and taking her father's money. Where was Katherine Morgan Sinclair now? Address unknown. Spencer thought about John Henry Sinclair. Had he taken his own life? It seemed likely, with his only daughter in a scandal. But what could be worse than a sixteen-year-old marrying an Asian man she'd never met and moving to New York? Maybe he really had died of heart failure. Spencer's own heart was weakening just trying to wade through the muck. Spencer needed to find Katherine Morgan Sinclair.

Kristina, Kristina . . . did you fight? Did you rage and scream into the good night, did you flail and gasp for your every last halting breath? Were you surprised by death?

Spencer drifted off, his head drooping to the side, and was awakened some time later by Dr. Innis, who held a manila envelope under his arm.

"Here it is," he said mildly. Spencer started, rubbed his eyes. He felt like shit, heavy-lidded and drained. Dr. Innis, on the other hand, looked refreshed and alert. He wasn't sweating anymore and he wasn't panting. He even had a glow to his cheeks. This man must thrive on cutting people open in the middle of the night, thought Spencer. There is a word for night creatures like that. Anne Rice wrote about them.

"I did a preliminary analysis of her blood," the doctor said. "I was right. There was no alcohol in her system at all."

Spencer nodded, his eyes burning. "What time is it?"

"Five-thirty," the doctor replied. "You should go home and get some sleep. I'll have the lab work for you by Monday, all right? You can hang in there till Monday, can't you?"

"What choice do I have?" said Spencer, standing up and reaching out for the death certificate. Dr. Innis pulled his hand back. "It's not ready. I can't figure out the time of death. No rigor, no decomposition until yesterday in the morgue, no stomach contents. Also the photographs and x-rays are not ready to go in the case file. I'll send everything to your office Monday."

Spencer felt as if he had cotton in his mouth and cotton for a brain. "Don't worry about the time of death," Spencer said groggily. "We know when she died. Put down between one-ten and one-thirty in the morning on Wednesday, November twenty-fourth, 1993."

"You're sure about this?"

"Yes. Last time someone saw her alive was fifty yards from the scene of death at one-oh-five."

"I see. She could've died much later."

"No. She was completely naked and it was cold. She would've turned around and come back home. I'm certain she never returned from the woods."

"Yes, you're right, you're right. Fine. Between one-ten and one-thirty it is." Innis scribbled something on the manila envelope. "By the way. It wasn't human hair under her nails. Probably dog hair."

"Oh," said Spencer. He was too tired even to be disappointed. "Just do the blood work for us, okay?" It was too much for him at five-thirty in the morning. He had been up on his feet for twenty-one hours. It felt like a hundred and twenty-one.

Spencer went home to Hanover. It was still dark out, but the sky had taken on the metallic hue of a winter sunrise. Spencer let himself in and looked at his chair, but it was too late, or too early, to think about sitting down in it. Too late, or too early, to eat or to drink whiskey. Spencer took off his big brown boots and his socks, and then looked in his empty refrigerator. He wanted to close the curtains, but it was morning. He went into the bedroom, wanting to think about everything, wanting to think about the blood under the long red nails, wanted to think about the knee marks, about Kristina, about her letters, about Howard, whom she had married, and Albert, whom she had loved, and Red Leaves House, which was probably going to end up with her fortune. Instead, he fell on the bed and was asleep in an instant.

———————

At ten-thirty Saturday morning, Spencer jumped up from the bed as if his military commander were walking through a barracks inspection and he had been caught napping. Then he realized the phone was ringing.

Will was calling to see if he was coming in today.

"I'm in the middle of a murder investigation. Of course I'm coming in."

"Okay. Because I'm already at the station. I'm only going to be here for a little while longer. Innis faxed us a copy of the death certificate. Very interesting."

"Yeah, I'd say interesting."

"Rules out a rapist."

"You could say that."

"We better check out those kids again. Don't you think?"

"Absolutely," said Spencer.

"Have you seen the papers, Trace?"

"No, you know," said Spencer, "I haven't had time."

"Don't be snide. You should pick one up if you can. Kristina is front-page news everywhere. They're all saying it was a rapist."

"Perfect," said Spencer. "In their ignorance, they'll print anything." He asked Will to call Frankie Absalom in Boston and ask him to return to Dartmouth immediately, and also to ask Frankie if anyone could vouch for his whereabouts at Feldberg the night of Kristina's death.

"What, you think maybe Frankie killed her?" asked Will.

"What do we know? We've never met this Frankie. Somebody killed her, why not him?"

"Motive, Trace?"

"Bring him in and we'll find out."

"Yes. I think we should check out the alibis of her friends, don't you think?"

"What alibis?"

Will didn't say anything.

"Will, listen, go to Feldberg Library, to the second floor, and ask any of the students there if they were studying late the night of November twenty-third."

"Well, it's only ten-thirty. I don't think any students are awake this early on Saturday," Will replied. "And I already talked to a bunch of kids at Feldberg, and all the kids who were out there when we found her. All fifteen of them."

"Yes?"

"Yes what?"

"Yes, I don't know. Like, yes, I saw a white male Caucasian, five-eleven, hundred and seventy pounds, shove her down, sit on top of her, and smother her."

"O'Malley, you're describing yourself."

"Will, go to Safety on Campus and have them put up some posters."

"To say what?" asked Will. "Wanted: Dead or Alive. Kristina Kim's killer."

"Yes, exactly. Or, if you can't swing that, reward money for any information leading to the arrest, blah, blah, blah."

"Reward money? Where do you think you are, New York?"

"Come on, we must have something in the budget."

"Yeah, your salary. I'll talk to the comptroller. I doubt it, though. Besides, you forget, these are rich Dartmouth students. You think they'll talk for two hundred bucks?"

"I was thinking more like two thousand."

Will laughed.

"Do what you can and I'll talk to you later," said Spencer.

"What are you up to today?"

"Me? I'm going to take a drive with Albert Maplethorpe."

"Sounds like fun. Can I come?"

"No, that's okay. Then I'm going to go to Red Leaves House. Talk to the woman who runs it. Want to come there?"

"No, thanks. Come noon and I'm going home till Monday. We don't have any blood work back yet. Or fingerprints."

Spencer grunted. "You know, in New York, the blood work on a homicide case comes back in two hours."

"Yeah, well, where's New York when we need it?"

Spencer wanted to hang up. It was already ten forty-five. The day was short.

"The prosecutor's office called," Will said.

"What took them so long?"

"They were short-staffed and busy—"

"Will," said Spencer tiredly. "It was a rhetorical question."

Will continued, "—but then they saw the coroner's report. All of a sudden it's a capital case."

"It was a capital case from word go," snapped Spencer.

"Well, you know, no blood, no struggle marks—but they wanted to know if you wanted them to send their own investigators—"

"Only if they want me to quit," replied Spencer.

"Spence, there you go again. They're only there to help."

"Yeah, to take over."

"To help. To find the killer. You know?"

"No," said Spencer. "What else?"

Will paused. "If we have a warrant for anyone's arrest yet."

"Yeah, tell them, my mother. I have a warrant out for my mother. She killed Kristina. What are they, kidding?" Spencer couldn't believe it.

"The DA asked if we have any suspects."

"Yes, call them back and tell them four thousand Dartmouth students and one hundred furloughed prisoners."

"Spencer, they're just trying to—"

"I know what they're trying to do," Spencer interrupted. "Call Innis, ask him to hurry on the blood work. And Landers too—the prints."

"Innis and Landers said by Monday."

"God! Is this usual—taking the weekend off during a murder investigation?"

"The labs are booked solid in Concord."

"Oh, yeah, I forgot, Thanksgiving is notorious for inciting felonies," Spencer said and hung up.

The phone rang immediately. "Just wanted to ask," said Will. "I didn't see the contents of her safety-deposit box."

"I entered them as evidence yesterday," said Spencer.

"That's not what I asked," said Will.

"Yes. Don't worry. Okay?" And Spencer hung up for the second time.

He showered, then dressed in khaki pants and a dark blue sweater. He strapped on the tan leather holster with his short-barreled Magnum in it. Looked in vain for Nescafé instant. Andie O'Malley never had had time to teach him how to use her coffeepot, though he kept it on the counter as a souvenir. Spencer got a can of Coke and sat down at his kitchen table. He swiped the old newspapers to the floor and emptied out the contents of Kristina's safety-deposit box.

He sifted through carefully. He was looking for something from her father and something from or to Albert. He was just looking, just feeling her be alive amid the papers.

There were her grandmother's letters, lamenting all the troubles, missing Kristina, missing the kids playing together at the lake.

Spencer looked at the photo of pre-adolescent Kristina holding a kite; she looked extremely neat and well attended to, her hair was short and brushed, she was smiling, and behind her was Long Island Sound. Between her and the sound was a low stone wall, and there was a stretch of beach. The time looked late autumn—the leaves had gone. Kristina looked very happy, smiling broadly at the photographer.

Greenwich, Spencer thought. Greenwich, Connecticut.

The phone rang again. Will had found some reward money in the budget and was about to ask the college to put up posters around the administrative buildings, libraries, and dormitories.

"How much money?"

"Five hundred bucks," said Will with emphasis, as if five hundred bucks were five hundred thousand bucks.

"Oh," said Spencer widening his eyes. "Oh, good. Well, if that doesn't get us the killer, nothing will."

Spencer continued looking through Kristina's things. He found nothing from her father. She must have thrown out his letter telling her she was no longer his daughter.

On the back of one of her grandmother's letters, he found a note addressed to *Dearest Albert.*

Spencer quickly picked it up. The letter on the front was of no consequence; the note to Albert had nothing to do with the grandmother's letter. *Dearest Albert,* the note read,

> *Please, please, let not the words of George Bernard Shaw apply to you—*
> *She makes you*
> *Will*
> *Your own destruction.*
>
> > *Love, Rocky.*

Spencer read the words over and over and over until he had them indelibly committed to memory. But they didn't make any sense, not the first time, not the hundredth time.

The note was written on the back of an old letter, hidden by envelopes and pictures and napkins, almost as if it weren't meant for anyone eyes but Albert's.

"Well, come on, Albert," said Spencer aloud, getting up and taking the letter. "It's showtime."

Spencer drove to Hinman Hall. It was one-thirty on a gray and cloudy December afternoon.

Albert was alone in his room. They nodded to each other politely. "Do you have a few minutes? I'd like you to take a ride with me," said Spencer. "I want to show you something."

"Sure," said Albert, putting on his leather jacket. "I'm glad to cooperate in any way I can."

"Can we take Aristotle?" Spencer asked.

"Rather not. He's a pain."

"He's a good dog. I'd like to take him."

Shrugging, Albert said, "Sure, go ahead."

They drove. Spencer made a right on West Wheelock, and drove across the river—the natural state line between New Hampshire and Vermont—across Interstate 91, through a quaint and tiny Vermont town called Norwich, and up the two-lane road, through the bare trees, through the snow, up the hill, past the farms and the whitewashed colonials.

"Where we going?" asked Albert pleasantly.

"You've never taken this way? To Thetford Hill?"

"This way to where?" said Albert, less genially.

"There's a little hilltop retreat around here somewhere. I'd like to show it to you."

They drove the rest of the way in silence. Aristotle panted in the back.

"Here, we turn here," said Spencer, making a left. "Recognize this place, Albert?"

"No," Albert said sullenly.

"Hmm. The dog sure recognizes it." It was true, the Lab was beside himself. His tail became an animate object.

Shrugging, Albert said, "Aristotle was Kristina's dog."

Spencer watched the dog as they drove up the hill on a dirt road. The first house did not excite him. He was staring straight ahead and panting. At the top of the hill there was a clearing with two wood country houses right in front of the Vermont hills.

Spencer parked and got out of the car. "Nice view," he said. "Very peaceful."

Albert said nothing. He too got out of the car, and stood mutely by the door. Aristotle became wild, running from house to house and barking.

"Happy dog," said Spencer.

"Yes, happy," echoed Albert.

Spencer turned to him. "Do you recognize this place?" he said.

"No," said Albert.

"Really? Let's go in and check the guest book, shall we?"

Albert didn't say anything, and Spencer watched him carefully before he repeated, "Shall we?"

"Yes, let's," said Albert and headed for the house closer to the top of the hill. He walked ahead of Spencer up the steep stairs and opened the door. Thoughtfully and slowly, Spencer followed.

The guest book was on a low dividing wall next to the door. The house inside was homey and warm, decorated in wood and books and corrugated iron. There were throw rugs on the floor and comfortable chairs. Books were everywhere. When Spencer called to inquire about Fahrenbrae, he had found out that the mother of the owner was a librarian in a local town. She obviously wanted to pass her love of books to all the people who stayed in her homes.

"Have a look," said Albert.

Spencer did. He went through the guest book as far as last summer. There was no Kristina Kim, or Kristina Sinclair, and there was no Albert Maplethorpe. That there was no Kristina, Spencer was not surprised about. He read all the names again, more carefully, and still nothing.

"Satisfied?" said Albert.

Spencer didn't like that. "Yes, very," he said. "Tell me one thing, though," he asked, slamming shut the guest register. "If you've never been here and this is all new to you, how did you know you could just walk right in without needing a key? How did you know the place wasn't locked?"

Albert was startled for a moment, only a moment, but it was all that Spencer needed to see. Albert was lying.

Laughing lightly, Albert said, "Look, this is Vermont, for God's sake, not New York. Everyone knows you can just walk in here, no one has keys. People are very trusting here."

"Yeah, right," said Spencer.

"What did you bring me here for, detective? Certainly not to read a guest book?"

"You want to talk here or would you like to be brought back to the police station and talk there?"

When Albert remained silent, Spencer said, "I thought so."

"What would you like to talk about?" Albert said. He put his hands inside his leather jacket pockets and smiled warmly. His black eyes were shining. Outside, Aristotle, unmindful of the cold, was trying to dig a tunnel under a wide oak.

"Tell me about Kristina."

"What about her?"

Spencer had to put all his feelings aside to ask Albert his question. It was so cozy inside the house, he almost wanted to light a fire and forget about the dead.

"Tell me," Spencer said, "did you love her?"

Albert stared at him for a moment and then, unfazed, said, "What are you talking about?"

"You should've told me," said Spencer. "You should've told me about you and her. When we last spoke, you should've."

"There's nothing to tell," said Albert, looking right at Spencer.

"Albert, did you deny her in her life, too? Why are you denying her in death? Be a man. She's dead. And she loved you so much. Why are you lying to me?"

Bowing his head, Albert said, much quieter, "I'm not lying."

"Oh, please." Spencer shook his head, disbelieving and fed up. "Things aren't looking good for you, not for you, not for Jim, not for Conni. Your friend Frankie, they're looking terrible for him—he's disappeared."

Albert just stood and watched the dog running in the clearing.

Finally, Albert, struggling with every syllable, spoke. "I didn't tell you because . . ."

"Yes?"

"Because," Albert finished, "it's a terrible situation."

"Couldn't agree more."

"No. I mean, Kristina is dead, but Conni is not dead. Jim is not dead."

"And you—you aren't dead."

"Oh, really?" Albert said in a shaken voice, stirring grief inside Spencer. "What's alive about me?"

Spencer thought about it. Albert was breathing—that seemed alive. Albert wasn't naked, he wasn't forgotten in the snow for nine days by his closest friends. She was a popular All-Ivy beautiful girl, and when she died, no one had come looking for her. Spencer's eyes hurt at the injustice. Or maybe just at the lack of sleep.

As if reading Spencer's mind, Albert said, "I don't need to be brought to justice. I'm tormented every day."

"Tormented!" exclaimed Spencer scornfully.

Albert shook his head, and his face was ashen. "Tormented," he whispered. His hands were shaking as he tried to get the cigarette into his mouth. "This impossible thing," he said, fumbling with a Marlboro. "We had this impossible love." Glancing at Spencer, he said, "I couldn't deny her in real life, and I'm not denying her in death. I just don't want to hurt Conni, I don't want to hurt Jim."

Spencer raised his hands as if to shake Albert and then put them back down. "Albert! Conni knows it's true. Jim knows it's true. I know it's true, and I hardly know you—"

"You don't know me at all," said Albert.

"Oh, I know you a lot better than you think I do."

"I don't think so, detective."

"Did you and Kristina go to Edinburgh together?"

"Not together," Albert said, blowing on his hands, cigarette dangling from his mouth. "But yes, we went to Edinburgh. We were both philosophy majors. We went on an exchange program."

"I see. Edinburgh meant a lot to Kristina."

"Yes."

"Kristina saved matchbooks from the places you used to stay in and napkins from the pubs you used to go to."

"She did?"

What was that in his voice? Regret? Tenderness? Worry? Albert was impenetrable.

"Albert, you can't stand here and pretend that Conni didn't know."

"I don't think she did."

"Really? Then why would she run out into a blizzard at one in the morning, desperately looking for you?"

"Sometimes she gets . . . overwrought. Conni is a very passionate person," Albert said.

"Passionate? Overwrought? She was frantic! Friends don't elicit this reaction in girlfriends. Lies do, lovers do. Deceit, betrayal. Did you betray Conni?"

"I betrayed nobody, I'm telling you. Nobody."

"Will Conni think you didn't betray her?"

"Yes, I think so. What are you getting at, anyway?"

"Listen," Spencer said. "You're so used to lying about you and Kristina, you don't know when to stop. I'm telling you, stop. Now. You're really pissing me off."

They walked outside and were now near an old hammock covered with snow. Albert visibly shivered and zipped up his jacket. Then he sighed. "Look, I'm not lying. I feel terrible about the whole thing."

Spencer let out a silent internal sigh of frustration. Here, the mountains, the snow, the valley lying below them, it was all so beautiful. Why didn't he feel relief, why didn't he feel at peace? Why did being here bring on feelings that were too intense to deal with in front of this stranger whom he was liking less every minute?

"Albert, what kind of a person are you? What kind of people were you and Kristina? It's obvious Conni's in love with you. And Jim loved Kristina—"

Albert snorted. Spencer went on, "Why would you just shit on them like that? Why? Why didn't you just break up with them and go out with each other?"

"Because we were all friends and we wanted to stay friends. Besides, Kristina and I were all wrong for each other. Detective O'Malley, listen, I am going to have to live with this the rest of my life. I'm trying to make it up to Conni, I'm trying to be a good friend to Jim, I'm trying to put all this behind us. Kristina and I just couldn't free ourselves from each other, but she's dead now, and it's all over. I have to take care of the living."

"The living, huh?" Spencer remembered the blood under Kristina's nails and the scratch on Conni's cheek.

"Let me ask you, Albert," Spencer said sharply. "When you were *all* still *living,* do you think it was possible for Conni to get so bent out of shape about you and Kristina that she went after her and killed her?"

Albert looked profoundly startled. "Detective, I—" he stammered. "I don't know—of course not—I mean, what are you talking about? Of course not."

"Of course not? There was blood found under Kristina's nails. I'm not going to jump to any conclusions. I'm going to wait till Monday, then I'll jump to all of them."

"Blood?" Albert became agitated. "Well, so? It's probably nothing."

"Albert, your lover has been murdered. Nothing is nothing."

Albert tried to light another cigarette, but his hands were shaking too much. "No, detective, no. I'm sure . . . I'm sure, it's just . . . really, just nothing. Believe me."

"Albert, did Conni kill Kristina? Are you covering up for her too?"

"No! Of course not, of course . . ." He trailed off. The cigarette fell into the snow. "God . . . I don't know what's going on."

"I'll tell you what's going on—you drove her crazy by your lies. Any sane person would crack."

"I didn't drive her crazy! And she didn't crack—we got engaged Thanksgiving."

"That's very convenient. What about Kristina?"

"I told you, Kristina and I . . . we were over, we were trying to be over. She didn't want to continue behind everybody's back, she just . . . she knew Conni and I were getting engaged. It was over."

"Why didn't you stay with Kristina?"

Albert didn't answer at first. "I told you, detective," Albert said quietly, sadly. "We were wrong for each other."

"Why?" And who the hell even thought about these things? thought Spencer. Wrong for each other? They were in college, for God's sake.

"Jim and Kristina were much better suited. He was going places. He was good for her."

"Are you? Going places? Better suited to Conni?"

"I don't know. Never thought about it, really."

"You haven't thought about it? How long have you and Conni been together?"

"Three years, about."

"And you haven't thought about whether you're good for her?" Spencer said incredulously.

"You know," said Albert acidly, "I guess I stopped thinking about it when I realized I wasn't good for anybody." His voice was dry and scratchy.

"Anybody? You mean not good for Kristina."

"Look! We were both broke, I didn't know what I wanted to do with my life, and she wanted stability, a career, a decent life. We just wanted completely different things."

"You were both broke? Well, you got that wrong, didn't you?"

"Obviously," said Albert sarcastically.

"She never told you she was going to inherit any money?"

"No, she did not."

"Don't you think that's strange? Your lover doesn't tell you she's going to become a millionaire?"

"Yes, I think it's very strange. But she didn't."

"I wonder why not."

"I don't know. Why don't you ask her?"

Spencer eyed Albert coldly. He pulled out Kristina's note and shoved it in Albert's face. "Tell me, does this make any sense to you?"

Albert backed away to try to read it. "What is this?" he said.

"I don't know. Kristina left her safety deposit box contents to you. Too bad for you she was killed and everything in it is now evidence for the state. What does this mean?"

"How the hell do I know?"

"She makes you will your own destruction. What is she talking about?"

"Haven't a clue."

"Did she put special emphasis on 'will' the way she wrote it?"

Glancing at the note again, Albert said, "I really have no idea."

"Kristina made a point of writing this to you on the back of an old letter. She dated it—look." November 23, 1993, the date read. "She addressed it to you and she pleaded that these words not apply to you. What does it mean?"

"Detective, how do I know?" Albert laughed thinly. "Kristina was an odd person sometimes."

"Yes, 'odd' would be one way to describe her. 'Dead' would be another."

Albert lowered his head. "Yes. Dead."

Spencer stuffed the note back into his jacket pocket. Albert said, "Can I have that?"

"Certainly not. *She makes you will your own destruction.* I want these words to make sense to me."

"Me too," said Albert.

Spencer became quiet and waited. Albert said nothing. Something else was bugging Spencer. "Tell me again how you met her," he asked.

"I told you, we had a class together."

"Class together," Spencer repeated. He became acutely aware of his chattering teeth. "When was that?"

"In our first semester, I told you."

Nodding, Spencer said, "Dartmouth. Nice college. Expensive, though. And you've got no family. How are you paying for this?"

"Scholarships, grants, loans."

Spencer stroked his face thoughtfully. "How is a philosophy major going to repay Dartmouth eighty grand?"

"I don't think I owe them eighty grand."

"No, you most certainly don't," said Spencer, and hoped that Albert heard the sarcasm in his voice. "How much *do* you owe them?"

"I don't know."

"Probably a lot?"

"Probably."

"Well, that money from Kristina—"

"What money from Kristina?" Albert interrupted rudely.

"Let me finish. That money from Kristina's accounts—your share would've come to over three million dollars. Would've nicely covered your debts. Don't you think?"

"Yes. I didn't want her money, though."

"I see. You're proud. Is that a recent thing?"

"What are you talking about?"

"What am I talking about? Do I look like an idiot to you?"

"No," said Albert, staring hard at Spencer.

"No, I think you take me for a real idiot."

"This is getting out of hand."

Coming closer to Albert, Spencer said through gritted teeth, "She paid your tuition, Albert. She paid it, and you don't owe the college a damn penny."

Albert didn't reply. The wind howled off the Vermont hills. The dog was lying in the snow, chewing on a stick. It was very quiet. No wonder she liked to come here, Spencer thought. But with *him*?

"What if . . . she did?" Albert said finally. "What if she did? There is no law against that."

"No, but there is one against lying to a police officer."

Silence.

"You think I'm an idiot?" said Spencer.

"No!"

Spencer said, raising his voice, "Albert, she paid for your tuition the very first year you were at Dartmouth."

"So?"

"Albert," Spencer said slowly, "she paid for your freshman tuition. How could she have paid for it if you only met in the freshman year?"

Albert didn't answer. Then he raised his eyes and stared at Spencer, who felt a chill run down his back. He was sure it had nothing to do with the weather. All of a sudden Spencer understood that he could die any moment, right now, right here, in the middle of the snow-covered mountains, and Aristotle sure as hell wouldn't be digging *him* up with his paws.

How could he have been so careless and come to a deserted place with someone he didn't know? He came without backup, without any knowledge of what or who he was dealing with. Spencer realized that while he was certainly going through the motions of an investigation, he was not taking any of Kristina's friends seriously.

Albert must have read his mind, because his cold brown eyes got colder as he said, "Don't worry, now. I didn't kill her and I won't hurt you." He paused. "Did you get scared there? Did you think that if I was backed into a corner, I might just strike out at you?" He laughed loudly. "Don't worry, Detective O'Malley. I'm not in any corner I do not want to be in. You're right, we did know each other briefly before we came to Dartmouth. I can tell you all about it, but I don't see how it has anything to do with Kristina's death."

"That's not for you to ask or decide, Albert," said Spencer.

"You're right. What do I know? I'm only a philosophy major."

You're a liar, too, thought Spencer. "Let's go," he said roughly.

Albert started to walk to the car and then stopped. "Wait a minute," he said. "Hold on. I'll be right back."

"You're not going anywhere."

"Wait. I just have to get something."

"No, Albert. You won't."

"I'll be right back," he said, and started to walk toward the house.

In an instant, Spencer was in front of him. "Albert. I said no, and I mean it. No. I don't know what you're going to get up there, and you aren't getting it."

Albert stared him down, not moving away, not flinching, not blinking. "Detective O'Malley, I want to get her coat," he said patiently, slowly, his black eyes flashing. "Kristina left her coat here and I want to get it for her. Come with me, if you want."

"Albert, don't make me arrest you. I'll gladly have you spend the night in jail."

But the words didn't have the same effect on Albert that they had had on Jim. Albert wasn't going into a career in politics. Albert didn't look as if he cared if he spent a night in jail, and his words bore Spencer out. "Detective," said Albert, "a night in jail for Kristina's coat. It's a deal."

Spencer stepped closer, pulling out his Magnum and pointing it at Albert's face. "Don't move," he said menacingly. "Turn around and walk back to my car, and get in. Don't take another step."

Albert did not back away, his steely expression fearless. "Or what, detective? Are you going to kill me?"

"Turn around and walk back, Albert," Spencer said through gritted teeth.

Albert smiled a wide-toothed, friendly smile. He and Spencer were standing four feet away from each other. Albert continued to smile. Then in one instant, his left leg flew up, knocking the Magnum out of Spencer's hands. The gun landed ten feet away.

Albert never stopped smiling. "I have a black belt in karate," he said.

Spencer stepped forward and punched Albert hard in the solar plexus, sending him down on the ground. Standing over him, Spencer grabbed Albert's arm and twisted it behind his back. "And I'm an officer of the law, you son of a bitch, and you will not threaten me, do you hear?"

Albert only panted in reply. Spencer yanked him up and, still twisting his arm up high, walked Albert quickly to the car, throwing him in the backseat. Then Spencer radioed Ray Fell to come right away.

Spencer picked up his gun and stood near the Impala, pointing the cocked Magnum at Albert.

At first they didn't speak. Albert just sat in the back, not looking at Spencer.

Through the car door, Spencer heard Albert's voice. "Good move, Detective O'Malley, but of course, if someone wanted you dead, you'd be dead already."

Spencer did not skip a beat, though his heart did. "And you'd be on your way to the chair, Mr. Maplethorpe."

Albert leaned to the window, flashing his white-toothed smile. "Who says I'd get caught?"

After thirty minutes of Spencer's standing out in the cold, Ray Fell finally came. Even Ray's car lumbered, but Spencer was glad to see him. Spencer told Ray to cock his gun and point it at Albert, and if Albert moved, to shoot him. Then he went in the house and searched every room, until he found what he was looking for in the walk-in closet in one of the bedrooms. It was the only thing in any of the closets. An old maroon cashmere coat. Spencer examined it closely—there was nothing in it.

He put the coat to his face. It smelled faintly of musk and soap. Spencer realized the coat smelled like Kristina. He put it to his face again and closed his eyes. He thought of not giving it to Albert, of keeping it for himself. He deeply breathed in the musk and the soap. It would've been safe to let Albert take it, but Spencer hadn't known that. Albert could've been hiding an Uzi in one of the closets, for all Spencer knew.

———•·•·•———

Spencer brought Albert back to the Hanover police station and, after reading him his Miranda rights, threw him in the small cell.

An hour passed. Spencer asked Albert if he wanted to make a call. Albert didn't answer at first and then said, "Look, I don't want any trouble."

"Good," said Spencer. " 'Cause you already got plenty."

"I haven't done anything wrong."

"Oh, yeah? Menacing a police officer? Hindering police investigation? You're lucky I don't bring you up on assault."

Albert looked at Spencer through the bars of the cell. "Lucky, detective?"

Spencer was so angry he accidentally knocked over a small table lamp when he bolted from the bench.

He called Will at home at eight o'clock in the evening and told him what had happened. "You're crazy," said Will. "How could you go there all alone?"

"I didn't go there alone," replied Spencer. "I went there with Albert, hoping to have a nice chat."

"I see. Is that why you now have him all locked up?"

"No, I now have him locked up for resisting me."

"What are you hoping to prove? It's Saturday night. The courts are closed, he can't get bail, he's got no money for a lawyer—"

"He should've thought of all that, shouldn't he?"

"He's a cocky kid, Spence," said Will. "So leave him. Go home. Don't worry about it."

But Spencer didn't go home; he couldn't leave him. He went back behind the offices and sat down next to Albert's single cell.

Finally Albert said, "Are you going to take the cuffs off?"

"I don't know," said Spencer. "I should probably cuff your legs, shouldn't I?"

Albert didn't answer, and after a while Spencer called him over and unlocked the cuffs. Rubbing his wrists, Albert sat back down on the bed.

Spencer said from his chair, "Give me one good reason I shouldn't keep you here till Monday morning and then charge you with Kristina Kim's death."

"I'll give you a good reason," replied Albert. "Because I didn't kill her."

"How do I know that?" said Spencer.

"Because I was sitting with some kid watching a stupid movie, that's why. Because I . . ." He paused. "I loved her, that's why." Spencer was quiet.

"Because I loved her more than anything in the whole world," continued Albert. "I would rather die than hurt her. I'd take a bullet for her. I'm not scared, detective."

"I see that," said Spencer.

They were silent. Spencer watched Albert, who sat on the cell bed and stared into his hands. "Albert, I don't understand. I just don't. Why would you be in love with Kristina and go out with Conni? I mean, what's the point?"

Albert shrugged, not looking up. "I love Conni," he said. "I'm just not *in* love with her. But she's a good person and she loves me, and there's no reason to hurt her."

"To hurt her? You don't think your not being in love with her hurts her?"

"I never kept that from her. She knows how I feel. She also knows I'd rather marry her than anybody, because she is a good person."

"A good person?" Spencer caught his breath. "Albert, do you understand what you're saying? Conni might have killed Kristina."

Albert shook his head vehemently. "No," he said. "No, that's not possible."

"If I were Conni? And you were tormenting me with your lies, and I was suspecting you were sleeping with my best friend? I would have killed her earlier. Her and you too."

Albert didn't say anything. Spencer waited. He knew he was grasping at straws. If only those three weren't going to leave the money to Red Leaves House, he thought. He'd really have something then.

But not much, Spencer realized. He didn't have an eyewitness. He didn't have a murder weapon. He didn't even have a motive. What he had was no case.

Also . . . what he had was a whole lot of emotions whirling in a frenzy around one dead girl. That was enough. That was plenty. Kristina had been killed. There had been two knees on her chest and there was blood under her nails.

Spencer was torturing Albert, and he knew it, but it was as if Albert were under Spencer's nails.

There was a time when Spencer could look at a person and know something important about him; Andie had said that was Spencer's special gift to the world. Not that he wasn't a smart man, she said, because he was, and not that he wasn't a handsome man, because he was. But Spencer Patrick O'Malley had an instinct in him like a lost wolf's. What happened to it? Spencer wondered.

"Look, I don't know anything about you," Spencer said at last. "Except that you lied to me and you struck out at me."

"I didn't strike out at you—you were pointing a gun at my face. I'm sorry about the incident up there. You just caught me off guard."

Spencer stood up. "I caught *you* off guard?" He laughed, walking toward the doors. "Good night, Albert. The night duty officer will bring you a sandwich and something to drink."

Coming toward the iron bars, Albert said, "You're going to leave me in here?"

Spencer smiled. "I thought you weren't afraid."

And with that he left and went home.

Spencer came back for Albert at seven o'clock Sunday morning. The patrolman who was watching him said to Spencer, "You know, the guy didn't lie down once. He just sat there the whole night with his head in his hands."

Spencer felt a twinge of guilt. Unlocking the cell, he opened the door and said, "Come on, Albert. Time to go."

Without saying anything, Albert got up and walked out.

"Need a ride home?" Spencer asked Albert.

Turning to Spencer, Albert said very quietly, "I need her coat, please."

Again, a twinge of guilt nagged at Spencer as he got Kristina's coat from the trunk of his Impala.

Spencer felt threatened by Albert. There was an unknown quantity to him that unsettled Spencer. Maybe because Albert wasn't afraid, and Spencer was always wary of people who weren't afraid.

They had so little to lose.

Chapter
Seven

CONSTANCE
TOBIAS

"W here have you been?" Will Baker whispered vehemently as Spencer walked in on Monday morning. "I've been looking everywhere for you."

Spencer nodded silently. "I've been . . . you know . . ." He trailed off. "I took a drive."

"A drive? Where?"

"Connecticut." Spencer paused and felt himself paling. "Will, I've got a lot to tell you. I found Kristina's mother. Katherine Sinclair."

"Who? God, Tracy! You gotta stop taking these drives in the middle of a murder investigation. First that Albert guy, now this. Plus you look like shit. What's wrong with you?"

Spencer threw his car keys on the desk. "Have you listened to a word I said, Will?"

"Very carefully. What does Kristina's mother have to do with this mess? Listen, I've got something to tell you, too."

"What's going on?" said Spencer, taking off his coat. He was unwilling to defend himself.

Will took Spencer by the arm and dragged him away into the hall. Through a partly open door, Spencer saw Frankie Absalom sitting alone in the questioning room.

"What's this?" Spencer asked. "What's going on?"

"He came back last night. I called and called you."

"What's up? He has something new to say?"

Will widened his eyes meaningfully. "He says yes. But he refused to talk to anyone but you."

Spencer made a move to go inside; Will held him back. "First the chief wants to see you."

"Immediately?"

"Sooner."

<hr />

When Spencer closed the door behind him, Ken Gallagher slammed half a dozen newspapers down on his gray Formica desk. "Tracy, where the *hell* were you yesterday?"

"I was—"

"Baker must have called your house a thousand times! Did he tell you? Franklin Absalom said he needed to speak to you urgently, and you were nowhere to be found!" Gallagher shouted the last part. "He said he wouldn't speak to anyone but you. So where the hell were you?"

"That's what I'm trying to tell you, sir—"

"So tell me! Goddammit, I thought you were conducting a murder investigation!"

"I was, and I am," said Spencer quietly. "I went to see—"

"Do you know that because of you we had to keep Absalom here overnight?"

"Why?"

"Tracy, I'm the one asking questions around here." But the chief answered him. "Because we don't know if we have a killer on our hands or what. Now where were you?"

"In Connecticut," Spencer said quickly, lest he be interrupted again.

"Why?"

"I went to talk to the dead girl's mother."

"The dead girl's *mother?*" Gallagher gasped and then fell quiet.

Spencer hurriedly continued, "Yes, sir. She is very ill, living in a convalescent wing of the Norwalk—"

"Tracy!" the chief exclaimed. "What do you think, I got quiet to listen to you? I'm goddamn speechless—I don't have time for this shit. We might have a murderer in custody and you're telling me about somebody's *mother,* for Christ's sake?"

Spencer willed himself to remain calm and persisted. "Sir, not just *somebody's* mother. The dead girl's mother. There are some very troubling th—"

"O'Malley! Perhaps I'm not making myself clear." Gallagher shoved a stack of newspapers toward Spencer. "What's this?"

"I don't know, chief," said Spencer. "What is this?"

"This, and this, and this." Gallagher was shoving the front pages in front of Spencer, banging his index finger at the cover stories. "Look. We're in every paper. Have you read this? Have you?"

Spencer looked up from the papers and quietly said, "No, sir. I've been too busy to read the newspapers. Sir."

"Don't you sir me, O'Malley!" Gallagher raised his voice. "When I left Thursday, I thought everything was under control."

"Everything is under control," said Spencer, thinking, except for me in about a minute.

"Is it? Then what's this?" Pointing to the lead story in the main local paper, Gallagher read, " 'The Hanover Police Department investigation has stalled; sources say there are no new leads and no clues in the crime.' "

Gallagher then showed Spencer similar cover stories in the *Dartmouth,* the *Concord Monitor,* the *Manchester Union Leader,* and the *Boston Globe.*

Spencer looked blankly at the chief. "So?"

"Tracy," said Gallagher ominously, "don't screw with me. I gave you this promotion, I thought you'd prove yourself—"

"Chief Gallagher!" Then Spencer lowered his voice. "I don't have *time* to prove myself." He was breathing hard. "I'm in the middle of a murder investigation. The papers have no idea. They're clueless. We're not going to be letting them in on every piece of evidence we have before we can make a formal charge. You do agree with that policy, chief, don't you?"

"O'Malley, don't patronize me. The papers are making us look bad, and this is our town. I don't want to be ridiculed by our people and by the college and by Concord because we can't do our jobs!"

"Who says we can't do our jobs?" Spencer gritted his teeth. "It's the papers who can't do their jobs."

"They're getting this information from somewhere, aren't they?"

"Yes, sir. Maybe a word with our men would be in order about discussing ongoing investigations with the press."

"Tracy, the DA's office is reading this crap, too!" Gallagher shouted. "They think we can't do our jobs either. The Dartmouth dean himself called Dave Peterson and wanted to know what was being done about finding the girl's killer."

"And the district attorney had no answer," retorted Spencer, "since he wasn't in the office. The deputy district attorney—ditto."

"Well, they were in the office this morning! I talked to Peterson; he's fuming. He's got a whole battery of people on their way here now."

Spencer thought it would be a relief to have some disinterested ADA take over the case. Spencer then could go back to driving around town and having coffee at Lou's, maybe having a meal again and going to Murphy's Tavern again. He could hibernate through the winter again, without having to think of Kristina or her broken family.

Spencer answered the chief. "Well, where were the ADAs when we really needed them? On Friday they were golfing, and on Saturday and Sunday they were having a weekend off." This was a dig at the chief himself, though Spencer didn't mention him by name. "Unlike Will and me, who have worked nonstop since Thursday."

"With no results! And I don't consider going off to Connecticut work."

Spencer felt himself getting hot. "What results do you want, chief?" he asked.

"I want the suspect apprehended."

"Well, I can certainly apprehend a suspect, sir. Immediately, if you want. Apprehending the actual killer will require more time."

Chief Gallagher shot up from the table. Spencer stood unmoving in front of him. Gallagher said nothing, Spencer did not look away. After a few seconds, Spencer bowed his head, gave a perfunctory smile and said, "If you'll excuse me, chief, I have to go and interview a witness."

"They'll be here soon, O'Malley. And then you won't have to interview anyone."

Spencer took that as a threat.

"Should I talk to Franklin Absalom or not?" he said, turning around. "Or are you taking me off the case, chief?"

"I'm not taking you off the case, O'Malley."

Will had come in and was standing quietly next to the open door. "Spencer, Peterson just called. He's apparently got some new information. He wants you to wait to question Frankie till Silas and Artell get here."

"Why?"

"We're not moving quickly enough, apparently."

"So waiting till they get here is moving faster?"

"We're not moving quickly enough," Will repeated stubbornly.

"For who?" Spencer was exasperated. "It's Monday morning and she was found Thursday afternoon."

"For the school," Gallagher said. "For Dartmouth. The dean of students and the president are getting a lot of pressure from the alumni and from the parents. A dead girl on campus, and the coroner's report clearly states it was murder. The papers have been carrying nothing but this story since Friday. Everyone's afraid it's an insane rapist."

"Did you explain to them she wasn't raped?"

"That's immaterial. They know she had had sex sometime in the last seventy-two hours of her life. In many frightened minds it's the same thing."

"Well, that's sick," Spencer said. "And it's not my fault."

"No one is saying it's your fault."

"How did the papers know about the sex, anyway?"

Will shrugged. "Someone in the coroner's office must have seen the autopsy report."

"Great. Just great," Spencer exclaimed. "Listen, I'm going to go and talk to Frankie. The ADAs can question him again if they want."

Will shook his head. Spencer walked past him, and then took five minutes to calm down near the soda machines in the adjacent fire department.

———

Spencer closed the door to the little white room behind him and stretched his hand across the round table to Frankie Absalom.

"I'm sorry you've been waiting for me so long, Frank. Or is it Frankie?"

"It's Frankie. But whatever you're comfortable with, man. I'm very relaxed about the whole thing."

Spencer sat down.

Frankie was quiet. "They kept me here overnight because I refused to talk to them. They think I did it, don't they?"

"Did you do it?"

"Of course not! Why did they have to keep me here, anyway?"

"My partner, Will, was suspicious. You should have just talked to him. He would have let you go then."

"Yeah, I guess," Frankie drew out and then fell quiet again. "You've got a cool name," he said. "Not after Spencer Tracy by any chance?"

"One and the same," said Spencer. "If I had been a girl, my mother was all set to name me Katharine."

Frankie laughed mildly. "Yeah, and my mom named me Frankie after 'Frankie and Johnny.' "

Spencer smiled. "In 'Frankie and Johnny,' Frankie was the girl."

"Isn't that just so ironic?" said Frankie.

Spencer couldn't help but laugh. Frankie had his legs on the table and was dressed in perfectly ironed loose plaid pants, a black-and-white-striped jersey, and a black cap worn backward. He looked like a bum, but a well-ironed bum.

"Frankie, could you get your feet off the table? So we can be semiserious about this."

Frankie moved his feet.

"So talk to me," said Spencer, taking a sip of hot black coffee. "Tell me."

"Just once. For you," Frankie said. "Right?"

"Frankie, you're going to have to tell your story another six times before we're done with you, and then you'll go to court, where you'll tell it once to the grand jury, once to the prosecution, and once to the defense. As a material witness, you're going to be taped, and if there are inconsistencies in your story, the defense is going to crucify you in court. So be careful, be accurate, and be honest. Tell me what happened."

Frankie lowered his voice, and his easy manner disappeared. "Well, this is the thing. I don't want to feel like a squealer here."

"Is this why you didn't come back to Dartmouth?" Spencer asked.

"Didn't come back? Oh, no, man." Nodding, he said, "Well, actually, yeah, I kind of . . . I was feeling real funny about the whole thing. I thought I'd stay home and get some perspective."

"Did you? Get some perspective?"

"Not much. Still feels like ratting on my friends. You know, the Mafia would garrote me for disloyalty."

"Frankie, this is not the Mafia, and your friends are not crime lords. There will be no garroting, I promise."

"Yeah, but I'm ratting on my friends."

"Frankie, we want to live in a universe where we are the first cog in the wheel of justice. So let's start dispensing some. Talk to me."

Frankie took his cap off, reconsidered, and then put it back on.

"You're not going to start lecturing me about good men keeping quiet while evil lives on, are you?" he asked.

"Certainly not," said Spencer. "Though I would not keep quiet."

Frankie slowly nodded. "No, I don't think you would, Detective O'Malley."

Spencer kept his eyes on Frankie. "Don't tell me you didn't tell me everything when we spoke on the phone," he said.

Frankie shook his head. "I didn't, man."

"Frankie." Spencer got up. "God! This looks bad for you. And bad for me."

"I'm sorry, I was extremely upset. You caught me off guard, calling like that. I didn't know what to do. I'm sorry, man, okay?"

Spencer sat back down. "How do I know you're going to tell me everything now?"

"Because I am. You'll see." Frankie bowed his head so far his hat nearly fell off, and he adjusted it. "Feels like ratting."

"You're doing the right thing. It's the right thing to do."

"You say that. Detective Baker said that. But it sure doesn't feel like the right thing."

"Frankie, did you kill Kristina Kim?"

"No, man, of course I didn't. What are you, kidding? I can't kill a cockroach, I'm, like, disturbed that way. Please. No."

"What happened? Did you see someone else on the bridge?"

Frankie lifted his eyes in surprise. "Yes. How did you know?"

Spencer didn't smile and got no satisfaction from knowing he was right. He was down on himself. "Was it Conni?"

"God! Yes. How did you know?"

"I suspected all along that Conni went out to find Kristina," said Spencer. "She was very vague about where she'd been, and she was gone from her room a long time. Go on, talk to me."

"Well, it's like this. When I came back from the bathroom and put my coat on to go back to my room, I looked out the window again."

"Why did you do that?"

"I wanted to see if Krissy was coming back. Or if she was walking the wall again. Or something. I just looked out the window."

"What time was that?"

"Maybe one twenty-five." Frankie lowered his head again. "I saw Conni," he said quietly. "I saw Conni walking very quickly down the bridge back to Hinman."

Leaning back and calming down, Spencer asked, "Was she alone?"

"Yes, alone."

"How was she walking?"

"Quickly."

"I mean, was she staring straight ahead, was she looking around? Was she close to running?"

"No, not any of those things. Maybe close to running."

"She wasn't staring straight ahead and she wasn't looking around?"

"I didn't notice. It didn't strike me as unusual—her head orientation. I suppose she was staring straight ahead."

"I see. Is that all you saw?"

"All. I swear." He crossed himself for emphasis.

Spencer leaned back. "My, my," he said. "We have an eyewitness."

"I didn't see her do anything, man. Nothing! That's the truth."

Spencer narrowed his eyes at Frankie. "I didn't say you did."

"Well, I didn't, no."

"Frankie, we don't have much time. The ADAs are a lot tougher than I am, and they're coming here to garrote you."

"I thought you promised no garroting, man?"

"Only if you tell me everything."

"I'm telling you everything. Everything," Frankie repeated.

"What did you think of it? Her being on the bridge?"

Frankie looked uncomfortable. There was an edge to his voice when he said, "Nothing. Should I have thought something of it?"

"You're not asking the questions here, Frankie. I don't know if you should have. As you know, the bridge leads to nowhere. Why would Conni have been on the bridge in the first place? Did you think of that?"

"No, I didn't think of that," said Frankie, uneasily shifting in his chair.

Spencer watched him very carefully. "Frankie, what?"

"Nothing."

"What else?"

"Nothing. That's it, I packed up my books and went home. I just thought you'd want to know I saw Conni there."

"You're right, I would want to know. What else, though?"

"Nothing."

"Frankie, I know you're hiding something from me."

"No."

"Okay, you see Conni. This is twenty minutes after you last saw Kristina. Aren't you wondering where Kristina is?"

"She could've already gone inside."

"But she didn't. And you left for home early on Wednesday morning. You didn't say good-bye to your house brothers, you didn't say good-bye to Albert. You didn't call Kristina to check if she was okay. You went home and didn't come back after Thanksgiving. When I called you two days ago, you broke down, but I bet you weren't surprised."

Frankie played with the crease of his pants but did not look up at Spencer.

"I bet you weren't surprised, were you?" repeated Spencer impatiently.

Frankie moved his head imperceptibly from side to side. "No."

Spencer studied Frankie for a long moment and then said, "Were you surprised to see Conni on the bridge?"

Frankie almost looked relieved when he answered. "No, I wasn't."

As I'm not, thought Spencer. "Why not?"

"You see, Detective O'Malley . . ." Frankie broke off, looking extremely uncomfortable again. "I've seen her there before."

"There where?"

"On the bridge."

Spencer paused, trying to formulate his next question. "You mean, late at night? In the middle of a snowstorm? Coming from the woods? Which one?"

"Seen her on the bridge before. In the middle of a snowstorm. Late at night."

"Also alone?"

Here Frankie hesitated.

"Not alone?" Spencer asked. "With someone else?"

"Sort of." Frankie sighed. "Shit, I don't want to do this."

"Frankie!" Spencer exclaimed. "You're very close, very close. Don't stop now."

"Is this being taped?"

"Yes."

"Will Conni hear this?"

"Absolutely. What was she doing on the bridge when you saw her there before?"

"Look, this is wrong," said Frankie uncertainly. "This doesn't feel right at all. This is not making the universe better, man, this is—"

"Frankie, let me ask you. Did you shove a helpless, hurt girl into the snow? Did you sit on top of her and hold a pillow over her nose and mouth till she suffocated, and then did you leave her dead and go home?" Spencer paused. "Your friend was killed. Someone killed her with his bare hands. It's a ter-rible injustice. Isn't that worth something?"

"Yes. But it's too late for Kristina. Nothing is going to right that."

"Except justice. The guilty should not go free."

"Well, it might make *you* feel better. But how can I right the wrong of a dead person by ratting on another person, who happens to be alive? Besides, all I saw this time was Conni walking back to Hinman."

"This time?" Spencer exclaimed.

Frankie went on, his voice lowered, surreptitious even. "It was last year in the winter. February, about. Yes, it was just before the winter carnival, which was in the middle of the month."

"Yes? Yes?" said Spencer, nearly shouting.

Frankie lowered his voice another notch and leaned into the table. "Conni," he whispered, "pushed Kristina off the bridge."

The assistant DAs arrived from Concord. Both wearing dark gray suits, John Artel and Daphne Silas were young, serious, and eager. They were clones of each other, and they came ostensibly to help Spencer with the case, but Spencer knew better.

What was it that bothered Spencer about the assistant district attorneys? It wasn't that they became involved. They always became involved in a capital case; after all, they represented the people, and the people had to send the guilty to prison. So the ADAs had to get involved. Their investigative teams were formidable, they had a large budget, and Spencer relied on their experts all the time to seek out assaulters and thieves.

But not killers.

This time, Spencer took it personally that they were here, because they were here not to help him, but to supplant him. They were here because Gallagher and they didn't trust him. It was murder in the first degree, and their moral fires were stoked. Murder meant a high-profile case, murder was a political ace in a reelection. They were here to win.

They all sat in the large conference room. Spencer held the tape recording of his conversation with Frankie in his hands. He was thinking of a way to tell these people about his talk with Kristina's mother.

However, Daphne had a plan. In a very businesslike tone she said, "We're going to thoroughly question the two men the victim knew—"

"What two men? She must have known more than two men," said Spencer, looking at John Artell. He raised his eyebrows. "Unless you mean biblically."

"O'Malley!" thundered the chief. Daphne and John did not laugh.

"Listen," said Spencer, gentler, trying to smile. "Before we listen to Frankie Absalom's interview, I want to tell you about Katherine Sinclair."

"Who?" said Daphne.

Will shook his head, mouthing, no, no.

"The dead girl's mother—"

"I thought her last name was Kim?" said John.

"It was. By marriage. She was Sinclair at birth. Her mother told me—"

"Well, I'm sure it is very interesting, detective," Daphne interrupted, "but we would just as soon talk to Howard Kim—"

"Howard Kim? Her ex-husband?"

"Yes."

"Well, you can find him at the funeral home. He's arranging for his ex-wife's burial. You can find him there till tomorrow," Spencer said caustically. "After that he'll be at the Pine Knoll Cemetery, burying her."

Daphne Silas had no sense of humor. Or if she did, she didn't show it. "What about this Frankie Absalom? Does he have an alibi?"

"Yes," Will interjected. "Someone saw him studying and then leaving the building around one-thirty or so."

Spencer said, "Why don't you guys question the Crimson women's basketball team? I hear they hated Kristina."

"Really?" Daphne livened up.

"Oh, please."

Gallagher coughed into his hand to get Spencer's attention, and then hissed quietly. Spencer shut up.

Then he said, "Why don't we listen to the tape, then? You might find it of interest. We have some time before Landers and Innis call. Or would you rather wait for the pathology and the fingerprints and have a look at those first?"

"I thought we could look at them together," said Daphne. If Daphne Silas hadn't been so proper and dry, Spencer could've sworn she was coming on to him. He looked at her carefully as she stretched her lips in a slight smile.

———————

Spencer hated the look on the chief's face when the Frankie tape was played. Gallagher looked like a man who had just heard he'd won four million dollars, or was getting a promotion and a raise. Even subdued Will became animated. Daphne and John remained calm, but their eyes sparkled.

"This is pretty incredible stuff, Tracy," said Gallagher.

"Well, I'm glad you think so, sir," replied Spencer. Gallagher's smile dulled a notch.

Daphne stood up. "John, call Dr. Innis. Tell him we need the results of the blood work immediately." She turned to Spencer. "Nice work, detective-sergeant."

Spencer swore under his breath.

Ed Landers called first, with the fingerprints. There had been numerous prints everywhere in Kristina's room, belonging to at least three people besides Kristina. All of them matched prints taken from Conni Tobias, James Shaw, or Albert Maplethorpe. The only prints on the bottle of Southern Comfort were Kristina's—and Conni's.

For some reason that seemed to excite Will. "She never liked to walk that bridge unless she was drunk," he said to Spencer. "Right, Trace? Conni could've given her that bottle to get her drunk, get her out there, you know?"

"Oh, Will," said Spencer tiredly. "That's a lot of conclusions from a little information. No one saw Conni bring that bottle to Kristina."

"Yes, but Frankie saw Kristina on the bridge. And he saw Conni on the bridge," said Gallagher.

"Yes, she was a jealous girl," said Spencer. "There was a triangle of sorts—"

"Are you saying Frankie's testimony is not compelling?" Gallagher said loudly.

"I'm not saying that, sir," said Spencer. "But compelling us to what? Over-look other things?"

"Other things like what?" the chief said unpleasantly. Spencer looked at Will. Even Will didn't seem to be on Spencer's side.

Spencer opened his mouth to try again with Katherine Sinclair. Wait, Spencer wanted to say. Listen carefully. Hear me out. But nothing he had to tell them would have given them the same intense, zealous look in their eyes.

The chief had to take a call. John Artell had to make a call. Will patted Spencer on the back. Daphne sat across from Spencer and stared at him.

And then the blood-work report came through the fax machine.

In the middle of reading the report and looking at the jubilant faces around him, Spencer broke off and excused himself. Will followed him out of the conference room.

"What's the matter with you?" Will whispered. "What the hell has gotten into you?"

"Nothing," said Spencer, quickly walking to his desk and grabbing his keys and coat. "I'll be back."

"Spencer!" Will exclaimed. "What the hell is going on? We are in the middle of a—"

"No, see, that's the whole trouble," Spencer said. "You all seem to be at the *end* of a murder investigation, and at the beginning of a people's case. *I* am still in the *middle* of a murder investigation."

"O'Malley," said Will, "what are you talking about? Did you see? Did you see all the evidence? Did you listen to Frankie?"

"I saw all the evidence. I listened to Frankie."

"So where the hell are you going?"

"I'm going to talk to Conni Tobias," said Spencer.

On the way to Hinman Hall, Spencer thought about Molly's potato skins, which he hadn't had yesterday for the first time in two hundred Sundays, because yesterday he had been in Norwalk State Hospital for the chronically ill. His only source of nourishment had been five cups of black coffee, which were lifting him off the ground, and Jack Daniel's, which he had stumbled on late last night after he returned from Connecticut.

Spencer knew he didn't have much time.

Conni was not in her room. Neither was Jim, nor Albert.

Spencer figured Conni had to have lunch eventually, so he walked to Collis Café. There was a big bay with four ten-foot-tall windows. Spencer waited at one of the round tables in the bay.

Constance Tobias, the nice girl from the right side of the tracks, from Cold Spring Harbor, from where only one kind of girl ever came—the loved, pampered, well-bred, well-educated kind. Cold Spring Harbor, where the trees were taller than the tallest house, where Long Island Sound peeked through the sycamores, shined, reflected, danced through the oaks and the pines. Cold Spring Harbor, where the driveways were an eighth of a mile long, where the houses had two maids' quarters and two guest quarters and seven bathrooms and heated, lighted pools and tennis courts and French-brick siding and slate roofs. Cold Spring Harbor, where Conni Tobias colored her hair lighter blond to look pretty for Albert Maplethorpe, where she put Lancôme blush on the cheek with the gash on it.

In high school Spencer hadn't even known girls like Conni. Spencer's high school hadn't had girls in her league. Girls who had thought they were too good for Spencer, who would walk past him with their books and their white sweaters and their upturned noses.

Spencer sometimes thought he had become a Suffolk County traffic cop so he could give all those girls speeding tickets as they raced by in their Trans Ams breaking eighty. Sometimes when he was in a generous mood, he let them go with a warning.

But this could not be one of those times.

After all, this was not about a Trans Am breaking eighty.

This was about being close to death.

Dressed in tight jeans and a high-waisted pink sweater, Conni walked in with friends Spencer didn't recognize. When she saw Spencer, she stopped smiling. Spencer nodded and stood up, thinking, she's hoping I'm not waiting here for her, but I can see by her face she knows I'm waiting only for her.

Spencer slowly walked toward her. Conni put on a brave face. "Detective O'Malley, can I have my lunch? I haven't eaten since seven this morning."

There she is, peeking at me out of the window of her black Trans Am, saying in a high-pitched, flirtatious voice, *What's wrong, officer? Was I going too fast?*

"No, Conni," said Spencer. "You can't. I have to talk to you."

"Okay, sure, anything. After lunch?"

"Not after lunch," Spencer said, raising his voice. "Now."

He caught her by surprise. She said, trying to smile, "I'm not going to lose my appetite, am I?"

"You might," replied Spencer.

His own stomach grumbling, aching from emptiness, he sat down, having bought a cup of coffee and nothing more. This time he drank it with lots of milk and lots of sugar. A liquid lunch, he thought, amused at the irony.

"Conni," he said, "I'm not going to beat around the bush. In about half an hour, maybe less, the chief of police is going to come here with a warrant for your arrest."

"Arrest?" Conni said, whisper-quiet. "Arrest for what?" She took a listless bite of her burger.

Their dark cherry-wood table was round; Spencer thought it was appropriate, as though they were back at headquarters. But this table was better suited for questioning, even over a burger.

"Conni, Frankie Absalom, you remember him?"

"Of course I remember him," she said. "He's a friend."

"Frankie saw you on the bridge the night Kristina died."

She didn't miss a beat. "So?"

Spencer looked away from her. "Conni, he saw you on the bridge minutes after Kristina disappeared from sight, and when he saw you, you were already coming back from the woods."

Conni didn't say anything, and Spencer didn't look at her.

"Do you remember going outside that Tuesday night?"

"I guess so."

Spencer lifted his gaze toward Conni. "You guess so? I've asked you where you were that Tuesday evening a dozen times in a dozen different ways. You never mentioned you went down to the bridge. That's an important part of your evening, wouldn't you say?"

"I didn't mention it because it had nothing to do with anything."

Spencer tried not to shout. "Yes, but you're not the judge of that, Conni. You can't be. Does that make sense to you? Haven't your well-educated parents taught you that when you're questioned about your alibi, you can't omit going to the scene of the murder because you didn't think it was important?"

"What do my parents have to do with it?" she snapped, and Spencer thought, that's right, what do they have to do with anything? But he thought of the sycamores in Cold Spring Harbor hiding Long Island Sound from view, and thought, they have so much to do with you, Constance Tobias. They've made you into what you are, thinking you're above the law and above me.

"Let me explain. You disappear for forty minutes and no one sees you anywhere, except Frankie, who places you near the scene of the crime. You want to tell me what you were doing on that bridge?"

"I already told you."

"No, actually. You never told me."

"Looking for Albert," she said, turning away.

"On the bridge?"

"Yes."

"Did you see him?"

"No."

"What about Kristina? Did you see her?"

"No," she said, picking up her burger with shaking hands.

Spencer laughed. "What are you doing, Constance? Are you saying you don't want to talk to me? That's fine. Because I'm about to leave."

She exclaimed, "Why are they going to arrest me?"

"For jaywalking! God, Conni, for the premeditated murder of a human being."

Now it was Conni's turn to laugh. "I didn't kill her, lieutenant, detective, whoever you are. I didn't kill her."

"No? That's fine. At your arraignment, you can enter a plea of not guilty. Make it heartfelt."

"Arraignment? What are you talking about? I didn't kill her, I'm telling you." She spoke so loudly that everyone at the surrounding tables turned to look at her. It wasn't often, Spencer guessed, that a Dartmouth College student would be proclaiming her innocence in a murder case during the lunch-hour rush in the middle of Collis Café. Maybe it was a first. People stared.

"Tell me what happened," Spencer said in a gentler voice. "Tell me."

Conni started to cry. "Don't I need a lawyer to talk to you? I'm not allowed to talk to you unless I have my lawyer."

"If that's what you want, have it your way. Just remember, there is no bail for those accused of murder one."

"I haven't been accused of anything by anybody yet," she said. "Except you."

Spencer sighed. "Miss Tobias. Do I look like a mean man? I'm here to help you. Why are you making this so hard on yourself? If you are innocent, tell me everything, and then I'll be on your side. That's my job."

"I'm innocent," Conni said quickly.

"Why should I believe you?"

"Because it's true."

"True?" Spencer searched for words. "You just aren't getting it, are you?" He paused as he waded through his jumbled thoughts.

"Why are you looking at me this way?" Conni said. "Like you think I'm guilty?"

Spencer shook his head sadly. "You just won't help me, will you? Why won't you tell me? Is it my bedside manner? I don't think so. I've been told I'm a decent interrogator. But still, not one of you volunteered information. Jim won't tell me why when he saw Kristina's black boots he ran the other way. Albert won't tell me about him and her. And you won't tell me what you were doing on that bridge."

"I'll tell you, okay? But if I tell you, will you believe me then?" she pleaded.

Spencer said calmly, "I don't know, Conni. Let's have it. But you won't start telling me it was because you were beside yourself with jealousy, will you? Because when you're convicted, you'll be hearing yourself tell that one in prison for the rest of your life. So tell it carefully. And think! Think of every-thing."

Conni stared at Spencer, dumbstruck. "There is no everything," she said, stammering over her words. Her fingers were pulling on her eyebrows and eye-lashes. It was painful to watch. "Look, I admit, I went out there—" Spencer saw the enormous effort etched on Conni's face.

"I went out there," she continued, "to look for Albert."

"For Albert."

"Yes, for Albert."

"Why would he be on the bridge?"

"Because," Conni said, struggling over every syllable, "where she was, he usually was."

"Ahh. I see."

"This is so hard for me."

"Yes, that much is clear."

"I went out there because I thought he might be with her, and I went crazy."

"How crazy, Conni?" Spencer asked her. "How crazy?"

She pushed the tray of food away from her, but pushed it too far, and it fell on the floor. They both looked at it but neither picked it up. Conni con-tinued, "Don't be stupid. I just went out there to confront him. Them."

"Confront them doing what?"

"I don't know. Having sex somewhere."

"Having sex in freezing temperatures? You'd have had to catch them quickly."

"Kissing, then. Something. I was completely at the end of my rope. You just have no idea what it's been like for me. The constant nagging suspicion. He's not in his room, she's not in her room. He's nowhere to be found, she's nowhere to be found. Or . . . she's at the library, he's at the library, she's walking Aristotle, so is he. She's at Collis, so is he."

Spencer was quiet.

"Look, I was crazy with jealousy. I couldn't see straight. Detective, I can't even deny it—I'm happy she's gone, I've wanted her to die for a really long time. She just made me crazy. That's what I felt. She'd always been in the way between Albert and me. As long as she was around, I was crazy."

Spencer listened in disbelief to Conni's words and stared in disbelief at her contorted face. "Conni, you just don't get it, do you? What you've just told me, together with the evidence we have—you're looking at life." He paused. "A life without Kristina Kim, but certainly life."

"What are you talking about? I said I didn't kill her. I just said I'm happy she's gone."

"Conni, no one will believe you." Then he added, slowly, "*I* don't believe you."

"I'm telling you the truth. Why would I lie?"

"Why would you lie?" And Spencer thought, is she stupid? "Why would *you* lie?"

Then she seemed to get it. "Okay, okay. But I'm telling you the truth now. I didn't kill her. I was looking for him."

"To kill him?"

"Don't be silly. To confront him."

"Confront him with what? And why?"

"So I would know once and for all if it was true."

"True?" Spencer laughed. "Constance, you can't—you just can't be this deep in denial. I have never seen them together, and I knew it was true three days ago. After speaking to you once and to Albert once, I knew it was true. You should've seen it long ago. Why did you take it?" Spencer was angry at Conni for letting Albert betray her and Kristina lie to her. "Why didn't you just break up with him, and end it there? Why did you stick around?"

"Why?" Conni seemed both surprised and embarrassed by the question. "Because I love Albert, that's why. I love him more than anything. Because I didn't believe it for a long time. I still kind of don't in a way. He always looked me right in the face, he sounded so sincere. I just can't believe he would do that to me, lie to me like that—"

"Believe it," said Spencer. "It's true."

"How? How do you know?"

"She told me. And he told me."

"*He* told you?" Conni breathed out. Something battled on her face, struggled, fought, and she finally said, "I—I can't—can't believe he'd tell you that."

"Why? He certainly didn't want to tell me. I had to ask him twenty times. But then that's par for the course for all of you. You don't answer anything the first nineteen."

"It's not important anymore," Conni said.

"You're wrong, Conni. It's very important," Spencer said.

"No, I mean it doesn't matter now. It's better between me and Albert. It's like, it's almost like she never existed, you know?"

"Oh, I know," said Spencer, making an effort to stay composed. "But she did exist, she was once alive. Can you imagine it, Constance, being alive and young, and then dying?"

Conni said, "I'm trying to forget her. I know it's only been a few days. That's why I thought giving her money to Red Leaves House was such a good idea. That way she's not always right there with us, you know? Buying us a house, paying for our wedding. Still in our lives."

"She'll always be in your life now."

Conni did not understand, or chose not to. Visibly upset, Conni said, "What kind of friend—I thought friends didn't do that to friends."

"Conni," Spencer said slowly, enunciating every syllable. "You're wrong, friends do that to each other all the time, it's the oldest betrayal in the book. But boyfriends don't do that to girls they love. What kind of boyfriend—"

"That's what I mean. Albert loves me. I didn't think he would hurt me like that."

"But he did, Conni. Kristina didn't owe you that much, but Albert owed you everything, and still he lied to you and cheated on you from the very beginning."

Conni, pale, her mouth twitching, said, "I don't believe it. I don't think it was from the very beginning."

Spencer was going to say, trust me Conni, from the very beginning, but instead he sat back. Will wasn't here to put his hand on Spencer's shoulder. He asked, "Those scratches on your cheek, Conni—how did you get them?"

"I told you, I was playing with my brother—"

"Conni!"

She moved back in her seat.

"Conni," Spencer said, quieter. He felt the veins in his forehead getting larger, and beating, coursing with frustration. "Conni, your blood, *your* blood, was under Kristina's nails. We found your blood under her nails, and there is the mark on your cheek to show us where she scratched you."

"Under her nails?" Conni said. Spencer could see she was about to deny it.

Spencer leaned closer, hollow-eyed, gaunt, pale, and, trying hard to stay in control, said, "Let me ask you, when you knocked her on the ground and put a pillow over her face to kill her, and she reached up with only one working arm to struggle for the last time and took that chunk out of your face, and you pressed the pillow harder into her, harder and harder, until her hand fell away and she stopped moving, let me ask you, did you then get off her, or did you sit on her for a while longer to make sure she was really dead?"

Conni nearly cried. "I don't know what you're talking about!" she exclaimed in a frightened voice.

Spencer said quietly, "Constance, your *blood* was under her nails. Do you understand what I'm telling you?"

Spencer could see by Conni's face she understood.

"Listen," she said uncertainly. "Things were coming to a head between us. We used to be really good friends. But you just came into our lives at a really bad time," she added, sniffling.

"Certainly a bad time for her," said Spencer.

"No, a bad time for both of us. I just couldn't take it anymore. I'd try so hard to believe both of them, but it was getting harder and harder. My relationship with Albert and her was getting out of control."

Spencer waited.

"But those marks on my face, I didn't—that wasn't in the woods. That was in her room. Outside her room. We had a fight."

"When?"

"Tuesday evening. Around midnight."

"Midnight you said?"

"Yes."

Spencer said, "You told me you didn't see her that night after eleven-fifteen."

"I did."

Spencer pushed his coffee cup aside. "Conni, I'd recommend calling your family and asking them to arrange for a lawyer."

"You think I still need a lawyer?" she asked lamely. "But I'm telling you the truth."

"The truth? What is that?" said Spencer. "I don't know what that is anymore. The three of you have made me doubt the truth of my own name."

Conni exclaimed very loudly, very insistently, "I did not put my knees up on Kristina's chest. I did not kill her! This is ridiculous. You know I didn't kill her."

Spencer shook his head slowly. "Do I know that? No. I know nothing. In any case, you won't have to prove it to me. You're going to have to prove it to twelve of your peers."

Conni got quiet, and then said, "Really, you must believe me. I didn't do it." Whatever facade she had had was gone. What was left was a Cold Spring Harbor sunny day that she couldn't see because she was inside the air-conditioned house. What was left, Spencer mused, was twenty-one years of instilling in your kids that they could do whatever they wanted if only they put their minds to it and then spoke loudly about truth. Well, Constance Tobias did what she wanted. She put her mind to it, and when at first she didn't succeed, she tried again.

Conni went on, "Why are you torturing me like this? I'm telling you the truth. We had a fight. I don't know what happened. I just lost it and went for her. She tried to push me away, and things got out of control for a second, but only for a second. I was angry, you know?"

Spencer leaned forward, wanting to grab her by the shoulders. "Angry enough to kill her?"

"I told you, I told you several times. Why won't you believe me? I didn't kill her."

Spencer went on, "Wouldn't be the first time you tried to kill her, huh, Conni?"

Falling back against the chair, Conni paled, her mouth opening. Spencer couldn't look her in the eyes and lowered his gaze.

"Lieut—Detective—O'Malley," she stammered, "I don't—please, you have to believe me. This time—no . . . I didn't kill her."

"You can't really confess to me, Conni, can you? You can't say, yes, I did it, because if you confess, there's only paperwork and sentencing left for you. No, you have to have a fighting chance. But you did kill her, didn't you?"

Rubbing her face and sounding frightened, Conni said, "Look, that thing, last year, what? Did Frankie tell you that, too? God, that Frankie. Who needs enemies, right? Well, that thing, last year—" She giggled uncontrollably, and then cried.

Spencer reached into his pocket and pulled out some tissues, handing them to her. She wiped her face. They said nothing. "Oh, God, it's really bad, isn't it? I didn't see it before, why didn't I see it? But it's just so bad . . ."

"Yes," Spencer agreed. "It's pretty bad."

"Does everybody know that?" Conni asked with a glimmer of hope. "Or just *you*?"

Just you, officer, is it just you who knew I was going too fast, why, aren't you handsome, maybe you'd like to go out sometime, you and your blue eyes, maybe—

"Miss Tobias, everybody knows it, everybody and their aunt. Besides, you weren't going to suggest that I keep vital evidence as to motive and your state of mind away from the DA's office?"

"No, of course not," she said dejectedly. "Look, it's true, obviously, I mean, I did—I was enraged, I did . . . sort of . . . you know, push her, I shoved her—"

"Like you shoved her into the snow?"

"The snow? What are you talking about? Please. No. That time, I pushed her legs—"

"Why did you do that?" Spencer interrupted.

"Why? I already told you. She drove me crazy. I loved her and hated her. I understood why Albert would be smitten with her and hated her for it, I just wanted her to go away—"

"Forever."

"Just go away!" Conni cried. "I admit, it was dumb, I don't know what got into me, but it's true, I pushed her off the bridge to make her fall. She was drunk—it was likely she'd just fall herself someday."

"What happened?" Spencer quietly asked.

"What happened? What, didn't Frankie tell you that part?"

Spencer said, "Obviously Kristina survived."

"Yeah, she survived," Conni said intensely. "I pushed her right near the foot of the bridge. I didn't realize the slope would break her fall. She was pretty banged up and everything, she looked like a—like a—"

"A pledge gone badly wrong," Spencer finished.

"Something like that. But she was okay."

Spencer scratched his head, nodding. "Conni, I don't get something. You pushed her, you tried to kill her. Why would Kristina leave you any money?"

"We made up, I apologized."

"How do you make up after something like that? How do you do it?"

"I said it was an accident, and she, I think she was too drunk, she believed me. You just go on, pretending everything is okay, pretending nothing happened . . ."

"Is that possible?"

"We did it."

"Not well, I see," said Spencer.

Conni remained silent. Spencer watched her. "If you didn't kill her, who did?"

"How should I know? A crazy man. I don't know. I wasn't there."

Spencer persisted, "It must've been hard for you with Albert. Lies can do that. Never knowing the truth can do that."

"No, you have no idea," Conni said. "This is such a small campus, and we were always together, we were such good friends. I trusted them so much, Kristina was a wonderful person, you know? I mean, how could she do that to me?" Conni lowered her voice. "It took me a long time to even get suspicious."

Spencer leaned closer to Conni and said, "Conni, who is Albert? What do you know about him? I tried to check out his background yesterday and had little luck. Did you know his infirmary emergency card has no emergency contacts on it? Just the name of a law firm here in town." Spencer sat back. "And when I called Clairton, Pennsylvania, to find a Maplethorpe, I was told there were no Maplethorpes in Clairton, Pennsylvania."

Looking perplexed, Conni said, "Clairton, Pennsylvania?"

Spencer nodded, tapping on the table with his coffee spoon. "Yes. That's where he told me he was from."

Conni laughed. "He's not from Clairton, Pennsylvania, he's from Fort Worth, Texas. And he doesn't have any family. He's an orphan—"

Spencer jumped up, knocking over his chair and dropping his spoon. "Oh my God," he muttered. "Oh my God."

Conni got up with him. "What's the matter?"

"Nothing, I gotta go, I'll . . ." He was already out the door and running to his car.

Spencer drove out onto Interstate 89, put on his police siren, and flew to Concord police headquarters, where Ed Landers worked. He asked Landers to show him the fingerprints from Kristina's room and to accompany him to the basement, where the FBI data terminal was kept.

"I've never scanned in anyone's prints," Spencer said, panting, as if he had run to Concord. "Could you help me with that?"

"Sure," said Landers. "I'm here to help. Is it the girl's prints you're interested in? I hear they're going to arrest her."

"No, the guys' prints. Albert Maplethorpe's and Jim Shaw's."

"Oh, okay."

"That's it," Spencer said, putting his hand on Ed's back, trying to hurry him along downstairs.

"Here, it's not so hard," Landers was saying when all Spencer wished was that Ed would get it done. "You put the picture of the prints facedown on this scanner, close the cover, push this green button—"

"This one?"

"That's right." Landers smiled. "You're getting the hang of it."

Get on with it, get on with it, get on with it, Spencer thought, smiling politely, blood draining from his tense fingers.

"We open up this scanning software, scale the photo of the prints. Is this sharp enough for you? Do you want them enlarged?"

Spencer nodded to everything.

"Now we choose a print path, now . . . here we go."

Spencer stopped listening and closed his eyes.

"Now we wait a few minutes. Let's sit down." Ed sat down in front of the monitor. Spencer sat down, and thought he wanted to bolt back up again, he willed himself to stay down. "It'll come up in a minute," Ed said.

It was one of the longest minutes of Spencer's life.

"Okay, look here. The prints are in the machine. Now the computer wants to know if we want to search for possible matches."

"Say yes, of course."

"Of course. We press F5 for search, and wait."

We sure wait a lot, Spencer thought.

The readout on the monitor said, *Can you narrow the criteria?*

"What does that mean?" said Spencer.

"It means it wants something more specific. Maybe there is another print close to this one but it can't be sure. Shall we say, male?"

"By all means."

Landers entered the data and waited. The same message for narrowing criteria came up.

"Oh," said Spencer. "How often does that happen?"

"Well, you have to be fingerprinted sometime in your life, like for citizenship or extensive traveling, diplomacy work, investment banking, and of course committing a federal offense. The last group is usually the first to be classified."

"Can you try all the categories?"

"Of course. Let's try male traveler."

They waited. The basement reminded Spencer of the Dartmouth-Hitchcock morgue. But this wasn't as clean and well-tended.

Now they had something. The hard drive cranked over and made some humming noises, then up came a photo of Jim Shaw, along with ten of his fingerprints and a short bio.

"How's that?" Landers asked.

"This is okay. Ed, can we scan in the other set of prints?"

"Sure, bear with me."

Spencer bore. His fingertips, white with strain, were pressing into his legs. Ed scanned in the prints. "What exactly are you looking for?"

"A name," replied Spencer. "Just a name."

"Is a name important?"

"I don't know," Spencer said in agitation. "Depends what it is."

This time they didn't have to wait so long. The computer cranked immediately, and on the screen appeared Albert's face. Spencer glanced at the name under the photo and let out his breath.

The name did not read *Albert Maplethorpe.* It read *Nathan Sinclair.*

Spencer stood numbly behind Landers. He heard the hum of the computer, and a printer in another room. He heard people talking; eventually he saw Landers turning around.

"Are you all right, Spence?"

Spencer came to. "Yes, yes, of course. I'm fine. Let me look at this some more." And he bent over the screen, trying to focus. The text was swimming in front of his eyes.

Nathan Sinclair had been arrested at age seventeen in Brooklyn Heights, New York, for juvenile delinquency. He and some friends got caught while bungling a convenience store robbery. He had served three months of a two-year sentence, and had been released on probation. According to police records, he had never reported to his probation officer, and, in fact, had never been heard from again.

"God, what was this person doing in Kristina's room?" said Ed.

Spencer leaned away from the screen, away from Ed. His emotions were as high-pitched as Conni's voice. "I don't know, Ed. But this is what I needed. Could you print that?"

After he received a copy of the report on *Nathan Sinclair,* Spencer, clutching the manila envelope, walked out of the building.

He wanted to go home. To think that only four days ago, he had sat behind his desk at work, bored, restless, and frustrated because a college girl hadn't called.

Four days.

Sometimes he didn't leave his apartment for four days, doing nothing, feeling nothing. He ate—eating, now that must have been a treat!—he drank, he slept, he watched sports on TV, four days passed, and absolutely nothing happened.

Spencer drove slowly back to Hanover. It was dark again; another day without food. He made himself stop and go into Murphy's and order a beer and a burger. He didn't eat the burger, but the Molson's tasted pretty good. He ordered another one. It was still early; the place was empty.

"Looks like you got troubles, pal," said Marty, his old friend the bartender.

"You could say troubles." Spencer smiled thinly. *Nathan Sinclair* rang through his ears.

"Have something to do with that dead girl?"

"Yeah. About everything."

"Well, you know—I'm sure you must—they made an arrest this afternoon. Incredible. Arrested some girl. Nobody can figure it out. I thought we were looking for a rapist. A girl. Can you believe it?"

"Almost no," Spencer replied.

"Apparently she's guilty."

"Well, we don't know that, do we? Let's not jump to any conclusions."

"What do you mean? They wouldn't have arrested her if they didn't have enough evidence. They gotta have enough to go to the grand jury with, especially for murder. I can't believe it."

"I almost can't believe it myself." Spencer liked Marty, but tonight he wished Marty would just go away. "Marty, how do you know all this stuff about the grand jury? Are you a lawyer on the side or something?"

Marty waved him off. "Nah. What you see is what you get, Detective-Sergeant Tracy."

Spencer sipped his beer.

"I hear she's not even denying it," Marty said, as if that closed his book on her guilt or innocence.

"She does have the right to remain silent, you know," said Spencer.

"Yeah, but I think she's not opening her mouth because if she does, they'll get a confession out of her."

Spencer knew he should go to the station, but he wanted another drink. He wanted to sit quietly at his usual spot in the subdued bar and go to sleep.

He hoped it would all be over soon.

"You really look like shit, pal. Even in this light."

"Thanks. You're too kind." Spencer smiled.

"Tracy, you know you're always welcome in my bar, and I'm happy to see you. But go and fight crime."

Before he left, Spencer took a long look at Marty and said, "You know what, Marty? One of these days I sure as hell wish you'd stop calling me Tracy."

"Ah, but Trace—"

"I mean it, Marty. It pisses me off."

Marty looked almost hurt. "Spencer, I've been calling you Tracy for five years."

"And it's been pissing me off for five years, Marty," said Spencer, unsmiling and tired. "Just thought I'd tell you. Good night."

Marty mumbled something.

Spencer walked slowly home to clear his head and change his clothes before heading down to headquarters.

Spencer knew he'd catch hell from the chief. He clutched the manila envelope tighter, turning the corner to Allen Street, slowly making his way home past Stinson's, EBA, and the Dartmouth Music Shop.

It was almost too hard to be alone with the knowledge of *Nathan Sinclair.*

Oh, if only Conni had known. If only she'd known. She would have run from Kristina and *Albert,* screaming, and told Jim Shaw, and he would have run screaming, too. As it was, Conni's hatred had gotten the better of her, and for what? For who? Spencer was almost sure Constance Tobias had done away with the wrong person. As Ruth Ellis—the last woman to be hanged in Britain—had done, Conni should have dealt with the disease, not the symptom.

Going up the stairs and turning the key to his apartment, Spencer wished he had someone to go home to. For someone to listen to him and then say, this is where you've gone wrong, this is where you're mistaken.

Secretly Spencer was afraid Will Baker was a better cop than he, because Will Baker had a wife. Will went home, and he talked about his day for ten minutes, and if there was something to add, Ginny Baker would add it, and then they would forget it and go on with their evening.

Spencer couldn't go on with his evening. He could only go on with himself. Usually he could bear it, but there were times when he looked at his dark, empty apartment and the forces of universe would combine and stifle him. When he wished someone else would be angry *for* Kristina and *at* Conni, and at *Nathan Sinclair.* When someone else would be mad at the chief for chewing him out and calling in the henchmen.

When someone would be angry for him.

When someone would be *anything* for him.

Spencer dropped his keys on the little table and, out of habit, looked in his refrigerator. Nothing. It was six on Monday evening, and no one would be home later, or tonight. Or tomorrow morning. No one but himself, and tonight he just couldn't stand himself anymore. He was sick of the sight of him.

He showered and changed, and then drove back to the station. He left Nathan Sinclair's manila envelope on the kitchen table.

286

Spencer was unprepared for the pandemonium at the station.

The press was everywhere with their cameras and lights and insistent microphones that had a life all their own. How did everyone get here so quickly? Spencer wondered. There were TV cameras from a station in Oklahoma, and two journalists from the *Los Angeles Times* shoving their live mikes at him. He pushed past them, muttering *no comment, no comment.* He barely even heard their questions, because his own questions were screaming in his head.

The blue-and-red lights of the police sirens flashed. There was still snow on the ground, and it was very cold.

Spencer went straight to the chief's office. Gallagher glared at Spencer as if he were mud.

"Where the hell have you been? We've arrested Conni Tobias."

"So I've heard."

"Goddammit! Where were you? Silas and Artell wanted you to go with them and Ray."

"Why? They seem to have managed fine by themselves."

"O'Malley, don't be a wiseass. You were heading this investigation. They needed your help."

"Well, well," said Spencer, his mouth stretching at the corners. "Why didn't you say so? That's what I'm here for. To help them."

"That *is* what you're here for," snapped Gallagher. "To help them. We all work together, Tracy. What's going through your thick head? You find the killer, they prosecute the case, remember?"

"Yeah, well, I didn't realize prosecuting the case involved making the arrest. I thought I was in charge of that."

"You weren't here!" shouted Gallagher, as Will stared at the carpet. "Maybe if you had been here, you could've made the arrest."

"If I had been here, I would have advised you to wait—"

Gallagher cut him off. "O'Malley, wait for what? Christmas? I'm tired of your shit. Want Baker to take over?"

Spencer glanced at Will, who didn't look up. "Is that another threat, chief?"

"Shape up, O'Malley! The DA's office needs you, your partner needs you, this station needs you. Don't let your personal problems overwhelm you every time we have a big case."

"Overwhelm me? Every time? What, out of the two we've had?"

"What, unless it's a murder, it's not a big case? What about the forty robberies we had last year? What about the burglaries? What about that near-fatal assault in the bar last winter? Every time things get heated up, you go off somewhere, doing God knows what."

Spencer considered the situation. "Is that why you brought in the ADAs? Because you think I'm off somewhere?"

"I didn't bring them in! We work together, goddammit! It was a suspicious homicide. Now it's murder one. Concord and Haverhill should've both been here on Thursday."

"Yes, but they weren't."

"No, and look what we got—I don't even know what!" Gallagher banged on his desk, stood, and sat back down. "Look," he said, in a calmer voice. "Baker seemed to indicate you might need some help."

Spencer cocked his head and studied his partner levelly. Will Baker flushed. "Baker seemed to indicate that, did he? Well, did he or didn't he indicate that?" Before the chief or Will could reply, Spencer said, "For your information, the help you've given me is too little too late, chief. I had only Ray on Thursday to process the scene, and there's no bigger screw-up in the department. No camera, no tape, no notebook, doesn't call Concord when told to, the coroner isn't notified till Friday evening, and frankly, where were you last week? If this was so important, where the hell were you? I don't know and I don't care, but one thing's for sure, you weren't here." Spencer's voice was becoming progressively louder. Had he been calmer, he would've understood that Gallagher's bluster and anger at Spencer was to cover-up for his own neglect of a murder investigation, but Spencer wasn't calm. And he didn't understand.

"I am the chief, Tracy," said the chief, raising his voice.

"Yeah, well, where was the chief last week when we were digging up a woman's naked corpse with our bare hands? Where were you when we found nine million dollars in her account, and where were you when we couldn't find a soul on earth to come and claim a dead girl, who was everybody's flavor of the month when she was alive, but dead must've given off quite a stink, because no one wanted anything to do with her! Let me tell you something about me going off somewhere. Yesterday I drove to Norwalk, Connecticut, and spoke to a woman who told me some pretty incredible things you don't give a shit about. Today I drove to Concord because—" He paused for breath. "Because one set of prints didn't match up. I've hardly eaten in four days. Where were you yesterday? Let me guess—playing touch football with your kids and having a nice Sunday roast with your wife. So don't tell me I've been going off somewhere," said Spencer with his fists clenched. "I've been doing my job."

It took a long while to blow Spencer's fuse, but once blown, it was blown. At Spencer's side, Will didn't look up from the floor.

Gallagher's voice when he spoke was remarkably calm, as if he were a parent trying to mollify a temperamental child.

"Now, Spencer," said Gallagher softly, through gritted teeth, and Spencer, had he been less angry, would've been amazed, for the chief never called him by his first name, not even when they were drinking.

"Ah, don't Spencer me," snapped Spencer. "I'm tired of it all. Just tired. I'm going home. You got your girl, so to speak. Go and talk to those mikes outside. They're clamoring for your opinion. Go and tell them everything you know about Conni Tobias. About Kristina Kim. And about Nathan Sinclair."

"Who the *hell* is Nathan Sinclair?" Will whispered.

"I'm sorry we can't all be as smart as you, Tracy," said the chief angrily. "But we're not idiots. And we'll all beg your pardon for having wives and families, but we do also try to do our jobs, as best we can, though of course not brilliantly and twenty-four hours a day like you."

Spencer did not want to have this discussion. He was overflowing with emotion. He hadn't felt this much since his wife died. He realized suddenly that Gallagher knew something very important about Spencer Patrick O'Malley, something that gave him the power of intimidation over Spencer, and this wasn't the first time the chief had wielded that power with glee.

Gallagher knew that Spencer O'Malley had no life.

Barely breathing, Spencer stood in front of the chief. Faced with a dilemma, a situation of mutually exclusive and equally unfavorable options, Spencer's only outward sign of emotion was a shaking of his fingertips.

"I quit," he said.

"O'Malley, don't be stupid," the chief said. "Every time I chew you out, you threaten to quit. I'm tired of it. One of these days I'm not going to call you back."

"Make that day today, chief," said Spencer, unzipping his holster with the Magnum and throwing it on the desk.

"O'Malley!" Gallagher exclaimed.

"Tracy, stop it, man," said Will quietly, coming over to him.

Spencer backed away, unclipping his police badge from his shirt pocket, and also throwing that on the table. "I know, I know," he said, much calmer now, and more relaxed. "It's always the same thing. I pretend to quit because I'm just fed up to here the way you treat me, the way you talk to me, the way you run this place. I've been waiting five years for you to retire so I can take over your job, but they seemed like fifty-five years. I stayed because I had no choice. But you know what? Kristina Kim has no choice. Katherine Sinclair has no choice. I actually have some. And I quit. You think I love this job too much—"

"I don't think that, O'Malley."

"Well, you're wrong. I do like this job. But then, I don't have a life to compare it to. That's why you treat me like shit, isn't it? Because I got nowhere else to go. Well, the hell with this place. I quit now. You can clean out my desk. I got nothing in it. If the DA needs me to testify, let them subpoena me."

"Tracy," Will whispered to him. "You're going too far."

"Yeah. Out the door."

And he turned to leave.

"Tracy," said Chief Gallagher, "I'm warning you, if you walk out that door, don't bother coming back. I'm telling you. That'll be it."

Spencer turned around long enough to say to Will and Gallagher, "And furthermore, don't call me Tracy. I hate that fucking name."

Spencer walked out into the cold night air, and stopped right outside the front door. He knew he could still come back. They needed him, he knew that. He hadn't told them yet about *Nathan Sinclair.*

But what would that change? he thought. So they would know. They wouldn't give a damn. But once the truth was out, Conni Tobias would know it. And Jim Shaw would know it. Conni would think only that her life had been ruined for nothing, and Spencer didn't want to make Conni feel even more hopeless. She needed hope to sustain her. Spencer felt some empathy for Conni. He didn't want to destroy her.

And Jim Shaw? He would become embroiled in a scandal that could wreck his potential public service. His countrymen would always come back to the time when he was young and involved in a vicious, incestuous quadrangle. As Ted Kennedy had never been able to live down Chappaquiddick, so Jim Shaw would never be able to live down Kristina and Nathan Sinclair. Spencer didn't want to drive the last nail into Jim's career coffin.

Slowly Spencer became aware of white flashing lights, of a hundred people, shouting, shoving black sponge balls into his face, bulbs going off. It looked like daylight. Fake daylight. But it was night, and cold. Once again, Spencer pushed past the swarm of reporters with nothing to say except in answer to the question "Are you the detective in charge of this case?"

"Not anymore," replied Spencer.

He drove to Hanover and did not look back at the tall and foreboding pines on the golf course near the police headquarters where he had passed five years of his life.

At home on Allen Street, he packed. It didn't take long; he had brought little with him and accumulated only a few things during his years in Hanover. Why didn't I grow roots here? he thought. Was it because I always knew I would leave? No, he had loved Hanover. He just hadn't gotten around to growing roots. He had been too busy surviving to be bothered with living.

Spencer haphazardly threw his stuff into suitcases. His mind was elsewhere. Oddly, he wasn't thinking about the job as detective-sergeant he just quit, or about what he was going to do next, or even about going home, a place he hadn't been to in years.

Spencer was thinking about the four friends, about the sleaziness, the trailer-trash vulgarity, of their relationship. The bad feelings kept washing over him like rain.

Jim Shaw. Conni Tobias. Nathan Sinclair. Kristina Sinclair.

Jim Shaw. Something barreled in loud and clear into Spencer's consciousness. *Jim Shaw.*

Why hadn't he reported seeing Kristina's black boots when he walked into them last Wednesday? He had said he was scared, but Spencer didn't buy it.

Rather, scared for whom?

Could Jim Shaw have known about the incident that Frankie had witnessed a year ago? Could they all have known about it, maybe even laughed about it during the low-minded games they played with one another when cards would no longer do?

Spencer threw on his parka and left the room. Disgusted with Hanover, he looked at nothing but his own feet as he walked to Hinman Hall.

Jim answered the door. He looked worn out and older than the student Spencer had met four days ago. He was unshaven and his hair was unbrushed. Spencer knew Jim had not been studying. Jim looked stricken. Spencer thought it was by the impending funeral, but Jim said, "Conni . . . she's been arrested."

"Yes, I know," said Spencer, nodding.

"It's horrible for her, horrible."

"Yes," said Spencer, wanting to say that it was horrible for Kristina, too.

"What do you think will happen to her?"

"To Conni? She'll get herself the most expensive lawyer her father can buy, and hope for the best."

"What do you think? Is there a way out?"

Spencer came in and sat down in the lounge chair. He looked around Jim's room.

"Jim, I know how you feel, but Conni *was* on the bridge and her blood *was* on Kristina."

Shaking his head and covering his face, Jim said, "No, no. I don't believe it. It can't be."

"Jim, she did it to herself. I know it's hard to deal with."

"She didn't do it, she didn't," Jim said. "I just don't believe it."

"You don't?" Spencer said. "Who, then?"

"I don't know," Jim said. "Someone else."

"Like you?"

Jim shook his head.

"Like Albert?" When Jim didn't respond, Spencer said, "Is there something you know?"

"I'm not saying it was him. I'm just saying . . ."

Spencer nodded. "What about last Wednesday? When you saw your girl-friend in the snow? Did you think Conni killed her then?"

Shaking his head defiantly, Jim said, "I don't know what you're talking about."

"No?"

Jim lowered his gaze. Spencer nodded and stood up. "I thought so."

"What did you come here for?" Jim exclaimed. "Did you come here to tor-ture me?"

"I came here to tell you that when you testify, you should muster enough courage to tell the court the truth."

"The truth?"

"Yes, the truth. You should tell them, to save your good name, that you ran away from your ex-girlfriend's dead body because you were afraid the girl you loved had killed her. That's correct, isn't it?"

"I don't know what you mean," Jim said loftily. "I told you I was afraid."

"Yes, but not for yourself, for her." Spencer said. "You knew about the incident on the bridge, didn't you? Last year? Conni could've killed her then, you know. She wanted to."

Jim lowered his eyes. Spencer nodded and walked toward the door. "Think about what I've asked you." And turning around, Spencer said to Jim, "Good luck."

Very quietly, Jim said, "Sending Conni to prison will not bring Kristina back."

"Of course not. It never does bring the victims back." Spencer shook his head and backed away through the open door. "You're allowing your feelings for Conni to cloud your judgment. The guilty have to be brought to justice." Spencer paused. "What's wrong with you? Kristina's life is over forever. And Kristina didn't ask to be killed."

Jim lifted his eyes. "No?" he said.

Spencer walked back into the room and moved close to Jim. "What the hell are you saying?"

Jim backed away. "God will forgive Conni," he said. "God should be the one to punish her, too."

"And God will," said Spencer. "Eventually. But here on earth, men enforce God's rules. And his first is thou shalt not kill."

Jim stared hard at Spencer and then said harshly, "How does it feel, detective? To just come in and ruin people's days—hell, their lives? Does it feel good?"

Looking down at Jim, Spencer said through gritted teeth, "You just have no idea. If I wanted to ruin your day, I'd ruin it good and proper. Hell, I'd ruin your Christmas vacation."

Spencer was nearly going to tell him about Nathan Sinclair, but in the end didn't want to waste one more breath on this kid.

On Tuesday morning, Spencer moved out of his apartment and got a room at the Hanover Inn, where Howard was arranging details for Wednesday's after-funeral buffet at the Daniel Webster Room.

Spencer was going to stay through the funeral and then drive back to Long Island. It was somehow fitting that Spencer should stay at the Inn on his last day in Hanover. After all, he had stayed at the hotel on his first day.

The hotel room had more furniture than his entire apartment. Through two Georgian windows, he overlooked the Baker bell tower and Dartmouth Hall. After eating lunch at the Ivy Grill, Spencer took an afternoon nap, under the covers of a king-size bed with a macramé canopy. He woke up exactly at three to the sound of the bell tower playing "Let It Snow, Let It Snow, Let It Snow."

He looked outside. It wasn't snowing.

It was cold but sunny when Spencer went outside. He could see Dartmouth Hall, its black shutters, its white paint, and felt a tremor of regret run through him. What had he done?

But the snow-covered common square, the Baker Library, with its white clock tower, and the students milling about Dartmouth Hall didn't give him the feeling of affection for Hanover he had once had. As he walked along Main Street under the green awnings, Spencer was aware of his own disenchantment. Hanover seemed to him like a straying mistress. She had once been beautiful, but now as he looked into her betraying face he felt only drab anger and saw none of the loveliness. The hell with it all.

He got into his Impala; the first thing he saw was the police radio and the siren on the seat next to him. One day he'd have to return those.

He drove to Red Leaves House. On the way Spencer thought about Kristina almost dying in a ditch near the reservoir, and he slowed down to a crawl at the spot where the accident had occurred. Someone behind him started to honk, so he moved on, trying to ignore the knot in his stomach.

Spencer drove through Lebanon and made a right onto a quiet street. He'd been to Red Leaves House twice before, both times to bring runaway pregnant teens to a place where they would not be judged. There was only one such place in the Upper Valley region. No wonder Kristina loved Red Leaves.

He got outside, walked past the establishment plaque, which was nailed to a post cemented into the sidewalk, and knocked on the door. A woman answered, led him to another woman, and another. The owner of Red Leaves wasn't here today, he was informed, but could anybody else help him?

When the counselors and the teenagers found out who he was, they gathered around him like churchgoers. They clucked solicitously, stuffed a cup of tea into his hand, put some tea biscuits in front of him, sat him down, and crowded around him.

A few of the women sobbed openly. They shook their heads, asked him to tell them what really happened, and kept interrupting him with exclamations, how unbelievable, how could it have happened, this sort of thing never happened in their part of the country. Spencer wanted to tell them that this sort of thing happened everywhere.

He wanted to explain to them how much Red Leaves had meant to Kristina, but he didn't have the words. The women, however, with their tears and kind words, clearly showed Spencer how much Kristina Kim had meant to them.

They would have claimed her body, Spencer thought. All of them, collectively, would have come in and rescued her from the anonymity of the metal gurney. They would have claimed her.

Spencer explained that it was probably a crime of passion, that the girl who the police department thought had killed her went temporarily crazy, that she had been crazy with jealousy for several years. One woman acknowledged that Kristina was a beautiful girl, there was a lot to be jealous over. Spencer halfheartedly agreed. He was being unexpectedly treated to an alive Kristina. It comforted him.

He asked them if they were coming to the funeral tomorrow. Then he asked if they had received news of the money coming to them. The assistant to the proprietor stepped forward and dabbing her eyes said, "Yes. She was extraordinary, wasn't she? Just extraordinary. To have thought of us, to have remembered us. It's really too much."

She told Spencer that after the local paper wrote on Sunday that Kristina's fortune was going to Red Leaves House, they'd had a remarkable response.

Today they must have gotten five hundred cards with checks in them. One of the counselors brought over three mail bags to show Spencer. He was impressed. Kristina had left a mark on this earth. Her good had begat good. Actually, it was Albert's—no, Nathan's—good that had begat good, but Spencer wasn't about to give that bastard a gram of recognition for anything.

Spencer sat for a while listening to them, nodding politely. The armchair was comfortable, he was warm, the last of the day's sunlight was coming in from the side windows and making him sleepy. He actually closed his eyes, and when he opened them again, his insides ached for home. Wherever that home was, he knew it wasn't in Hanover.

After Spencer bid them all good-bye and walked out to his car, it occurred to him that until today he had never drunk tea in his adult life.

———•·••·•———

Spencer treated himself to an expensive dinner at the Daniel Webster Room. He knew this would be the last night of his life in Hanover.

The consequences of quitting the only job he'd ever loved hadn't hit him yet. Would the chief give him a reference, or was Spencer planning to be a security guard for the rest of his life?

Will had been a good friend through the years; Spencer was sorry he hadn't made a better departure. Maybe Will could've thrown him a party.

He thought of going back to the headquarters to say a proper good-bye to his old partner and to drop off the last of his police gear, but didn't want to come close to Conni Tobias sitting in her jail cell.

Spencer didn't want to face Conni. Too often he would close his eyes and see Kristina, naked, nearly out of time, standing on the bridge while a fully dressed ranting young woman thrust her hands forward.

What kind of denial did Kristina have to live through twelve months continually facing a girl she knew had tried to kill her?

Kristina had lived too close to death for too long, thought Spencer, trying to work up an appetite for the braised duck he had ordered. Mostly he drank. He drank alone at the table, and when his glass was empty he would motion for another. He sat quietly without disturbing a soul and drank to dull the pain, drank to forget. By two in the morning, Spencer had drunk enough whiskey to forget pretty much anything, and mostly he had.

Except he couldn't forget *Katherine Morgan Sinclair.*

ONCE UPON
A TIME IN
GREENWICH,
CONNECTICUT

The memory of Katherine Sinclair tugged at Spencer's whiskey-laden heart.

Spencer saw Katherine Sinclair for the first time sitting calmly in her wheelchair near a white-framed window.

She probably had been a beautiful and stylish woman. Now there was only a glimmer of a life long gone, a life once well lived and well loved but now past. Katherine's hair was untended. He imagined how it had looked when there was color to it and a brush ran through it, and shampoo and conditioner every day; when the hair was set in curlers or left loose, blond and wavy around the shoulders. Katherine Morgan Sinclair. Her name still had glamour. It didn't matter where Katherine was now, it didn't matter what she looked like or what she wore, or how she talked. What mattered was that her name still said everything.

I am Katherine Morgan Sinclair, it said. And I once had a life.

It was a miracle he had found her. He had spent two and a half hours on Sunday morning calling every hospital in Connecticut until he found a Katherine Sinclair at Norwalk State Hospital. The director was protective of Katherine and her fragile health and was extremely reluctant to let Spencer in to see her, badge or no badge. Spencer had to threaten Katherine with a subpoena before he was allowed in.

When he came to see her, he didn't know what to expect. "I'm much better now," Katherine had told him. "I could leave anytime, really, but it's comfortable here, and they take good care of me." She had agreed immediately to see Spencer without knowing who he was or what he had come to tell her, and now sat there stoically, regally, her back firmly against the wheelchair. She occasionally turned toward the window, outside which was a park, a meadow, a lake.

Katherine was blind. She sat there quietly, her white cane propped behind her wheelchair. Spencer guessed the white cane was redundant. The nurses probably brought it because she asked for it, but it looked as if Katherine Sinclair never rose from her wheelchair. Her body had the weak look of long atrophy. Her limbs were loose beneath her skin.

Spencer cleared his throat.

"Don't bother, Detective O'Malley," Katherine said quietly. "I know you came to tell me she is dead. Didn't you?" she said without inflection.

Spencer nodded, and then, realizing she couldn't see him, said, "Yes."

They sat. A twitch passed through Katherine. It started in her eyelids and passed all the way down through her mouth and her neck and her arms and legs and ended in her feet. Then Katherine was still.

She stared at the space to the left of Spencer's head, and he stared at the blanket that lay limp on her lap. He couldn't bear to look at her.

Finally, Katherine asked Spencer to get her a glass of water.

When she had taken a sip, she whispered, "My baby. My baby." Spencer reached out to touch her, and she said, "No, no, detective. Please. It'll be harder with your comfort. I'll be all right. Just give me a minute."

He gave her two minutes, and then five.

"Did you know my daughter, Detective O'Malley?"

He nodded. He had to stop doing that. "Yes, Mrs. Sinclair. I did. Not well, unfortunately."

"She was still quite beautiful, was she?"

"Very beautiful."

Katherine smiled. "Yes. She was really exquisite as a child. It used to break my heart to look at her. I just couldn't believe she could be so beautiful. Or do you think every parent thinks so about her children?"

Spencer's own mother thought the world never had more beautiful children than her own. "Kristina was objectively lovely," he said.

She nodded. "Yes. You know, I'm happy now I can't see. I had seen her, and that was enough. Now I won't have to see her dead." Her eyes filled with tears.

Spencer turned away.

"How did she die, detective? Was she in a car accident? Did she freeze? Was she murdered?"

Spencer wanted to say yes to all three; he was profoundly upset. "She froze," he said. "How did you know?"

"The snow, she loved the snow," Katherine said brokenly. "She used to run outside in her pajamas the mornings after it snowed. And fall on her back into the snow. Get up, I used to shout. You'll freeze to death."

Spencer shuddered.

It was a miracle Kristina had lived at all, Kristina's mother told Spencer. Katherine was a diabetic, and Kristina and her twin brother were born eight weeks premature.

The boy didn't make it; he had been born too weak.

Kristina, meanwhile, spent the first three months of her life fighting for it. Katherine buried her baby son and then day after day trod to the Greenwich Memorial Hospital to sit next to the incubator that warmed her only child. Kristina weighed one and a half pounds when she was born, but she held on for dear life. "How she held on, Detective O'Malley," said Katherine Sinclair with misted eyes, her fingers furiously tearing at the worn cotton blanket on her lap. "Every breath she took, I thought it would be her last. I listened to her and I thought I would go insane hearing her gasp for breath, up, down, short, short, long, too long, another labored breath. But she came through in the end. We took her home on her four-month birthday. She weighed eight pounds then." Katherine smiled. "She grew up nice and tall, didn't she?" She stopped smiling suddenly. She stopped tearing at the blanket and turned in the direction of the window. "She grew up so nice. So neat. And she wasn't a diabetic. She was healthy as anything after her first year. Didn't ever get chicken pox or any other childhood disease. Rarely caught cold, never had the flu. You'd never know she'd been on the edge of death."

"No, you certainly wouldn't," agreed Spencer. "She looked a little like you," he added, trying in vain to make the woman feel better.

After some time Katherine continued, "For the first seven years of her life she grew up as our only child, spoiled like you can't imagine."

"I can imagine, Mrs. Sinclair," said Spencer.

"She had two governesses. At four she began piano lessons on her own Steinway grand piano, at five ballet and gymnastics, at seven she wanted to play violin, so my husband and I bought her the best instrument available. She learned to ride horses, had her own horse in a stable we built in the back of our property. My husband ran a very successful business, and I came from money. My mother was very well off."

"Yes, I know," said Spencer.

"Everyone doted on Kristina. I hovered in the background constantly, wanting her, needing her, loving her. She would brush off my kisses as she concentrated on Mozart. I didn't mind. She was my only child—can you imagine how I loved her?"

Spencer could only imagine—not the wealth; the mothering. Ah, shit, he said to himself, shaking his head.

"When Kristina was seven, my husband and I realized we were ruining her. Completely. Our attention was harming her. She became self-involved, independent. She needed a brother or sister. But having children of our own was no longer possible, not if I wanted to live to raise them, and I did, you see."

"Yes, Mrs. Sinclair, I see."

"We adopted a child from an orphanage in Texas. We went all the way to Fort Worth to find just the right boy."

Spencer could only nod.

"He was a perfect little boy, dark, thin, well-behaved; he even looked a little like our Krissy. He was desperately in need of a home, and that suited us just fine, because we desperately needed to give him one. The sisters at the orphanage said he had been found three years earlier on the shoulder of a local highway in the middle of the night. At the orphanage at first he didn't speak. For the first year, not a word. Then two years before we adopted him, he started to speak. He didn't have a name, he didn't know his parents, he didn't know his date of birth. The sisters called him Billy. We renamed him Nathan. After our dead boy. We made his birthday a day before Kristina's, just like her older twin, who was born at ten minutes to midnight."

Katherine must have sensed Spencer's reaction, because she said, "Yes, I know. That old superstition. You shouldn't name a living child after a dead one, my friends told me. Well, why not, I said. Jews do. So I did. We were God-fearing people, not superstitious. We went to church every Sunday, and we said grace at our dinner table. We didn't believe in old wives' tales."

"I don't either," Spencer agreed.

"Ah, but we should have," said Katherine. "We adopted him, we gave him our name, we gave him everything we gave Kristina. Actually, we gave him more. He was a needy little boy."

"I'm sure," said Spencer.

"Kristina wasn't needy at all—as I said, she was too independent. She really thought her daddy and I cramped her style, hovering over her constantly as we did. But Nathan was another matter. He lapped up our love and got very attached to us. He didn't like to go anywhere without us, or be in the house at night without us. He was an affectionate boy. A beautiful boy.

"The children took to each other instantly. Kristina was the aggressor, and I always had to intervene on Nathan's behalf. Kristina, don't tease your brother, Kristina, don't make fun, Kristina, leave him alone, Kristina, act your age. Kristina, Kristina, Kristina . . ." Katherine caressed her daughter's name as she spoke.

"But secretly I was glad. They played, they fought, they watched TV, they played in the yard. Kristina taught Nathan how to swim. He didn't know how. He taught her how not to be afraid."

"Afraid of what?"

"Of anything. If there was one quality that described him, it was dauntlessness. Nathan wasn't afraid of anything. Unlike Kristina, who had a number of childhood fears, of the dark, particularly. Nathan taught her to hold her breath underwater, long past the time the lifeguards would come. Nathan was the boy who climbed a tree and jumped from one tree to another, he was the one who broke his leg hopping the fence and didn't tell anybody for three days, he was the one who got straight As on everything without ever looking inside a textbook. He was our shining star. We couldn't believe God would bless us with such a boy."

All Spencer could think of was that Nathan hadn't taught Kristina *that* well, because she had continued to be afraid of the dark.

"Kristina wasn't jealous?"

"Are you kidding? She must've been pretty lonely her first seven years. *We* were jealous of *them*. They were inseparable. They seemed to have a bond that we couldn't even understand, much less penetrate.

"They excelled in school. They were impeccably mannered, even Nathan, who learned well despite coming from nothing, from a garbage can somewhere on the plains of Texas. Three years passed, then five, then seven. I got back into my charity work, my husband worked hard on his imported textile business, we went out, we threw dinner parties, at which Kristina played the piano and Nathan sang. He had a beautiful voice.

"Even now, after everything, I look back on those years and think we had a perfect life. We had a life most people only dream of. Most of our friends were many times divorced, many times remarried, with children, stepchildren, half siblings coming together or coming apart, doing drugs at thirteen, rehab at fifteen, getting caught for stealing, stealing from their parents, rude, spoiled, indulged children, unhappy mothers, drifting, restless fathers. We knew women who were having affairs with nearly everyone who came to their front door, and their men worked all day and looked the other way at night. Except one man who shot and killed his wife."

Spencer raised his eyebrows.

"John and I thought we had shielded our children from all that. We thought we'd given them a good life."

"You had."

"Well, we thought so then," said Katherine. "Even now, I don't know where we went wrong. Should I have paid more attention to them? Less?

Given Kristina more attention? Given Nathan less? Adopted another child? What?"

Spencer didn't know what to say. Still, something was called for, so he reached over and patted Katherine's hand. She didn't move.

"It sounds like it was a good life, Mrs. Sinclair," he said, and in response she made a rasping sound, a strangled cry.

"Sure does, doesn't it?" she said. "We loved that boy as our own. Do you understand?"

"Absolutely," he said.

"My husband was priming Nathan to take over our family business when he was older. And in our will, we divided our assets equally between the kids. They both had trust funds that would become available to them when they turned twenty-one."

Spencer nodded, once again belatedly realizing she couldn't see him.

"Nathan and Kristina—" Katherine swallowed hard, as if it physically hurt her to say the two names together. "Little by little they started drifting away from us. Nathan stopped wanting to spend time with us. Kristina never did want to. Oh, well, we said. Just normal growing up—what do they want with old fogies like us, anyway? By the time they were fourteen, they were more withdrawn from us than ever. We attributed it to their being teenagers. Sometimes teenagers are just like that. Their schoolwork hadn't suffered, they still got along, they had dinner with us. But something was different. I don't know. Maybe it was my little girl. I thought I knew her. She was always such an outspoken, forward child, but lately—then, back then," she corrected herself quickly, "she was getting inside herself and not coming out much. You know? I still heard Nathan's voice in the house, but Krissy stopped talking back. It used to make me smile to hear them argue, but now they were silent upstairs, silent in the family room, and pretty silent at the dinner table, too. Very polite, both of them. Too polite.

"Was this teenage rebellion? My husband and I wondered. If it was, it wasn't too bad, we decided. Many parents we knew had it much worse. You grow up indulged, the excesses just have to show themselves on teenagers. They show themselves in adults surely enough."

"What excesses?" said Spencer, almost not wanting to know.

"That's right. I didn't see anything wrong either. Now, with perfect twenty-twenty vision—isn't *that* ironic?" Katherine smiled in his direction. She must have been so beautiful once, thought Spencer. "I say these things to you, but then I went along blithely, I did my charity work, I threw my small and large dinner parties twice a week, we went to New York for charity events, social functions, plays, parties."

She was intent on telling him more and more about her past life. Spencer already had a good idea of what kind of life they had led in their estate mansion in Greenwich, Connecticut. But she wasn't through. She needed to talk about it. She went on at some length about Kristina's piano and violin lessons, about her ballet dancing, about the money she spent on ballet shoes and tutus, about Nathan's making the varsity basketball team.

"I first thought something might be wrong when Kristina was fourteen and a half. And she came to me—no, she didn't, our governess did, Mrs. Pitt came to me and said that Kristina had quit her music and dance lessons. All of them. When I confronted her, Kristina said she'd become bored. It was very strange, you have to understand. She's been playing the piano since she was five. Now she wants to quit? I didn't buy it. My husband didn't buy it. But what could we do? She didn't tell us anything was wrong. We sent her to our family psychologist, who said she was closed-mouthed. He seemed concerned, and that concerned us. He said her behavior could be a response to something. He asked if anyone had recently died. No, we said. The kids are very happy. There isn't a problem.

"Every summer they went to Lake Winnipesaukee in New Hampshire, to my mother's house. She adored them both, was ecstatic to have them, but Kristina had always been her undisputed favorite. I was my mother's only child. I think she felt like she was raising another daughter. The kids loved going there, she loved having them. But when Kristina was fourteen and a half, she quietly told me she'd prefer not to go. It was inexplicable. Not go? But why? Grandma loves you. Oh, I know, she said, and then hesitated and didn't say any more. I couldn't get another word out of her on the subject. She went. The following year, she said again that maybe she could do something else this summer. I knew my mother would be devastated not to have her—she'd had Kristina every summer since she was born. When Kristina didn't offer me any explanation for why she didn't want to go, I insisted. I said it was ridiculous." Katherine paused. "So she went."

Spencer asked, "She went, or—"

"No, they both went. Of course. They both went. I thought nothing more about it, but when they came back, Kristina was more into herself than ever. Even my mother had mentioned Kristina's moodiness. We talked about it and decided it was just adolescence. You have sisters, detective?"

"Yes, three of them."

"Didn't they go through adolescent angst?"

Actually, he didn't remember. They were always the same to him, and he was too young to notice how they acted with other people. When Spencer was young his world had been his family, and his sisters had been his surrogate mothers. *When I was born, Kathleen, the oldest child, was twenty, Maureen, the fourth, was fourteen, and Sinéad thirteen. By the time I was old enough to understand anything, they had long grown and flown and married. Kathleen, in fact, had my nephew Harry two years before I, the uncle, was even born. Some uncle I was to Harry. He is now thirty-two and calls me his little Uncle Spencer.*

"I guess so," said Spencer. "I guess they seemed different during that age."

"Yes, that's right," Katherine exclaimed sharply. "I'm sure your mother didn't think anything of it."

"I am *sure* my mother didn't," said Spencer.

"I didn't either. Kristina and Nathan returned from New Hampshire, started school, everything was okay. I kept busy. There are many charity fundraisers to organize before Thanksgiving and Christmas in Greenwich."

Spencer understood. "And then?"

"Then? Then nothing. Sometime in October of 1988, in my own house, in my own great room, on my new couch, my husband came to me on a Thursday night, after a long business dinner, and said, 'I have to talk to you. It's about Kristina.'

"Absentmindedly, I said, sure, what is it? I was stuffing envelopes or mailers, or whatever. John said people had been saying terrible things about Kristina, so awful that he'd punched his brother Jeff earlier that evening because he was so upset. Jeff apparently passed along some information.

"Now I looked at him. I put my mailers away, and looked up at John. If he said he hit his brother, it had to be serious. John had never hit anybody in his entire life. Then.

"John told me vicious rumors have been flying around North Street. People were saying—it was just too horrible—that Kristina was pregnant.

"I laughed. That was my first reaction. I just laughed. Don't be ridiculous, I said. You interrupted me to tell me this? Don't be so ridiculous. She doesn't even have a boyfriend. And he just stared at me so hard that I got very scared. I shook my head and laughed again. What's gotten into you, John? I said. Cut it out. What are you talking about? I might have screamed at this point. It can't be true, you know that.

"Call her, he told me. Call her down. It was late, but I did call her down. I heard her slowly walking down the stairs, and then she stood in front of us, in her white robe and slippers, looking tired and beautiful. 'Krissy, Daddy is driving Mommy crazy,' I said. 'Look how late it is and we got you out of bed.' She asked us what was the matter, and I felt better for a minute, until I said, 'Daddy's been hearing things around town, some awful lies, I can't even believe I'm repeating them to you. Daddy—your father and I—we wanted to know—' I couldn't continue. I was shaking badly by this point. It was just so absurd. I laughed again, and then John got up off the couch and asked our daughter, 'Kristina, they're saying—someone told me you might be pregnant. Is that true?' "

Katherine bowed her head, as if five years and blindness could not hide the bare humiliation she felt then.

"And she said yes.

"I looked at my daughter as I've never looked at her before, or since. I looked at her and saw her, saw her good and proper, maybe for the first time in her teenage life, I saw her as she was—gaunt, pale, with circles under her eyes, with tired lips and sunken cheeks, and that loose white robe.

"Apparently it was the talk of the town. Greenwich is really a provincial town, when you get right down to it. A small-minded town. This was the whisper topic of the cocktail parties and the dinner parties and the indoor tennis games."

Spencer patted her hand. Katherine did not move it away. Her body was motionless.

"That child, she was mine. She was mine, do you understand? How did we go from her being mine to being pregnant at fifteen?"

As if that was the worst of it, thought Spencer glumly, and Katherine must have read his mind, because she nodded and said, "Yes. Pregnant at fifteen, by *him*.

"I had to face her. I can't forgive myself for what I did then. I came up to her and slapped her hard in the face. She fell to the ground. I was going to hit her again, but my husband held me back. I couldn't even look at John. And eventually—much too soon—I had to face Nathan. I could barely speak when I faced him."

She could barely speak now, remembering it.

"Too awful, Detective O'Malley. Too awful. Nathan looked at me with remorseless eyes, he looked at me as if he just couldn't understand what all the fuss was about, and I knew then, I knew my husband would kill him if he saw that look in his eyes. He would kill him. And I knew how he felt. I understood. I wanted to kill Nathan too, seeing him stare shamelessly at me."

Spencer shook his head. He was glad Katherine couldn't see him.

"I packed him up, very quickly—two hours maybe? I packed him up and sent him on a bus to New Hampshire to be with my mother while we figured out what to do with Kristina. I was on serious medication by this time. I must have been taking Valium every two hours, I was a zombie, but it was the only way to get through it all. Medically induced lack of feeling. We thought

Kristina would have an abortion, but would you believe it, she plainly refused. Refused. And do you know why? Because of the worst five words in the English language a mother can possibly hear. Kristina said, *'But Mom, I love him.'* "

Spencer sniffed loudly and shook his head. Katherine blindly sought his hand with hers. He gave it to her, and she took it and squeezed it. Tears were in her eyes. " 'But Mom, I love him,' " Katherine whispered. "Can you imagine anything worse?"

"No," said Spencer frankly.

"We couldn't drag her against her will to a clinic. I even told Kristina I'd gladly perform the operation myself. But she didn't want it. She wanted—can you believe it?—to keep the baby." Katherine laughed silently. "I had been more proud of my daughter than of anything else in my life, she was my crowning achievement, but the Sinclairs have a proud tradition of finishing high school before they become pregnant by their brothers."

Red Leaves House. Spencer wanted to tell this destroyed woman that her life's work had not been in vain. That Kristina had tried to do something with her life, tried to ease the pain she had caused. But he couldn't. Katherine's daughter was dead, murdered; her husband was dead, and her mother was dead. Only Nathan Sinclair remained.

"How did Kristina get to marry Howard Kim?"

"Well, tongues were wagging all over Greenwich. The whole town had become one big wagging dog. Wag, wag, wag. We had to do something. And soon. My soon-to-become ex-friends, they may have known that Kristina was pregnant, but they didn't know by whom. They guessed it was some high school boy. If they were to guess at the truth—" She swallowed hard. "Have you met Howard Kim? He is a good-looking man."

"Yes," agreed Spencer. "He is."

"He practices tai chi chuan. He was in good shape, mentally, physically. Also, he took his responsibilities seriously. Which is why my husband trusted him and went to Hong Kong. Howard had wanted to come to America for a long time. Finally he had his chance. So you see?" she said, trying to smile. "Everybody won."

Spencer didn't say anything.

"How is he now?" she asked.

"He is very well. Successful."

"Good, good," she said without emotion. "I'm glad for him. Did she die still married to him?"

Spencer shook his head. "No," he then said quickly, remembering she couldn't see him. "They were divorced in November."

"This November? Just past?"

"Yes."

"When did she die?"

"November twenty-fourth," said Spencer, and watched the mother shudder.

"Two days after her birthday," she said, her voice breaking.

"Yes."

"Did she—" Her voice broke. She whispered, "Did she die a good death, detective?"

No, she died a violent death, he wanted to tell her, and she fought for every last breath, for every aching, icy breath, but in the end, her shoulder was too weak and her arm too sore, her ribs couldn't hold off the pressure, her throat was fragile, full of fragile life, and it gave out in the end, though not without a railing fight.

"Yes," he said aloud, but couldn't add anything more.

Katherine stared into space. "I always thought she would die young," she whispered. "I don't know why. She lived too much life when she was too young. She didn't save any for later."

After a silence, Spencer asked, "Did marrying Howard quiet the wags?"

"Oh, you know." Katherine waved dismissively. "It really didn't matter. The following month, the son of one of my friends went into drug rehab, another's was in the hospital for overdosing, a couple more kids were arrested for drunk driving on the interstate. Life went on. That is—other people's lives.

"We just kind of stood still—lost at that moment, suspended in our house, without Kristina, without Nathan, and really without each other. My husband blamed me. I blamed myself. A few months later I overdosed on Valium myself and spent a month in the hospital. I think John was hit harder than I was— if that's possible. He thought of Nathan as his son, you see."

When Spencer didn't say anything, lost in his thoughts, Katherine said, "Marrying Howard was the right thing to do. Even if she had had the abortion, detective. Big deal. That's like killing the devil's child. There is still the small matter of the devil. And what? Should he have continued living in our house?"

"Of course not. Of course not."

"And if we sent him away, how would we have explained that?"

"But Mrs. Sinclair—you *did* send him away. How did you explain *that*?"

"His sister got married, and he wanted to be closer to her. We sent him to boarding school in New York."

"Ahh."

"It was really the best possible course."

"Of course."

Katherine didn't speak after that, just sat there and kneaded her old cotton blanket. Spencer finally said, "Where is he now? Nathan? What happened to him?"

"I don't know. After my mother found out why Nathan was with her—"

"How did she find out?" Spencer interrupted.

"Believe it or not, Nathan told her." A little smile crossed Katherine's lips. "He was just dauntless. He told her, she said, because he wanted her to be appalled at the way *we* had treated Kristina. The gall." Katherine snorted, but her unseeing eyes betrayed some other emotion—shame? Guilt?

"My mother kicked him out of her house, into the middle of winter. He was sixteen, and she took out a gun from her nightstand, my seventy-eight-year-old mother, who had me when she was forty-four, and told him to get out or die. He got out. No one has heard from him since."

"Did Kristina hear from him?"

"No, I don't think so. He didn't care about any of us. Besides, my husband forbade her. Nathan's trust fund had been dismantled, and John had set up a separate one for Kristina to be administered by Howard, a trust fund for her living expenses, college, and whatever else. But John stipulated that if there was one sight of Nathan, Kristina wouldn't get a penny of that money."

Spencer said that if Kristina had loved Nathan she would've figured out a way to see him.

Katherine scoffed. "Love him! She didn't love him. Sixteen-year-old girls don't know the first thing about love. Money was too important to her. She wouldn't have risked it, not even for him."

"You don't think so?"

"No, absolutely not."

"How can you be so sure?" he asked.

Katherine was slowing down. Spencer could see she was becoming less interested in answering his questions, and generally less interested in sitting with him altogether.

"Because . . ." She sighed wearily, ruffled her blanket, and went on, "John knew some people. He hired a private investigator to find Nathan, but he had disappeared from the face of this earth. No one could find him. We assumed he'd left the country or changed his name. Or both."

"Or died," said Spencer wishfully.

"Died." She sniffed. "We wouldn't be so lucky, detective. Besides, the evil he brought lives on eternally. Nothing would've changed. My husband was consumed by what had happened. You know, he would regularly disappear for weeks at a time, coming back thinner and sicker than ever. John said he was out looking for *him*. I think that when my husband didn't kill Nathan right then and there, he just couldn't live with himself anymore."

Spencer understood that.

"I've been in and out of hospitals ever since Kristina left us. I haven't been well, you know. My diabetes—it's wrecked my eyes, my arms, look—" Katherine showed Spencer her right forearm, black-and-blue, swollen and peppered with needle punctures. "Does it look as bad as it feels? They give me morphine to deal with the pain. I don't think I'm leaving this place. Why? What for? Even without my mother's money, I can still afford to stay here."

"Your mother's money?"

"Yes, my mother's. She was so furious with us for Kristina, she cut us out of her will. I must say I was shocked. My mother had sisters, aunts, cousins, nieces, and nephews. And me. No one got a penny. We were all upset, I tell you."

"Do you know who got her money?"

"Of course I know who got her money, detective," Katherine said. "I did not just fall off the turnip truck. What I want to know is, who gets the money now? Do I get some of that money?"

Spencer shook his head. "Kristina made a will before she died. She didn't speak of you." Spencer peered into the blind woman's face. "Mrs. Sinclair, you and your husband . . . you disowned Kristina, didn't you?"

"We were angry!" Katherine shouted. "We were furious. Do you have any idea how betrayed we felt?"

Spencer said quietly, "It works both ways, you know. If you disown her, you can't get any of *her* money, either."

Katherine breathed out and then shrugged with a humph. "Who'd have thought she'd have any money?" She sat quietly and then said, "She was killed, wasn't she, detective?"

Spencer didn't have the heart to tell her.

Patting the blanket on her lap, he said, "Mrs. Sinclair, don't blame yourself. Please. You did the best you could. Don't blame yourself. Don't sit here feeling guilty. How could you know about Nathan?"

"I could have known. Should have. Why, everyone knows that orphaned children are emotionally screwed up. I read up on it. The attachments they form are few and shallow, the affection they feel is fleeting, their gratitude nil. Their moral code is missing and their social restraint is torn to pieces. That was Nathan, but we thought miraculously he was different. But he wasn't different. He was the stereotype."

"But Mrs. Sinclair, not all orphaned children grow up to be morally and socially deviant."

"It's the norm, detective. No, not all. But they are the exceptions. We didn't get the exception. We got the normal kid. The kid we're all scared of having. It's the monkey. The monkey with a bottle but without the wire mommy. You know. Harlow's famous experiment with monkeys with and without surrogate moms. Nathan had the bottle, but didn't even get a wire mommy to cling to."

Spencer patted the cotton blanket again, at a loss as to what to say or do. "That's no excuse. You didn't know you were going to be this unlucky."

Katherine's mouth stretched into a grimace. "Actually, Detective O'Malley, I'll tell you something. When Nathan was first found, he had with him a small cat, which he was allowed to keep. He had that cat for two years. The cat slept with Nathan and ate from his hand, and followed him around the orphanage. They seemed very attached to each other. When Nathan was six, the silly animal was run over by a truck or a bus, or a small industrial vehicle. When Nathan was told of the cat's death, he immediately threw out all the cat-related paraphernalia, the cat bowl, the litter box, the toys, the catnip, asked for his sheets to be changed, and never spoke of the cat again." Katherine stifled a sob. "When I heard that story, my heart just filled with love and pity for poor Nathan. Now, there's a boy who needs to be loved, I thought. But in the end, the joke was on me, wasn't it? I was the only one who cared about the stupid cat. No one else did. Certainly not Nathan. He never got attached to anything in his life."

Carefully, Spencer said, "Maybe he got attached to Kristina."

Katherine scoffed, "Not so much that he wasn't willing to ruin everything he had going for him."

"Maybe he was willing to risk everything because he loved her."

"Yeah? Well, where is he now, if he loved her so much?"

"Thank God he's not around," said Spencer, feeling strangely bothered. "Just one more loose end."

Katherine said, "You think that because he might have loved her it was okay? As if that justifies everything? Anything?"

"Not at all. It justifies nothing. He is despicable," said Spencer fiercely.

Katherine groaned with despair.

"Forget him, Mrs. Sinclair," said Spencer intensely. "Nathan is unfathomable to us. But you're not. You loved your kids. Please don't blame yourself. There are many parents who treat their children much worse than you treated yours and yet nothing like this ever happens. It was just a freak thing."

"I don't believe you, Spencer." Katherine called him by his first name. "We breed what we plant. We reap what we sow. It's not an accident, and you and I both know it. I just don't know what I could've done to prevent it from happening."

"Nothing," said Spencer. "It was just an accident."

"It's not an accident. If I were dead, it would be an accident. It's not an accident. It's my life."

When it was time to go, Spencer got up and kissed Katherine on the cheek. "Good-bye, Mrs. Sinclair."

She grabbed him by the arm and pulled him to her. "Spencer," she whispered to him, her thin hand reaching up and touching his face. She touched his cheeks, his eyes, his lips, his cropped hair; she circled his eyes again and again with her long dry fingers. "Spencer," she repeated. "Promise me something. Promise me," she said before he had a chance to reply, "that you will find who killed her."

Spencer recoiled, but Katherine pulled him back. "I know somebody murdered her, I know you wouldn't be here unless my baby was murdered. Promise me you will not *rest* till you find him," she whispered.

Spencer tried to extricate himself, but she held on to his arm. "Please, Spencer, promise me."

"I promise," he said, sighing, pressing his forehead against her hair. "I promise."

While driving back to Hanover, Spencer stopped feeling sorry for himself, stopped lamenting his dead wife. He actually began to consider himself lucky. Compared to a blind woman who had lost everything she ever loved, he was lucky.

In the three-hour trip back to Hanover, Spencer thought, God, I'm just like Katherine, behind a window, in a small room, looking out with unseeing eyes, wondering where my life went wrong, wondering what I ever did to make my life go so wrong.

But I don't want to give up on my life just yet. I don't want to give up on it. There is still a bit of it left, and I'm not blind, and I'm not dead.

Chapter Nine

RED LEAVES

S pencer slept poorly in his Hanover Inn bed after a night of drinking. The goose-down quilt was too hot, the pillows were too many, the sheets were too crisp.

In the morning he felt thinner and older when he put on his only suit to go and bury a girl he had known mainly in death.

It was windless, sunny, and bitterly cold out. The snow was iced into the silver ground. The tips of the trees barely moved at Pine Knoll Cemetery on the outskirts of Hanover. Howard had bought a beautiful plot on a raised plateau amid the tallest pines, which stood majestically over Kristina's grave. Spencer thought it was appropriate for her to be buried in a place similar to the one where she had died. Appropriate, yet eerie. Spencer wouldn't want to be her, looking up at the pine trees that she had seen on the edge of death.

About three hundred people turned out for Kristina's memorial service at Rollins Chapel, the Dartmouth College church. There were too many people to fit inside, and many had to stand outside in the cold, just to watch her coffin being carried into the church and then back out. Albert, Jim, Frankie, and Howard were among the six pallbearers. The ornate coffin was black lacquered oak with brass handles. Howard had spent a lot of money to have Kristina buried in style.

A gaunt and restrained Jim Shaw eulogized Kristina. He looked somber but didn't cry. His voice did not break. After he was done, he sat far away from Albert and Frankie.

Then the vice captain of the Big Green women's basketball team stood up and lifting her hand high up in the air, said that Dartmouth basketball would never be the same without Kristina's hair in her opponents' faces. That Dartmouth basketball would never be the same without Kristina.

The women from Red Leaves tried to speak but were too emotionally overcome, except for a girl named Evelyn, who lumbered up to the altar with her twin infant sons, showed them to the coffin, and wailed, "Krissy, they let me keep my babies. Thank you. They let me keep them." Sobbing, she was led away by her father.

Albert wore a dark suit, with a dark shirt and tie. His hair was tied back with a shiny black ribbon. Black sunglasses adorned his face. He didn't get up to speak, and what must have seemed odd to everyone else felt right to Spencer.

He wanted to talk to Albert.

Spencer's mouth went dry. He didn't care about propriety anymore. There was a young girl held in custody, awaiting a trial for her life, and there was another girl dead because this man had consumed them both, this orphan who, with his orphaned heart, had ruined a whole family. What was Spencer to do? He didn't know. But he had promised Katherine Sinclair he would do something.

The burial service at Pine Knoll was slow and less well attended. About a hundred and fifty people, including Spencer, Will, and Chief Gallagher.

Albert wore no overcoat. He stood near the priest with his head bowed. He held something in his hands. Standing behind him, Spencer couldn't see what it was.

Spencer wondered, looking at Albert's back, if *Nathan Sinclair* regretted Kristina's dying. He wondered if Albert had maybe loved her, too, and been swept away by her long dark hair and her beautiful eyes, swept away by her heart that sacrificed her whole family for him. Did Albert, too, save matchbooks from Edinburgh?

Spencer didn't have to wait long to get his answer. Albert came up to the closed coffin, knelt down, brushed the flowers off the top, and tried to lift the cover. The priest and Howard Kim stopped him. What are you doing? they said. Stop, stop. He shook them off, his own shoulders convulsing. *Her coat,* he said quietly. *It's her coat. I want to cover her with it. It was one of her favorite things. Please let me cover her with it. She'll be cold.*

They helped him unlatch and lift the coffin cover, and with trembling hands, *Nathan Sinclair* placed Kristina's maroon coat gently, tenderly into the casket, and then pressed his fingers to his lips in a final kiss.

After the funeral, Spencer checked out of the Hanover Inn and drove to Long Island. He didn't talk to Nathan Sinclair.

Will and Ken Gallagher had approached Spencer to talk him out of going. Gallagher promised him a raise and his own office, while Will appealed to their friendship, but Spencer flatly refused. He was finished with Hanover.

At home, however, there were more urgent matters. His family was together but not intact. A few days earlier, a deranged madman had shot up a Long Island train car full of people coming home from work, killing six and maiming nineteen. Spencer's brother Patrick had been in the train car. He had been wounded in the shoulder and was to spend several weeks at the Stony Brook hospital. He didn't die, and this was the only thing the family talked about during dinner for many weeks. Though Spencer had not seen anybody in his family for five years, he sat down with them at their rectangular wood dinner table that reminded him of Collis Café at Dartmouth. Spencer sat down in his old seat, and was served food and was talked to, and was treated as if nothing had ever happened, as if he had never left.

He thought it felt just right.

He lived with his mother for three months while he worked as a security guard in an office building and as a bodyguard for a local Republican politician. Spencer tired of visiting the local bars at midnight, and then he got tired of his jobs, so he applied again to the Suffolk County police force and was reinstated after several months of psychological tests and a number of ringing references from Ken Gallagher, who seemed eager to provide them. Spencer became one of twenty senior detectives. No individual case was ever his own, but Spencer liked being lost in the shuffle.

In the course of the following year, he went back to New Hampshire several times while *New Hampshire* v. *Constance Tobias* case inched toward trial. Fortunately, the courthouse was in Concord, not Hanover.

Whatever troublesome doubts Spencer had about Conni's guilt were relieved before he could take the stand. With the trial due to begin on the anniversary of Kristina's death, Constance Tobias, through her attorneys, pled momentary lapse of reason and was sentenced to five to fifteen years for voluntary manslaughter, which was less than the twenty-five to life for murder two, and much less than the life without parole for murder one. Her lawyers knew it was a good deal, and Conni took it.

With Frankie Absalom a reluctant witness for the prosecution, all the defense team could do was continue to say she hadn't done it, but Conni did not have an alibi. She couldn't even say she was sleeping or in the bathroom or studying. She didn't have an alibi. And she had a motive.

Nathan Sinclair testified to that for the grand jury. *Albert Maplethorpe* testified to that.

Jim Shaw, a hostile witness for the prosecution, if there ever was one—he had gone to the local courts in Delaware to try to quash the grand jury subpoena—was forced to say under threat of perjury and jail that he knew of the incident the year before Kristina's death when Conni pushed Kristina off the bridge.

Conni Tobias pled voluntary manslaughter, committed under the influence of drugs, alcohol, or uncontrollable emotional forces.

Spencer was glad he did not have to testify and reveal to the defendant Constance Tobias that the crime she had committed was for a scoundrel and a wasted life, though he was prepared to tell the truth on the stand about *Nathan Sinclair.*

Spencer's relief at the plea bargain was short-lived. At the sentencing, Spencer saw Nathan outside the courtroom, deftly fielding questions from reporters. He looked well and smug in his smart suit and with his slicked-back hair. Slimed back, thought Spencer, as he walked up behind Nathan, who was in the middle of some long-winded, pseudo-intellectual answer about the dangers of reason on an emotional heart, and whispered fiercely, "I know all about you, *Nathan Sinclair.*"

And then Spencer continued walking down the court steps. The best part was turning around and seeing Nathan's face, its usual inscrutable blank stare twisted. Nathan stopped talking. A few moments later, he got rid of the reporters and rushed down the stairs after Spencer.

"What did you call me?" he said.

"You heard me," said Spencer.

"I don't think I heard you," he said. "Now what did you call me?"

Spencer stopped walking and faced Nathan. They were eye to eye. Spencer was a little taller and a little thinner. "I spoke to your mother. I know who you are."

"Now I know that's impossible," said Nathan. "My mother is dead."

"No. Katherine Morgan Sinclair is not dead," said Spencer.

"She is not my mother," Nathan replied.

Spencer swallowed. "No, Clairton, Pennsylvania, huh? What, did you stick a pin on a map to come up with that one?"

When Nathan didn't answer, Spencer said, "You keep in touch with your mother?"

"I told you she was not my mother."

"Who was she, exactly?"

"Kristina's mother."

"You keep in touch with Kristina's mother?"

"Now and then," he said evasively, his hands in his suit pockets. "What do you need from me, detective?"

"Nothing, Nathan. Nothing. But Constance Tobias could use something from you—the truth. Don't you think?"

"No," he said firmly.

"No?"

"No. Hasn't she suffered enough?"

"I don't know," said Spencer bitingly. "Has she?"

"Yes," replied Nathan, not flinching. "She has."

"I'm going to go back up to the reporters, Nathan, and I am going to tell the world about you."

"Fine," said Nathan. "You're going to destroy Conni, you're going to destroy Jim, and you're going to destroy what little is left of the Sinclair name and family. I am going to be just the same."

"But maybe you'll talk to reporters a bit less."

"No, actually, I'll talk to them a lot more. I'll be a lot more interesting."

"You're not interesting, you're pathetic," said Spencer.

"Am I the one trying to hurt a girl going to prison for five years? Who's the sad one, detective?"

Spencer was surprised at the intensity of his own feelings. He wanted to kill Nathan. He was usually dispassionate, but this time he took it personally, and the feeling didn't pass. He clenched his fists and gritted his teeth, remaining barely in control.

Nathan smiled.

"I'm not worth it, detective," he said, looking at Spencer's fists. "I'm not worth losing a job over, am I?"

"You're not worth losing a night's sleep over," replied Spencer.

Conni Tobias was taken to a medium-security New England prison, and Spencer went back to Long Island, where life was quiet and comfortable. Spencer was glad to have left Hanover behind. It was good to be around family again, except on those occasions when one of his eighteen nieces and nephews would say, "Uncle Spencie, how come you don't have any kids?"

Spencer went on with his life as best he could, as if he had never left Long Island, never lived in a little town called Hanover, and never stumbled upon a pleasant black-haired girl named Kristina Kim putting on her black boots in the middle of Main Street. In the beginning, it was almost easy. His days were busy, his nights too—two million people in Suffolk County as opposed to ten thousand in Hanover meant little idle time behind a desk. Local bars took care of his rare free time. Occasionally he went to the movies with his brothers.

But Spencer's mind wasn't quiet, his soul wasn't at peace. In the year after Conni's sentencing Spencer spent his free time going over the minutia of Kristina's case. He went over every crumb like a hungry dog looking for food on the kitchen floor.

During the second year, his memory began to dim. He forgot how long Kristina had lain on the ground unclaimed. He forgot about the knee marks on her chest. He forgot how long Conni had been gone from her room. He started to forget the sound of Conni's squeaky voice, and the look of Jim Shaw.

But Spencer could not forget Nathan Sinclair.

Sometimes Spencer would flash back to a face across from him on the steps of the Concord Courthouse, in the middle of the afternoon, saying, "I'm not worth it, detective. I'm not worth losing a job over, am I?" And the feeling of rage, raw and untamed, would spring back at him.

Spencer had missed something, and he kept going over it in his head, until it became a tic with him that followed him throughout the day and made him sleep badly at night.

Nathan Sinclair. Nathan Sinclair. Spencer wanted to tell him how much Kristina had loved him. How she had loved him more than anything in the entire world, how she had given him everything and risked losing everything to have Nathan near her.

He couldn't breathe when he thought of Kristina and Nathan Sinclair.

Spencer began dating a fellow policewoman. She was young, very attractive—too attractive for him, Spencer thought. She was ready, and wanting. She was his age, and he agreed with her that it was about time to get back into the human race.

He didn't like living with himself.

Dreams of Hanover wouldn't go away. He dreamed of the pine trees looking down at Kristina, in death as they looked at her in the last moments of her life, and he dreamed of running through the dark path behind the Feldberg Library, hearing the noises from below.

Every night Spencer would wake up in a sweat, asking himself the same question over and over.

Could Nathan Sinclair have killed Kristina?

He would then turn on the light, open the top drawer of his nightstand, and take out a torn and many-times-folded sheet of paper to reread the inscrutable words: *She makes you will your own destruction.*

Then he would throw it back in the drawer and turn off the light.

Kristina's safety-deposit box screamed her love for Nathan, but oddly, she hadn't left him her full inheritance, hadn't even told him she was coming into an astounding sum of money, the kind of money that would mean freedom from grandmothers and Howards, freedom from Conni and Jim, freedom from work. They could have taken that money and flown to St. Bart's, never to be seen again. Why hadn't she told him?

Not only had she not told him, but the day after her near-fatal crash, Kristina had gone to the bank and specifically made sure he wouldn't get all of her money. Why?

Had she died intestate, everything would have gone to Nathan, her nearest living relative. Nathan would have had to come out of Albert Maplethorpe's skin, but to get nine million dollars, he'd have come out and pledged into a sorority.

She makes you will your own destruction.

Kristina had typed the will, gone to the bank, had the will notarized, and put it into her safety-deposit box. It was probably then that she had scribbled the seemingly meaningless words to Nathan.

He was getting three million dollars. What was she warning him about?

Why would Nathan give the money away? All that money must have seemed like a fortune to a pauper orphan from Texas. Yet he had given his share away as if it were an extra shovel in the sandbox. Had he been angry with her for not leaving him everything? But surely his pointless gesture would mean nothing to Kristina when she was dead.

If he had not killed her for the money, why would he kill her? And if he had killed her for the money, why would he give the money away?

One night, Spencer thought, *he could have killed her. He could have slipped out unnoticed with the pillow under his coat and waited for her in the bushes near the bridge. Maybe that's why he went to Frankie's the afternoon before Kristina died. Not to see his friend but to walk through the woods, to plan his attack, to time himself getting back, throwing out the pillow, maybe even the coat. He could have slipped out that night, waited for her, killed her, quickly walked back through the woods, thrown the pillow and his gloves into the trash compactor, maybe even brought a garbage bag with him, put his coat, gloves, and the pillow in the garbage bag, and then tossed the bag in the compactor. This way he wouldn't have to return the coat and gloves to his room. He would just go back into the lounge where the kid was sleeping and pretend he was there all along, watching TV.*

Spencer laughed out loud. His tortured mind was overacting. All he wanted to do was ease his pain. Even drinking heavily before bed was only good while he was actually drinking.

And still he returned to *Nathan Sinclair.*

Nathan waited in the woods for her, and then called her, and she came, because she didn't fear him and she didn't fear the night with him, nor the dark woods, nor the snow. She came to him in the snow. Did she kiss him? Did she smile? Did her eyes, looking at him, know it was the last minute of her life? Did she get scared and run?

Did she scream?

Spencer got stuck on her scream—night in and night out. What if she screamed and no one heard? To quiet her, he shoved her helpless body to the ground and knelt on top of her and put a pillow to her face. And she tried to roll away from his hands but couldn't move with her bad ribs, bad shoulder. Spencer didn't know, but he may have cried in the night, thinking about Kristina fighting against death.

She makes you will your own destruction.

It made no sense. Why would Nathan kill the only person who took care of him, who loved and nurtured him, who took him out of the tattooed gutter of juvenile courts and paid to change his name and move him to live close to herself?

He couldn't have wanted her money, for he gave away his share as if it were a quarter to a homeless bum.

Why would *he* kill her? Spencer understood why Conni would. The irrational emotion was blazing in Conni's eyes. She had been lied to so often and so long, she could no longer tell reason from insanity. Everything was jumbled up. She was out of control the first time she went to the bridge. The second time she decided to be more thorough. She brought props. Spencer could understand that.

But why would Nathan kill Kristina?

Then he remembered his own words to Kristina Kim the Sunday afternoon they had coffee together. *"Power and intimidation," Spencer had said to Kristina. Suffocation was an act of power. During their final years together, Kristina had all the money, therefore all the power. Albert didn't want to have the money doled out to him anymore by a girl who may have been fed up, who may have wanted out. Who knows, maybe Kristina stopped loving Albert, maybe that's why she didn't leave him all her money in the will. Albert wanted the last interaction between them to be one of him wielding his power over her.*

Conni's words, "I didn't do it," started to ring in Spencer's head like church bells, unexpectedly breaking into a high-pitched song and bruising Spencer's insides.

His work was suffering.

Finally, after an acute episode that lasted most of a rainy Sunday in March, Spencer sent Conni a short note, saying he hoped to come and see her soon. A few weeks later, having given her ample time to receive his letter, Spencer set out for New Hampshire.

It had been two years since he had seen her, and she had changed considerably. Gone was the young girl. Her face was drawn now and full of bitter disappointment. Gone was the happy smile, gone the long blond hair. She was thinner, paler, tougher-looking. Conni was twenty-three; in another two and a half years she'd be eligible for parole. She smoked heavily now, as she had once nervously pulled out her eyebrows.

"How've you been, Conni?" said Spencer, sitting down across from her. They were separated by a glass partition, but they could see and hear each other without phones.

"Fine, as you see. You look different."

Spencer ran his hand through his hair. "My hair—it's not a crew cut anymore."

"Yeah, that's it. You don't look as tough."

"Very deceiving," said Spencer.

Conni smiled. "You look good. Really."

Spencer hadn't come three hundred miles to talk about himself.

"Get a lot of visitors?" he asked.

"Sure, my parents come all the time. My brother comes, like, five times a year, which is pretty good for him, since he lives in LA and all." She paused. "That's not what you meant, is it?"

Spencer shook his head.

"My lawyer comes, too. Not too often. If I'd been convicted, we would have appealed and then I would see him a lot more often. Now there's nothing to appeal, and I'm out one visitor." She paused again. "It's nice of you to come."

He waved her off. "It wasn't nice of me to *not* come for so long."

"Well, why should you come?" Conni said mildly. "The district attorneys don't come."

"Of course they don't. But they . . ." Spencer was stumped. They what? They don't wake up with sweats?

"What, detective?"

"Spencer. Call me Spencer."

"All right, Spencer," said Conni. "Why did you come?"

"I came . . ." He looked down at the gray countertop. "Well, you know, I've been thinking of you a little bit."

"You have?" She smiled. "Good or bad?"

"Neither. I've been thinking of you here, been thinking of you back at Dartmouth, too. Do you ever see your old friends?"

"You know, I was just going to ask you the same question. Do you ever see my old friends?"

"No, never. Haven't been back to New Hampshire since the sentencing."

She fell quiet, as if she were struggling with how to find a way to say what she wanted and needed.

Spencer wanted to help her, but he didn't know how either. Years of work had made him adept at interrogation, not conversation. And years of no personal relationships had made him wary and introverted.

They sat there for what seemed like a long time, while Spencer battled with himself. Finally he looked at her and quietly said, "You didn't do it, did you, Constance?"

Conni's voice cracked when she replied. "No," she said.

Spencer nodded. Somehow he was finding it easy to believe her. "You did try to kill her a year before her murder?" In his detective mode, Spencer was more comfortable.

"Sort of, but not really."

"So why did you plea-bargain?"

"It was either that or face a life sentence on conviction. Five years somehow seemed better than a life." Conni bowed her head.

"Conni, if you didn't do it, you should've stuck to your guns and gone through with the trial. Taken the stand. Told your side. Innocent people don't usually get convicted."

"But sometimes they do, don't they?"

"Sometimes," Spencer allowed.

"Spencer, listen, there's nothing I can tell you except the same old thing, and you must be so tired of hearing it."

Spencer, who'd heard the same old thing day in and day out for the last two years, nodded.

Conni leaned into him. "Go look up Albert, Detective O'Malley. Look up Albert. See what he's up to these days."

Spencer's face hardened and he leaned back. "I doubt Albert's up to much."

"Look him up, detective. Find out what Albert Maplethorpe is doing these days."

Placing his hands palms down on the table, Spencer sighed. "What do *you* think he's doing these days, Conni?"

"I don't know," she replied. "But he has never come to visit me here."

"Did you think he would?"

"I thought he would, yes." And she almost started to cry; her eyes remained dry, but her face became contorted.

"I'm going to tell you something, detective, something I haven't told anybody before today, not even my brother, not my parents, not Jim, nobody."

She paused.

"The night Krissy died, I ran out. I was half crazed with anger, with jealousy. Kristina and I had just had a big fight. I went looking for Albert, but he was nowhere to be found, and neither was Kristina. It was just too much coincidence, and it was always the same. When she was missing, so was he, and vice versa. And now again."

"What time was this?"

"After one. Maybe one-ten, one-fifteen."

Spencer was trembling. "Go on."

"You don't understand what I was feeling. I had called Albert's room at twelve-forty five. Busy. I called again, and again, and again. Busy, busy, busy. Finally, I went up there a little after one. You think I didn't knock on Kristina's door? Of course I did. Only the dog was there. Then I ran down to the lounge. Tim was there, but Albert wasn't. I didn't stay long, but there was no noise in the hall, no noise coming from the bathroom." She paused. "I did notice a beer bottle on one of the tables. But it could have been anybody's."

"It could have, yes. But it could also have been Albert's."

"Yes, but where was he? How long does it take a guy to pee? I ran back upstairs, called his room again, called Frankie, called Jim. I was crazed. I thought he and Kristina were together. I took my coat and ran outside."

"You didn't just run outside. You put on your coat." Spencer was thinking about hiding the pillow Kristina had been killed with.

"It was snowing outside. I just threw it on."

"Did you put a pillow under your coat?"

"A pillow? What are you talking about?"

"A pillow. A little twelve-inch-square pillow. Soft. Just enough to cover Kristina's face with."

Sighing, Conni said, "No, I didn't. Can I tell you what happened?"

Gently Spencer said, "Please."

"We'd just had a fight."

"I know. Your skin was under her nails."

"Yes, we had a fight. It was terrible, I don't know what came over me. She had as usual denied everything—" Conni paused, hurt and conflicted. "Well, not everything. I think she really was trying to tell me the truth. I just didn't want to hear it. That's why I got so upset. I thought, sure, tell me the truth, I want to know, but when she told me, I just freaked. I realized I didn't want to know. I wanted to believe Albert. Why *should* I believe her? He was my boyfriend. Who was she to me?"

"You must have suspected it was true about them."

"I didn't want to think about it, Spencer," Conni said firmly. "I chose not to think about it."

"Why?"

"Why?" She seemed upset by the question. "Because," she answered sadly, "then I would've realized that Albert was lying. I would've realized that he had every reason to lie and had been lying to me for a long time, and if I realized that, I would have had to break up with him—and I didn't want to break up with him. You know?"

Spencer was incredulous. "Even if it meant living an out-and-out lie?"

"Yes," said Conni quietly. "Even if it meant that."

Spencer had nothing to say.

Conni continued, "Anyway, after we had the fight, I left, but then I couldn't find him, then her, and I—I just went crazy. I ran out, looking for them.

"I ran out, first to the parking lot, then down the stairs that led to the boat ramp, then back up the stairs, and I went to look for her on her bridge. I didn't see her or him. I started calling her name. I went to the end of the bridge and looked to my right." She swallowed. "You know, I thought I saw something. Someone. I wasn't sure. I don't know if you've been back behind Feldberg at night. It's dark."

Speechlessly, Spencer nodded. He knew the darkness behind Feldberg.

"But still, I thought I saw something moving in the woods. I slowed down and moved down the path. There was no path anymore, only snow, and my footsteps made no sound. Suddenly I got scared. I can't explain it. Just scared. Like I was a child out in the dark with the boogie man. It was whisper-quiet. Then I heard something. Or thought I heard something." Conni coughed. "I thought I heard the breaking of branches down the slope in the woods. Like footsteps."

Spencer stopped breathing, hanging on to her every word. "The noises, they could've come from down below, from Tuck Drive."

Shaking her head, Conni said, "No. There were branches breaking. And they sounded very close. So close that I thought I might walk into someone. I stopped hearing the footsteps because my heart was pounding too hard, you know?"

Spencer knew.

"I had forgotten my anger, my jealousy, everything. I was just terrified. I stopped walking and listened for the noise again. There it was, but much farther away now. It was the sound of someone walking fast through the forest, toward the dorms."

"Did you see anything?" said Spencer, literally at the edge of his seat.

"You mean who or what it was? No. It could have been a wild animal. But it didn't sound like one. Not that I know what one sounds like. I just know what a person sounds like. And this sounded like a person walking fast through the thick bushes. I didn't hear any footsteps, only branches breaking." Conni paused. "The noise got fainter and fainter and eventually died out. Weird as it sounds, I wasn't any less scared. There was something else I feared. Like . . . badness. Evil. I can't explain it."

"You don't have to," said Spencer. He had no doubt at all that Conni Tobias was telling the truth. "Did you turn around and go back?"

"No, I didn't," she replied. "Not then, anyway. I was just so scared in the darkness. There was no other noise coming from down the hill. I didn't think there was anyone else down there. I just wanted to see if I was right, if there were footsteps, or if I was just imagining awful things, the way people sometimes do in the dark."

Spencer nodded.

"I was taking little steps, keeping to the path behind Feldberg, trying not to make any noise myself. I reached just about the place I first heard the sound come from. I stopped and looked down the hill, but it was very dark. Not pitch-black, you understand. The trees were pitch-black. But there was light coming from some of the windows in Feldberg. The snow reflected light back to me. It wasn't dark dark out. I could see the white snow and the cluster of pines about twenty feet down the hill. I took a few steps, then a few more. I wanted to see but didn't. Do you know what I mean?"

"All too well," said Spencer, holding his breath.

"I walked down to that cluster of trees. It took me, like, I don't know, five—six minutes maybe. I'd take a small step, then stop and listen. Another small step. Listen again. There was no noise, I just wanted to be sure I hadn't gone deaf or something." Conni swallowed hard and stopped looking at Spencer.

He was transfixed on her face.

"I was about five feet away when I saw, I thought I saw, I wasn't sure, it's only later that I can say I saw, but back then, I wasn't sure at all of anything, I *thought* I saw . . . a pair of black boots."

Spencer breathed heavily out and fell back against the chair. "No," he whispered.

Conni still didn't look at him. "I couldn't even place them at first. They made no sense to me. They were like two ink blots, I couldn't place them at all. They almost looked like small tree stumps, or ears sticking out of the ground. But I stopped walking because I got scared again. I was paralyzed. I couldn't take another step. Even before I realized what they were I couldn't take another step."

Spencer said nothing, breathing heavily, almost panting.

"It took a couple of seconds, but I remember my thoughts exactly, because when it became clear to me that the black things looked like boots, it took me a second to place the boots, and the very next second I pushed back so hard, I fell in the snow and couldn't even get up. I crawled on my hands and knees up the hill, scrambled. Then I turned my back on what I'd just seen. I don't know how I turned my back, but it was like trying to frantically wake up out of a nightmare. I've never been so scared in all my life. When I was at the top, I stood and, never turning around, ran back home. I wasn't walking hurriedly on the bridge, detective, as Frankie said. I was running with all my might. Thank God I left my door open. I couldn't have used the key, my hands were shaking so badly. No one was there. It took me a while to calm down. Then I called Albert's room, busy. Frankie's room, Jim's, no answer. Then I went down to the lounge again and found Albert. I was so relieved to find him. He told me he'd been in the lounge all along, and I believed him."

Spencer didn't say anything for a long time.

"Did you see—her?" he asked at last in a small voice. Naked, dead, with the snow falling on her.

Conni shook her head vigorously. "Absolutely not. I never got past the black boots."

Spencer wanted to splash water on his face. That's why Conni hadn't looked for Kristina when they came back from Thanksgiving. She had known there was no point.

"Conni," he asked, "why did you keep this to yourself? Especially in the light of what followed? Had it been nothing, I'd understand your not telling anybody, but since Kristina was found dead, why didn't you say something?"

"Like what? To who?"

"Why didn't you say something to Albert that night?"

"I was really, really scared. I was physically sick the whole night, and then we left and I tried hard not to think about it. I started to think maybe I was wrong."

"Why didn't you say something to Albert the next day, in the morning, so you could both go and check it out?"

Conni bowed her head. "I couldn't tell Albert. I don't know. I couldn't tell him."

"Why?"

"I don't know."

"I don't buy it."

"It's true."

"Why didn't you tell your lawyers this? Why didn't you say you were innocent?" As Spencer said it, he thought, not so innocent. And in that instant, he stopped feeling sorry for Conni, stopped pitying her.

"How could I prove I was innocent?" Conni said. "The circumstances were against me. I'm seen running from the scene of the crime, I can't account for nearly an hour of my time, which happens to be the time she died. And you were convinced I was covering something up."

"You were," interjected Spencer.

She nodded. "I was. Plus my face is under her fingernails. What do I have, except my word? Albert testified against me," she said broken-heartedly. "Jim testified against me. *You* testified against me."

"I was wrong."

"You didn't think you were wrong."

"Doesn't make me any less wrong."

"You weren't on my side, and I knew it."

"Your side? Conni, you saw a dead human being in the snow and you didn't tell anyone. You didn't even tell Albert. You should've told him."

Spencer and Conni fell silent.

Then Spencer asked, "Did Albert have a pair of gloves?"

"Gloves?"

"Yes. Leather or any kind of gloves."

"Yes, yes. I don't remember very well, but he had a pair of brown leather gloves he wore all the time." She bowed her head. "Something other than the gloves." She quietly stared at the table in front of her. "He had a brown leather coat."

"Yes?"

"It disappeared."

"It what?"

"It disappeared. I tried not to think about it then. We were ready to drive home for Thanksgiving, and he took his ski jacket with him. I asked him where his leather coat was. He said he couldn't find it. After we came back I asked him if he'd found the coat, and he said no. We had a little bit of a thing about it. I didn't understand how he could lose a leather coat. I was upset.

You see, I had given him that coat for Christmas the previous year." Conni looked up, an ashamed look in her eyes. "I just didn't want to think about where that coat might be."

Spencer nodded. "No, I'm sure you didn't." He saw the pained expression on her face. "It's all right now," he said. "It doesn't matter anymore." But he was lying.

Primping her short hair and touching her face, Conni said, "So what now?"

"What now?" Spencer was surprised by the question. "I don't know. You might want to go to your lawyer and tell him what you just told me."

Her manner became agitated. "And what? What good is that going to do?"

"Conni, ask him to reopen the investigation."

"To what end? I plea-bargained!" she exclaimed shrilly. "But I'm not guilty. Not guilty of anything."

Spencer coughed gently. "I wouldn't go so far as to say that, Conni."

"I told you, I didn't kill her."

"No, you didn't. But—" And here Spencer paused again. He was having difficulty coming up with the right words. "You did see her—dead." He willed his eyes to remain dry. "You knew whose boots they were. You knew it was her. I know you didn't want to think about it right then—though I really wish you had—but the next day you didn't see Kristina. You must have known what you saw in the snow was her, and yet you left, with her dog. Left to celebrate Thanksgiving. Left her in the snow for over a week—" Spencer couldn't continue.

"I couldn't say anything. It was too long already."

"Yes. Which is why I say you should've gone for help immediately. I doubt you could've helped her, because she was probably dead when you saw her. But maybe not. Think about that. Live with that. Had you gone for help immediately, you wouldn't be sitting here for five or more years of your life."

"I couldn't go for help immediately! Don't you understand?" Conni sounded helpless and desperate.

"No, actually, I don't. I know you were scared."

"Not just scared. Terrified. More frightened than I've ever been."

"You didn't have much to be frightened of before that night, Conni," said Spencer. "But what we are only comes out in crises. It's so easy to be passive in everyday life, which doesn't challenge us. There are no risks. But once or twice in our lives, our name is called. And when it's called, we have to stand up. Not run the other way." Spencer fell silent.

She stared at him, uncomprehending.

"So you're not going to help me, detective?" she said coldly. "Why did you come here, then?"

"I came here to see if I was right."

When he didn't elaborate, Conni asked, "Were you right?"

Slowly he bent his head. "I was right."

Spencer didn't feel like a young man anymore. Their web had entrapped him and held him prisoner for nearly four years, and he couldn't extricate himself from it. He couldn't be young again. He was graying at the temples of his light brown hair, and the lines of his face were becoming pronounced. These kids were going to make him old, but he wouldn't let them. He needed to let them go.

"Conni," he said resolutely, "I know why you didn't tell Albert the night you ran back from the bridge. You didn't tell him because you thought he'd killed her. And when he didn't speak of her, and when days passed and he hadn't mentioned her, when she was obviously missing in plain sight and he said nothing about her, you *knew* he'd killed her. And you didn't say anything. What were you hoping? That she'd never be found? If you thought he'd killed her, did you then realize you'd be shacking up with a murderer, or did you not care?"

"Don't say that," Conni gasped. "Don't say any of this. Stop talking."

Spencer continued, louder than before. "You kept your mouth shut, hoping your suspicions were wrong. Were you hoping that if you took the fall for him, he'd come around and start to love you, too?"

"He did love me!" she exclaimed.

"Oh, Conni!" Spencer was so tired. "For God's sake! He never loved you. He never loved anyone his whole life." Then Spencer remembered Kristina's maroon coat. "He loved only her. Don't you see that? You thought you could make him love you by your sacrifice, but he forgot you as soon as you went to prison, and now you want revenge. You should have tried to put him away, not woo him."

Conni started to cry.

"Don't cry. What do you want me to do now? We don't even know for sure, we don't know anything for sure. You don't, I don't. Don't cry. Maybe I'm wrong. Maybe he isn't the one."

Conni wept, not even bothering to wipe her face. "Find Albert," she sobbed. "Find him."

"Find him? And then what?"

"I don't know," she admitted. "In your heart you'll know what to do."

"Leave my heart out of this, please," he said. Then Spencer softened.

"What do I do when I find him? Kiss him on both cheeks?"

"You'll know what to do, detective. I'm confident in you." Conni sniffled.

Spencer understood she was placing her hope in him. "You think Albert is going to fess up to the deed? You don't know him, Conni."

"I do. I know him."

Shaking his head, he said, "You don't know him at all." Again he thought of telling her about Nathan Sinclair. But hadn't she been punished enough?

Changing the subject slightly, Spencer asked about Jim.

"Yes," she replied. "Every Sunday. He comes here."

"You're kidding," said Spencer. "Every Sunday?" But he wasn't really surprised. "What's he up to?"

"Not much. He's working as a bank manager."

"He went to Dartmouth to become a bank manager?"

"No," said Conni. "He went to Dartmouth to go into law, but he's . . . reconsidered."

"Reconsidered? Did he graduate?"

Conni said thoughtfully, tenderly, "He reconsidered that too."

"I see," said Spencer. "Conni, have you reconsidered Jim?"

She nodded, looking ashamed. "He comes every Sunday." Her voice broke at those words, and Spencer wasn't sure if it was because of what Jim had done for her or because of what Nathan Sinclair had done to her.

He wanted to reach out and pat Conni's arm. "I'll do what I can, Conni," Spencer said.

"I know you will, Spencer. That's the kind of person you are."

"But so you understand—not for you. For Kristina." *And for me. And for Kristina's mother, whom I promised.*

"I understand," she said eagerly.

"I'm not promising anything, you understand?"

"Fully," she said, smiling sadly. "Thank you."

Spencer thought her thank-you sounded heartfelt. He stood up. "You're welcome." He wanted to say, it's the least I can do, but what he was actually thinking was that it was the *most* he could do. The very most for himself.

"I don't think we'll see each other again, Conni," he said. "Take care."

Here he was, putting himself back into the quagmire of those four people's broken lives. And his own. He'd thought when he left his once beloved Hanover he'd be leaving them behind too, but he carried them with him all the time, stacked sloppily into the old suitcase of his soul.

They had ruined Hanover for him. They had sullied it with their fractured lives and their complex miseries.

Three months later, in June, Spencer O'Malley found A. Maplethorpe in the white pages of the Greenwich, Connecticut, phone book.

A. Maplethorpe lived off Sound Beach Road, on the shores of Long Island Sound, about a quarter mile from the exclusive Greenwich Point Park. Spencer called first before coming out to see him. Nathan seemed curiously pleased to hear from him. "What took you so long, detective?" he said, inviting Spencer to lunch.

Before he went to see him, Spencer thought about the encounter carefully and decided to tape a microphone behind his shirt pocket. He also brought his police Magnum. He didn't go anywhere without it, even while off-duty.

Pauper Nathan Sinclair had really come a long way since the orphanage days of Fort Worth, Texas, and the juvenile jail days of Brooklyn Heights.

The house looked magnificent from the outside. Secluded and covered by lush greenery, it was a three-story country cottage with white-grilled windows, dormers on the third floor, and ivy over the fence. The landscape included mostly sugar maples and oaks with Long Island Sound peeking through them.

Nathan met Spencer outside, where Spencer was looking at the trees and breathing in the briny air. Pointing to the sugar maples, Nathan said, "I've had them transported from New Hampshire and Vermont. You really can't find beautiful ones like these in Connecticut."

They nodded to each other with cool detachment. They did not shake hands. Spencer could hear the tiny hum of the recorder. He touched his lapel.

Nathan looked grown-up. Spencer supposed that returning to a Greenwich full of Sinclairs, Nathan could hardly help but be A. Maplethorpe. In all other ways, however, in his demeanor, in his clothes, in his polite and refined speech and his neatly groomed, cut, nearly manicured hair, Nathan had become a Sinclair. His clothes and his house and his speech were evidence of much money well spent.

"Still a Maplethorpe, huh, Nathan?"

"I'm hardly anything else." Nathan stretched his mouth in a white-toothed smile. "Where should we go?" he asked.

"I thought we could stay here."

"No. Today is not a good day. I just fired my cook and cleaning lady. Why don't we go to a place in town? It's charming. I think you'll like it."

Spencer didn't care where they went. He wanted to stay at the house. He wanted to see inside. What did he expect—right there in the sunroom, amid the flowers and the potted plants and the bookshelves and knickknacks? Did he expect to see the square pillow lying placidly on the sofa?

They went to a diner and sat on the southern side, where the sun pleasantly shone on the tables covered with red-and-white-checkered tablecloths. The waitress, wearing a red-and-white-checkered apron, came over with some coffee.

As the two chatted idly for the first ten minutes, Nathan smoked nonstop. Spencer became aware that Nathan's cool demeanor, calm speech, and polite manners were hiding tense fingers, gripping cigarette after cigarette.

"So what do I owe this visit to, Spencer?" Nathan said after a while. "May I call you Spencer? Are you writing a book?"

"I've never been much for writing," said Spencer.

"Ahh," said Nathan, his question unanswered. Not wanting Nathan to be on guard—though it was obviously too late—Spencer said, "I went to see your old girlfriend, Constance Tobias. Remember her?"

"Of course I remember Conni," said Nathan flatly. "How is she?"

"Very well, she's doing well. She was wondering why you never come to see her."

Shrugging attractively, genteelly almost, Nathan said, "Well, you know. It's been very difficult. It was a difficult time for me, too."

"Oh sure, difficult. Are you working?"

Nathan smiled. "Nah. A rich wife. She bought us our house."

"Ahhh," Spencer drew out. "Wife. So you've married."

"Yes," Nathan said solemnly. "I had been married."

Spencer struggled to understand. "Had been? Nathan, it's only been two years."

"Actually, it's been nearly four, detective," corrected Nathan. Was that a hint of sarcasm in his voice?

"Are you already divorced?"

"No, I'm widowed."

"Widowed?" Widowed! Spencer's hands began to shake. He struggled to remain composed.

"Is that black-widowed, Nathan?"

Nathan didn't answer, smoking and smirking.

"Well, I'm very sorry to hear that. I was just about to congratulate you on your marriage."

"That would've been less than appropriate."

"How did your wife die?"

"She lost control of the car. Just a freak thing. Went off the road, turned over."

Spencer sat and absorbed what he'd just heard. He hoped his face didn't show what his heart was feeling. He hoped he didn't sweat himself into an electric shock with that microphone taped to his chest.

"Waitress!" Spencer called. "I think I'll have a whiskey."

"We have—"

"Anything. As long as it's whiskey," Spencer interrupted her.

She brought it to him.

"Let me ask you," Spencer said finally. "Did anyone investigate her death?"

"Certainly. The insurance company." Nathan leaned over and smiled thinly. "It really *was* an accident, Detective O'Malley."

"Yes, and Kristina really *was* naked in the sub-freezing temperature. She could've very well frozen to death."

"What are you talking about?" said Nathan. "You know she didn't freeze to death."

"Yes, but that was strictly an accident itself. Kristina was meant to look like she froze to death."

Nathan lit another cigarette and flung his groomed hair back. "Detective O'Malley," he said, "I'm not saying it's not pleasant to see you, but why are you here? Conni Tobias is in prison."

"Yes, Conni Tobias is, isn't she?" said Spencer pointedly. If it weren't for the fact that Nathan was into his second pack and it had only been about thirty minutes, Spencer would've thought he had wasted his time by coming. But Nathan was smoking the cigarettes so mechanically, so tensely, so systematically, that Spencer suddenly became sure, *sure,* that his gut feeling was dead on.

"Nathan—"

"I really wish you'd call me Albert," said Nathan. "I haven't gone by that name in years."

"Strange. You went by that name in Kristina's letters to her grandmother, and in her letters to you that she never sent, and in the other things she left behind, except her will. You are Nathan to Kristina's mother. Let me ask you, did your bride—what was her name?—know you by your rightful name?"

"No, because it is not my rightful name and hasn't been for years."

"What was your bride's name?"

Nathan lit a cigarette before he said, "Elizabeth."

"Elizabeth. Elizabeth. That's a beautiful name. What was her last name?"

"When she died, I believe she was Maplethorpe."

"How about before she died?"

"I really can't remember, detective. Why are you so concerned?"

"I'm not concerned at all. I'm concerned she's dead, I'll be honest with you."

Nathan smiled. "Well, don't be so concerned."

Nathan Sinclair was very cool on the exterior. Spencer was so shaken, he didn't want to pick up his bourbon; he didn't want Nathan to see his unsteady fingers.

Where did one go with these pointedly bad feelings?

Did one crawl away, did one die with them?

Spencer didn't want to crawl away. He wanted to know more about Elizabeth. Nathan, though, was very closemouthed on the subject and only acknowledged that it was hard to be a widower at twenty-five. Spencer stared at Nathan to see if there was genuine emotion behind the words. When he looked across at Nathan, all he saw was a cool young man in trendy clothes, chain-smoking Camels. He said the right words, certainly, but Nathan did not seem to be suffering a tragic loss. And Spencer knew something about loss.

"Let me ask you a question. Was there suspicion of foul play?"

"No, why? Should there have been?"

"I don't know. Should there have been?"

Nathan looked mystified. "On whose part foul play?"

"Yours," said Spencer bluntly.

Nathan first tilted his head back and then smiled broadly. "No, detective. There was no suspicion of foul play on my part. You see, I was in the car with her."

Spencer nodded, unconvinced. "It seems that no matter where you go, Nathan Sinclair, you leave death in your wake. Kristina is dead—"

"Are you accusing me of killing Kristina, detective?" Nathan laughed.

"Death follows you like Aristotle used to," Spencer said. "How did you manage to get your wife to die, too?"

"Ah, well, this is not such a friendly visit after all. Detective, as I told you a number of times, my wife was driving. It was an unfortunate accident—"

"Unfortunate accidents seem to be your MO."

"Unfortunate accidents are not my MO at all," said Nathan, mimicking Spencer. "What happened with Kristina—"

"Which time is that now? The time you got her pregnant? Or the time you . . ." But Spencer stopped short of accusing Nathan of murder.

There was no profit in it.

He didn't want to get Nathan's emphatic, condescending denial on tape. Instead Spencer fell quiet, wanting whiskey, but having black coffee instead.

Having lost his wife in an accident, Spencer knew what a grieving man behaves like, and Nathan did not behave like one. He might as well have been speaking about a spring break loss by the Red Sox. Nathan didn't care. He looked straight at Spencer with insolent eyes, as if to say, *I dare you. You've been trying so long to catch me in something, and all this time you haven't caught me in shit and now you're coming to me again, and I'm telling you, you will again go away empty-handed to your apartment in the suburbs while I will continue to live on Sound Beach Road, in a house you can only dream of. I won't even allow you to step foot in my house. I won't allow you into my house, and do you know why? Because you really, really want to come in. But I will not let you in.*

But Spencer knew there was something in their conversation that would open a door for him.

"A philosophy major, weren't you?" said Spencer. "I'm surprised your sense of guilt isn't more developed."

Nathan laughed dryly. "Sense of guilt? It has nothing to do with philosophy. It has to do with religion and mothering. And I've had neither. Philosophy has to do only with rationalization. I've had plenty of that."

"You've had plenty of mothering, too."

"Who? Katherine?" He scoffed mildly. "If you call going to charity functions four times a week and entertaining friends the other three mothering, then yes, I've had plenty."

"She loved you very much."

"Is that what she told you? Well, I'm sure she believed it."

"She took you into your home and made her house yours," said Spencer in an impassioned voice. "How can you be so ungrateful?"

"What should I be grateful for? Did I ask her to do that for me? Who said I wasn't happy where I was? I had friends, I had three nuns who took care of me better than Katherine Sinclair ever took care of me. I went from a warm place to a gilded cage with no supervision and no discipline. A lot of show. A lot of manners. But what besides that? I was seven when I came to the Sinclairs. They thought I had just been born, but I was already somebody before them. Then all of a sudden they didn't like the somebody I was and threw me out. Not just me but their own daughter, too." He sounded angry when he said that.

Spencer was surprised. He hadn't seen much emotion in Nathan.

Except for the maroon coat.

Spencer said, "They didn't throw her out."

"What would you call it? They arranged a marriage for her just so there would be less of a scandal. They couldn't keep their only child in their home? It was so important to make nice for the neighbors. God forbid the Sinclairs should become the talk of the town. They discarded her as they had discarded me. And it was the worst moment of her life."

"Well," said Spencer caustically, "she didn't have much of a life. I'd say dying an unnatural death at twenty-one was the worst moment of her life, wouldn't you agree?"

Nathan flinched, barely, and it was this wincing that stayed with Spencer. Nathan flinched. Spencer hadn't been prepared for that.

Shrugging and outwardly calm, Nathan said, "I don't know. I'm sorry she's gone."

"Of course. She is the only family you ever had. The only one who treated you like family."

Nathan smirked. "See, here you're wrong, detective. You're romanticizing our relationship. I'm an orphan, or have you forgotten? Every female I ever meet melts at the sound of that word. 'Or-phan.' Oh, they say, poor baby, let me take you home, let me show you to my mommy, let me love you as if you were mine, let me cook you a meal, let me make your bed. Kristina was this way, Conni was this way. Elizabeth was this way and then some. Every protective fiber of their female souls is shaken by the word 'orphan.' They want nothing better than to take care of me. To bring me into their family circle."

"That's because they don't know what you are." Spencer was becoming convinced that Nathan had murdered Kristina. He was the only one capable, the only one remorseless and heartless enough to snuff out the life of a young woman who loved only him, and then go on as if it didn't matter. Like his old dead cat. It didn't shake him up one bit. He killed her and went on with his life as if she had never existed. This broke, poor kid from nowhere killed the hand that fed him and then quit the college she had paid for.

He was obviously well off, thanks to his late wife. He was now alone and seemingly happy about it, ensconced in the same social sphere that had spit him out as an adolescent. Nathan Sinclair didn't need to go to Edinburgh to learn the philosophy of rationalization. He seemed at peace with everything he'd ever done, and there was nothing that made Spencer's Catholic soul sicker. Had he shown some remorse, her death would have been less meaningless. But he acted like a man for whom the act of murder was as forgettable as taking Aristotle for a walk.

With an amused expression, Nathan said, "I know *who* I am. But what *am* I, detective?"

Spencer leaned across the table, his fists clenched underneath, and said, "The Sinclairs adopted you! How can you be so heartless?"

"Who's heartless? They adopted me and changed my name, calling me after their dead kid. Every year on November twenty-first, Thanksgiving or not, they would bring me to the family cemetery and make me put down flowers at the grave of *Nathan Sinclair*. Every year since I was seven. Boy, that was fun," Nathan said dryly. "According to the tombstone, I was already dead."

Spencer listened. It wasn't what he had come to hear. "Did you have a name before?"

"I'm sure I did. I don't know it. The nuns called me Billy."

Shaking his head, Spencer said, "Billy, Nathan, Albert. Do you even know who you are?"

"Do you know who *you* are?" Nathan retorted. "You say your name is Spencer, but I heard your cop buddies call you Tracy, and when you introduce yourself you say Spencer *Patrick* O'Malley. No one includes his middle name in an introduction."

"That's who I am," said Spencer, beginning to tremble in helpless anger. "Spencer Patrick O'Malley."

"And that's who I am—Albert Maplethorpe."

"Kristina chose that name for you, didn't she?"

Blinking twice, Nathan said, "We chose it together."

"Did you get the tattoo on your arm together too? With her initials on it? Have you tried since her death to have it surgically removed?"

"What are you talking about, detective? Why would I do that?"

"Tell me, Nathan-Albert-Billy, did you love her?"

Nathan answered him fast, without thinking. "Yes, I loved her," he said.

"Did you kill her?"

The reply came instantly. "No, I did not."

The tape recorder whirred.

"Are you lying?"

"No, I'm not."

"You've lied your whole life to everyone about everything. Are you lying now?"

"No, I'm not."

"I see."

"I have an alibi, detective. You know that."

"Yeah, alibi." Spencer was tapping furiously on his empty glass.

Nathan laughed.

Then they were quiet. Nathan ate his turkey club with no mayo and no bacon, while Spencer nursed his coffee. He thought of something else, the grandmother.

"Yeah? What about her? We stayed with her every summer. It was a lot of fun. The lake was nice. She was a good cook. Kristina was sad when her grandmother died."

"Did you know Louise Morgan had a will?"

337

"Of course I knew she had a will. These are the Sinclairs and the Morgans. They're born with a will." After taking a big bite of his club, Nathan continued, "When Kristina was living in Brooklyn Heights she told me that her grandmother was furious at the way the family treated Kristina—Grandma's only grandchild. Louise couldn't believe Kristina had been thrown away with the baby, so to speak, just to maintain appearances on North Street. So Louise turned her back on her family after they turned their backs on Kristina. She vowed to cut them all out of her will, including Kristina's mother."

"Did Kristina tell you who Louise Morgan was leaving her money to?"

Nathan paused. "Krissy said she didn't know."

Spencer shuddered at the diminutive of Kristina's name on the lips of Nathan Sinclair. There was something sacrilegious about it.

"You sound like you feel Louise Morgan was right to disinherit the whole family."

"Absolutely. They had treated Kristina horribly. Me, I don't care, I expected it. Who am I to them? But she was their princess, she was the pinnacle of their dreams. All of what they both were, John and Katherine, was sublimated into Kristina."

"I thought John was sublimated into you."

"Is that what *she* said?" He scoffed. "Yeah, right."

"Nathan, you can't ignore the fact that because of what happened between you two, the entire family completely fell apart."

He shrugged. "They were a weak family." He was silent for a second and stopped eating. "When I was very young, maybe a year, something happened to my mother. She died. My mother's sister wanted to take care of me, but my father would have none of it. He was living with other women then. One day my aunt took me with her after school. We had been living in Colorado and she drove to New Mexico. We lived in Albuquerque for a little while, until my father hunted us down. I don't know what he did with my aunt, but it was the middle of a summer night. He took me from her, and we hitchhiked for a long time till we got to Texas. Then something happened to him at a truck stop. He got into a fight, I think, because I found him in the back lot. I sat by him all night, and when I realized he wasn't going to get up, I got up myself and left. I went out onto the highway to find my aunt." He paused. "Go figure, I ended up with the Sinclairs."

Spencer listened quietly. Nathan picked up his sandwich.

"I don't know their names; I don't know my own name, or where my aunt is, or where in Colorado we first lived. I'm not that sure it was even Colorado. It could've been Wyoming. In any case, what happened with the Sinclairs was unfortunate, certainly, but it was not death. In fact, there was a baby. It could've been much worse, and shame on the Sinclairs for not seeing it that way. How many grandkids are they going to have now?"

Spencer was too dumbfounded to speak. How could a man be so devoid of humanity? When he found his voice, he said haltingly, "They thought of you as their son, don't you understand that? What good would a grandchild from their son and daughter do them?"

Nathan shrugged and went on finishing his club sandwich. "Whatever," he said.

"Did you understand then, or now, that what you did had consequences?" Spencer asked angrily. "Listen, you didn't just take up with each other in a vacuum. This world isn't a black amoral hole where your actions have no meaning, and where nothing you do matters. Did you ever think of the people you hurt?"

"They weren't strong. I didn't ask them to be hurt."

Spencer said, "Had you not behaved like an idiot, you would have had a trust fund worth millions when you turned twenty-one."

"I did not behave like an idiot," Nathan said indignantly. "How did I know they were going to overreact?"

"Because you should have known your little dalliance would break their hearts. Knowing that would have set you apart from an animal."

"Knowing that and doing it anyway?" said Nathan sarcastically.

"Knowing that would have been a beginning," said Spencer, seething.

Nathan just smiled.

"The whole world is pretty dispensable to you, isn't it?" said Spencer.

"Don't know what you're talking about."

Spencer wanted to smash the table with his fist. "Let me ask you, Nathan *Sinclair*," he said, "in the quiet of the night when you're alone, are you ever, tell me, are you ever simply *revolted* with yourself?"

Wiping his mouth and putting down his napkin, Nathan said gruffly, "What did you come here to accuse me of, detective? Because if I'm not under arrest, I think I'm about done."

"You're not under arrest," said Spencer, disgusted.

"I didn't think so."

Nathan got up from his chair. As he stood up, he gave Spencer a kind of half mock salute, half obscene gesture.

Spencer sat quietly in his chair and tried to stay in control. He didn't want to lose his temper in a public place, and when he realized that, he got scared. He thought, *I don't want to lose my temper in front of all of these people and have a fistfight that everybody in the restaurant will remember.* Spencer calmed down after realizing this, but not before he said, "Watch out, Nathan Sinclair."

Nathan leaned down menacingly. "No—you watch out, detective," he whispered.

Spencer said, "You destroyed a family. You ruined Conni Tobias, who is sitting in jail for five years of her life. Don't you give a shit?"

Spencer saw Nathan's face. He saw Nathan did not give a shit.

Nathan reached into the back pocket of his pants for his wallet and pulled out a fifty-dollar bill. He threw it carelessly on the table and said, smiling, "Thanks for a pleasant lunch."

Spencer cursed under his breath as he paid for lunch out of his own pocket and left the fifty-dollar bill as a tip for the waitress.

He didn't go back home. He couldn't. It was midafternoon, and Spencer drove around Greenwich, chanting a mantra to himself, *What am I missing? What am I overlooking?*

He went to the registry office of births, marriages, and deaths and looked up the date of the marriage of Nathan Sinclair and Elizabeth—Elizabeth Barrett, as he found out. They had been married two years earlier, on June 12, 1995. Elizabeth had been a June bride. Then Spencer looked up her death. She had died on April 13, 1996. Nothing more was said about it, so Spencer went to the local library, where in an old issue of *Greenwich Time* he read a short article about the death of Elizabeth Barrett Maplethorpe.

In the middle of the day, on an open country road, going about forty-five miles an hour, a sober Elizabeth Maplethorpe lost control of the car and went off the road. Her passenger had survived. She herself, however, was not wearing a seat belt and went through the collapsible steering wheel, suffering massive head injuries. Members of her family were quoted as saying they could not believe Elizabeth was not belted in, because she would not put the car into drive unless she and all her passengers were wearing seat belts. It had something to do with a bad accident years earlier. Albert Maplethorpe confirmed that his wife usually always wore a seat belt, but she had been getting more lax with them lately. Sometimes she would just forget, he said, and this was one of those times. Mr. Maplethorpe was largely unharmed except for a gash on his nose and bruises where the restraint had dug into him to keep him alive. There was not much in the article about her family; she was from New Hampshire. She was survived by Mr. Maplethorpe. There were no children. There was no photograph.

Spencer sat in the library and thought for a long time. He knew it was in there, right there, somewhere, right between those lines, right in those words, but he didn't know where, he didn't know what. Elizabeth had died intestate, which meant all she had went to her surviving spouse. But what did she have that made disconnecting her seat belt worthwhile?

On a clear day, Elizabeth was taking a Sunday drive with her husband, who was properly belted in. Spencer was sure she was, too. Until just before the "accident," Elizabeth was belted in. Then he unbelted her. All it took was five pounds of pressure from his pinkie finger, and then he could have done a million things to make her lose control of a vehicle. They weren't on a highway, they weren't on an interstate. Nathan couldn't ensure his own survival as easily if their Jaguar had been doing seventy instead of forty. No, they were humming along on a country road, breezy, springy, sunny, and then all of a sudden she was dead and he wasn't. The investigation was closed after the insurance company made sure the seat belt had not malfunctioned. And it hadn't. He was in the car with her, the ambulance came and took them both away, and he went home and took her money.

Spencer wasn't sure Elizabeth Barrett had had money, but he was certain Nathan Sinclair hadn't had a penny. That was the whole point. Poor penniless Nathan always had to mooch off the women who loved him, thought Spencer.

Elizabeth Barrett's name sounded familiar. The brief article said she was from New Hampshire. Where in New Hampshire?

He left the library and drove out north on I-95—in the direction of New Hampshire. Spencer was not going home until he found out about Elizabeth Barrett.

Absentmindedly, Spencer listened to the radio. Occasionally a song he knew would come on, and he'd hum it. He hummed to Bruce Springsteen's "Dancing in the Dark," Nirvana's "Come as You Are," and Elton John's "Benny and the Jets."

In Massachusetts, about forty miles south of Brattleboro, Vermont, Spencer was humming to Kim Carnes's, "Bette Davis Eyes," *She's got Bette Davis eyes . . . she's got Bette Davis eyes . . .*

Something exploded inside his head, and he swerved, almost hitting the car to the right of him. It took him fifty-three minutes from the time he heard the song to fly ninety miles to Lebanon, New Hampshire. When he came off onto I-89, it was not yet dark. It was only a few miles to Lebanon, and Spencer broke every local speed and traffic law. He skipped two red lights and neglected the stop signs. Finally, he drove around the roundabout, made a right off it onto Wheeler, and then another right.

He drove to Red Leaves House.

And there it was. On a sunny, quiet street of other older, well-kept, lived-in houses, what had been Red Leaves House sat shut and boarded up. There was no glass in the windows, only old wooden boards with rusted nails. The front door was covered with graffiti. The asphalt in the driveway was broken in places, and grass and weeds grew through the cement cracks.

Spencer sat behind the wheel for a long time, his head in his hands. And then he turned the ignition off slowly, got out of the car, and walked across the street to the house. He had seen everything there was to see; there was nothing left. The establishment plaque that had once hung on a post outside the house had been torn down. Spencer found it near the front step on the grass. He picked it up. RED LEAVES HOUSE, EST. 1973, PROPRIETOR, ELIZABETH "BETTY" BARRETT.

For another hour, Spencer sat motionless in front of the house. He now understood everything. Then he left.

He drove out of Lebanon and took Route 10 to Hanover. He was going to visit his old partner, Will, and then he was going to visit Ken Gallagher, maybe have a drink, tell him what he had just found out.

Will would shake his head. Gallagher would nod politely. Then they would talk in hushed voices between themselves, pointing to him and shaking their heads. They would think he was nuts, and they'd be right.

He turned around before he reached Hanover, and drove back to I-89, taking it southeast to Concord. He was headed for the DA's office. It took him thirty minutes and fifteen miles to reconsider. How could one person be tried for a crime another already had pleaded guilty to?

And what did Spencer have, anyway?

He had nothing.

Nothing except the truth.

But what would the district attorney do with the truth? The truth, Dave Peterson would say. You got a boarded-up house with a beat-up sign, and you want me to arrest a man? For what? For not caring about pregnant teenagers?

But but but, Spencer would say. He married her, don't you see, he saw everything, he wanted everything. Don't you see?

I see, Peterson would say. And you got proof of it? Oh, it's a hunch you have. Well, if it's a hunch, let's put him right in jail for life then.

Spencer shouted and hit the wheel in frustration.

Peterson would be right. He'd tell Spencer to get a confession out of the bum, and he'd buy Spencer a nice, long, cold drink, and then he'd send Spencer on his way.

Spencer got off I-89 back onto I-91 and slowly made his way down to the Brattleboro mall, where he got lost in the crowds. First he bought himself a pair of shin-high black workman's boots. Then he purchased three black sweatsuits in three separate stores. He also bought a generic black travel bag and, in a small boutique, he laid out seventy bucks for a pair of black leather gloves with a waterproof lining on the inside. He paid cash for everything.

Back in the car, Spencer drove to the outskirts of town. In the bathroom of a gas station, Spencer put on his safety vest and changed into two of the sweatsuits, one on top of the other, and put the black boots on. The microphone was still taped to his clothes—he hadn't bothered to take it off. He took it off now, spooled the tape of his conversation with Nathan out of the casing, burned it in the sink, and then ran water over the ashes.

Back in the car, he placed the recorder, the wires, and the small mike in his glove compartment.

Spencer put on the brown gloves and opened the trunk, rummaging through it until he found a cheap Saturday-night special he had confiscated in a drug bust two or three weeks ago. He had about a dozen of them in his police vehicle and had not bothered to turn them in yet. The rest remained in the trunk of the cop car. The gun was very poorly made. Spencer hoped it would work. He placed it carefully in a plastic bag under the seat of the car, then holstered his police Magnum .357 to his back and drove back to Greenwich to see Nathan.

Spencer was going to talk to him again, but without the tape recorder and without the pretense of lunch.

———

At about eleven at night Spencer arrived in Greenwich. He parked his car in the commuter parking lot for the Old Greenwich Metro North Station and walked the two and a half miles to Nathan's house.

He knew he had to be very careful. Nathan was probably armed to the teeth, living alone in a big old house. Who knew what ghosts Nathan was expecting to pay him a visit? The house was dark in the front; it almost looked as if no one was home. Spencer suspected Nathan was home, for he had nowhere else to go.

Between Nathan's house and a neighbor's, there was a tree-covered little path that led to the beach—Spencer had seen it when Nathan was giving him a tour of the grounds.

Now Spencer took that path and made his way to the back of Nathan's house, which, unfenced, faced Long Island Sound. All the windows were dark except for a small pair on the left, lit by the blue flicker of a television. The windows were too high up for Spencer to look into, but he went up the steps to the back door and tried the knob.

The door wasn't locked.

Spencer opened the door and walked in. The television was on loud. Spencer moved quickly through the big kitchen to the left and stood in the entranceway to the den, where Nathan was lying on the couch under the windows watching TV.

Nathan saw him but didn't move. "Well, well," he finally said. "I don't remember inviting you in."

Spencer was too tense to speak.

"I knew I should've locked the back door."

"You should have," agreed Spencer.

Nathan slowly got up to a sitting position. "What do I owe another visit to, Spencer Patrick O'Malley?"

Spencer said, "I went by Red Leaves House."

"You did. Good. You came here to tell me that?" Nathan reached over to turn on the lamp, but Spencer stopped him. "Don't move, Nathan," he said. "Don't move at all." Spencer's feet were apart, and he was holding the Magnum in his hands.

Nathan smirked but stopped moving. "Are you going to take me in, detective? Are you going to arrest me?"

"No, Nathan Sinclair. I'm not going to arrest you."

Nathan laughed, carelessly, insolently. "No, of course not. You don't have a case. And you know it."

Spencer nodded. "I know it."

"If you think you're going to get a teary confession out of me, you're sadly mistaken."

"I have no such illusions, Nathan. I know you too well."

"You don't know me at all, *Spencer*," Nathan said.

"I want to know—I see you here, living the life of luxury, and I want to know, was it all worth it?"

"If you know me so well, you should be able to answer that."

"Listen, tell me something," said Spencer, pointing his gun down. "Tell me you didn't kill her for money. Tell me you loved her too much. Were crazy about her—I could see that. You were afraid she didn't love you anymore, you were afraid she loved someone else. You were afraid she was pulling away and after Dartmouth she might marry Jim Shaw and you'd never be together again. Tell me you killed her in a fit of passionate madness. But don't tell me you killed her for money. Don't tell me that. I can't stand the thought of that. I'll go nuts thinking that's why she lost her life. Tell me you loved her, you hated her, tell me your feelings for her were too much, too strong. Tell me you loved her too much!" Spencer said passionately.

Nathan didn't reply.

"I'm just deluding myself, aren't I?" Spencer said coldly. "You knew Kristina's grandmother left her the money, and that's why you killed her. You were hoping she made a will leaving it all to you. How cozy and convenient *that* would have been," Spencer said through gritted teeth. Sweat dripped into his eyes. "Or if she died intestate, you would have reared your head then, wouldn't you? To get her nine million, you wouldn't have continued to pretend you were Albert Maplethorpe, would you?"

Nathan said, "I don't know what you're talking about."

"What I want to know is how did you know Betty Barrett would fall in love with you?" Spencer asked. "And Red Leaves was her life. How did you get her to close the business?"

"I didn't *know* she would fall in love with me," Nathan mimicked. "We were both dealing with Kristina's death, we were grieving and came together naturally. She was very grateful that Conni, Jim, and I donated Kristina's money to Red Leaves." He paused, smiling, still sitting on the couch. "As for your second question, she wasn't as crazy about running Red Leaves as you think. Five minutes of discussion made up her mind. She had always wanted to live near the water."

Spencer felt Nathan's darkness descending on him. He put his Magnum back in the holster, keeping his hand on the Saturday-night special stuck in the back of his sweatpants. Spencer couldn't bear to think Kristina's life had come to an end over money. Couldn't *bear* it. And not just *her* life.

When Nathan didn't reply, Spencer said, "You're not worth the life you were given. Your own life is worthless to you—why should Kristina's life have meant anything? You know, it would've been better if Conni had killed Kristina. At least she had passion. She had conviction. She was made crazy by you, by your lies and betrayals, and by Kristina. It would've been better if Kristina had died for passion, not greed."

"Better for who?" said Nathan. "And who would it matter to? Not her—she's dead. Better for who, detective?"

Shaking his head at Nathan, Spencer said, "Is this what you wanted, to live on the water in a soulless house, all alone, surrounded by your flower gardens?"

"You have to admit," said Nathan, sounding almost jovial, "this isn't half bad."

Darkness engulfed Spencer.

"She makes you will your own destruction," he whispered. "I get it. She *was*

warning you. I was right. She was warning you not to be greedy. She was telling you you had plenty, but three million wasn't enough for you."

Nathan said nothing.

"Why didn't she leave it all to you, Nathan? You were her true love—why didn't she leave it to you?"

Shrugging, Nathan said, "It hardly matters now, does it, detective?"

"She didn't leave it all to you because she wanted you to redeem yourself, to see clear through the day, to change your heart. To be a human being."

"She already thought I was a human being, detective. She loved me, remember?"

Spencer was having trouble breathing. His heart was stopping and pounding, stopping and pounding.

"Then why didn't she tell you about the money? She was afraid of you. She was afraid you'd kill her for it. She didn't trust you, and she was right."

Nathan smirked in the darkness. "She wasn't afraid of me at all. But it hardly matters now, does it?"

Spencer circled the air with the hand that held the Saturday-night Special. "Don't you see? She's still here. Her death bought you this house—you'll never be rid of her. You think you're not in prison? Look! Look around you!"

There was only the light from the TV, but as Spencer's gaze moved around the room, it fell on the end table near the sofa. Next to the table lamp and the phone lay a semiautomatic pistol. Spencer thought it was fortunate the TV had been on loud and Nathan hadn't heard him come in; otherwise, now he would be being buried in Nathan's flower gardens.

Spencer lowered his gun and said, "How do the dead philosophers justify that to have nothing you took a life of someone who loved you? You gave up love for death. You would rather have nothing than have love. Have love from Kristina. Don't you think her love was worth something? The little matchbooks that she saved from Edinburgh—they were worth something. The little smiley faces on napkins with the names of pubs engraved on them—they were worth something. They were worth more than this place you live in, looking out on the shores where you used to fly a kite when you were children."

Nathan's eyes glistened, and he stood up, fast, fluid, facing off against Spencer. "You know, it just occurred to me," said Nathan. "You're trespassing. And I've decided I don't want you here anymore. Get out or I'll call the police."

"No need," said Spencer. "I'm here."

Nathan took a step toward the phone and the gun.

Hair rose on the back of Spencer's neck. "Don't move."

"Or what? I'm tired of your games." Nathan took another step.

"Nathan, I'm warning you. Don't move." Spencer put both hands on his gun, cocked it, and assumed his firing stance. Nathan was now a few short paces away from his own gun. If he lunged for it, he'd have it in his hands.

"Spencer Patrick O'Malley, what are you going to do?" Nathan said with such rude malevolence that Spencer started to shake. "Am I worth losing your job over?"

"Nathan, I've told you, you're not worth losing a night's sleep over."

At the next instant, Nathan dove for his pistol, hand outstretched. Spencer pointed the Saturday-night special at Nathan's thigh and fired. Nathan fell, swiping his own gun with his hand onto the floor, and then tried madly to find it on the carpet. But in the darkness, he couldn't see where it had fallen. Nathan's gaze lowered on his leg, and then his frantic hands went around his wound.

Shooting in the dark was Spencer's specialty.

"What have you done?" Nathan gasped. "What have you done?"

Even in the dark, Spencer saw blood flowing from the thigh through Nathan's gripping hands, onto the carpet. Spencer had shot out the femoral artery.

Nathan Sinclair had about four minutes before he bled to death. In the blue flashing moment, Spencer wondered if Kristina had had four minutes.

"What have you done?" Nathan whispered, his voice empty of anger. He was lying on the floor, holding his leg. The blood was as slick and thick as in a slaughterhouse. But it wasn't in red. The den wasn't in color. The harsh lights of the TV made the room appear black-and-white. Nathan's blood was black.

Spencer lowered his gun. He knew he'd no longer need it. Coming up close to Nathan and squatting down a few feet away from his head, Spencer said, "I didn't come to arrest you, and I didn't come to get a confession out of you. Underneath these clothes I wore my safety vest. I knew you would try to kill me, and I was right."

Nathan's eyes were glazed.

"Can you still hear me, Nathan? You know you're going to die. Kristina Sinclair was the only person in the world who would've mourned you dead. But she is gone, and now you'll die too, and not a single soul on earth will grieve for you, not a single soul on earth will claim your body when it's found here months and months from now by a disgruntled UPS man, or by the gardener. You will lie here in your own blood, dead, with no one asking for you, no one calling your name, no one wondering where you are. You will not have a little boy sitting by your side till morning, waiting for you to get up, like your father did."

Spencer nearly cried.

"And when you're found," he continued in a broken voice, "and the coroner takes your body away, you will lie in the state hospital until the state buries you in a pauper's grave, or cremates your body and leaves your ashes in the furnace. No one will shed a tear for you, because you've brought nothing but grief and death into this world. You're leaving it a worse place. You did exactly what you wanted, and that was the only absolute truth you knew. You're going to die in about two minutes, and you will never see Kristina again."

Nathan didn't speak, and then he whispered, "Well, that's not true, detective. You're—you are shedding a tear for me."

Spencer almost fell back. "Not for you, you bastard. Not for you."

The seconds ticked by. Leaning down to him, whispering, Spencer asked, "How did you do it? How did you get her, naked, cold, frightened, to come to you in the dead of night?"

Nathan's hold on his leg slipped, and he answered, "I don't know what you're talking—" And then, much softer, "She was afraid of the night, but she wasn't afraid of me. She would've come to me anywhere."

Spencer couldn't speak. He smelled blood, other odors, he was feeling nauseated. "Nathan," he finally said. "What are you hiding now? I'm not taping this, and you're, well, you're—what are you afraid of?"

And Nathan answered, "Death."

Spencer said, "Kristina, you think *she* was afraid of death?"

"Yes," he replied. "She was." And very quietly, "She didn't want to die."

Spencer helplessly groaned aloud.

"You're dying for her, and for her mother, and for her grandmother, and for her father, and for Elizabeth Barrett, and for Constance Tobias. And for me, too. God gave you free will, and look at what you've done with it. You left her alone in the snow . . . she didn't even have a priest bless her—"

And here Nathan interrupted him. "Bless me," whispered Nathan hoarsely.

"The devil, is he ever blessed by God?" said Spencer. "No, my sainted mother of eleven said. The devil chose his fate, and with his own hell he must pay. I looked and beheld a pale horse: and his name that sat on him was Death, and Hell followed with him."

Nathan tried to shake his head, but couldn't. "Something else," he moaned, breathing convulsively.

"I have no pleasure in the death of the wicked," said Spencer quoting Hezekiah.

He heard Nathan's hoarse voice, "Eyes. Her eyes. I can't erase them from my memory. I can't close my own eyes without seeing hers. Will they be staring at me for eternity in hell? Lord have mercy on me. I don't want to see her eyes ever again, those black pools of comprehension and pain. . . ."

With his weakened knees nearly giving out, Spencer finally whispered, "Believe in the Lord, and you shall be saved."

Nathan let go his leg and sank to the floor, his body slowly emptying of life. Spencer crossed himself and waited.

Almost inaudibly, Nathan Sinclair said, "For her, I deserve it."

—•••—

Five minutes later, Spencer left the house, carefully locking the kitchen door behind him. He walked on the side of Sound Beach Road toward the intersection and then he made a left and walked another mile and a half to the train station, where he took off the top layer of his clothes outside his car. He took the Saturday-night special and put it into a black plastic bag. With his knife, he ripped apart the clothes he had worn to Nathan's house, the gloves, and the boots. He put everything into the black travel bag and drove toward Long Island. On the way, he stopped in the Bronx in Co-Op City—a minimetropolis of anonymous thirty-story buildings and vast parking lots. He threw the plastic bag with the gun in one of the overflowing public trash receptacles near the multiplex theater. He burned the black travel bag in another trash can in an empty lot. Then he went home and did something he hadn't done in the three and a half years since Kristina Sinclair had died. Spencer slept through the night.

EPILOGUE

The children were sitting on the bench up at the castle *afterward*. They didn't usually stay in the enclave covered by yellow forsythia. This afternoon also, they came out and sat on the bench overlooking the peaceful water. After a few minutes, the girl's hands steadied. She primped her hair and touched the creases on her jeans, as if for comfort. There was comfort in neatness, in orderly things. It made her feel in control. Control was important to her.

"How come you don't like to swim?" she asked the boy.

He shrugged. "Never learned how."

"So why don't you learn now?"

"Not interested."

"Why not? Swimming is such fun."

"I don't like it."

"Are you scared of the water?" she said teasingly. But he didn't smile, and the smile fell from her face. "I'm sorry," she said quickly. She didn't like the look in his eyes. It was cold, almost hateful.

"So why do you walk that stupid wall? There's water on one side of it—you could fall in."

He laughed. "I'm not going to fall in."

"How do you know?"

"I'm steady on my feet," he said, "and I'm quick."

"You could fall in."

"I'm not going to fall in. You, now you might fall in."

"I hate walking that thing," she admitted.

"Scaredy cat!" he teased.

"Not scaredy! Just . . . careful."

"So? Be careful not to fall in," he said, and she flinched; she didn't like his playing with her words like that.

"If I fall, who'll save me?" she said petulantly.

"I would."

"You would? But—"

"I'd run with all my might and call for help."

"I'd be dead and drowned by the time you got somebody."

"I'd run fast. I'm very fast. Very quick."

"You can't swim," she repeated. "You should learn how."

"What are you so afraid of? If *I* fell in, who'd save me?"

"I would," she said without hesitation. "I'd jump in and save you."

He laughed. "We'd both die."

"We wouldn't," she said, offended. "Princesses can rescue their princes, too."

He shook his head. "Yeah, and we'd live happily ever after."

"Yes, we would," she said earnestly.

He looked at her, equally earnestly. "Promise?"

She crossed herself. "Swear."

"Don't do that," he said quickly. "Just say 'swear,' that's enough. You don't have to cross yourself." The girl saw him shudder. She fell silent. Sometimes she didn't understand him, not one bit.

"Can I ask you a question?"

"Uh-huh."

"Did you ever know your real mom and dad?"

The boy paused. "No, never did. Don't remember them at all."

"That's too bad," said the girl, looking out onto the sound. "That's kind of sad, isn't it?"

"No, not really. I mean, how can you miss what you've never had?"

"I guess," she said uncertainly, thinking. "You have it now, though, don't you?"

"Yes," he said.

"You know, with you around," said Kristina, "I'm not lonely anymore."

"I know," he said.

"Before you I was so lonely," she continued. "Now I feel like I have a brother for life."

"You do," he said. "For as long as you live, I'll be your brother."

"Thank you," she said in a heartfelt voice. "I know Momma and Daddy love you to death, too. They've always wanted a little boy, you know."

"I don't believe it."

She kicked a stone hard against a low stone wall. "It's true. They only wanted a son. They love me and everything, but I overheard them talking one night, just before you came to live with us. Daddy was saying that if they were meant by God to have only one child, why couldn't my real twin brother have been saved instead?"

"And what did your momma say?"

"She said she was happy with whatever God had given them, but she just wished she could have another little baby to love."

"She's really nice, your momma."

Kristina smiled. "Well, she's your momma now."

He smiled, too. "I suppose she is," he said, sounding unconvinced. "I suppose she is."

"Do you like me?" she asked him.

"You know I like you," he replied, adding, "You're the only thing I like."

"Is that true?"

"That's true."

"What about Momma and Daddy?"

"They're nice. But they're kind of busy a lot, aren't they? Your mom, she's never home."

Kristina smiled. "She likes to keep busy."

"We've got to stick together," said the boy.

"I know."

He stood up from the bench. "In sickness and in health, for better or for worse, for richer or for poorer, till death do us part."

The girl was silent. "Isn't that what married people say?"

"They say it because it makes sense," the boy replied. "And *I'm* saying it because it makes sense."

"Okay," said Kristina. "Till death do us part." She fell silent again.

"But," she said, disturbed, "I don't really want to die."

"Who does?" he said. "We're not going to die. We're too young to die."

"So maybe we don't have to say that part?" she asked.

He sighed. "You're a pain. Okay, we won't say that part. Come on, let's go. It's getting late."

The children left their secret place amid castle ruins, rolled down the hill, and ran down the stone stairs.

There was no one else in the park. Only a little boy balancing himself on the wall that separated the land from the sea, and a little girl, arms out, stepping carefully behind him, looking at her feet and at him. The salty air carried the sounds of the wind and the rustling leaves, and the girl's voice, calling out, "Wait for me . . . wait for me . . ."

ACKNOWLEDGMENTS

This is a work of fiction. Any inaccuracies are intended, and any mistakes are mine.

To Bob Wyatt, for being my friend, for making me laugh aloud in the most unexpected places of the edited manuscript, and for living this book with me for nine months, and to Joy Harris, thank you.

Thanks to police officers Patrick O'Neill and E. Douglas Hackett for your details and patience.

To Oron Strauss, editor in chief of the *Dartmouth Review*, for letting us play with your Labrador.

To Clint Bean of the Hanover Chamber of Commerce, and to Kris Wielgus of the Dartmouth women's basketball team, thank you.

A heartfelt thanks to Jackie Feldmann and Kerri Basso for looking after our little Mishie-guy. Where would I be without you guys?

Natasha, Misha, and our yet unborn—Mommy loves you.